A . . . My Name's Amelia

This Large Print Book carries the
Seal of Approval of N.A.V.H.

A . . . My Name's
Amelia

Joanne Sundell

WHEELER PUBLISHING
A part of Gale, Cengage Learning

GALE
CENGAGE Learning·

Detroit • New York • San Francisco • New Haven, Conn • Waterville, Maine • London

GALE
CENGAGE Learning·

LIBRARY OF CONGRESS CATALOGING-IN-PUBLICATION DATA

Sundell, Joanne.
    A... my name's Amelia / by Joanne Sundell.
    p. cm.
    ISBN-13: 978-1-59722-790-2 (pbk. : alk. paper)
    ISBN-10: 1-59722-790-0 (pbk. : alk. paper)
    1. Deaf — Fiction. 2. Large type books. 3. Psychological fiction. I. Title.
    PS3619.U557A63 2008
    813'.6—dc22   2008014505

Published in 2008 by arrangement with Tekno Books.

Printed in the United States of America
1 2 3 4 5 6 7 12 11 10 09 08

— For my mother, Shirley Gregg Dean
No greater heroine in life or in death —

ACKNOWLEDGMENTS

To Angela Taylor, for her words of wisdom, guiding me on every page.

To Kathie Gonzalez, Colorado School for the Deaf and Blind, for her assistance with research and access to school archives.

To *The Perigee Visual Dictionary of Signing* for the illustration "The Manual Alphabet" and their descriptive definitions of American Sign Language. (See copyright page.)

The Manual Alphabet

It is highly recommended that the manual alphabet is memorized at the outset of learning sign language. The right hand is preferred to form the letters of the alphabet, although if you are left-handed the left hand may be used. The letter signs are illustrated as seen by the observer, or in some cases at a slightly different angle for the sake of clarity. Generally speaking, the hand should be held comfortably at shoulder level and in front of the body, with the palm facing forward.

A

B

C

D

E

F

G

H

I

J

K

L   **M**   **N**   **O**

P   **Q**   **R**

S   **T**   **U**   **V**

Z

W   **X**   **Y**   **Z**

"There's a language that's mute; a silence that speaks."

— Deaf-Mute Index
June 19, 1875

CHAPTER ONE

Colorado Springs — Summer 1880

The door of the *Gazette* swung wide, its bell jingling louder than usual. The editor, Benjamine Steele, looked up from his galleys, then nodded to his junior reporter to see to the front desk. The regular clerk was out sick. Harvey Pratt, ever eager for a story, greeted the cowboy who'd just entered.

"Hullo, sir. What can we do for you?"

The cowboy said nothing as he shuffled slowly toward the desk. He removed a paper from his vest pocket and began to unfold it. His hands shook but not enough for anyone to take notice.

"Fire! Fire at the Livery Feed Stable!" A young man burst open the door of the *Gazette* long enough to shout his news, and then disappeared, jerking the door closed. The bell jingled loudly for a second time in as many minutes.

Harvey grabbed up his pad and pencil and

whirled around to face the editor.

"Mr. Steele, I'll —"

"Yes, Harvey. Go," Benjamine Steele broke in. "Ladder Number One should be there quick. Get going, son."

The cowboy forgotten, Harvey was across the floor and out the door, slamming it shut behind him, before another word could be said. The door jingled a third time, this time vibrating hard in its frame.

Amelia looked up from her engraving block. She worked at her desk behind the presses, and was almost through with her drawing of the Cliff House Hotel. After the success of her illustrations of the Colorado Springs Hotel and the Iron Springs Hotel, Mr. Steele wanted her to complete a series of illustrations of the best tourist spots in the area. Colorado Springs and Manitou Springs could readily boast thriving resort hotels, trips to the Garden of the Gods, and mineral springs. Folks in the East should have pictures to go with copy covering the health resorts and near-perfect climate in the Pikes Peak region.

Surprised to see Mr. Steele hurrying toward her, Amelia jumped a bit when he tossed a note atop her work and then abruptly turned and left. She scooped up the editor's note and read it:

Gone to help Harvey cover fire at Livery and Feed. Back soon.
Please cover front.

While she hoped the fire would soon be out and everyone safe, particularly the animals, Amelia didn't look forward to covering the front. She'd done it before, but never liked the responsibility. Putting her work aside, she scooted her chair out, stood, then took a deep, resigned breath. The ties of her work apron had come loose. She set the ties right again as she walked between the now-dormant presses toward the front of the Gazette Newspaper and Job Printing office. Soon enough the presses would be rolling again, cranking out the next day's edition.

A customer waited.

Amelia's heart sank. *Of all the luck.* Someone already needed her help.

"Ma'am." The tall cowboy touched the edge of his Stetson when she arrived behind the news counter.

The stranger's imposing presence caught Amelia off guard. She'd no idea why. There was no reason for her reaction to him, none at all. She'd seen handsome cowboys before, maybe none as tall — this one, well over six feet — and of such fine physique, but

15

certainly he wasn't the first good-looking man she'd seen. True, she rarely socialized in town and didn't cross paths with too many folks on a daily basis. If she were a little uncomfortable now around the stranger, she refused to admit it to herself.

Much as she tried not to, she studied the roughened cowboy further. The smell of news ink evaporated. In its place Amelia's nostrils flared slightly at the rich scents of earthy trail dust and new-tanned leather. The hint of fresh tobacco coated the air, too. Without meaning to, she stole another breath. It struck her as odd that the cowboy didn't keep on talking. Most customers rattled on so fast it was all she could do to try to follow their meaning. But this man seemed to be studying her, too, and in no hurry to make his reason for visiting the newspaper known. Amelia shifted on her feet and swallowed hard, fighting the urge to make sure her ever-disobedient hair was in place. Straightening her back, she felt the grosgrain ribbon touch at her nape, and knew most of her hair was secured. More than once during her busy day, she'd have to re-tie her thick, raven hair, as tendrils always managed to loosen. She never bothered to take the few minutes necessary either to braid her hair or pin it into a bun.

16

Now wasn't the time to start. Nor was it the time to berate herself for her foolishness.

Amelia studied the man's hands instead of his face. They were tan and weathered, doubtless hardened from years of being outdoors. His callused fingers looked strong and masterful. They trembled slightly. So did her insides. The longer she gazed at his hands, the warmer the room became. She hoped the stranger didn't notice her flush. A little afraid now, Amelia had no idea why she reacted so to this stranger. The sooner she found out what he wanted, the sooner he could leave. Then she could go back to her comfortable, predictable life where little broke into the safety and routine of her day.

The cowboy grasped an unfolded piece of paper in both of his hands, as if holding on for dear life. She'd wait for him to hand her the paper, suddenly wanting to know what troubled him so. It seemed utterly incongruous to her that someone so rugged, so strikingly handsome, and who cut such an impressive figure could be nervous about anything.

Her gaze traveled back to his face. Beneath the brim of his black Stetson, before his intelligent eyes hooded over again, she saw they were a rich, rust brown. His hair, the

17

same color as his eyes, was cropped at his shoulders. She imagined him taking a Bowie knife to cut his own hair instead of going to a barber. A day's growth of whiskers covered his face, giving him a shadowy, roughened complexion. Instinct told her he always looked this way, routinely forgetting to shave. His mouth was strongly set and firm. Instinct told Amelia, too, that he rarely smiled. Her heart wrenched.

She studied his clothing. A red bandanna hung loosely around his neck, just covering the edges of his worn chambray shirt collar. His weathered leather vest was the same color as his hair and his eyes. She pictured him in chaps of the same leather, knowing that cowboys wore them for roundups. He looked like a cattleman. In fact he looked like he'd lived outside most of his life. A hard life, for sure. But then, Amelia knew many folks had hard lives. This cowboy was no different. Or was he?

"Ma'am," the cowboy began. He reset his hat with one hand, keeping his note clutched in the other.

Amelia looked up at his face.

"Ma'am," he said again.

Amelia nodded her interest and focused on his lips.

"I . . . I want this in your newspaper." He

18

put the note down in front of her on the desk.

Amelia put her hand over the note, momentarily looking away from the cowboy. It was all she could do not to read the note right away. She returned her gaze to his face, watching him, studying him.

"Here's a dollar for the advert." He reached in his vest pocket for the coin and put it on the counter. "I'll pay up later if it's more. I'll come by every month regular, to see if there's something here for me." The cowboy shuffled his feet and reset his hat yet again.

Amelia followed his every move. If anything, he seemed more nervous now than before. Her heart went out to him. He struck her as shy, even boyish.

"Bye, ma'am," he mumbled with a curt nod in her direction, as if in a hurry now to get out of there. He turned away from the counter and was across the room in a few strides.

When the cowboy opened the *Gazette* door, Amelia could see a dog waiting just outside. The dog looked like an impossible cross between a wolf and a coyote. *Both wild,* Amelia thought. Leaving the door ajar, the cowboy gave the dog a quick pet before the two vanished from sight.

Moments passed. Amelia didn't take her eyes from the spot where he'd stood. Something drew her, held her, spoke to her. It was the queerest feeling she'd ever experienced. She closed her eyes and held herself still, waiting for the feeling to pass. When it did, she was relieved and refused to give the matter another thought. She'd already wasted too much time today on foolishness. The cowboy had left the door open. Remembering his note, she smoothed the paper out on the counter, oddly reluctant now to discover its contents. She took slow, deliberate steps across the room to close the front door and even slower ones on her return. The same queer feeling of only moments before returned with her.

Steeling herself against goodness knows what, Amelia picked up the cowboy's note and carefully read it:

Personal Advert
Looking for a wife to live on cattle ranch in Colorado. I'm twenty-six years old and in good health. Will pay your fare to travel. Contact me at the Colorado Springs *Gazette.*

Yours truly,
Aaron Zachary, A-Z Ranch
Forty miles northeast of Colorado

Amelia read the ad once, then again, in utter disbelief. Yes, men still sent away for so-called mail-order brides, even though more women populated the West now. She'd seen an ad like this one before in the *Gazette,* but was not in the habit of paying attention to such matters. Even though she'd turned eighteen a few weeks ago and was a full-grown woman now herself, she refused to waste time dreaming about romance. No good at all could come from it. None at all.

Aaron Zachary. Amelia repeated the cowboy's name to herself. It suited him, she thought. Aaron Zachary suited the big cowboy. It was a good name, a strong name, a handsome name. Like the cowboy. It didn't make sense that someone like him was looking for a wife. He was a good-looking rancher who surely had many girls chasing after him. She studied the note more carefully, struck by his penmanship. Writing was important, critical in life. To read and write well was of the utmost importance. Evidently Aaron Zachary was an educated man.

Amelia looked again at the location of his A-Z Ranch. Forty miles northeast of Colorado Springs. It suddenly dawned on her that he lived on the open range, the sea of grass, away from towns and most folks. Maybe he didn't have time, working so hard on his ranch, to come into town and court anyone. Maybe he'd taken the time before, but no woman wanted to live outside of town. Maybe he'd been rejected before by someone he loved. Amelia's heart went cold. It did little good to dwell on such matters. None at all.

And it served no purpose for her to speculate on any customer coming into the *Gazette* with an advertisement. It wasn't her business. Her job was to help set type, help with the printing presses, and draw and engrave illustrations for the *Gazette*. On occasion, like this one, she covered the front desk. She'd no business worrying and wondering over what was in the advertisements brought to the newspaper.

She looked up at the clock over the front door. *Fifteen minutes to five! Oh my!* In a hurry now, she pulled a blank piece of paper from a nearby pile and hastily scribbled a note for Mr. Steele, all the while praying her boss would return within the next few minutes. In her note she explained that Aaron Zachary wanted his personal advert to go in the newspaper, paid a dollar for it, and that he'd be back and check . . . every month she thought, but wasn't sure.

Amelia put her note on the counter along with Aaron Zachary's, then quickly stepped back to her desk behind the presses. With great care, she put away her drawing pencils and wood blocks. It was a painstaking process to attempt her own engraving, but with Gabriel's help at the *Index* newspaper, she was able to get her assignments for the *Gazette* completed to everyone's satisfaction. For the most part, artists drew illustrations for their papers, and then engravers transferred the drawings onto wood blocks. Sometimes, however, the results didn't satisfy the artist, as their work might be obscured. Amelia tackled the engraving process, grateful for her friend Gabriel's expert assistance. She took great care with her drawings, wanting to make sure her illustrations appeared clearly in the *Gazette.*

Once her desk was in order, Amelia double-checked her type settings. The presses would be rolling soon. As with her illustrations, she wanted to make sure the print for which she was responsible would be accurate. It took her little time to check her work. She was a fast reader. This skill came in handy, indeed, in the newspaper business. She was also an accurate reader, taking in every word. Rarely did Amelia forget anything. Her quick mind served her well.

She glanced at the clock a second time. Five on the dot! She hated to be late. The idea of not being on time had been drilled into her for many a year. Her young charges back at the Institute, their recreation hour now over, would just be sitting down for supper. She liked to make sure all was well with them first. In particular, she liked to make sure they'd completed their schoolwork and were all set for the next school day. Advanced students had study hour from seven to eight in the evening, but not the little ones of nursery age. The primary students needed mentoring in most everything. Bless their hearts. Her charges would be going to bed at seven. For sure, she'd see to their bedtime. The fact that Amelia was now missing her own supper was lost on her.

Truth be told, Amelia relished time she spent with the young girls in her care. She thought of them as her little sisters and put their happiness above all else. If any of the primary students needed her for anything, she was there. She helped them wash, dress, comb their hair, get ready for school, and brush their shoes, and she tutored them in their schoolwork. She wanted to be there to put her arms around them when they were scared, praise them for their good work, gently correct any misbehavior, take care of them when they fell ill, and give them encouragement in all their tasks. Whenever one of the little ones would run up to her for a hug, Amelia's heart filled with joy. These children meant everything to her. She didn't question why — not anymore.

Amelia's day, like everyone else's at the Colorado Institute for the Education of Mutes, began at five in the morning. After breakfast, when both advanced and primary students began their school day, she'd head down the hill at eight sharp to begin her workday at the *Gazette* on the corner of Tejon and Huerfano Streets in Colorado Springs. Due to her new, full-time job, she no longer studied with the advanced students. Her hours at the paper were eight-thirty to four-thirty, around which hours she made sure to complete her long list of daily chores at school, as well as take care of her young charges. Thanks to Mr. Harbert, her teacher and mentor in the print shop, as well as editor of the *Deaf-Mute Index* at the Institute, she'd secured a job at the *Gazette* in March.

Benjamine Steele agreed to take her on, on a trial basis only — "her being deaf and all" — at the *Gazette,* given that Mr. Harbert had so highly recommended her. Like many in the hearing community, Mr. Steele mistakenly believed deaf people were perhaps not as intelligent as those who could hear. Mr. Harbert appealed to Mr. Steele to hire Amelia, as she was "the brightest and most promising student I've had in the print shop." Mr. Harbert went on to say that "Amelia Anne Polley bests all the boys in the print shop and I think the *Gazette* would be lucky, indeed, to have her." Mr. Harbert only made an appeal to the *Gazette* at Amelia's insistence. The first female student in the print shop at the Institute, and the first student to insist on trying to work at the larger, well-established paper in town, Amelia badgered Mr. Harbert until he gave in and approached the *Gazette* about a job for her.

Amelia had been well served for being a dutiful student and employee of the *Deaf-Mute Index* at the Institute. The weekly paper circulated not only among the students at school but also to other schools for the deaf. The *Index* helped the deaf in Colorado communicate with one another and with the rest of the deaf community in the country. News from Maryland, from Kansas, from New York — all made its way to the deaf school, started in 1874 in Colorado Springs by the Kennedy family.

Jonathan Kennedy came from Kansas, where he had been the steward of the Kansas school, the Asylum for the Deaf and Dumb, for several years. Three of his own children were deaf and were enrolled in the new school in the Colorado Territory at its inception. Supported by the Territorial Legislature in 1874 and then the new state of Colorado in 1876, an appropriation of five thousand dollars funded the Institute. General William Palmer, the founder of Colorado Springs, donated ten acres for the site. The school that began with twelve students in 1874, ranging in age from six to twenty, had at least thirty-six pupils registered by 1880. Jonathan Kennedy served as the steward and his wife, Mary Kennedy, as the matron.

From the school's outset, the boys were encouraged to pursue certain trade skills and the girls to excel in homemaking. For boys, pursuits included printing, carpentry, baking, mattress making, broom making, piano tuning, chair caning, shoe repair, painting, and barbering. For girls, dressmaking was high on the list, followed by needlework, hammock weaving, and general housekeeping. In fact, the girls' tasks seemed unending. Classroom hours for primary and advanced pupils, both boys and girls, began at eight in the morning and ended at four in the afternoon. On Monday afternoons, rather than academics, the girls were put to the task of learning dressmaking. Though instructed by a seamstress, there was little time for any fancywork. The girls sewed dresses, undergarments, aprons, sheets, towels, pillowslips, cloaks, and comfortables (comforters made of calico and cotton batting). Muslin sheeting was used to make undergarments for the poorer students.

The older girls, the advanced pupils, also had charge of the pupils' dining room, chamber work, ironing, mending and general sewing, and the cleaning of all of the woodwork above the basement. Added to these tasks, the older girls were each entrusted with the care of a small number of primary-age pupils. The older girls helped their wards get ready for the day and generally looked after them.

From the start, Amelia balked at her assigned tasks — all of them, that is, except the care of her primary pupils. Admittedly, she wasn't a good role model for the little ones. She'd never liked cooking and sewing, even before she entered the Institute, and didn't particularly take to the girlie tasks now. It didn't matter. She'd little choice and obediently attempted to become skilled in dressmaking and kitchen and dining room duties, as well as anything else she was told to do. The classroom was a different story for Amelia, ever attentive to her studies.

She'd always loved school before entering the Deaf Institute, despite her tomboy ways. Though she'd gaze fondly out the classroom window of the little Grout School in Colorado City, dreaming of riding a wild stallion over Pikes Peak and beyond, she'd return to her geography or arithmetic studies without regret. Her favorite subjects had always been reading and writing. Every story transported her to another place, another time. She never tired of reading, happy to curl up with a book under the nearest tree. Used to being teased by the girls for her tomboy ways and for being Miss Smarty-Pants, reading all the time, she'd toss away her book the moment the boys gathered to roughhouse and play nearby. They never teased her about anything, and she made friends with them much more easily than she did with the girls her age. The boys never called her names for being smart.

That sat well with her.

After her first year at the deaf school, Amelia was determined to work in the print shop and study with the boys. She didn't want to pursue girlie tasks for a trade. When Mr. Harbert took charge of the print shop, he approved her joining the boys-only print profession. Presses were loud. That was no bother to the deaf students. And so it was that the trade of printing was an ambitious yet fitting vocation for the deaf.

Before the school moved to its new building in 1876, the print shop was up and running. An early issue of the *Deaf-Mute Index,* printed at the school on June 19, 1875, announced that the Colorado Deaf-Mute Institute was "open to all Deaf-Mutes of the Territory between the ages of seven and twenty-five years. Term begins on the second Wednesday of Jan., and closes on the second Wednesday of Oct., of each year." Over time, the calendar would fluctuate, depending on the term set.

The Institute employed the use of sign language, finger spelling, and written English in its classroom instruction. Eschewing the use of speech and speech therapy to date, the school avowed that sign language allowed pupils to see their mode of communication, their mode of expression, in sign or lip movement. The school aspired to help its pupils "obtain a fair knowledge of language, be able to express their thoughts, learn arithmetic, reckon in the daily transactions of life, support themselves, and add to the general good." Faithful instruction and work was "the universal remedy for all ills to which the flesh is heir."

The oral movement in deaf education had not yet broached the doors of the Colorado Institute for the Education of Mutes, although talk of using speech and speech therapy was in the air. Deaf students under oral instruction would not be allowed to use sign language, doubtless making their communication all the more difficult since the deaf instinctively use their faces, hands, and body to communicate. This new oral method required spoken English only, in schools where deaf students were expected to learn their lessons and communicate — some without ever having heard English, and without having a good grasp of the English language.

In manual, residential schools like the Colorado Institute, where signing was considered the natural language of the deaf, the English language, spoken (speech-reading) or written, challenged deaf pupils on several levels. Teachers were aware that whether born deaf or deafened at an early age, children deprived of their hearing have no sounds, no speech, to imitate. Many words in the English language look alike, making English a truly difficult language to speech-read. Only a certain number of deaf pupils would ever speech-read effectively. Written English, too, proved difficult for deaf pupils to master. The location of words in written English differs from the instinctive location of word order in the deaf standard of expression. Only those hearing impaired at the Colorado Institute who were able to become fluent in both sign language and the English language could expect to reach a higher reading and writing level. The older the pupil when he became deaf, the better his mastery of the English language.

Deaf pupils referred to themselves as mutes, meaning they lacked the ability to speak. This reference did not mean the inability to think, or to excel, or to lead a productive life, as some in the hearing world might have thought. Indeed, deaf pupils were challenged in the classroom since, unlike their hearing counterparts who relied on listening for most of their learning, the deaf could not listen and learn. Though limited due to the lack of information received, deaf pupils learned to cultivate other learning skills. Quick at imitation, with a keen eye for form and outline, pupils worked to improve their already-adept powers of observation. The deaf, thinking more in terms of visual and logical concepts than verbal and auditory concepts, possess skills well beyond the ability to speak.

Set apart by their deafness from the bulk of society, deaf pupils came together in residential schools like the Colorado Institute for the Education of Mutes to learn, to socialize, and to graduate with the skills necessary to lead a productive life beyond school. Deaf pupils, aspiring to learn and function to their potential, were isolated from their surroundings in a way that hearing pupils were not.

Determined to break out of the isolated world, a world in which she'd lived for the past six years, Amelia had badgered her mentor and teacher at the Institute, Mr. Harbert, until he helped her find a job outside the school, in the hearing world. Though she enjoyed predictability, routine, and the safe arms of the deaf community at school, she longed for more. She'd never liked being confined, even before she'd become deaf, and somehow she felt the need to break out of the confines of the deaf world, if only for a time. The job at the *Gazette,* she hoped, would be just the thing.

At the moment Amelia hoped for something else: that either Mr. Steele or Harvey Pratt would return to the paper now! It was five-fifteen and dinner at the school would be well under way. Anxious to see to her charges, Amelia paced back and forth in front of the news counter. She imagined the look on Minnie Gilbert's face when she arrived late to the dining room.

Seventeen-year-old Minnie, for some reason known only to Minnie, saw responsibility for the younger girls as some sort of contest. She always wore a stern expression, which Amelia thought was a shame. Minnie's long, blond hair, delicate features, and pleasing shape easily made her the prettiest girl at school. Too bad her sour disposition didn't match her good looks. Minnie was already at the Institute when Amelia entered, and the two never became friends. This was not just because Minnie was rather ill tempered, but because Amelia had never been successful at having girls her age as friends. Her classmates had teased her at the Grout School, much the same way Minnie did at the Institute. *Some things have changed in my life, while other things most definitely have not,* Amelia mused.

The door of the *Gazette* swung open, with Harvey Pratt right on the heels of the editor, Benjamine Steele.

Amelia stayed only long enough to exchange nods with Mr. Steele before she flew out the door herself. She was in such a hurry, she neglected to point out the note she'd left on the counter, right next to Aaron Zachary's personal advert.

CHAPTER TWO

"C'mon, Dogie," Aaron called over his shoulder to the animal, when Dogie lagged behind to lap up water from a horse trough. Aaron wanted to ride out of Colorado Springs quick as he could. It already gnawed at his gut that he'd left the cussed advert at the newspaper. Aw, hell, he shouldn't take out his upset on Dogie. Aaron stopped and reached down to give Dogie, who'd come running, a scratch behind his ears. "Hey, ol' pard. Good boy." Dogie licked Aaron's hand. Aaron couldn't remember what life had been like before he and Dogie partnered up.

It was right after Aaron decided to ranch in Colorado, some two years now, that Aaron spotted Dogie on the Goodnight-Loving cattle trail up from Texas. When the dust settled from the Texas longhorn herd, Aaron couldn't believe his eyes — that he was looking at a dead wolf. It was hard for him to believe the wolf had been trampled. A wolf should have been long gone. Shore as hell, something had killed it. Aaron rode up to the dead animal for a closer look, regretting how damned hard life was for some out west, man or beast. The truth of it was that he worried more over beasts than he did most men.

The animal whimpered. Aaron thought he'd heard wrong and slid off his horse. How in blazes the wolf could have lived through being underfoot the cattle herd was a pure mystery. He looked closer and sure enough, the poor animal was still alive, its scrawny, bloody, torn body barely moving with each shallow breath. But for a gray blaze on its face, the wolf was all black. It looked like maybe a hoof or two had struck him — a miracle in itself — but the wolf's throat said it all. The animal must have been in a bad one with another wolf. Could have been a bear; but then the wolf would be dead for shore. Only a pack could best a bear. The poor fella must have mixed it up with another male over being leader of the pack, or over a mate. Aaron's heart tugged a little, as much for his own longings for a mate as for the poor creature's desperate state.

Instinctively Aaron squatted down next to

the wolf to see what he could do to help. Likely he'd have to shoot the poor thing to ease its suffering. The wolf growled. Aaron moved back a bit, surprised the animal could still be fighting for life. The wolf's eyes were closed and it lay perfectly still, except for quick pants moving its bare-bones rib cage. Moved by the animal's courage, Aaron acted quickly. He put his arms under the growling beast and gently lifted it up, laying it across his saddle. He'd take the injured dogie back to camp and tend, as best he could, to its wounds.

The name Dogie stuck, Aaron seeing no need to call the wolf anything else. Out on the trail, he'd come across more than one dogie — a skin-and-bones, starving, left alone, motherless calf — in his time. Yep, the name suited his newfound companion just fine. For sure, Dogie took to Aaron, and Aaron only. If anyone else got too near, Dogie bared his teeth and snarled, ready to fight. Aaron would have to calm him down, glad that they didn't mix too much with others anyway. Never forgetting Dogie was a creature of the wild, Aaron didn't tie Dogie. If he woke up one day and found Dogie gone, he wouldn't be surprised. He'd miss the wolf like hell, but he wouldn't be surprised.

With plenty of late-August daylight left, Aaron giddy-upped his horse, intent on putting as much distance between himself and the pretty gal at the newspaper as he could. He'd make camp at nightfall and be back at his ranch soon after first light. He didn't like leaving his place, and his herd, unattended. Trouble had a funny way of visiting whenever he was away.

Trouble might come in the way of weather. Blizzards could bury livestock, or at the very least, trap them, leaving them to starve. 'Course Aaron didn't expect any blizzard waiting for him. Not yet anyway.

Trouble might come in the way of rustlers. He'd already found six of his cattle over the past months with his A-Z brand changed to L-A-Z-Y B. Aaron's branding had very distinct lettering. He knew enough about lettering to tell his herd from somebody else's. Somebody else's branding iron had added the L, Y, and B, not his. At roundup, when all the ranchers got together to herd in their cattle from the open range, he'd deal with the cattle thief. Only one rancher in the area claimed the name LAZY B Ranch: Ned Bingham. Aaron couldn't figure why someone like Ned Bingham, a respected, wealthy rancher, would be stealing from him. Bingham had more cattle and grazing land than anyone else Aaron had come across in Colorado. He couldn't even count how many sections and acres Bingham laid claim to. It didn't make sense. There was a code among cattlemen — decent cattlemen, that is — and Aaron never figured Bingham for a thief. No matter, Aaron would settle up with Ned Bingham soon enough.

Trouble might also come Aaron's way from range pirates trying to fence his cattle off from their watering places. The local livestock association frowned on range pirates and after roundup, if any of the range pirates' cattle were included in the roundup, they'd be turned back out onto the open range.

Aaron didn't socialize much with neighboring ranchers. The Gannon ranch was the closest, some ten miles from his. The Gannons ran a modest general store and post office on their place. Aaron rode over once a month to take in supplies like fresh vegetables and such. He didn't keep a garden.

The only time Aaron had occasion to get together with his other neighbors was during roundup time, in spring or the fall. Coming up from Texas, starting with six hundred and forty deeded acres in Colorado, Aaron soon doubled the size of his ranch and ran a herd of well over two hundred cattle. He made sure to have at least five acres for each cow in order to have decent grazing, needing only three acres per cow if the grass was real good. So far, he was all right with grazing land, the gramma and buffalo grasses providing fodder year-round, but he needed ranch hands to help with his growing spread. He dreamed of grazing a larger herd. But for that, he'd need more land. In time, he'd be able to hire men and afford to buy more land — if nothing went wrong and if he kept finding a market for his cattle. Cattle ranching had become big business, and he could get up to fifty dollars a head in the Denver stockyards. There was a good market, too, for beef up in the mining camps. Aaron planned on the cattle business being a big business for some time to come. It was all he'd ever known, and all he'd ever wanted. Until now, that is.

Now Aaron wanted a wife. He'd grown up in bunkhouses or been out on the trail most all of his life. Once he'd made a choice to settle down and get his own ranch, he wanted a wife. He wanted to put down roots. He had Dogie, and a more loyal companion no man could boast, but he didn't have the one thing he knew he should have at this point: a wife and a family.

This was a whole other kind of trouble waiting for Aaron.

With darkness falling, Aaron slid off his horse to set up camp for the night. He'd been so caught up in his worried thoughts that he didn't stop earlier as he should have, to bed down. Dogie took off like a bullet the moment Aaron was out of the saddle. He'd be back with something soon enough.

Aaron searched out wood scraps for a fire. In little time, he had the gathered kindling and firewood ablaze, ready to skin and cook whatever Dogie brought back. He had plenty of jerked beef with him, but right about now the taste of fresh rabbit watered in his mouth. There was no cookie waiting at the chuck wagon with good eats before turning in. Pulling his saddle off Old Blue, Aaron set his horse out to graze where it wished. The big buckskin wouldn't venture far. After Aaron placed his saddle near the campfire, he took out his bedroll and laid it flat. On roundups he brought along his sugan, a kind of quilt laid underneath and on top for sleeping on the ground, but for this short trip in good weather, a blanket was just fine.

"Good boy." Aaron praised Dogie the moment the wolf returned to camp, a dead rabbit tight in its jowls. "You earned half of this," Aaron said, and reached down to retrieve the rabbit. Dogie always held onto his kill a moment before relinquishing the spoils of his hunt. Whimpering slightly, Dogie hunkered down next to the fire, never taking his eyes from the dead rabbit. Aaron took out his Bowie knife to skin it and then cook it up. Dogie licked his chops, waiting, just like Aaron, for his supper.

Aaron, not a bit sleepy, reached into the back pocket of his Lee jeans for his tobacco makings. He needed a smoke. Dogie was asleep, or at least quiet for now, his ears pricking at every sound carrying across the open range. Aaron picked up a twig from nearby and poked it into the still-burning embers of the campfire to light his rolled tobacco. He leaned back against his saddle gear, and took a deep draw.

The night sky had never looked so beautiful. Stars blazed as far as the eye could see, seeming to pick up the glowing embers of the campfire and scatter them over the heavens. Aaron warmed to the sight. The western sky had been the roof over his head on many more nights than any bunkhouse ever had been. He always felt at home when he was outdoor — whatever a home was.

Aaron could only imagine.

He thought of the pretty gal back at the *Gazette,* suddenly wondering what her home must be like. She must be married with lots of littl'uns underfoot. A gal as pretty as her for shore was already snapped up. He didn't have any illusions that he'd ever end up with the likes of her. She worked, too. Had a job at a newspaper, of all things. Aaron hadn't come across any other females with jobs like men had. The gal must be special, all right.

He'd bet the ranch on something else about the gal: she had to be smart to work at a newspaper and all. He never figured to end up with somebody smart. Aw, hell, he hadn't thought about that at all. Aaron inhaled deeply then blew out smoke. His lungs burned a little. Now he wondered if his advert said everything right. Maybe he should have said something more instead of talking about his age and his health.

Dammit!

He threw what was left of his smoke into the fire.

Unbidden, his thoughts returned to the dark beauty at the *Gazette.* He'd never seen any gal so pretty; never in all his life. Smelled good, too. Like clover and spring sage. His innards stirred just thinking about her. Funny, he'd never felt this way before, except maybe when he was sick. But then he didn't really feel sick, just queer inside. He tried to shake the feeling, but it wouldn't go away. His thoughts wandered back to his first time with a female, when the boys at the bunkhouse practically tied a lariat around him and dragged him into a saloon with fancy women and all. Aaron was fifteen. The next thing he knew he was shoved into a room with a whore — and not a very pretty one at that. He remembered being stirred up by the whole thing, but not scared or upset by the experience, as some youths might have been. He'd been with other whores since then. Some pretty, some not. Some nice, some not.

The dark-haired beauty at the newspaper had to be as nice as she was pretty. Her husband was one lucky fella for shore. Certain the beauty had never worked in a saloon or any other kind of brothel, Aaron found himself wishing — for the briefest of moments — he'd been lucky enough to have somebody like her before. The queer stirrings in his belly suddenly grated against his gut. He swallowed hard, not liking the feeling one bit.

Serves me right for thinking such about a gal like her.

Aaron shut his eyes against the starlit sky and pulled his hat brim down far over his brow, then stretched out on his bedroll. He tried to get comfortable but he couldn't — not with thinking so hard on the dark beauty. His eyes might be shut, but his thoughts weren't.

The bluest eyes he'd ever seen. Like cobalt. Drawing him in, they sparkled and shone like the clearest of days, promising to lead him to a beautiful, happy place — a place Aaron was certain he'd never been in his life. Held captive by her luminous eyes and thick, sooty lashes, Aaron sucked in a breath. The strange feelings of moments before returned. He shifted on the hard, unforgiving ground, still unable to get comfortable. Her olive skin, flushed and glowing, mesmerized him. He'd never seen a female with such a look — all healthy like being outside, yet all smooth like being protected from the sun and hard weather. Her long, raven hair, thick and shiny down to her waist, would be wavy, he could tell, once set free from its ribbon. He imagined the sight and shifted again on his blanket.

He remembered her mouth. Her full, ripe lips, all rosy and soft-looking, forming a gentle pout, lured him most of all. It was like she was thinking, was about to say something, but held back. It made him all mixed up, trying to imagine what it was she would say. Her voice had to be as beautiful as she was. Aaron gritted his teeth, suddenly hating her son-of-a-bitch husband — the lucky bastard.

Aaron couldn't help remembering the whores he'd been with, comparing those fancy women with this dark beauty. Most of the rouged whores he'd known were taller with fuller shapes and big bosoms. This slender, small-yet-shapely-breasted gal, with her tiny waist and narrow hips, barely came up to his shoulders. Her hands were prettier, too, than any whore's. Had ink on 'em and pencil marks, but it didn't take away from the fact that they were pretty. Funny, he felt like they talked without talking. Now that, for shore, was something he'd never expected to come up with.

"Shoot, A-Z, you're the sorriest thinking cowboy in Colorado," Aaron berated himself, and turned hard onto his side.

Dogie opened one eye, but didn't move otherwise.

Aaron locked gazes with the wolf.

"Yep, you heard me. Sorriest thinking cowboy in Colorado. Now go to sleep," Aaron grated out, more for his own benefit than the wolf's.

Dogie whimpered at Aaron's harsh tone.

Aaron reached out and gave the wolf a scratch behind his ears.

Dogie settled.

So did Aaron, finally.

Amelia rushed inside the dining hall only to find it empty. She wasn't surprised. The clock just outside the door read six! Pivoting on her heels, she made a beeline for the girls' dormitory upstairs. She took the polished wooden steps two at a time. The boys' dormitory was right next door. The moment Amelia reached the landing, her three little charges — Della, Gracie, and Mary — came running. No doubt they'd been on the lookout for their "big sister."

All three of the little ones tried to hug Amelia at the same time, each latching onto her wherever they could. Amelia knelt down to hug them back. Della and Mary were smiling. Gracie was not. Immediately concerned, Amelia stood and took Gracie by the hand, motioning to the other girls to follow.

Ignoring the smug look on Minnie Gilbert's face the moment Amelia and her charges entered the dormitory, Amelia continued past Minnie, walking between the rows of iron beds toward the back of the

48

extended, spacious room. Indicating to Della and Mary to sit on their beds, Amelia sat down next to little Gracie on her bed.

With Gracie watching her, Amelia passed the tip of her right index finger down over her left, flat hand from her index finger to her little finger. Next she moved her right "I" hand forward from her mouth. Then she placed her "Y" hand on her chin with her palm facing in. Taken together, Amelia had signed, "What is wrong?"

Gracie's elfin face puckered into a worse frown, appearing on the verge of tears.

Amelia, anxious to know, repeated her signing. "What is wrong?"

Gracie slowly put up her "I" hand. Then she put her little right "A" hand thumb on her lips and moved her right hand straight, forward. Next she placed her right middle finger on her forehead and her left middle finger on her stomach. Taken together, Gracie signed, "I am sick."

Quickly now, Amelia held her right index finger up with her palm facing forward and shook it rapidly back and forth, from left to right, asking Gracie, "Where?"

A tear escaped and ran down Gracie's dear little face. She slowly placed the palm of her right, flat hand on her chest. Then she placed the fingertips of her right, bent, hand against her right temple and moved her right hand downward in an arc until her fingertips touched her jaw. Taken together, she had signed, "My head."

Amelia tried not to panic. Of her three charges, Gracie's situation was the most concerning. Deafened by acute congestion of the brain at age two, Gracie still suffered aftereffects. Like Gracie, Amelia had been deafened by brain fever, but much later, at age twelve. Unlike Gracie, Amelia didn't suffer from fits. Also referred to as "acute congestion of the brain, or cerebrospinal meningitis," the disease sometimes caused major changes in the body close to the brain, eyes, and ears. Hearing loss, ranging from mild impairment to complete and profound deafness, was a common aftereffect, but less common was epilepsy and blindness. Afraid that little Gracie would suffer another fit, Amelia gathered the little girl in her arms, gave Della and Mary a reassuring smile, then quickly left the dormitory and went down the stairs to the matron's quarters. Mrs. Kennedy would know what to do.

The doctor had just departed. Amelia only left Gracie's side once, to check on Della and Mary and make sure they were properly tucked in for the night. She also made sure to console the girls, telling them that Gracie would be all right. A quick kiss to each of their foreheads, and Amelia was back downstairs with Gracie. Thank the Good Lord, Gracie's fit was a mild one, and she would, in fact, be all right.

For now.

Only for now.

Feeling guilty all over again that little Gracie suffered aftereffects of brain fever — deafness aside — while she did not, Amelia gave Gracie a kiss on her forehead, tucking her in for the night, much as she'd done for Della and Mary. Gracie would stay at the matron's until morning. Amelia felt reassured Gracie was in good, motherly hands.

Motherly. Humph!

Agitated with herself for allowing the word *motherly* to slip into her thoughts, Amelia stomped back upstairs. Her upset had nothing at all to do with the attentive, kind matron.

It was dark now, so dark in fact that Amelia couldn't even see the big-faced clock on the wall downstairs. She guessed it was well after midnight. She'd no candle or kerosene lamp with her. Anyway, she knew the stairs by heart, as she did the rest of the school and its grounds. Getting to bed without the benefit of light would not be a problem. Once in the dormitory, she knew how to sidestep the slop pails, wash stands, and wardrobes. There was little in the way of clothing in the big wardrobes. Mostly muslin sheets, toweling, and comfortables filled the wooden shelves. Some pupils had means, and some did not. Amelia's iron bed was next to her charges, at the very back of the dormitory. She loved the fact that her bed was by the only window at that end of the room. Given to staring out that same window for some six years now, she'd dream of another life, of another world — much the same as she'd done when she gazed out the window of the Grout School in Colorado City, before she contracted brain fever, and lost her hearing. Tonight was no exception.

Had the stars ever shone so brightly? Amelia thought not.

Quickly changing into her nightdress, Amelia climbed into bed and nestled under her covers. It would be time to rise soon enough. A cloud passed across the moon, momentarily darkening the heavens, but for the stars. She let her imagination run wild, as usual, picturing all sorts of ways the stars were formed in the heavens. Even the moon itself. Of course the Bible taught how God created the world in six days, resting on the seventh; but still, Amelia was prone to question most everything she read. Her mind, as scientific as nature itself, worked over all the possibilities. Sometimes all that thinking got her into trouble, sometimes not. No matter, Amelia's nature was her nature. There was no getting around that.

Today her practiced routine broke. As much as she didn't want to think about why, she couldn't help herself. The tall, handsome cowboy. What could it mean, her getting upset over the stranger? It shouldn't matter at all, but somehow it did. Maybe she should mention this to Gabriel tomorrow. Like the brother she never had, she valued Gabriel's opinion above everyone else's. He'd been her steadfast friend and confidant since she'd entered the Institute. In the habit of discussing everything with Gabriel, she decided she'd mention her concerns to him tomorrow evening, during the advanced students' study hour.

Amelia flipped onto her stomach and batted her fist against her pillow before laying her cheek against the thin muslin. She hadn't told Gabriel everything, actually. She rolled onto her back again, unable to get comfortable in bed. The straw ticking seemed out to get her. Never once had she mentioned Avery Bingham to Gabriel.

Avery had been her childhood friend at the Grout School, before she became deaf. From first grade on, they'd been close. Avery always included her in the boys' games, looking out for her as much as roughhousing with her. Some time around age eight or nine, Amelia had developed an infatuation with Avery. She was mad at herself for getting such an infatuation — her being one of the boys and all — but at the same time, she mooned to herself over how handsome Avery was, with his thick, blond hair, and, how strong Avery was, when he wrestled with the other boys. He always beat them.

Once, during recess in fifth grade, Avery held her hand when none of the other kids were looking. Amelia remembered how her breath caught in her throat. To this day, the thought of Avery could do the same thing to her. She remembered, too, how she went home that very evening that Avery first let her know he liked her — and dreamed of him all night long. Like her, Avery was a bright student. His family had a large ranch outside of Colorado City; she didn't know where. Avery's favorite subject being geography, he'd tell her of all the places he'd take her one day when they grew up and got married. Amelia remembered blushing so, her face turned pure crimson. Even now, she put her hands on her cheeks to cool them. Not so much from liking Avery, but from hating him with every fiber of her being.

She hated that he still had any effect whatsoever on her. She hated that she'd ever liked him, and that he'd pretended to actually like her. She just plain hated Avery Bingham. As soon as he learned she'd come down with brain fever and was deaf, he stopped coming to see her. He stopped liking her. For the rest of her days, Amelia would never forget the look of pity, and then disgust, on Avery's face when he first came to see her after her illness. She knew then that she and Avery were not meant to grow up and get married. Never again would she hum herself to sleep, repeating her romantic rhyme: "A . . . my name's Amelia. I'm going to marry Avery." His rejection was all the more painful since he didn't even want to be her friend. He didn't want anything to do with a deaf-mute girl. She hadn't laid eyes on Avery in six years, and didn't care ever to see him again. Hopefully, he'd moved far, far away from Colorado by now.

Time passes. Wounds heal. At least, most wounds heal. Amelia had yet to get over all of her painful memories. It would soon be five o'clock, and time to get up. She flopped back onto her stomach, this time determined to go to sleep. Sleep was ever the best medicine for whatever ails a body.

Nothing should be on her mind right now except Gracie. Amelia wished with all her heart that she could make Gracie better. She wished the child could grow up and lead a normal life, free of fits and bouts of illness. As soon as she thought of it, Amelia rolled back over, took her arms out from under her covers, and fixed her gaze on the stars, signing as she offered her silent prayer to God: "Please, Dear Lord in Heaven, watch over little Gracie. Hold her in your loving arms every day of her life and every day after she leaves this world."

For the time Gracie had on this earth, Amelia would make sure the little girl knew how much she loved her. The greatest gift is love. Unconditional love. Amelia's heart suddenly went cold. An old, painful memory — the worst of all — overtook her thoughts. She tried to push it away. Nothing worked. Nothing that is, until she thought of the tall, handsome cowboy, Aaron Zachary.

That same queer feeling she'd experienced earlier in the day when she'd encountered him at the *Gazette* struck her. Though unnerving, it helped her breathe more easily to think on the stranger, rather than dwell on painful memories. Able to settle in bed now, she was not as worried as she'd been moments before; the straw ticking no longer poked and irritated her. Utterly exhausted, Amelia fell fast asleep.

CHAPTER THREE

Happy to see Gracie doing well in the morning, Amelia stepped lightly in her black lace-up boots on her way to work. The day was bright, just like her mood. Dressed in a navy cotton skirt down to her ankles, and a long-sleeved, high-button, white blouse, she'd no need for a shawl or cloak. Not yet. The weather should stay nice for a good two months before the cold came to stay.

Dry and sunny most of the year, at an altitude of over six thousand feet, the climate of the Pikes Peak region attracted many settlers and tourists to the area. The warm Chinook winds kept winter temperatures moderate, helping to quickly melt fallen snow. Winters could have dry, sunny days just like in spring and summer, though certainly not as warm.

Amelia thought of the Indian meaning of *Chinook:* snow-eater. She loved winter. Snow covered the earth in a beautiful blanket, with Mother Nature holding one and all in her arms. Amelia always felt as if Mother Nature slipped a beautiful white cloak around her, especially for her, and only her. Then, quick as the thought came, she let it go. No good in wasting time on such foolish, childish thoughts.

Winter simply meant cold weather, and cold weather meant needing to take care of things yourself, and cover up. Struggling with her sewing and mending, Amelia had, at long last, finished her black wool cloak. She'd fashioned a gray collar to go on her cloak, just to be different from the other girls. Maybe Minnie Gilbert thought her cloak looked silly, but Amelia didn't care. She liked what she'd made.

Suddenly Amelia pictured the wolf, the dog, waiting outside the *Gazette* yesterday for the cowboy, Aaron Zachary. The dog had a dark, sleek coat, all black but for its gray blaze. Mother Nature evidently made that dog the same cloak. Amelia's mood picked up even more at the thought. *Now this, Minnie could call silly,* Amelia joked to herself as she continued down the footpath to town.

Amelia, for the second time in as many days, broke with her normal routine and picked up a copy of the day's *Gazette,* hot off the presses, the moment she entered the newspaper office. She whisked a copy off the stack by the door, left there for customers to come in and buy if they hadn't already received their copy. Tucking the paper under her arm, Amelia hurried past a curious-looking Harvey Pratt to her desk behind the presses. She hoped Harvey wouldn't come back and find her, asking her questions as he always did.

The cub reporter didn't need a reason to ask her questions, following her around when he had time every day, wanting to know about being deaf. "What is it like? How do you learn? Is sign language hard? How do you manage? Can you understand when people talk to you? Is it hard to read lips? What causes deafness? Can you hear any sounds at all?" On and on Harvey would go, every day. Amelia, ever polite, since she liked Harvey and knew he meant well, tried to answer his questions as best she could. She'd jot down an answer or two, and then follow her answer with:

Sorry, Harvey. I have to work now.

This morning would be different. Amelia knew Harvey smelled a story.

Unfortunately Amelia wasn't able to shove the newspaper into her desk drawer before Harvey showed up. She didn't look up at the lanky, red-haired youth, dressed in his same, ill-fitting, store-bought suit. Most of the time he made her smile, inwardly of course, especially when she glimpsed the part straight down the middle of his slicked-down hair. There was always a cowlick. She wondered if he even realized it. Well, she didn't feel like smiling now, inside or out, and she certainly didn't feel like having any kind of conversation with Harvey. She knew his questions wouldn't be about being deaf today.

Beating Harvey to the punch, Amelia jotted down her own question and shoved her pad toward him. Still, she didn't look up. She didn't want to give him a chance to say anything. Most of the time she could read his lips pretty well, and he knew it.

Harvey snapped up the pad, read her question, then took out his pencil from his jacket pocket. Amelia hadn't looked up at him, so he knew he'd have to write this morning. Quick as he could, Harvey penciled his answer beneath her question and set the pad in front of her.

The fire was put out fast. No body or animal hurt. Things fine. Hook and Ladder Number One did the job in record time.

Guilt-ridden, Amelia had forgotten all about the fire yesterday, what with everything else occupying her mind. She scribbled fast and handed Harvey the pad, this time looking up at him.

The young reporter took the pad from her and read her comment aloud.

"Wonderful," Harvey repeated her notation flatly, then made sure to have Amelia's eye before he said anything else. "Amelia, what's going on with you this morning?"

In her own defense, Amelia looked away, wishing with all her heart that Harvey would do the same. Well, she knew he would not. Nothing was to be done for it. An idea popped into her head. Maybe she should just tell him and get it over with. Maybe if she told him the truth, he'd pay the whole thing little mind. Harvey had a way of giving up on things as soon as he got an answer. Most of the time, anyway.

Amelia looked at Harvey again, this time smiling as best she could. If she appeared matter-of-fact about things, Harvey would likely feel the same. Besides, what was the big deal anyway? My goodness, all she wanted was to see if a certain advert made the paper or not.

Amelia took the newspaper from her lap and set it on top of her desk. She unfolded the paper, taking care now to scrutinize every page. When she found Aaron Zachary's advert on page four, she spread the paper out full. With a sinking heart, she reluctantly pointed to the advert in question.

Harvey looked surprised, even suspicious.

Amelia grabbed her pad from him and scribbled her intent.

Harvey read her note to himself, once, then again. Instead of writing his reply, he made sure she was looking at him and spoke. "You wanted to make sure the advert made the paper?"

She nodded her head, wishing Harvey would write back instead of forcing her to speech-read. How much easier it was for her to just write things down and have others write back, Harvey couldn't know. She'd never told him, since she wanted to fit into the hearing world — for work purposes, that is. It was ever a relief, at the end of each working day at the *Gazette,* when Amelia passed back through the entrance to the Institute and could use sign language again. Signing and writing were her preferred means of expression and communication. For her, they were her natural means of socialization with others.

Truth to tell, trying to fit into the hearing

world at the paper exhausted her every bit as much as the work itself. It sapped a lot of her energy each day, and forced her to remain alert to each and every thing in her surroundings. Any moment someone might need her, might want to speak to her, or might want her to do something. Ever alert to her tasks at work, without the ability to hear — unable to really relax during the day — she always looked forward to returning to the deaf school where she could, at last, be at ease and sign with everyone.

Unlike some at the Institute, Amelia never tried to talk when she signed. She had no interest whatsoever in trying to speak. Her speech, she knew, had been affected when she'd come down with brain fever. She'd found that out the first time she tried to say something. The looks on everyone's faces said it all. She felt like a monster. She knew she sounded like a monster. She was more afraid of the monster now living inside her than she was of anyone else in the room. Never could she run from such a monster. From that time on, Amelia had never tried to utter even one word.

Drawn out of her reverie by the persistent cub reporter, Amelia jumped a bit when Harvey touched her arm to get her attention. She looked at him, keeping her composure and showing absolutely no emotion. Difficult, but necessary.

"What's so important about this advert?" Harvey's expression, contrary to Amelia's, was permeated with questions and suspicion.

Amelia, frustrated and growing impatient now, jotted down her reply.

Harvey read it to himself:

I had the desk. Just wanted to make sure job done right. Sorry, Harvey.
I have to work now.

The second Amelia saw that Harvey had finished reading her note, she closed the newspaper on her desk and shoved it into one of the desk drawers. She didn't look back up at Harvey, but took out her engraving projects and set to work, dismissing him.

Practice told Harvey she was through talking with him. *For now, Amelia,* he thought as he walked back to the front of the *Gazette.* She was up to something and he knew it. He'd make sure to find out soon enough. It wasn't in his nature to leave any story unreported.

Amelia looked up at the clock on the *Gazette* wall. Noon. Where had the morning gone? Finished with her drawing of the Cliff House, she'd turned her attention to her typesetting duties, but that seemed only moments ago. Not three hours. She'd often immerse herself in her work, forgetting to eat or take a breather. Losing track of time was nothing new to her.

She stepped between the moving presses to return to her desk and take up her drawing yet again. She wanted to make sure her illustration was perfect before taking everything to Gabriel this evening. Now that her illustration was drawn onto wood blocks, Gabriel could carve the engraving for her, ensuring that the Cliff House illustration would come out letter perfect in the newspaper. Gabriel was a talented woodworker and printer, and Amelia relied on his skills. He never let her down.

Suddenly reminded of the other issue she wanted to discuss with Gabriel, Amelia put her things away and took out her lunch. She'd brought a ham sandwich and an apple, both wrapped in red checked cloth. Carefully unwrapping the cloth, she wished it were later in the day instead of only noontime, sure that she'd feel better once she'd conversed with Gabriel. About Aaron Zachary, that is. About having met him, about worrying over the advert he'd placed, and, most of all, about what was eating at her regarding the rugged westerner. Amelia put her sandwich down and wrapped it back up, losing her appetite. Mindlessly, she picked up the apple and took a bite, chewing slowly. The moment she swallowed, her stomach rebelled. Tossing the apple away, she got up and walked over to the nearby water pitcher and poured herself a cup. The cool liquid soothed her upset stomach.

She sat back down at her desk and fixed her gaze on the rotating presses, imagining how loud the sound of their clanking must be. Remembering sound, or at the very least, its concept, Amelia shut her eyes and concentrated hard. She kept her body as still as she could, waiting to see if any noise might penetrate her silence. She visualized the presses, waiting for a noise, any noise, to reach her deaf ears. Eyes remaining shut, she put her palms flat on her desk to feel the vibrations from the presses, thinking this might help her receive some sound, some knocking from the door of the hearing world.

None came.

Frustrated, disappointed, and disgusted with herself, Amelia opened her eyes and straightened in her chair. Never, in all the years since she'd become deaf, had she engaged in such a waste of time and energy. If anything, Amelia was practical. A dreamer, perhaps, but only on rare occasions. To waste time just now trying to hear again upset her more than any mere swallow of her apple.

What could possibly cause such foolhardy behavior? *Buttons and bows,* Amelia exclaimed to herself, the saying coming up whenever she was upset. From the first stitch of the first dress she'd tried to sew, whenever she pricked her finger with a needle, she repeated the utterance. Always she'd put her finger in her mouth to stop the bleeding and throw her sewing onto her worktable. Right now she felt like doing the same thing, only her finger didn't appear to be bleeding and she had no mending to toss aside. Would that she did; then maybe she could make sense of how she'd just behaved.

Buttons and bows! Why she'd have any inclination to try to hear again unnerved her beyond anything she'd experienced in years. Yes, her workdays were now spent in the hearing world, but Amelia had no desire to hear because of her job. She did her job just fine without hearing, thank you very much. And as far as the people at the *Gazette* went, she managed to understand them and communicate with folks quite adequately through writing and speech-reading. She'd never gone to work hoping that today she would hear what folks say. Why on earth, today of all days, did she imagine, no matter how briefly, what it might be like to hear again?

All she'd been doing, for heaven's sake, was trying to eat her lunch and think on talking to Gabriel this evening about the stranger, Aaron Zachary.

Gabriel sat across from Amelia in the advanced study room. The clock read seven-fifteen. The wiry, dark-haired, twenty-year-old had watched her for fifteen minutes now, going on about a man she'd met — some Aaron Zachary. Gabriel knew Amelia was bringing him engraving tonight, but he never expected her to bring him news of meeting someone at the *Gazette.* Someone good-looking. Someone not deaf. Gabriel took his wire rims off, set them down hard on the table, then put them back on. While he wasn't bad looking, no one ever called him good looking, least of all Amelia.

Dispirited, Gabriel tried to appear interested in what Amelia signed. He wanted to look anywhere, at the moment, but at her. Even though Gabriel knew Amelia considered him a brother, he'd never considered her a sister, liking her from the first.

Upset himself now, he couldn't — he wouldn't — offer his opinion on her encounter with the unknown, intruding cowboy. He'd be polite to Amelia and sit there and pretend to be interested, but he didn't have to like it.

When she got absolutely no response at all from Gabriel, Amelia repeated her question, more forcefully this time. Using firm, precise motions she passed the tip of her right index finger down over her left, flat, hand from her index to her little finger. Then she pointed both "C" hands down in front of her, a little above waist level, and moved her "C" hands simultaneously, first to one side and then the other. Next she pointed her right index finger at Gabriel, then made a counterclockwise circle with her right index finger just in front of her forehead. After this, she held her flat, left, hand in front of her with her palm facing right, then moved the little finger of her right "I" hand into her left palm. To finish her question, she placed the fingertips of her right "V" hand in the palm of her left, flat, hand, with her palm facing upward.

Gabriel signed Amelia's question back to her, his gestures even sharper than hers. "What do *I* think it means?"

Puzzled by his apparent anger, which she deduced from his hard facial expression and irritated demeanor, Amelia waited for him to continue. She didn't understand his response, almost forgetting the question she'd just asked him — almost.

"Amelia," Gabriel finger-spelled, trying to maintain his composure and not let on his true feelings for her. He knew she didn't like him — not like *that* anyway — and he sure didn't want to risk losing her as a friend. Smart as a whip, his beautiful, beloved friend, Amelia. No, he sure didn't want to trip things up with her.

"Amelia," he signed again. "It's just that I'm better with my hands than my heart."

"Your heart?" Amelia signed back to him, dumbfounded at his response. "What does your heart have to do with anything, Gabriel?" Signing as fast as she could, to hurry and get her point across, she followed one question with another. "Why on earth are you talking about hands and hearts when all I want to know is if you think there's something odd about the rancher, Aaron Zachary?"

Gabriel sighed heavily, wanting to be careful with his answer. "It's just an old saying, Amelia. All I meant is that I don't know much about what things mean or don't

71

mean. I'm good with hard, honest work, but not with puzzling over why things happen or don't happen. That's all I meant to say." Gabriel signed slower than was usual for him.

Amelia had never seen this side of Gabriel. She'd never known him to hesitate about anything, or trip over his words. It made sense though, what he'd just told her. And if he didn't want to talk about the why of things with people, it was all right with her. She would have valued his reasoning and sage advice, but she understood that he wasn't comfortable with the discussion.

But buttons and bows, why not?

Nothing about this day, so far, made any sense whatever to Amelia.

She softened her features and relaxed in her chair, sending Gabriel her best heartfelt, apologetic smile. Her drawing and wood blocks already on the table, she reached over and gathered them closer and set them right in front of Gabriel.

He returned her smile, apologizing himself with his easy expression, then studied her work. Reaching into a pocket, he took out the knife that he used for precision work and set the carving implement next to Amelia's drawing of the Cliff House Hotel. Amazed by her artful handiwork, he'd do his best to see that her illustration was the best it could be for the *Gazette*. Looking up momentarily to gesture for Amelia to bring the kerosene lamp closer, Gabriel quickly set to work.

Completely engrossed in their conversation and in the task at hand, neither Amelia nor Gabriel noticed that Minnie Gilbert sat so close, at the table right next to theirs. Minnie's presence was lost on Amelia and Gabriel, but Minnie hadn't missed a word exchanged between the two.

So, Minnie jealously concluded, *Miss Smarty-Pants is interested in a cowboy — a rancher, no less. A rancher looking for a wife. Humph.* Minnie smirked. *Well, no matter. This time Amelia Polley won't get her way. She might have Gabriel wrapped around her little finger, but she won't ever have the cowboy. No one will want a wife who can't hear!*

Minnie loved the fact that Amelia wouldn't win this one. Of course, Minnie drew her own conclusions from what Amelia told Gabriel. She had no way of knowing for sure what Amelia intended or felt. Amelia hadn't signed that she liked the cowboy at all, *but we girls know these things,* Minnie told herself. *Maybe Amelia is pretty, and smart, and talented, and her three little wards love her, but this time Amelia Polley won't succeed.* Smug satisfaction filled Minnie's unfortunately dark heart. Laughter bubbled up, as if from a boiling caldron.

Amelia and Gabriel finally looked up when Minnie brushed by them, bumping intrusively against their table as she passed. Neither knew why, or cared to know why, their usually ill-tempered classmate laughed so hard. Amelia and Gabriel forgot about Minnie the moment she exited the study hour room.

"Good night, ol' pard," Aaron said and gave Dogie a scratch behind his ears before shutting and latching his ranch house door. Dogie curled up just outside the door every night, never wanting to come inside. He'd had opportunity enough, but never crossed Aaron's threshold. Born wild, been wild, staying wild, Aaron figured. Didn't matter if the temperature dropped and a blizzard blew across the plains, Dogie stayed put, content to sleep outside under the night sky.

Aaron hadn't slept too well last night under the night sky. It wasn't because of any cold or storm or cattle thieves, either. It was because of that pretty gal at the newspaper. Why the hell he couldn't get her off his mind, he couldn't figure. Shore, she was pretty, but so what? He'd seen prettier before, hadn't he? Well, maybe he wasn't so shore about that. He wished he knew her name.

"Aw, hell," Aaron muttered and walked over to the fireplace. He poured himself another mug of coffee from the cast-iron pot hanging over the blazing hearth, and then sat down at the sawbuck table nearby. He ran a finger over the big chip in the mug's rim before he took a sip. The hot liquid hit his stomach hard. He shoved his mug aside and got back up. Supper hadn't gone down too well, either. Aaron didn't like change and upset. Never had, never would. He liked his routine, his cattle-ranching life, and his privacy. Except for Dogie, that is.

Then why the hell do I want a wife?

Me and my stupid, stupid ideas

That must be what gnawed at his gut — not the pretty gal, but the idea of *any* gal, living here with him at his ranch, robbing him of his tranquil solitude. Except for the boys in the bunkhouses where he'd lived, he'd been alone, on his own, most of his life. He was used to it. It suited him. Something hit him, though, after he got the deed to his place in Colorado, and it told him he had to do more now besides buy land and raise cattle. On other ranches back in Texas, the ranchers had wives and families at the ranch house, besides ranch hands living in the bunkhouse. Some of the hands said howdy on occasion and talked with the family members. Never Aaron. Aaron always watched the wives and kids from a distance, with no desire to go too near. He'd never known much about women and littl'uns and such, and didn't want to know. Maybe he didn't feel welcome. Maybe he was gun-shy because he never had a ma and pa to hold their arms open to him when he'd come running, like he'd seen when the ranch kids ran up to their folks. The sight always tugged at him. He steered clear.

Until now. Until he'd become a rancher himself.

Now he needed to complete the picture — the picture of a rancher with a wife and a family. It was how things were supposed to be, wasn't it?

So what gnawed at his craw, then?

Aaron looked around the well-built, spacious cabin. This larger room had a stone hearth, while the smaller bedroom did not. There was a loft overhead, and Aaron thought to maybe, one day, build onto the ranch house, adding a needed room or two. Room needed for a family.

Boys would be a big help on a ranch. Yep, a couple of boys would be good. But then, what if girls came along? Other than the cooking and mending and such, what good were girls? Suppose they could make a nice garden with vegetables. Flowers, too. 'Course, flowers were of no use at all, especially on a cattle ranch. Nope, a flower garden had no place on a ranch, for shore. Boys . . . boys were best to have.

Littl'uns would be all right, Aaron figured, once he got used to them. But it was the wife to get littl'uns with that worried Aaron. How in blue blazes would he get used to a wife? Aaron paced across the dirt floor. One side and then the other. Something else hit him, and he stopped and knelt down, touching the smooth, hard earth.

No wife is gonna like this, no sirree. He hadn't thought about it before, being so intent on finding a wife. He hadn't thought about the fact that a wife wouldn't take to a dirt floor. A puncheon floor is what a wife needed. And a cook stove. Aaron stood back up and eyed the fireplace. He'd used it like he did a cook fire outside. Had a pump and everything just outside, real convenient and all. All his life he'd cooked over an open fire. Did the same inside his ranch house. But a wife wouldn't take to cooking over the fire. A wife would want a stove. Aaron remembered seeing one advertised in the mercantile window in Colorado Springs for fifteen dollars. Next trip into town, he'd buy the stove.

His dishes, or lack of them, nudged at him now, too. The few plates he had were cracked and chipped just like his two mugs. He had four Mason jars for drinking, and they were good as new, no cracks or nothing. His only eating implements were a wooden spoon for eating and cooking, and a second Bowie knife for cutting. He could make more spoons easy enough. When he got to town for the stove, Aaron would also buy new plates and mugs, and a new iron skillet. He had the money.

Aaron made a beeline for the bedroom and reached under the iron frame bed for the money jar he kept hidden there. It wasn't a very good hiding spot, but he didn't feel the need for more security. He counted two hundred and five dollars. Yep, plenty enough for what he needed to buy for a new wife. Good with numbers and with money his whole life, Aaron knew how to save and when to spend. He never squandered his hard-earned coin. Only for necessities would he part with his money. He wasn't a spendthrift, because he'd always believed that a penny saved is a penny earned. Too much of a body's blood and sweat went into life on the open range to squander even one penny on something unnecessary.

Taking in supplies for a wife was a necessity, Aaron figured. If a stove and some dishes were what a wife needed, Aaron would make shore she had 'em. He put his money jar back under the bed and stood, surveying the room. Not much there but a bed, a straw-ticked mattress, a slop jar, and an old bench for his things. He'd put wooden pegs above the bench, too, for his clothes. Right now, the few clothes he owned were thrown in a pile in the corner near the bench, but not on the bench. His buckskin jacket, however, hung from one of the pegs. Suppose he'd try to be neater for a wife. "Humph." Aaron shrugged when he spied the slop jar. At first light tomorrow, he needed to put in a proper outhouse. No wife would settle for anything less.

Aaron stalked back into the living area, his jaw clenched. Not even considering the dirt floor, this room wasn't exactly fit for a wife. The room's only bench was shoved now under the sawbuck table. In the habit of throwing a bedroll down wherever he was, Aaron never made any rocking chairs and such for his place. He'd just hunker down on some old saddle blankets, lean against the cabin wall, light up a smoke, and take his ease from the day's hard work. But this wouldn't do for a wife, Aaron knew. After he finished with the outhouse, and the puncheon floor, Aaron would have to start on making some furniture.

Yep, boys were best on a ranch. Boys didn't need stoves, and dishes, and fancy outhouses, and extra furniture. Aaron didn't know anything about the soft ways of a female, and never figured, until now, that he'd have to learn. But if he wanted a wife, a happy and content wife, he'd have to learn. And fast. It was almost time for fall roundup.

CHAPTER FOUR

Amelia wrung her hands and paced back and forth outside the matron's door. It had been two weeks since Gracie's last fit. More worried for her little charge now than ever before, Amelia's heart broke for Gracie. Every day the child had left was precious. Every day she grew weaker, and her once-bright smile dimmed.

"Dear Lord," Amelia signed as she paced. "Gracie is only five. Please give her more time. In your mercy, grant her more time to be a child, to play, to learn, to love and be loved."

Amelia stopped short and shoved her hands into her skirt pockets. Love and be loved by loving parents. The thought stabbed at Amelia's heart. Little Gracie didn't have loving parents. Mrs. Kennedy, the matron, had said as much. Whether Gracie had been left on the Institute's doorstep or sent there by some charitable group, orphaned was orphaned. Deserted was deserted. Short of Gracie's parents being dead, Amelia thought their sin in deserting their own flesh-and-blood child was unforgivable.

Mrs. Kennedy opened the door to her quarters and motioned for Amelia to enter. She darted past the matron and the doctor and hurried to kneel at Gracie's bedside. The child appeared to be sleeping. Amelia put out her hand and touched the top of Gracie's brown mop of curly hair. The child had the most beautiful curls Amelia had ever seen. Natural and springy, yet soft and cuddly — just like her. Sobs welled in Amelia's throat. She choked them back, fearful that Gracie would awaken and see her crying. Using both of her hands, Amelia gently, privately, signed, "I love you," to the peaceful, sleeping child, and then stood up.

Facing the doctor and Mrs. Kennedy now, Amelia addressed the pair. Struggling to keep her hands steady, she pointed the fingers of both of her bent hands down and placed her hands back to back. Then, revolved her hands in and upward together, until her palms were flat and facing up. Next she moved her right "I" hand forward from her mouth. And then, she traced her right jawbone from her ear to her chin with the palm side of her right "A" thumb, followed by pointing her index finger forward. After this, she moved the middle finger of her right "H" hand along her left, upturned, flat, hand from her palm to her fingertips. Taken together, she signed, "How is she? Honest."

Mrs. Kennedy and the doctor talked for several minutes. The doctor had turned from Amelia to face the matron, and Amelia couldn't speech-read any of his comments. Amelia's insides tensed. When Mrs. Kennedy motioned and said, "Thank you," to the doctor, Amelia tensed even more. The doctor turned and offered a weak smile to Amelia before leaving the sick room.

"Amelia, dear," Mrs. Kennedy spoke so that Amelia could read her lips. "Sit down and we will talk."

Amelia nodded "yes" and followed Mrs. Kennedy to the nearby deep rose and mahogany settee. Morning sun splashed across the floral carpet, illuminating the attractive room. Usually Amelia would have taken note of every detail in the well-ordered, lovely room, from the china washbasin and pitcher, to the sparkling-clean mirrors, to the fine detail of the well-crafted wall sconces. But this was not a usual morning. Nervous, and a bit faint, Amelia didn't take her gaze from Mrs. Kennedy.

"Amelia," Mrs. Kennedy repeated. "Gracie is doing poor —"

Amelia firmly shook her head, then grabbed up Mrs. Kennedy's hands, only to quickly let them go. "Sign please," Amelia insisted through gesture.

An apologetic expression covered Mrs. Kennedy's kind features, and she nodded "yes" before continuing with the doctor's prognosis in sign. "Gracie's fits are growing worse. There is no cure. It is part of the damage done from the brain fever. The doctor believes there could be other things wrong with Gracie, too. When the brain is ill, it is hard to know. There is so much that doctors do not know about fits."

Amelia paid careful attention to Mrs. Kennedy's every gesture, her nerves on end.

"The doctor says that all we can do for Gracie is try to keep her safe when she's having a fit. She might have them more often, or she might not. But the doctor says that the truth is, Gracie is never going to get bet—"

"How?" Amelia interrupted Mrs. Kennedy. She began signing as fast as she could and still be understood. "How do we keep Gracie safe? Tell me! I will keep Gracie safe!" Hot tears were streaming down

Amelia's face.

Mrs. Kennedy tried to soothe her, taking Amelia's shaky, clammy hands in her warmer, steadier ones.

Amelia slumped against the matron's chest, letting all her heartbreak spill out. Long moments passed before Amelia straightened, wanting to know exactly how she could help Gracie.

Mrs. Kennedy then carefully explained to Amelia what she should expect, and how to help the child. Amelia filed away every detail in her quick brain. After hearing all about fits, and what to do during and after the episodes, Amelia felt better. Now she could be of help to little Gracie. Now she could keep Gracie safe.

"A teacher, Principal Kinney?" Stunned by the principal's comments, Amelia took the seat in his office he'd just offered. She had been on her way out the front door of the Institute, worrying she might be late this morning, and she wished the principal hadn't stopped her. Now, she *really* wished he hadn't. Mr. Harbert, her professor and mentor, had warned her that Principal Kinney had mentioned to him that Amelia Anne Polley would make a fine teacher here at the Institute. She'd completed her advanced studies in record time, and she was smarter than most, certainly. Mr. Harbert, knowing how much Amelia loved printing and illustrating at the *Gazette,* tried to hint back to the principal that Amelia was content at her new job and trade. She already earned a fair salary, too.

When Principal Kinney finished signing his intent to Amelia — to hire her as a teacher — he sat back in his chair, seemingly satisfied with his offer of a teaching job. He'd explained how the school was growing — so fast, in fact, that he needed to hire a new teacher right away. Since Amelia's advanced studies had been completed and she was a graduate now, it was the perfect time for her to enter the teaching profession. Yes, yes, he knew she liked her job at the newspaper, but surely the print trade wouldn't hold her interest the way teaching would. And since, most unfortunately for her, Gallaudet College, the National Deaf-Mute College of Liberal Arts in Washington, D.C., did not accept female students, Amelia's best choice was to become a teacher at the Colorado Institute for the Education of Mutes.

Amelia thought she saw genuine regret on Principal Kinney's face at his mention of women not being admitted to Gallaudet

College. It would be wonderful to travel east and study with other deaf scholars, men and women alike. *Imagine the possibilities if I could!* It wasn't just the idea of being able to go to college alongside other academics that sparked Amelia's interest, but the idea of going east, to new and unknown places. The notion stirred her, reminding her of her imaginings as a child at the Grout School, when she'd stare out the window at the majestic Pikes Peak and dream of what lay beyond. Buttons and bows! Nothing to be done for it. Amelia knew a few other apt exclamations to express her opinion of women not being able to enter Gallaudet College, but she dared not repeat them, even to herself.

Her thoughts returned to Principal Kinney's offer of a job. How could she explain things to him, when she'd yet to understand things herself? She didn't know what she was looking for. Something eluded her, just beyond her reach. It was as if she had a hole — a sad, empty place deep down inside her — that she wanted, that she needed, to fill. What did she long for? She wished she knew. What did she search for? What could complete her? And bring her contentment? It could be more education and professional fulfillment. It could be travel. It could be new people and places. Certainly, most everyone at the Institute had been nothing but kind and generous to her. They'd become her family. Maybe not her real family, but her family nonetheless. *Humph, my real family.* The thought agitated her, and her head began to ache. She got up from her chair.

"Principal Kinney," she began to sign, "thank you for your offer of a teaching job, but I cannot accept. For now, I'd like to stay at the *Gazette* and continue to live here, if, of course, this is all right with you and the Board. On occasion, if you need me, I'd gladly substitute teach for as long as you require. I do hope you'll search for another teacher. May I recommend Gabriel Moore to you, sir? He'd make an excellent teacher, and it happens that he just completed all of his advanced studies. He's certainly helped me enough over the years. And his temperament, Principal Kinney, why no one is better with pupils than Gabriel." Suddenly self-conscious about her refusal of a job and her bravado at putting Gabriel forward, Amelia stood, hands folded now, and obediently waited for the principal's reply.

"Gabriel is an excellent suggestion!" Principal Kinney beamed at Amelia, as if the idea suited him well. "I'll speak to him this very morning, Amelia. Now you run along to the *Gazette.* Mustn't be late, you know. Punctuality is key, Amelia Anne Polley. Yes, indeed," he finished signing, checking his pocket watch as he got up, dismissing Amelia from his office with a quick nod and wave of his hand.

Amelia eyed the clock in the reception hallway, glad to be away from Principal Kinney's scrutiny. Seven-forty-five. If she hurried, she'd make it to work on time. Luckily, the weather hadn't taken a turn and she'd have little to slow her down on her path to work. The cloudy, crisp day hinted of rain, and possibly snow. No matter. Snow didn't stay on the ground long in winter — in town, that is — and it was only September. It might sleet a mix of rain and snow, but nothing more.

Realizing only now that she might need her wool shawl, Amelia didn't bother to go back and get it. She'd beat the rain to work. Something else spurred her down the hill from school into town and to the *Gazette.* She wanted to check today's post at the newspaper. Maybe someone had replied by now to Aaron Zachary's advert. She saw nothing wrong with her interest; it was only professional. Wasn't it part of her job to sort through the mail for Mr. Steele? Yes, her interest in checking for a response to Aaron Zachary's advert was purely and simply professional. Nothing more.

Her heart skipped as she hurried down the well-trod footpath. This, too, Amelia decided, was purely and simply because she ran down the hill, and certainly not from any thought of the tall, handsome, intelligent-looking cowboy.

The moment Amelia entered the newspaper office she snatched up the pile of mail on the counter and took the post back to her desk. The clerk hadn't come in yet, and even when she did, Amelia still had charge of the post. Usually Amelia sorted through it at the counter, only after she'd gone to her desk and readied it for her day's work. Just as she'd broken with her normal routine the morning she snatched up a copy of the day's *Gazette* upon arrival at work, she'd broken with her routine this day, in taking the mail back to her desk, well behind the presses. None of this would be of any consequence to anyone but Amelia, if it weren't for cub reporter Harvey Pratt's curious, discerning presence.

Harvey held his note right under her nose, and right over the post she'd been studying with such care.

Riled, Amelia jerked the note from him, nearly ripping it as she did so. Much as she'd no desire to, she read the intrusive note:

What's so interesting about the post this morning?

Amelia huffed as she scribbled her answer.

I'm just doing my job, Harvey Pratt!

Harvey's sly smile told Amelia he didn't believe her. She waited impatiently, yet reluctantly, for Harvey to annoy her further. He didn't disappoint.

Amelia, you're curious about that cowboy, aren't you? The one who put the advert in the paper for a mail-order bride.

Nonsense! she penciled quickly to Harvey.
No, I'm right, Harvey insisted.
No, you're not! Amelia penciled, so hard that her lead broke. She fumbled in her drawer, exasperated when she couldn't find another pencil. One magically appeared in front of her: Harvey's. Letting out a resigned sigh and calming somewhat, Amelia slowly,

deliberately, and in her best script, wrote:

Sorry Harvey. I have work to do.

Annoyed now himself, Harvey snatched his pencil from her hand and walked toward the front of the *Gazette* office. He knew when he was being dismissed by Amelia Anne Polley! At least Harvey had the satisfaction of knowing he was dead-on right about his friend Amelia. She was interested in the cowboy, Aaron Zachary, for sure. Harvey always loved a good story. This was going to be a really good one.

Roundup was over. Most everything had gone well for Aaron, with few surprises. He'd had his talk with Ned Bingham about his A-Z brand being messed with, but the old man swore he knew nothing about Aaron's brand being changed to L-A-Z-Y B, Bingham's brand. Bingham advised Aaron, "Either your mind is playing tricks on you, young fella, or some no good cowpoke is playing tricks on you." Aaron shook hands with Bingham, believing the aged, successful rancher had nothing to do with Aaron's troubles. The two men said their goodbyes, peaceful-like.

Aaron cut his A-Z herd out from the other

cattle rounded up, and got his cattle to market, to Denver and the stockyards. Next year he'd take some to market up in the mining areas. For now, he'd done well in Denver. Once he'd grown his herd, increasing its numbers, there was no telling how well he could do, and how many changes he could make on his ranch.

'Course, he hadn't thought too much about changes until he'd decided to get himself a wife. Before roundup, he'd put in the outdoor privy and put down a puncheon, planked floor inside the ranch house. Didn't have new dishes yet and such, or the cook stove, but he'd lay in those goods during his next trip to Colorado Springs to check on his advert. By now there must be some letters there at the *Gazette* waiting for him.

Despite the presses rumbling, despite her complete focus on her drawings at her desk, Amelia jumped the moment the *Gazette* door opened wide, its bell jingling to signal someone entering. No vibrations had emanated from the door when it closed in its frame. The queerest feeling hit Amelia, and she instinctively looked up. At first she glimpsed only the rotating presses, then Mr. Steele talking to Harvey at the front counter, and then . . . the cowboy, Aaron Zachary!

Harvey turned away from the editor a moment to throw Amelia a knowing smile.

Amelia quickly looked down at her trembling hands. Buttons and bows! That Harvey Pratt! She'd show him. She'd keep working and just show Harvey Pratt that the big, roughened cowboy meant nothing at all to her! The longer she stared at her drawing, the longer she tried to hold her drawing pencil in her sweaty palm, the more her curiosity was piqued about Aaron Zachary. She just had to steal one more look at the handsome rancher — just one.

The moment Amelia dared look up, her gaze met Aaron Zachary's. The drawing pencil slipped from her hand. She couldn't find her breath. Swallowing hard, she tried to pull her gaze from the cowboy's, but it was no use. Held to the spot, and to the moment, Amelia's heart thudded in her chest. Warring emotions battled inside her, leaving her feeling exposed and vulnerable, her nerves on edge. She'd never felt so uncomfortable in all her life, yet pleased, at the same time.

When she'd first encountered Aaron Zachary, he didn't have this effect on her. She didn't understand. It made no sense. But the way he looked at her now, his intelligent brown eyes full of mischief, wrapping her in their warmth, drawing her in, most definitely affected her. There was something else in his penetrating expression, something un-readable, something beyond the moment, hidden from her. She thought of his advert for a wife. Her heart went out to him, and she was suddenly more concerned over him than over herself — more aware of his troubles than of her own flustered state. Now this really made no sense to her. That she should care and worry over a perfect stranger was ridiculous.

Amelia took her gaze from his, needing to settle her nerves and make sense of the mo-ment. Something inside her was changing and it stirred her, but equally, it scared her. Didn't she thrive on routine? Didn't she relish her normal, ordinary life? Didn't she have everything figured out in her life — that she'd work at the *Gazette* in an admi-rable trade, and live at the Institute and watch over little Gracie? Wasn't that all that mattered to her? Surely this stranger made little difference to her. The truth was Amelia wasn't sure about anything in her well-ordered life anymore.

Sorry for him — that's all this is. Yes, definitely. He's coming in here looking for a wife, Amelia lectured herself in her head.

And there was no wife for him — not yet. She squirmed in her chair, this time because she felt badly for Aaron Zachary. No letters from prospective mail-order brides had come for him. It had been over two months since his advert ran in the *Gazette,* reaching as far as Denver, Cheyenne, Kansas City, and the like. Every morning Amelia checked the post, looking for mail for Aaron Zachary. Every morning, when none arrived, she'd breathed a sigh of relief.

Buttons and bows! Amelia chided herself, all the while keeping her gaze downcast. She'd not yet looked back up at Aaron Zachary, because she was unprepared for what else might happen to her if she did. She'd had her fill of the jitters and quivers for this day, thank you very much. The very idea that she experienced relief when the cowboy didn't get mail was absurd. Stuff and nonsense. Wasn't she upset now by the fact that Aaron Zachary stood at the *Gazette* counter and was about to discover there was no mail for him, and no mail-order bride on her way to marry him? Wasn't that why she felt sorry for him? *Of course it is,* Amelia resolved to herself. She chose that moment to chance another look at the surely disappointed cowboy, her heart sinking as she did.

But it was Amelia who was disappointed. He was gone. She strained to see if Aaron Zachary had merely stepped to the side of her line of vision. She got up from her chair, came out from behind her desk, and ventured toward the front counter. He was gone. The front door had just shut. Amelia stared at the jingle bells, watching them settle into stillness. She fought the urge to cross the floor, throw open the front door, and search up and down the street for Aaron Zachary and his wolfish dog.

Amelia Anne Polley, you've gone plum crazy! Plum crazy! Stiffening her spine, turning quickly on her heels to go back to work, she ran straight into Harvey Pratt.

Backing away from Harvey, startled and unnerved, Amelia began walking right past her annoying, agitating friend.

Harvey locked his fingers around her elbow and turned her to face him. He wanted her to be able to read his lips. He made sure to erase the sarcastic "I told you so" smile from his face first.

"Amelia, he left. The rancher is gone. I told him no one had written to him. He just nodded to me and then left. That's all."

Amelia studied Harvey's mouth closer than she'd ever done before, not wanting to miss a word. A little frustrated that she

97

might have, she wrested her elbow from Harvey and, nodding her head firmly at him, signed "again" with both hands.

Harvey didn't know sign language, but he thought he got her meaning and repeated his words, speaking as distinctly as he could.

Abysmally self-conscious of her actions, she shot Harvey a cursory nod and hurried back to her desk. For the first time in as long as she could remember, she'd no idea what to do or what to sign. Harvey knew! Harvey Pratt knew something was wrong. *She* didn't know what was wrong! How could she tell Harvey, for heaven's sake! Unsure what to say to Harvey, she ran away. Unlike her, to run away from anything. Of one thing she was certain: Harvey knew the rancher got to her, whatever on God's good earth that meant.

Aaron turned his loaded buckboard away from town. He'd had enough of Colorado Springs for this month. He had a full load of supplies for the winter, and so the trip was worthwhile. It irked him a little that he'd bought things he surely didn't need — like a fifteen-dollar cook stove and five dollars' worth of new skillets and dishes!

No letters.

Nary a one.

I'm nothing short of a hell-fired idiot, Aaron castigated himself, unaware he jerked hard on the reins. His team of two horses whinnied in objection.

"Whoa now," Aaron soothed. "Sorry boys," he cooed and eased up on their reins. "I've got no cause to take out my troubles on you." Aaron spoke as if the big animals understood every word. Their ears did prick whenever he spoke. Aaron didn't like stirring up his animals. There was enough in this wild land to spook them. He didn't want to add to their worries. Aaron glanced behind him, spotting Dogie. The wolf had taken off when they cleared Colorado Springs, and Aaron was happy to see him return. One day Dogie might just up and take off to run wild, and that would be that. Hell, maybe Dogie would take off today, leaving him in the lurch just like any consarned, would-be, mail-order bride just did.

Right now Aaron regretted that he didn't take Charlie Goodnight up on his offer to go with him to the Colorado Cattle Growers Association Ball in Denver. The dance was the crowning event after roundup and market. Supposed to be lots of fillies there, according to Charlie. Aaron didn't cotton to socializing, pretty fillies or not. Besides, he'd already sent for a wife in his advert.

He'd no need to go to any dance to find a wife, he'd told his longtime friend.

Fact is, it was Charlie who helped him get the note writ down in the first place. And it was Charlie who'd told him that it would do him a world of good to go to the dance in Denver. Maybe Aaron would meet a gal there that would suit fine for a wife. Charlie didn't give up on the conversation until Aaron had promised to go to the Cattle Growers Association Ball next year, at least. Of course, in his heart, Aaron knew there would be no need. He'd have a wife at his ranch come next year. Or would he?

Right now, he wasn't so shore. Not if no gals answered his advert. Aaron soured on the whole idea — almost. He'd give it one more month, one more ride into town to the *Gazette.* If no gal had answered his advert by then, if no letter waited for him, he'd reconsider his plans. Maybe it would be enough to get his pleasurin' from fancy women and run his ranch alone, family or no family.

His horses whinnied again, more rebelliously this time. Aaron eased up on the reins, yet again. The leather strapping grated against his palms. Why he didn't wear his gloves now purely mystified him. He put the reins in one hand and reached down to scoop up his gloves from the floor of the buckboard with the other. Once he had them on, his hands felt better, but not the rest of him.

Much as he tried to shake the dark beauty at the *Gazette* from his mind, he couldn't. She shore got to him. There was something about her that reached out to him; that spoke to him. It wasn't just that she was the prettiest gal he'd ever seen, either. It was more than that. Drawn to her the moment he'd first laid eyes on her, Aaron hated her husband all over again. He hated that she wasn't available to become his bride.

The rest of the trip home, including stopping to camp for the night, Aaron could think on nothing but the dark beauty living at his ranch. In the kitchen at her new cook stove, setting out her new dishes, sitting in the rocker he'd fashioned, or in his bedroom — sharing his bed.

The whole way back to his ranch, Aaron couldn't find one comfortable seat or easy breath. The entire drive home he fought yearnings for the unknown gal. A stranger to him, an already-married stranger for shore, the lovely girl would stay just that. The best Aaron could ever hope for was that some other, unknown gal would have a letter for him at the paper, promising to become his wife.

For the life of him he couldn't picture any female, other than the one at the *Gazette,* living at his ranch. He'd best sort this out, and fast. No good came from wishing after things that weren't meant to be.

CHAPTER FIVE

Amelia's heart was in her throat. Her chest pounded and her head ached. In her hand she held a letter — a letter for Aaron Zachary. Her first impulse was to toss the wretched paper away, but that would be wrong, even illegal. Amelia was first to arrive at work, thank heaven. Harvey was nowhere in sight. Neither was Betsy, the ever-late clerk.

This morning Amelia didn't resent that Betsy was, in fact, late. The editor's cousin, Betsy no doubt got her job because she was a relative, and not because of her punctuality or her skill. Amelia tucked the letter for Aaron Zachary in her skirt pocket and picked up the empty coal bucket. She hurried outside, around back of the *Gazette* office to the coal bin, to fetch the needed fuel.

Once the potbelly stove was lit and warming the chilled, spacious area, Amelia went back to her desk and sat down. She lit the kerosene lamp on her desk, turning the wick up high, not caring about the smoky discharge from doing so. How could she see anything through the envelope addressed to Aaron Zachary if she didn't have light? Besides, she always needed a lamp anyway, as there were no windows in her work area. She just never turned the wick up high. The smoke always made her cough when she did. No matter this morning.

Her hands trembled, making her feel really, really foolish. She not only was doing something wrong, she didn't want Aaron Zachary to find a wife. The realization stunned her. The very idea stunned her. Aaron Zachary finding a wife shouldn't mean a hoot to her, but somehow it did. Looking up once more, making sure she was still the only one in the room, Amelia took the envelope from her pocket and held it up to the kerosene lamp. She coughed once, then again. Bothersome smoke. She'd little time before Mr. Steele, Harvey, and even Betsy would come in the front door. Others would soon follow. Hurrying now, coughing the entire time, she held the envelope as close as she'd dare to the lamp. But nothing. She couldn't see a thing. She couldn't read a thing.

Slumping in her chair, she shoved the horrid letter into her pocket, coughing all the while. Once she'd turned down the wick, the lamplight, less smoky now, irritated rather than soothed. "A fine help you are," Amelia signed sharply to the lamp, unaware she'd done so. *Serves me right,* she thought to herself. *I shouldn't have pried in the first place.* She sucked in a breath the moment she thought of Harvey Pratt. He'd be there any moment. If he caught her with Aaron Zachary's letter, there would be no end to his teasing.

She shot out of her chair and rushed to the front counter, hastily putting the now well-crinkled letter to Aaron Zachary at the bottom of the morning's post. It would be hours before Mr. Steele would get to the mail. He never read any of it first thing. He'd directed Amelia to sort through the mail, in case there was something that needed his immediate attention. She'd open the mail, and arrange the post according to priority. A bit relieved, not only that she hadn't been caught reading someone else's mail, but also that the letter wouldn't be discovered for hours yet, Amelia calmly walked back to her desk. No sooner had she done so than she turned right around and hurried back to the counter.

Why, she hadn't even gone through the

mail and sorted it, for mercy's sake. Focusing on the task at hand, she grabbed up the nearby letter opener and opened the first piece of mail, careful to leave the envelope for Aaron Zachary at the very bottom. That letter wasn't for the *Gazette* so she'd no right to open it for Mr. Steele. *At least,* she thought dryly as she worked her way through the day's post, *at least the letter isn't perfumed.*

Time for the noon meal, and Mr. Steele had yet to finish going over the day's post. Amelia couldn't sit still a moment longer. She set her uneaten chicken sandwich back down on her desk and scooted out her chair. In no time she stood at the counter, absent of Betsy, of course. Betsy always took an hour for lunch and always went to a nearby local restaurant to buy her dinner. No one was around, not even Harvey. Amelia retrieved Aaron Zachary's letter and slipped it back into her skirt pocket. Then she took it back out, looked at it, and returned it to her pocket. What to do now? Should she read it? No. Should she get rid of it? No. Should she put it back? Probably. Nailed to the spot and to the moment, Amelia didn't know what to do. She hated not knowing what to do.

Just then Harvey came through the *Gazette* door, back from dinner. He immediately deduced that something was upsetting his friend. He could tell by Amelia's desperate expression, if nothing else.

"What's wrong, Amelia," he scribbled and held up his pad in front of her.

She pushed the pad away, with little desire to answer.

"Amelia, what's wrong?" Harvey spoke this time, making sure her eyes were on him.

Amelia looked away.

Harvey put his hand under her chin and turned her face toward his.

She didn't protest, understanding his concern. Heaving a sigh of utter resignation, she slowly took the letter from her pocket and handed it to Harvey.

Harvey understood Amelia's upset the moment he saw that the letter was addressed to Mr. Aaron Zachary from a Bertha Hildebrand in St. Louis. He knew instantly what the letter meant, to Aaron Zachary and to his friend Amelia. Aaron Zachary had his mail-order bride and Amelia would never be that bride. He'd known from the start that Amelia liked the cowboy, a lot. Harvey didn't really know what Amelia saw in the rough westerner, but then, he didn't know too much about the way females think.

What he did know was that Amelia's present gloomy mood had everything to do with Aaron Zachary, and nothing else. Life wasn't fair. Not now, not ever, to Harvey's thinking. It for sure wasn't fair that Amelia should miss out on getting to know Aaron Zachary, and having a chance at happiness. But there it was, right in his hand, the very paper thwarting Amelia's chances with the cowboy.

Harvey took out his pad and pencil again, not wanting Amelia to struggle in understanding his words. He jotted down his intent and handed the pad to her.

I'm sorry.
I'll take care of this.

Unwittingly, she motioned "thank you" in sign rather than nodding her head. She touched her lips with the fingertips of her right, flat hand, then moved her hand forward until her palm faced up.

Harvey said, "You're welcome," and did his best to give her a smile.

His lopsided grin usually made her laugh, but not today. What a kind, good soul Harvey was. She'd never realized before.

Nothing unusual about this late November

morning to Aaron, except the temperature. Ten o'clock and it had to be at least fifty degrees, pretty high, he thought. He'd been gearing up his place for the coming cold, putting feed in the barn for his horses and other livestock, keeping his remaining herd close, making sure their pathway to the Big Sandy was open, with no range pirates fencing his steers off from water. A small creek ran through his property, but it wasn't sufficient for his herd. When temperatures dipped below freezing, the little creek bed would freeze solid. Temperatures were already below thirty-two degrees most nights; cold would soon set in to stay.

No, nothing at all unusual about today except that Aaron was on his way to Colorado Springs to see if news of his future wife waited for him. It had been weeks since he'd last passed through the doors of the *Gazette,* and Aaron didn't look forward to doing so again. He'd faced a lot of things in his life that were way tougher than this. But for the life of him, he couldn't think of even one of them right now. He couldn't remember even one stampede. He couldn't remember one time he'd been caught in a blizzard on the open range, one gun on him, or one Indian skirmish. One snake ready to strike, or even one time curled up in a ball on yet another bunk, a child of no more than three or four, fighting back tears — alone and lonely.

Aaron giddy-upped Old Blue. Suddenly he wanted to get to the newspaper, and get this over with, one way or the other. Dogie ran on ahead the instant Aaron picked up his speed. The wind picked up, too, blowing the dry prairie grasses into shimmering pathways as if they, too, understood the urgency of the moment.

"Hullo, sir," Harvey greeted when Aaron came through the door of the *Gazette.* Harvey had just returned from his noon meal, glad he was alone now at the front desk. Amelia, he knew, would be hard at work behind the cranking presses. Harvey hoped she hadn't noticed the cowboy's entrance. If he could get the matter over with quickly, so much the better . . . for Amelia.

"Howdy," Aaron returned, and tapped his Stetson in the reporter's direction. A quick glance told him the dark beauty wasn't there. Relieved, he'd get to his business and leave before she showed. Embarrassed to have her know what he was up to, it hadn't occurred to him until now, that she already did. After all, he'd given her his advert. Aw, hell.

"A letter's come for you, Mr. Zachary,"

110

Harvey quickly said, and took the letter from his jacket pocket. "Here." He held the crinkled envelope out for Aaron to take.

Aaron eyed the envelope but didn't take it from Harvey. Surprise didn't say it. Shocked did. Shocked . . . and humiliated. Except for Charlie Goodnight, nobody in these parts knew that he couldn't read. Good with sums, Aaron had learned quickly how to count and to make accounts of cattle and money earned. But reading and writing: those things he'd never learned. Occasionally, those cowboys who had learning tried to help him with his ABCs and such, but for some gall-darned reason Aaron kept messing things up, even getting his letters backward. After a time, he plain gave up. Shore, he could recognize his letters and even knew some words, but full reading and writing would never come easy to him.

Right now Aaron wished he'd had formal schooling. Then maybe, just maybe, he could get through this. Reluctantly, Aaron took the outstretched envelope from the reporter. If he went over the writing maybe he would be able to read some of it, at least enough to get by. Why in blue blazes had he worried so over outhouses, puncheon floors, stoves, and such, and not this? The clock was against him now. Any moment the raven-haired beauty could come in. He didn't want her knowing he was ignorant of reading and writing. He shouldn't care. Hell, he didn't even know her.

Aaron didn't have any time left to linger at the counter. He shoved the envelope back under Harvey's nose. "Read it to me, will you?"

Harvey scrutinized Aaron Zachary, not critically, but with critical interest. He got it. He understood. A grudging respect for the rough westerner welled up inside Harvey. It had to be hard for the cowboy to admit such a thing. Well, he'd help Aaron Zachary as best he could. Not just for the cowboy's sake, but for Amelia's. Amelia liked the cowboy. Amelia would want him to help the cowboy.

"Of course, sir." Harvey spoke quietly and took the letter from its envelope. He wanted to hurry with the letter, reading it before Amelia noticed what was going on. The presses were loud, and so others working wouldn't hear him, but any moment, ever-alert Amelia could discover the two of them. "Let's see, sir." Harvey made sure he had the cowboy's full and complete attention. "The letter is from a Bertha Hildebrand in St. Louis," he explained, then opened the letter full to read it:

" 'I am replying to your advert for a wife, to live on your ranch in Colorado. I am young and strong, a widow with two adorable children. They're precious and will be no trouble. If you send the fare, we will travel to Colorado Springs and meet you. Telegraph the time and place to me. I am sure we will get on fine. Bertha Hildebrand, St. Louis, Missouri.' "

Barely listening to the reporter's words, Aaron wanted to finish this business, worried like hell the dark beauty would find him out. "Here." Aaron reached in his pocket for the money to send to . . . Miss What's Her Name, in St. Louis. "Would you send this for me, and telegraph that I'll meet her here in three weeks' time?"

"Sure thing, Mr. Zachary," Harvey agreed and took the money. "I'll take care of this right away for you."

"Appreciate it." Aaron tapped his Stetson again and nodded. "I'll be back three Mondays next."

Harvey nodded his acknowledgement and watched the proud westerner leave the *Gazette.* Indeed he would take care of everything right away, mostly to keep things from Amelia. Her knowing any of this would do her little good. He knew instinctively she wouldn't press him on the subject and ask,

113

"What happened to the letter?" or "Did Aaron Zachary come in for it?"

It wasn't until Aaron was halfway back to his ranch that he remembered exactly what the letter said — a widow with two children. A widow named Bertha. He didn't like the name, but he was more worried about the two children. Not at all shore of taking on a wife, he shore as hell wasn't certain about littl'uns.

It was already ten o'clock, and Amelia was good and late for work. Nothing to be done about it this morning. Little Gracie had needed her; she had not been feeling at all well upon awakening. Thank God the child didn't have another fit — a bad headache, yes, but not another debilitating fit. Gracie finally fell back to sleep, a blessing indeed. Amelia's other charges, Mary and Della, had been upset over Gracie, too. Amelia tried to console the children and hurry them off to breakfast and their classes to occupy them and help them get over their upset. Since Gabriel now taught half of the primary pupils, Amelia knew Mary and Della would be in good hands. She'd alert Gabriel to the situation before leaving for work.

Minnie Gilbert, however, had been no

help at all this morning. It irked Amelia that Minnie, her quarters being close, never did show interest in Gracie's plight. Cold-hearted through and through, Minnie was. Amelia almost felt sorry for Minnie. Almost. Minnie's family was well to do, lavishing her with gifts and attention each time they visited. Amelia would watch from her window at the end of the dorm, as Minnie and her brothers and sisters and parents would picnic outside on a warm day. It always made Amelia's nose cold — pressed so against the pane. Her heart, too, went cold, watching the family scene. During those moments, Amelia supposed she could be accused of being coldhearted, herself.

Breathing in the crisp morning air, Amelia shrugged off her melancholy and hurried down the path into town. She turned her focus onto something pleasant to rid her of unpleasant thoughts. Pikes Peak. The majestic mountain towered in the distance against the western sky. The sight of its snowy caps warmed her, melting any icy introspection. Amelia marveled at such mountainous beauty, imagining herself at the very top of Pikes Peak. How wonderful! She imagined the splendid view, a view of the whole world! This wasn't the first time Amelia pondered such a prospect. From her vantage through the window at the Grout School in Colorado City in her primary years, she'd dreamed of climbing Pikes Peak. And beyond. Avery Bingham had talked of that.

Avery had promised to lay the world at her feet and take her far beyond Pikes Peak to see all the wonders of the world. Once, she'd wanted that. As a child, she'd wanted that. Now she was a grown woman, and she didn't want that. She didn't want any part of Avery Bingham and the promises he'd made her. Disappointment wasn't new to Amelia, but the manner in which Avery had abandoned her, rejected her, and hurt her, child or no, was unforgivable. She stared at Pikes Peak, her thoughts turning even darker, imagining Avery Bingham right off the edge of Pikes Peak. Not dead exactly, but close to it.

The day quickly turned as dark as Amelia's thoughts. She gathered her cloak tightly about her, steeling herself against the chilly gusts. An ill wind, for certain, she thought, and picked up her step.

The instant Amelia opened the door of the *Gazette,* flying newspapers pelted her. Then a child, a girl of about seven or eight, bumped into her, nearly knocking her off her feet. What on earth? Amelia had never seen the room in such disarray. The post, she noticed immediately, was scattered over the counter and the floor. Papers and letters flew willy-nilly. Where was Mr. Steele? And Harvey? And Betsy? What in heaven's name was going on? The room was devoid of any employees that Amelia could see. Likely they were at the presses. Out of nowhere another child, this time a boy about the same age as the girl who'd just bumped into her, tore across the room, in chase after the girl. Now the two children ran round in circles, around Amelia. A woman, Amelia finally noticed, sat calmly on the bench provided near the entry. The plump, matronly woman sat still, as if nothing at all was amiss. Could this sour-faced woman actually be the little rapscallions' mother?

The door swung open behind Amelia, the cold air having no effect whatsoever on the miscreants encircling her. Harvey, Mr. Steele, and Betsy piled into the newspaper office, and at once attempted to bring order to the room. Amelia was never happier to see anyone in her life, even Betsy. Mr. Steele, Amelia could discern, ordered the children to sit next to the woman on the bench. The children, Amelia could also discern, did not want to listen to the imposing editor. He said something to the woman and she motioned for the children to sit down next to her. Oddly, the woman huffed at Mr. Steele instead of the children. Amelia couldn't understand how anyone could be so foolish and rude.

Free now to help clean up the mess, Amelia scooped up as many papers as she could, working alongside Harvey. Harvey gave her a knowing, yet questioning look. Amelia sensed something else was amiss, something beyond the mess all around them. She'd never seen Harvey appear so upset. What could be wrong? Anxious for her friend and confidant, she hurried with her cleaning. When they had a moment to spare, she'd find out what troubled Harvey so.

As for the venerable editor Mr. Steele, Amelia didn't wonder what troubled him. He looked like he'd take the very heads off the children if he could, his face was that red with anger. Amelia giggled inwardly. It was funny to see Mr. Steele in such a state. She didn't find the chaos or the potential damage to the day's post funny, but Mr. Steele looked mad enough to spit nails. She could only imagine what he'd said to the shocked-looking woman, who had thrown an arm around each of the children sitting by her, as if trying to protect them. More giggles stirred inside Amelia. The woman was the silliest, most pompous, unattractive soul she'd seen in the whole of her life. If the dowdy, sour woman in widow's weeds was the hellions' mother, Amelia felt sorry for the children. Almost.

At his first opportunity, Harvey knew he had to tell Amelia everything that had taken place between him and Aaron Zachary in the past weeks. Everything, that is, except that the cowboy couldn't read or write well. He had no reason to withhold this particular fact other than his gut feeling. Amelia had enough on her hands with the news of the arrival of Aaron Zachary's mail-order bride.

Bertha Hildebrand!
   That woman with her impossible children was going to be Mrs. Aaron Zachary!
   Abject panic consumed Amelia. She'd plopped down in her desk chair seeking some ease, but the hard wooden chair, cushion or no, hadn't helped her frayed nerves. Never in the whole of her life had she experienced such a moment, such a tangle of emotions. One minute fearful, the next angry. One minute distressed, the next, even more distressed.

What to do? What to do? What to do?

Maybe there wasn't anything she could do, or should do. It wasn't any of her business to worry over Aaron Zachary. The rancher was a grown man who, after all, put an advert for a bride in the *Gazette* in the first place.

He deserved this.

No, he didn't.

In her heart, Amelia knew that no man deserved to be saddled with such a woman, and such children, least of all Aaron Zachary. Despite her upset, Amelia went over the facts of the situation one more time.

Bertha Hildebrand was supposed to arrive Monday next. Not today. Not Friday. She was supposed to be young and strong, with two adorable children. Lies. All lies. Bertha Hildebrand had lied to Aaron Zachary. If she were a day younger than thirty-five, Amelia would eat her hat, if she had one on at the moment. Not that looks mattered, but Bertha Hildebrand was the sourest-looking human being Amelia had ever laid eyes on. And her out-of-control children were the worst behaved she'd ever seen. Even the naughtiest child at the Institute didn't possess such a spoiled, mutinous demeanor.

What to do? What to do? What to do?

Harvey showed up at her desk. Amelia hadn't noticed that he'd left.

He shoved his pad under her nose.

She read it, despite her distracted mood.

Amelia, I'm sorry about this.
Wish we could keep that horrible woman from marrying that nice rancher. Too bad there's no way out of this for Aaron Zachary.
Too bad you can't help him out of this.

Amelia froze — the import, the suggestion, in Harvey's words shocked her. Harvey Pratt hinted that she should do something about this dreadful situation. But what? What could she possibly do to prevent the roughened, handsome, intelligent rancher from marrying the arrogant, untruthful, and, doubtless, unkind widow?

Amelia locked stares with Harvey. In that instant she knew precisely what he implied — that she should marry Aaron Zachary instead! Ridiculous. Impossible. Unthinkable! She ripped her gaze from the cub reporter, still feeling the brunt of his meaning despite looking away. She'd not give the matter one more moment of thought. Not one!

Out of the corner of her eye she could see

Harvey scribbling furiously on his pad. He broke one pencil, then pulled out another. Well, she had no interest in anything else he might say or suggest. None whatsoever. She had a lot of work to do today, being so late and all, and Harvey's intrusive, annoying, agitating presence provided no help whatsoever. Quickly now, she picked up her notepad and penciled her intent to Harvey. She put her note on top of his pad, interrupting his writing.

Harvey, I have work to do.

He scrunched up her note and threw it away, continuing with his own.

Amelia got up from her chair and picked up the tossed note, straightened it out, then stuck it directly under Harvey's nose.

He acted oblivious.

Furious with Harvey, she wanted to leave, but where could she go? Where could she go, that is, without everyone at the newspaper wondering what was wrong? She plopped back down in her chair so hard that the drawings on her desk scattered. Mindlessly, she re-gathered her work, knowing full well she'd no ability at the moment to get anything done.

What an impossible day this had become.

How could things get any worse?
How, indeed?

CHAPTER SIX

Alone, pacing back and forth in front of her desk, Amelia had worked herself up into a good and agitated state. She couldn't focus on her job. She couldn't think straight. She couldn't make a decision about anything at all, not even whether to sit back down at her desk or keep up her marching. Time stood still, though she herself found it impossible to do the same. Ever practical, realistic, clear-minded, and in control of her emotions, Amelia knew she was none of those things at the moment. Unlike her. Most unlike her.

The very idea that she might put herself forward as Aaron Zachary's mail-order bride struck her as preposterous. Harvey had to be jesting. But then, Harvey wouldn't. Not about . . . this. He, more than anyone else, even Gabriel, knew she did like Mr. Zachary. She didn't know the rancher at all, but she did like him. Heaven knew why. The last time she'd liked anyone, it had gone terribly wrong. Avery Bingham had left her with nothing but open wounds and wretched memories. For all she knew, all men would do the same thing.

Suddenly Amelia stopped pacing. A pain hit her stomach, as if she'd been smacked with a mean fist. She walked slowly toward her chair and gingerly sat down. Thinking about Avery Bingham raised issues other than romance, issues that hit her harder than his leaving had — the *reason* he left her.

I'm deaf. That's why. I'm deaf, and I can't talk right.

Amelia put her hands to her temples to try to ease her throbbing head. It surprised her that old hurts could return with such a vengeance. She might have been only a child when deafened, but she'd been old enough to understand rejection, even revulsion, on the faces of others — faces other than Avery's. Amelia, after a time, accepted what had happened to her. She wished she could say the same for others.

Rising slowly, she went for a drink of water. The cool liquid soothed her, and calmed her enough that she began to tie her scattered thoughts together. She sat back down at her desk. For the first time in over an hour, Amelia chanced a peek, through the revolving presses, at the front counter. She knew Bertha Hildebrand must still be there, since Harvey hadn't informed her otherwise. Bertha Hildebrand and her two spoiled, misbehaving children waited for Aaron Zachary to come and marry her and take all of them back to live with him on his ranch.

Amelia knew then with certainty that she did have to help Mr. Zachary. Somehow, she would. She'd figure it out. There had to be a way other than marrying him herself. There just had to be. The longer Amelia pondered the situation, the more she realized there was no other way. She shut her eyes to help her think as much as to shut out life's harsh realities, if only for a moment.

Suddenly she was in her dorm room, peering out the window at Minnie Gilbert's large family, longing to have the same thing, wishing with all her heart she had a family to picnic with on the school grounds. Was it so wrong of her to want the same things? To have a husband and a family and children, and be surrounded by loving arms. Would it be so wrong?

Amelia thought hard, keeping her eyes shut and sitting dead still. Never in her life had she asked herself to make such an important decision, a decision affecting the rest of her life. She'd never thought of being anyone's mail-order bride, but the thought of being Mr. Zachary's mail-order bride sent shivers down her spine, awakening feelings she didn't even know she had. Could this be her chance? Could this be right?

Amelia opened her eyes, sure now of what she would do.

"Amelia, Amelia," Harvey said, making sure she looked directly at him, at the same time trying to still her rapidly moving hand signs. He'd no idea at all what she was trying to say. He'd come back to her desk to see if she'd made up her mind about the cowboy, agreeing or disagreeing to marry him.

Frustrated, Amelia stomped her foot, and labored to free her hands so she could let Harvey know how he had to help her. There was so much to do and so little time.

"Amelia," Harvey tried again, hoping to reason with her, to communicate with her.

Amelia dropped her hands to her sides, only now realizing she'd been signing to Harvey when he didn't understand a word. This was unlike her. Very unlike her. She'd been so intent on getting her point across to Harvey that she'd reverted to her first choice in communication: signing. She should have known better. She knew full well that people who did not know sign language couldn't understand, and that her own preferred means of communication certainly wasn't the preferred language of the hearing. Nothing to be done for it. Doing her best to calm down and go slowly, she heaved a sigh and sat back down at her desk, taking out her pencil and pad. It took effort, but she managed to still her shaky fingers enough to pencil her intent. She finished and handed her pad to Harvey.

He pulled a nearby chair up to Amelia's desk and sat down before reading her note.

You must ask Bertha Hildebrand to leave.
She and her children have to leave.
Tell her that Mr. Zachary is sorry but he had a change of heart.

Harvey smiled at first, knowing Amelia's decision now, then shook his head and wrote an answer.

That woman won't go quietly.
If she leaves, she'll demand money for the train and her trouble.

Buttons and bows! Amelia hadn't thought that she might need money to get rid of the dowdy, sour-faced widow. Her hand instinctively went to her throat, feeling over her clothing for her necklace, which usually brought her some solace. The necklace was the only remnant, the only tie, to her past that she'd kept. Wherever would she get the money to get rid of Bertha Hildebrand? Amelia earned a salary and saved what she could, but she had spent most of her hard-earned coin on Gracie, Mary, and Della. They were her family, especially little Gracie. Amelia didn't have any extra money to put the Hildebrands on a train back to St. Louis.

She could ask Harvey to help. No, she couldn't. That wouldn't be right. Harvey worked hard and didn't have much, either. What to do? What to do? What to do? She ran her hand over her necklace, absentmindedly pulling the chain out from under her blouse. She ran her fingers over the familiar ridges in the little gold nugget, seeking comfort as much as an answer to her dilemma.

There it was! Right in front of her. Right in her hand. She had to part with her necklace. It was the only way.

Fast as she could, she penciled her

thoughts to Harvey, and removed her necklace the moment she'd finished.

Take this, please, to the assay office, and get the money. It should be enough to cover all the expenses.

Harvey nodded his agreement and took the outstretched gold nugget. If he had questions, he kept them to himself. He messaged to Amelia that he'd go right away and return soon. Then, he'd deal with Bertha Hildebrand. *After that,* he mouthed so that she would understand him, *we'll finish our talk.*

To this, Amelia nodded in agreement. She watched Harvey pass through the presses to leave for the assay office, taking a treasured part of her — a piece of her past now gone forever — with him.

Unable to concentrate since she'd just, by her own choice, turned her life around and absolutely upside town, Amelia had begun sorting out everything in, on, and around her work area. She'd have to beg Mr. Steele's forgiveness and quit her job. She loved her job. She took pride in her job, having accomplished a lot and working hard to get where she was. And what of Mr. Harbert? Oh, she hoped he'd understand that she was getting married.

Married. The idea of it made her tremble, inside and out. Fear piled upon fear until she worried she'd throw up. She couldn't imagine having a conversation with Mr. Steele or Mr. Harbert or Gabriel or anyone else about getting married. It was all embarrassing and unexpected. What would any of them say? What would they think of her? *Amelia Anne Polley, you've no time for this,* she lectured herself. *You've no time to worry over what people will think. Maybe you don't exactly have to say mail-order bride. You'll have to explain things as best you can. You certainly don't want everyone worrying over you, for pity's sake. You must be clear and certain and calm. Yes, calm.*

Amelia's newfound calm, unfortunately, was soon interrupted by the most important matter in all of the day's tortuous decision-making — *Gracie.* Amelia could resolve to leave the Deaf Institute behind. She could resolve to leave her wonderful friend Gabriel. And even, God forgive her, little Della and Mary. Bless their hearts, they were healthy and smart. They could grow up to do anything. That was the pity of it. Little Gracie wouldn't grow up to do anything — she wouldn't grow up. The hourglass had

131

overturned long ago for Gracie. Amelia had no idea how many precious grains of sand the child had left.

She couldn't leave Gracie. The child was a part of her heart. What to do? What to do? The situation presented complications. The situation required all the stars being aligned in proper order. First and foremost, Mr. Zachary would have to agree to take Gracie, too. Next, Principal Kinney and the Kennedys, the steward and matron of the Deaf Institute, would have to agree to let Gracie become her ward on an official basis. They would have to agree to entrust Gracie to her care. And, my goodness, Gracie would have to want to go with her. Amelia almost changed her mind about everything. Almost.

Amelia realized she couldn't put first things first. She had to work backward. Everything must be straightened out and settled at the Institute and at the *Gazette,* with all parties involved, before Mr. Zachary would know about any of it. My gracious. Before he even agreed to marry her.

What if he didn't want to? What if Aaron Zachary took one look at her and turned on his heels? What if he found her wanting? What if he couldn't accept her deafness? Certainly she should tell him that she didn't hear. But then, in the very next moment, Amelia was certain she should not. With everything else going on, with leaving her job and the Institute and her friends, especially with Gracie entrusted to her care, Amelia didn't think she had enough left inside her to deal with Aaron Zachary's reaction when he learned she was deaf.

She remembered the look on Avery Bingham's face.

And by her actions in becoming Mr. Zachary's mail-order bride, was she doing something far worse to him than being sentenced to a life with the likes of Bertha Hildebrand?

For the first time in this whole impossible day, a tear escaped down Amelia's feverish cheek. One, then another. She wiped them away. Tears didn't help anything.

Amelia decided to look on the positive side. If she was steadfast and confident in her choice, then so, too, would Mr. Zachary be. After all, he was an educated man. His penmanship was good. He'd obviously gone to school and reaped the advantages of an education. He wouldn't mind, after he thought about things, writing to her. They could easily communicate through writing. She'd been able to read his lips, at least partially. Taken together, writing and lip-reading should suffice. And hadn't she adjusted well enough to a hearing world in the past months? Mr. Zachary, given time, would adjust to her deaf world.

Yes, it will all work out.

It has to.

The clock near Amelia read two-thirty in the afternoon. Through with tidying up her things at her desk, she had to wait for Harvey before anything else could be done. She'd communicate with Mr. Steele at the close of the workday, but, not yet. She wanted to venture to the front office, to the front counter, to see if Bertha Hildebrand still waited. *I'm nothing short of a coward,* Amelia scolded herself. The very thought made her charge to the front counter, mindless of the stares from her coworkers as she did.

The ax fell. The guillotine sliced off another head.

There sat Bertha Hildebrand, exactly where Amelia had left her hours ago! Amelia's heart dropped to her feet. Dear Lord, what was going on? Where was Harvey? *My, oh my.* Both children hopped off the bench and came running over to Amelia, mischief, no doubt, on their minds. They started running around, playing chase, and once again knocking papers off the counter. Amelia shot a disapproving look at Bertha Hildebrand, who did nothing and made no attempt to say anything. Was there ever a ruder woman on the face of the earth?

Amelia hurried out from behind the counter and put herself in between the mischievous children. She managed to grab an arm of each one, then marched them over and sat them down next to their ineffectual mother. At this, Bertha Hildebrand rose from her chair, glaring at Amelia with eyes like those of the devil himself. She began gesturing and saying things to Amelia, but Amelia refused to take any of it, turning on her heel and walking back across the room. She wanted nothing more to do with the woman.

At the same time Bertha Hildebrand let go her tirade at Amelia's back, Harvey walked in. Just when Bertha Hildebrand screamed, "What's the matter with you? Are you deaf?"

Harvey couldn't help himself. "As a matter of fact, she is." The instant he said it, he regretted revealing anything about Amelia to the horrible widow. If he weren't a gentleman, he'd wipe the smug smile off Bertha Hildebrand's face with the back of his hand. Her equally horrible children then got up and began running around the space teasing, "The lady is a dummy. The lady is a dummy."

For the first time since he'd met Amelia, Harvey was grateful she was deaf. In no way did he want her to catch on to any of this cruel mocking.

When Amelia turned around, eye to eye with Harvey, he motioned her away. She understood. He would now deal with the Hildebrand brood. She prayed it wouldn't be too much of an ordeal for him. *Bless Harvey. I couldn't do any of this without him today.*

Amelia carefully penned her letter to Aaron Zachary. If everything went according to plan, Mr. Zachary would believe that her letter arrived after Bertha Hildebrand's. And that Bertha Hildebrand had had a change of heart and telegraphed that she wasn't coming. Instead, she, Amelia Anne Polley, was answering his advert for a mail-order bride. Nerves on edge, Amelia finished her letter and read it back to herself:

Dear Mr. Zachary,
My name is Amelia Anne Polley. I'm eighteen years old, strong, and healthy. I'd like to marry you and learn about ranching. I reside in Colorado Springs.

No travel fare will be necessary. I have a ward, five-year-old Gracie, I'd like to bring, too. If you agree, I'll meet you Monday next, at the Gazette. The justice of the peace is close by.

Respectfully,
Amelia Anne Polley

Amelia couldn't believe her boldness in suggesting the justice of the peace was close by. But then again, that's what this day required — brass and boldness. She had two days to sort everything out and be ready for Monday morning.

On his way back to his rooming house late that same Friday evening, Harvey's thoughts were troubled. Glad for most everything that had happened for Amelia today, he remained unsure of one thing — he'd didn't tell Amelia that the rancher, Aaron Zachary, couldn't read or write. He should have. He knew it. But his gut had told him not to. So, he didn't.

And there was one more slight on his part. This one, perhaps, was at the expense of the rancher. Amelia didn't want Aaron Zachary to know she was deaf. The man was sure to find out soon enough, Harvey argued. He tried to reason with Amelia, but in the end, he gave in to her. She flat out thought it wouldn't be the right time. She would find the right time and, of course, Mr. Zachary would know. Harvey accepted that Amelia knew what was best. She was a goodhearted young woman with a good nature. If she thought her way was the best, then so be it.

Still, Harvey couldn't take in a full, easy breath when he thought on the matter.

Aaron shook off his driving glove, and tried to loosen the collar of his only boiled shirt. He gave up and unbuttoned the top button. Hell, was any of this trouble worth it? He pulled his glove back on and shared the reins of his team of horses with both hands. The December morning was bitter cold. Hadn't warmed up to more than twenty degrees, he suspected. A little different from his last trip into Colorado Springs, in more ways than one. He'd broken camp this morning before dawn and would arrive in town sooner than expected.

Aaron hadn't donned his dress clothes since that funeral back in Texas that all of the cowboys on the Big Hereford Ranch had to attend. It took most all of Aaron's money at the time to buy the gall-darned store-bought clothes. At least he hadn't thrown out the scratchy brown wool vested suit. This occasion called for it, he supposed. Still, he kept on his weathered leather boots and Stetson. Wouldn't change those for any new wife. No, sir.

New wife. His new wife was a woman named Bertha Hildebrand. Damn, he sure hoped all of these doings were worth it. Nervous as hell inside, he couldn't even enjoy his coffee this morning. If he loved anything in life — more than Dogie, that is — it was his morning brew. Well, not this morning. The mere thought of getting to know the woman, a stranger to him, and her two littl'uns ate at him.

Suppose she's a real talker, like most females. Suppose my peace and quiet days are long gone.

But then again, he'd have a ready-made family. Isn't that what he wanted — a family with a decent, good woman who'd cook and clean and mend and such — a woman who could be a part of his ranch, in his bed and his life for the rest of their lives?

"Yep, the thing to do here . . ." Aaron talked to his horses now. He knew they listened, the way their ears pricked back. "The thing to do, boys, is to look on the bright side. I'll have me a wife and two kids. I'll have my own family." Aaron, for the briefest of moments, thought back to his childhood. He thought back to those days when he'd play outside the bunkhouse, staring at the ranch children and their parents. He never got tired of it. He never tired of seeing how happy they always seemed to be. The parents never invited him inside their ranch house. The other kids never invited him to play. But Aaron determined, always, to one day have his own family. He determined, too, never to turn his back on anyone. It wasn't in his nature.

"So, boys," Aaron continued to his team, "looks like we'll be a family soon enough." He tried to relax at his own words, and settle his nervous innards. All of this would be over soon. He'd meet Bertha Hildebrand and her littl'uns and have the ceremony and they'd all be heading back to his ranch before noon. Any moment it would snow. The cloudy sky and chill, moist air told him as much. His team would do all right in the weather, but he wasn't so sure about his new family. He giddy-upped the horses, turning behind to whistle for Dogie to do the same.

Dogie wasn't there. Aaron figured right away that the wolf had run off to hunt. He wasn't worried. Dogie knew the way home, when he was ready. Blue blazes! Aaron almost pulled his team up short at the thought that just hit him. *Dogie!* Dogie was a worry. How would Bertha Hildebrand and her littl'uns take to a wolf? More to the point, how would Dogie take to the woman and her littl'uns?

Aaron would need to do more than unbutton his shirt collar to take his ease about this worry. His instincts told him to turn his buckboard around and head back to his ranch, and give up on the whole crazy idea. Going against his instincts, however, he kept on going.

"You look so pretty," Amelia signed to little Gracie.

The child grinned ear to ear, apparently happy over Amelia's doting and her new adventure. She threw her arms around Amelia, who still knelt before her.

Amelia started laughing, finding it hard to catch her breath with Gracie's arms wrapped around her neck that way. She untangled the child's arms and gave each of her little hands a kiss. Then she signed to Gracie that they needed to hurry and say goodbye once again to Della and Mary.

Gracie nodded yes and scurried over to her bed to fetch her dolly.

Amelia's heart broke all over again for

Gracie. Why didn't she buy Gracie a new doll before, when she'd had the money? Why didn't she use her necklace for Gracie? Guilty that she hadn't thought of it before, Amelia couldn't undo what she'd done, or hadn't done. She hadn't bought Gracie a new doll. And now she didn't have the funds to do so. As it was, Gracie's doll was a little straw concoction that Gabriel had helped craft. Amelia had made a calico dress for the straw doll, but somehow it didn't seem enough. Gracie didn't complain. Gracie smiled at everything. Amelia knew she should do the same. If she had only a little of Gracie's zest and positive spirit, she'd be a far better person for it.

With a heavy heart, Amelia rose and straightened out her black wool skirt. It wasn't new, but it was her best. And she'd polished her prized black lace-ups. Sticking out one toe from beneath her ankle-length hem, she assured herself that her boots nearly sparkled. She'd put on her very best white blouse, too. She'd added lace at the collar, which, for her, was quite a feat of sewing. Everything in dressmaking class had taken effort for her. Not to worry. Her blouse was fine. She didn't have a cameo to place at her neck, but that was fine, too. Such frivolities were unnecessary.

Of one thing she was glad. Her black wool cloak was not only pretty, she prided herself in thinking, but very serviceable. She'd need a warm cloak for this day. The air outside was bitterly cold, and her shivers inside needed warming, too. If only her stomach would stop flip-flopping. As for her hair, Amelia wore it the same today as always, caught up in a grosgrain ribbon. She'd chosen a black one to match her skirt. She reached under her bed for her worn satchel. She'd packed it the night before and just wanted to make sure her things were in order. As for personal effects, she'd none to leave behind at the Institute, having given her only treasure to Harvey to sell.

Glancing over at Gracie, watching her pack her straw doll with such care, Amelia knew the straw doll must mean as much to Gracie as her necklace did to her. But still, it was a shame Gracie didn't have a proper doll. She'd love that one, too.

Mercy sakes! Amelia looked at the clock in the downstairs hallway. Eight on the dot. She'd arranged with Harvey to be at the *Gazette* at eight-thirty, the start of her regular workday. And she'd no idea exactly when Aaron Zachary would arrive, but she knew it had to be soon. With little time to make her good-byes, yet again, to Gabriel

143

and Della and Mary, Amelia directed Gracie to put her small satchel down next to Amelia's, near the front door of the school. Then she caught Gracie's hand up in hers to hurry and find Gabriel and the children.

It took everything she had in her not to think about her upcoming meeting with Aaron Zachary. It could be the best moment of her life, or the absolute worst.

CHAPTER SEVEN

Where were their satchels? Amelia looked all around the reception area, panicked now. She pictured Mr. Zachary waiting on the bench inside the *Gazette,* impatient for her to appear. What if he left? He might. What if he had a change of heart? He might. Gracie tugged on her skirt, seemingly trying to get Amelia's attention. Amelia took Gracie's hand away, gave it a gentle pat, and then scurried inside the reception office.

Signing quickly to the receptionist, Amelia asked Mrs. Beale if she knew where the two satchels went. Near frantic, Amelia didn't notice at first when Gracie, again, tugged at her skirt. Motioning to Mrs. Beale — "One moment, please" — Amelia turned her attention to Gracie. Gracie tugged harder on her skirt, wanting, no doubt, for Amelia to come with her. Amelia, despite her anxious state, did so.

Gracie tugged on Amelia's skirt across the

main hall of the school, out the front door, and down the steps. Intent on following Gracie, and making sure the child didn't stumble, Amelia didn't look up until they'd reached the bottom step. Once she did, and she saw Mr. Higgins, the school laundry man, sitting in the driver's seat of the school buggy, she understood why little Gracie had dragged her outside. In the back of the buggy, loaded next to both satchels, was Amelia's packed crate of books. Mercy sakes. She'd forgotten all about her precious store of books and school supplies for Gracie.

Principal Kinney not only offered her the use of duplicate books from the school library, but he let her take primary books for Gracie, including *Peck's Arithmetic, Peet's First Lessons for Deaf Mutes,* and a small *Webster's.* Besides nearly forgetting the necessary supplies for Gracie's schooling, Amelia scolded herself. She couldn't believe she thought to leave for an isolated ranch out on the open prairie without her own books. She quickly ran down the list in her head. She'd selected some, but not all, of her favorites. They included *Moby-Dick, Jane Eyre, The Scarlet Letter, The Last of the Mohicans, Essays and Nature* by Emerson, *The Pickwick Papers, A Tale of Two Cities,*

On the Duty of Civil Disobedience by Thoreau, *Uncle Tom's Cabin, Madame Bovary,* and *Silas Marner.* Two she'd not brought, there being no extra copies, were *Letters on the Equality of the Sexes and the Condition of Woman,* and *Narrative of the Life of Frederick Douglass, An American Slave.* She did pack her Bible. The Institute had given her her own Bible when she'd graduated from primary to advanced. And she took a duplicate of *'Twas the Night Before Christmas* for Gracie.

Unlike her. Very unlike her, to forget such things.

It's a wonder I remembered Gracie, at the rate I'm going this morning!

Intent on her upcoming marriage, so nervous now she felt faint, Amelia had allowed the supply crate and the offer of a ride to the *Gazette* to slip her mind entirely. Right now, if she were not careful, she feared she might be in danger of losing her mind. Buttons and bows! Suddenly petrified, feeling more inept than ever before, Amelia couldn't fathom how on this earth, she was to become anyone's wife.

Nodding to kind Mr. Higgins, she indicated that she'd be right back. Besides his duties with the laundry at the Institute, Mr. Higgins was in charge of taking care of the lamps, scrubbing the floors, and helping to look after the younger boys. Amelia appreciated his help this morning. Gracie scrambled into the buggy. Amelia signed to Gracie that she'd return in a moment, then hurried back inside to let the receptionist know, "All is well."

Lord in Heaven, Amelia thought. *If only that were true!*

"Not coming, you say?" Aaron repeated to Harvey Pratt at the counter of the *Gazette.*

"Not coming, Mr. Zachary," Harvey said again. Quickly now, before the cowboy reared up like a wild stallion and turned and left, Harvey put forth the contrived explanation. "The widow Hildebrand telegraphed to say she was sorry, but she'd had a change of heart and couldn't move away from her family and friends. She refunded your money, which I have here," Harvey said, and he pulled the right amount from his pocket — money left from the sale of Amelia's necklace.

"Thanks," Aaron muttered and took the money, more disappointed than he let on. "I best be going," he said quietly to the reporter, and turned to leave. His business at the *Gazette* was definitely *over.*

"No, sir, wait," Harvey implored, and

pulled yet another envelope from his pocket. "This is another response to your advert. From someone here in Colorado Springs. She's coming this morning to meet you and, maybe, marry you." Harvey didn't mean to sound so urgent. He didn't want to raise the cowboy's suspicions.

"Hold on," Aaron said in a low voice, and faced Harvey full again. "Are you fooling with me?" Aaron had had about enough of the *Gazette* and this reporter and the whole crazy idea of finding a mail-order bride.

Harvey swallowed hard. He didn't want to get into a tangle with the tough-looking cowboy. He'd lose for sure. "Sir, the *Gazette* doesn't fool with anybody." He tried to keep his voice even. "This is a bona fide letter for you in answer to your advert. Would you like me to read it to you?" Harvey asked this last as respectfully as he could, not wanting to further raise Mr. Zachary's ire.

Aaron stared long and hard at the letter in Harvey Pratt's shaky hands. If this was a joke, the reporter would see his fist soon enough. "Yeah, read it," Aaron said, wary of what the letter might say.

"Yes, sir. Of course, sir." Harvey, grateful no one else was at the front counter, carefully read Amelia's letter to the agitated rancher.

"One more time," Aaron said, his voice losing its angry tone.

Harvey did so.

Aaron shook his head, a little disbelieving, but interested all the same. He'd come for one wife and was about to meet another. Maybe. This one didn't have two kids, but one, a ward or some such. This one was eighteen. This one wanted to learn to ranch. This one had a much prettier name. Amelia. Aaron shore liked the sound of it. If all of this were a joke, he'd find out soon enough. The lady and the littl'un were supposed to arrive any time now, according to Harvey Pratt.

Aaron, his wagon tied out back of the *Gazette,* took a seat on the nearby bench to wait for Amelia Anne Polley to come through the door. He did his best to focus on Amelia, rather than the pretty gal with raven hair that worked at the newspaper. If she showed up, he might not be able to go through with marrying some gal named Amelia, his soon-to-be, mail-order bride. Nope. At best, this wasn't going to be easy. He shore as hell couldn't go through with any of this in front of the dark beauty.

People came and went. The door of the *Gazette* opened and closed more times than Aaron liked. His jitters got worse every time someone entered. He started feeling like a stalled, spooked horse. If the beauty with black hair came in before Amelia Anne Polley, what the hell was he going to do?

The door of the *Gazette* opened wide, its bell jingling loud and clear.

Aaron had just lit a smoke, needing one for shore. He took a deep inhale at the sound of the door opening, dreading what or who he'd see had come in.

Amelia left Gracie in the buggy out front with Mr. Higgins, wanting this meeting to be as private as possible. She wished she'd arranged with Harvey to meet Mr. Zachary out back or somewhere away from curious eyes. Staring hard at the toes of her black lace-up boots, she'd yet to find the courage to face Aaron Zachary and the *Gazette* staff. She didn't know if she could even face Harvey at this impossible moment.

Her heart and head had filled with regret, doubt, trepidation, and guilt over leaving the Institute and the *Gazette,* replaced by a complete and utter lack of self-confidence. Never had she been so frightened. Not even when she was ill and lost her hearing. Not even when she found she was alone in the world. Not even when Avery Bingham deserted her. And, God forgive her, not even

151

when little Gracie teetered on the brink of a debilitating fit. Guilty for her focus on herself now, and not Gracie, Amelia straightened her shoulders and raised her head.

Aaron stamped out his smoke, pulled off his Stetson, and stood up the moment he saw the raven-haired beauty. Dammit. Blue blazes! Why the hell did she have to get here before his bride?

Frozen to the spot, Amelia stared up at the cowboy. She hadn't remembered how he towered over her. But yes, her head only came to his shoulders. She had, however, remembered how handsome he was. His looks didn't disappoint. In fact, she realized now that he was even better looking than she'd thought. With his hat off, his thick brown hair, cropped at the neck, framed his shadowy face perfectly. His face, as before, hinted of a day's growth of beard, as if he'd forgotten to shave. She liked it, and imagined what it might feel like to touch him there. *Buttons and bows, Amelia Anne Polley!* She scolded inwardly. *Remember decorum! Remember you are a lady!* But when she looked at the cowboy, she didn't feel like a lady.

He was impressive — well muscled, with broad shoulders — in his Sunday suit, Amelia thought. She had never seen someone fit his clothes as well as Aaron Zachary did. And his eyes, the way they captured hers in their intelligent yet mischievous gaze, sent tingles up and down her spine. His mouth drew her attention, too. His lips, all smooth and gentle looking, almost formed a smile. Almost. Nervous beyond anything she'd ever known, she knew that any moment she'd lose what little breakfast she'd been able to swallow. How would that be, right in front of Mr. Zachary?

For his part, Aaron, too, stood frozen to the spot.

Never having had Bible learning, he had no idea what angels were supposed to look like, but to his way of thinking, for shore this was an angel. No matter that he had devilish thoughts when he looked at her. There wasn't any gal prettier in the West than this one. She looked all new and clean, and made just — *for me.* Yep . . . right at the moment, Bible learning or no, Aaron thought for shore God had made this female for him, and him alone. Instantly possessive, he forgot all about the fact that she wasn't his mail-order bride. She wasn't Amelia Anne Polley. In fact he couldn't think on anything but taking this gal back with him to his ranch, and getting her into his bed quick as he could.

He imagined her without her cloak, without her outer clothes, her hair tie gone, with her boots off, and in her undergarments . . . waiting for him to remove them. Suddenly he wanted — he needed — to hear her moan for him, and him only. Her ripe, full lips were meant for him to kiss. Her smooth complexion was made for him to touch. Her shiny black hair was made for his fingers to thread. Her cobalt eyes were made for him to lose himself in their alluring depths. Her slender, shapely body was made for him to kiss and stroke and enter and call his own. Aaron swallowed hard, unmindful that he'd unbuttoned his collar button yet again. He tried to suck in a deep breath, but couldn't. Like a bucking bronco ready to come at anyone daring to cross him, he felt good and corralled — by the situation as much as the gal in front of him.

Harvey chose that moment to place himself in between Amelia and the cowboy.

"Mr. Aaron Zachary," Harvey spoke as quickly as he could, and still be understood. The urgency of the moment required it. "Mr. Aaron Zachary," he repeated, "may I have the pleasure of introducing you to Miss Amelia Anne Polley?"

Amelia held her breath.

Aaron finally let out what little breath he had.

The pair stood motionless, time standing still along with them.

Harvey broke into their shared reverie. "Please, shake hands or something," he suggested, forgetting that Amelia couldn't hear him, and feeling more awkward than he could remember. Somebody had to get this train to leave the station.

Amelia hadn't noticed what Harvey said, but Aaron heard him, all right. At first it didn't sink in, that this beauty was Amelia Anne Polley. But now it did. If he were a Bible-believing man, he'd thank God for such a gift. He had to thank somebody.

"Thank you, Harvey Pratt," Aaron said to the stunned reporter, before he could stop himself. So addle-brained now, Aaron hardly realized what he'd said.

Harvey smiled, understanding. Sort of. "You're welcome, Mr. Zachary," he replied, and held out his hand to shake the cowboy's. Quickly, Harvey withdrew his hand. How ungentlemanly! They were both acting as if Aaron Zachary had just bought a new horse or something.

Amelia shot Harvey a quizzical look. Was she being introduced to Mr. Zachary or was Harvey? She didn't have much time to find out. Her stomach threatened to rebel at any moment. Nauseated and a little dizzy, she held out her hand to her future husband. Or so she hoped. After all, he might not agree to marry her.

The instant Aaron Zachary took her trembling fingers in his strong, warm grasp, she forgot all about her nausea. She forgot about everything but his tanned fingers covering hers, spreading his warmth through her, calming her shivers, only to replace them with new ones of a different kind. Her insides quivered at his touch, at the suggestion of what his touch could do. At that moment she understood the power a man could have over a woman. Was it good or bad? Unsure, Amelia pulled her hand out of his. She did her best to smile as she did so, not wanting him to think her unwilling — to marry him, that is.

"Ma'am," Aaron said, unable to think of anything else to say to the blushing woman. She seemed shy of him. That was all right. He was a mite shy himself. When she didn't say anything back, he didn't mind. In fact, it eased his mind that she didn't throw him a bunch of questions. He didn't feel like saying too much about himself, leastways not yet.

The way Amelia Polley looked at him now,

bashful, beautiful, almost smiling, told Aaron all he needed to know about her, for the time being. She took to him, too. If she didn't want to go through with this marriage, she for shore would have turned tail and run by now. He wasn't about to marry her if she didn't want to marry him, plain and simple. It struck him that maybe he should ask her, all proper like. No matter that the reporter stood close by. Hell, none of this was private anymore.

Aaron turned his Stetson round in both of his hands, studying his action, instead of her. How the hell should he do this? It wasn't any damn business deal or nothing. Mail-order bride or Sunday-go-to-meeting bride or shotgun-wedding bride, he should ask her if she's willing. Tongue-tied, Aaron couldn't figure on what to say. Before he lost his nerve, he'd best do something; say something.

He put his Stetson back on, then yanked if off and dropped it on the bench behind him. Swallowing hard, he straightened his spine and looked into Amelia's mesmerizing blue eyes. She stood so still, so quiet, like an angel. *My angel.* He wanted to take up her hand again, but he sensed that if he did, she'd spook, just like a skittish horse. Nope, he didn't want to chance that. Clearing his throat, his gaze locked with Amelia's, unmindful of Harvey Pratt. Aaron wanted to do this right. He figured he only had one shot at it.

"Ma'am, are you willing?" He spoke low and slowly.

Amelia studied the movement of Mr. Zachary's lips, wanting with all her heart to understand him. She fought the urge to shove a pencil and pad under his nose to make sure of what he'd said. But when he spoke, his lips clearly conveying his intent, the urge faded. Elated that he was proposing — actually proposing to her — asking her if she was willing, surprised her, touched her, and humbled her. This man, this roughened westerner, showed her respect by officially asking her if she was willing. She liked that. Respect was important. She hadn't expected it, especially from the tough cowboy. Maybe he was just being polite. Still, that was being respectful. Amelia relaxed a little — only a little. She could tell from the way Mr. Zachary's tender brown eyes gently shone on her that he approved of her. She approved of him, too. After all, he wanted to know if she was willing.

Amelia nodded her agreement. A simple "yes," but one that would determine her entire future. Her head suddenly felt heavy, as if she couldn't nod again if her life depended on it. But then, it did.

The smile on Mr. Zachary's face should have been reward enough for Amelia. He looked like Christmas morning. It made her happy and proud to see him so happy. She liked that he was shy, unlike her. She didn't consider herself timid. Well, not exactly. Well, maybe sometimes. Then and there, Amelia was absolutely and completely sure she'd done the right thing in sending Bertha Hildebrand and her bratty children packing. She couldn't have lived with herself if she'd let that horrible woman insinuate herself into Mr. Zachary's life. Amelia refused to know another moment's guilt over the part she played in preventing the disastrous union.

Less anxious now, even lighthearted, Amelia felt happy, truly happy, for the first time in a very long time. She felt like Christmas morning, too. Well, at least what she imagined Christmas morning must be like. She'd shut down such memories long ago. Yes, at the Institute, everyone celebrated the joyful holiday, but it wasn't the same as sharing it with a family of her own. It wasn't the same as waking up Christmas morning, stoking the fire, sharing a Yule cup of warm cider, and opening a special gift around the gaily decorated tree, which the family had gone over hill and dale to find. It wasn't the same as sharing a Christmas turkey with family, and devouring all the goodies made especially for the holiday meal.

The Institute had become her family, of course. She'd never been treated badly there. But still, it wasn't the same as your very own family. Of late, Amelia had fallen into melancholy at Christmastime, having trouble finding much joy in anything. But here, now, standing in front of Mr. Zachary, agreeing to marry him, she felt joyful. And yes, joyful like Christmas morning.

Harvey had just said something to Mr. Zachary. Amelia tried to follow the conversation, but neither man's face was turned toward her. She could take out her pad, but then again, that could wait. It would be simple enough, if that's what the two discussed, to walk to the nearby justice of the peace, sign the license, have the quick ceremony, and be on their way.

Mercy sakes! Gracie!

Only then remembering that the poor child waited outside in the buggy, in the cold, rekindled Amelia's nerves and jitters. Without a glance, or even a gesture, for Harvey or Mr. Zachary, Amelia turned on her high-polished, booted heels and hurried outside.

Harvey and Aaron Zachary were right behind her.

Gracie hopped out of the school buggy the moment Amelia stepped outside. The mop-headed urchin put her little arms around Amelia's legs and hugged her. A more affectionate child, Amelia had never known. She bent down to Gracie and scooped her up in her arms, giving her a quick kiss on her cold cheeks. She was suddenly concerned Gracie might take a chill, a chill that could lead to a fit, a fit that could lead to —

Amelia set Gracie back on her feet, refusing to take that distressing thought a step farther. Gracie was going to be all right. She would thrive on a ranch. She'd be healthier on a ranch. She'll be all right. If Amelia repeated it to herself enough, she might just believe it.

Gracie protested at being put down, seemingly wanting Amelia to pick her up again. She stamped her feet and hugged Amelia's legs again, squeezing hard. Her bright smile from moments before disappeared.

Amelia untangled the child and stooped back down to Gracie's level. She needed to calm her, to ensure that nothing would trigger a catastrophic fit. Gracie needed to get stronger, and it was Amelia's responsibility to make sure she did. "Gracie." Amelia finger-spelled the name. "What's wrong?" she signed, by first passing the tip of her right index finger down over her left, flat, hand from her index to her little finger, and then placing her "Y" hand on her chin with her palm facing in.

Gracie's mouth puckered. She was about to cry. She held up her right hand to Amelia and positioned her "I" hand with her palm facing left and her thumb touching her chest. Her little shoulders shook slightly, revealing her upset state.

Amelia was scared for her.

Gracie kept on signing. She placed the thumb of her right "A" hand on her lips and moved her right hand straightforward. Then she moved both of her "and" hands simultaneously across her little chest, from the sides in opposite directions. During the movement she changed her hand positions to open hands. Taken together, she signed, "I am scared."

Amelia hugged the child closely. She was scared, too. Scared for Gracie, and scared for herself. It was her fault that little Gracie suffered so. All her fault. *Oh, Dear Lord, please tell me I'm doing the right thing. For*

162

Gracie, and for me.

Amelia pulled Gracie's arms from around her neck, and signed that she, too, was scared. But Amelia was quick to sign her reassurance. "We're going to a new life on a ranch. A wonderful adventure! We're going to live with kind Mr. Zachary. I'll be with you all the time. I'll never leave you."

Gracie's frown left her. She grinned at Amelia, then rushed to the buggy to retrieve her straw dolly.

Amelia waited, still kneeling, and watched.

Gracie rushed back over to Amelia and held up her dolly, only to give it to Amelia so she could sign. "Will my dolly like it on the man's ranch?"

"Yes," Amelia nodded, relieved that Gracie didn't appear upset anymore, or to be on the verge of a fit. God willing, Gracie wouldn't have a fit again for a very, very long time.

Intent on Gracie, giving her full attention to the child, Amelia forgot all about Aaron Zachary and that she was about to become his wife. She was already married to her worries over Gracie.

Aaron hadn't forgotten about Amelia, his soon-to-be wife. In fact he stood right behind her now, her and the littl'un. As soon as he'd stepped outside and seen the child, he remembered about her. In her letter, Amelia Anne Polley said that she had a ward. Was it five years old she'd said? Aaron couldn't remember. Wait. Yeah, Gracie was five. Glad he thought of the littl'un's name, Aaron didn't have any idea what was going on with the girl. Appeared she talked with her hands or something. He'd heard of it before, maybe. Still, he wasn't sure.

He turned to Harvey Pratt for answers.

Before he'd said a word, Harvey knew exactly what Aaron Zachary was thinking. He could tell by the puzzled look on the cowboy's face. Anxious himself over this revelation, Harvey sure didn't want to let anything on to Aaron about Amelia before Amelia wanted him to know about her hearing loss. But as for the child . . . well, the situation spoke for itself.

"The child is deaf, Mr. Zachary. She's from the school up the hill a piece, a deaf school. Amelia has taken on her care, just as she said in her letter." Harvey tried to keep his voice steady, wanting to give nothing away. He watched the cowboy closely as he spoke. Mr. Zachary sure wasn't giving any of his thoughts away. Harvey couldn't gauge them, because his expression was too stony. "Amelia is using sign language with the little girl. Gracie can't hear or speak."

Aaron tensed at the word *language*. Anything to do with language and learning made him nervous. He didn't want to give up his secret. Not yet anyway. Enough time for his bride to know he didn't have book learning, and that he was real poor at reading and writing. Worse, what little he could do, he got backward. He knew Amelia would be surprised that he couldn't read and write, but he figured her to get used to it in time. Nice as she seemed, she wouldn't care. He hoped.

Damn.

What if she does care?

The longer Aaron studied Amelia and Gracie, the more worried he became. Maybe this whole thing wouldn't work. He didn't know anything about taking care of a wife, much less a littl'un, a deaf littl'un to boot. Hell, he couldn't read and write, and he shore as hell didn't know anything about any sign language. How in blue blazes could he take proper care of Gracie if he couldn't speak to her? Or understand her?

And it worked both ways. She'd have no idea what he was saying, either.

"Mr. Zachary." Harvey interrupted Aaron's apparent dark reverie. "Did you hear me?" he asked, though somehow it didn't sound right to use those exact words at that exact moment. Mr. Zachary looked so perplexed, Harvey felt he had to take it upon himself to find out how this was all going down with him. In all good conscience, Harvey couldn't let his friend go off with the rancher, if the rancher was set against Gracie because the child couldn't hear or speak.

"Mr. —"

"Yep, I heard you." Aaron didn't mean to snap.

Harvey's worries mounted. Obviously the child's deafness did matter. Amelia was going to be very, very disappointed. But better to find out about Aaron Zachary's prejudice now — sooner, rather than later.

CHAPTER EIGHT

"Say, Pratt," Aaron spoke low to the reporter, not wanting Amelia to hear him. "Would you step inside the newspaper with me?"

Harvey nodded that he would, seeing that Amelia had yet to notice them, and led the way back through the *Gazette* door. He had a few things himself that he wanted to say.

Mr. Steele was at the front counter, intent on the day's post and not his reporter and the stranger. People came and went all day long at the newspaper. Unless something specifically required his attention, Benjamine Steele paid little heed.

Harvey could tell Aaron Zachary wrestled with his thoughts, the way he shuffled from foot to foot and wouldn't look him directly in the eye. *Cowards can't look people in the eye,* Harvey thought.

"You know my problem," Aaron finally spat it out to the reporter.

I sure as hell do, Harvey wanted to spit back. *You're gonna go out there and disappoint the hell out of Amelia and that little girl.* It grated hard on Harvey, too, that Amelia had given up so much. She'd given up her school, her job, and her savings — the gold nugget she'd kept around her neck. And for what? For who? This ignorant, cowardly, no-account rancher.

"I never learned to read and write good." Aaron had trouble keeping his words steady. Damn, it embarrassed him to have to say such a thing. "I've got no reason to believe I'll learn to read and write with my hands, neither. That littl'un out there, little Gracie. Her being deaf and all, how can an ignorant son of a bitch like me take decent care of her?"

At that moment, a feather could have knocked Harvey Pratt over; him being so surprised at Aaron Zachary's stated problem. He'd been dead wrong about the man. And there was something else. Harvey didn't think he'd ever met a bigger man, a man of finer character, or a man with more grit. If it wouldn't sound so foolish, Harvey would have come right out and told Aaron Zachary how he felt. But, as it was, he didn't.

"Amelia can do your talking for you with

Gracie. She'll sign to the little girl," Harvey reassured, all the while guilt-ridden. He wasn't being honest like Aaron Zachary. Harvey didn't exactly lie now, but he didn't tell the whole truth, either.

"Shucks. You're right," Aaron breathed a little easier. He'd been so focused on what he didn't know, he forgot that Amelia could help with things. Amelia could help them all talk. "I damn near forgot that. Sorry, Pratt," Aaron said, and held out his hand to underscore his apology with a handshake.

Harvey reluctantly shook the man's hand. Mr. Zachary didn't have anything to be sorry about, but Harvey sure did.

Harvey had followed Aaron back outside.

Amelia and Gracie stood now, apparently waiting for them. Mr. Higgins also waited, still in the driver's seat of the buggy.

Harvey needed to help things along quick as he could, with Amelia's direction, of course. He spotted her things in the back of the buggy and realized the satchels and the crate of books needed to go into Aaron Zachary's buckboard. With Amelia watching his words carefully, he told the driver to take Amelia and Gracie's things around back and put them in the rancher's wagon.

Amelia understood most of Harvey's

meaning, nodded her agreement, and offered a wan smile to Mr. Higgins as he started for the back of the *Gazette.* Her gaze shot to Mr. Zachary right afterward, as if he might not approve of the move — her belongings going into his wagon. After all, they were not married. Yet. Mr. Zachary might believe her to be bossy or some such. Well, she was, a little. Sometimes, she thought.

Her breath caught in her chest when she looked at Mr. Zachary, seeing the way he looked at her. The day was cold, even bitterly cold, but Amelia wanted to unfasten her cloak and toss it into the back of the disappearing school buggy. She tried to moisten her lips, but her mouth was so dry, she could not. She fought the urge to rush into the *Gazette* for a drink of cool, soothing water. Yanking her gaze from the devastatingly handsome rancher, she took up Gracie's hand, in hopes of getting back to her normal self. *Ha, whatever that is.* In truth, Amelia didn't think there was anything normal about anything so far on this, her wedding day.

"Come in, come in," the round, jolly Mrs. Appleton greeted when the four guests knocked at the door; Mrs. Appleton's husband was the justice of the peace. Bestowing her biggest smile upon Harvey Pratt, whom she knew, Mrs. Appleton smiled kindly and politely at the other man, the young woman, and the adorable, sweet little girl. "Good morning, all. Do come in. The day's that cold!"

Amelia entered last, Gracie in tow. The entryway of the modest white-clapboard house was welcoming enough, with its lace-curtained windows, multicolored rag rug, and small yet beautifully crafted oak table, a kerosene lamp resting atop its well-dusted surface. The table stood out a bit from one wall, with room enough for someone to stand between the rectangular table and the floral-papered wall. A pretty table scarf draped the oak table surface under the flickering kerosene lamp. Almost like being in church or something.

A church.

A wedding.

My wedding!

Amelia's nerves couldn't possibly fracture another centimeter. She wouldn't faint. She couldn't. Squeezing Gracie's hand for courage, she was glad at least that she could swallow. A calming breath followed. There. Better, she thought. Harvey disappeared with Mrs. Appleton into another room.

Alone now with Mr. Zachary, whose back was to her, Amelia forced herself to remain calm. She took another breath, this one deeper. *Good. This will all be fine. Just fine,* she tried to reassure herself, all the while grateful beyond anything that Mr. Zachary didn't turn around and face her.

Harvey came back in; followed by the cheerful woman; followed by Mr. Appleton, the justice of the peace. *Here we go, Amelia Anne Polley,* she told herself as if she were a primary pupil on the very first day of class. *You're going to become Mrs. Aaron Zachary in a matter of minutes. You're going to live with him on his ranch, with little Gracie, and everything will be fine. Just fine.* With Aaron's back still to her, Amelia actually believed her newfound bravado.

Amelia needed all her senses for this moment. Not being able to hear, she required a keen eye and acute sensitivity to all parties involved in this adventure, and everything that went on in the entryway — the wedding parlor. Mr. Zachary could not find out she was deaf, not yet. He'd for sure leave her at the altar. Well, at the oak, scarf-covered, kerosene-lit table altar, anyway.

The justice of the peace smiled at her. All she could do was return the friendly, kind-looking gentleman's smile. When he, standing now behind the oak table, motioned for her to come forward, she did. She noticed that he made the same gesture to Mr. Zachary, who obediently stepped forward as well, and the two of them stood side by side in front of the justice of the peace.

Instinctively turning around, Amelia held out her hand for Gracie to join her.

The child happily ran up to Amelia and took her hand, positioned now in between Amelia and the nice man.

When Amelia turned back around, she found Harvey close by, standing in front, to her left. The wife of the justice of the peace stood to her right, in front of Mr. Zachary and next to her husband. They would bear witness to the upcoming union. Amelia took courage from Harvey's nearness. Although only a recent friend, he'd turned out to be one of her best. Not as close as Gabriel, certainly, but he was a trusted friend none-theless.

I should at least look at Mr. Zachary, Amelia scolded herself.

But she couldn't.

She tried to glimpse what he was doing out of the corner of her eye. She thought he looked at her, and she immediately knew that he was far more courageous than she. It pleased her that he was, and that her soon-to-be husband didn't suffer her misgivings.

The justice of the peace began talking. Amelia strained to catch his every word, or, at best, half of what he was saying. He didn't hold a Bible, but then this wasn't a wedding in a church, sanctioned by God. This was a civil wedding, to be sanctioned by the state of Colorado. When she was younger and in love with Avery Bingham, she'd dreamed of a wedding in a church with flowers and family and friends gathered round, all in good cheer. Tomboy or not, she'd also dreamed of a beautiful white dress and a bonnet with a white veil. That all seemed silly now to Amelia, although the memories tugged at her heart, if only a little. Shaking off old memories, Amelia stiffened and faced forward, focusing on the justice of the peace.

She quickly glanced at Harvey, hoping he'd gesture or make some indication if she wasn't doing everything properly or in the proper time. Noticing only his encouraging smile, she tried to relax and concentrate on — everyone's actions.

The justice talked on. The obligatory words for any wedding, Amelia figured. She'd prepared herself, or so she thought. The moment the justice indicated to her to nod her head "yes," she was unprepared to do so. She wanted — she wished — she knew she should say "I do" at such a moment. That she couldn't say her vows upset her more than anything had so far on this day of trials and tribulations. For the first time in six years, she wished with all her heart she could speak, in order to say "I do" to Mr. Zachary, repeating her vows the way a bride should to her future husband. But if she did, if she let the monster inside her out —

Unable to finish her agitated, monstrous thought, Amelia couldn't remember being so unraveled about anything. The pain in her chest connected with the one growing in her head, and both threatened to send her tumbling to the floor. Oblivion would be more welcome than this reality. It wasn't fair to Mr. Zachary that he didn't know she was deaf, and it wasn't fair to him that she couldn't say "I do" and become a proper wife. He deserved better. She knew it. She just hadn't wanted to admit it.

As carefully and respectfully as she could, Amelia nodded her head yes. In the next instant, she tensed, turning her head toward Mr. Zachary just enough to see if he would do the same, if he would answer "yes," too. When he did, saying the word as well as nodding his head, she wondered if he'd answered "I do" or "yes." She hated that she didn't know. And she hated that she'd no idea what Mr. Zachary was thinking about this moment and about her.

Angry as a hornet at himself for his forgetfulness, Aaron knew what was coming next. The ring. Damned if he'd forgotten, and not bought a ring. If he hadn't been so blamed worried over a stove and pots and a privy, he might have remembered — only the most important thing a bride would want. His index finger on his left hand still hurt from when he'd driven a nail into it by accident when he was pounding in nails to set down the puncheon floor for his new bride. *Serves me right,* he thought. *I should have pounded one through my thick skull. Maybe then a clear thought could get through and set my thinking straight.* More than he wished he could read and write, more than he wished he knew how to talk with his hands to Gracie, Aaron wished he'd bought a ring for Amelia Anne Polley. She deserved a gold band. It killed him that she'd think badly of him. Here they were, first starting their lives together, and he'd already got it wrong.

"I now pronounce you husband and wife," Mr. Appleton cheerfully declared to the new bride and groom.

Amelia gulped hard.

Aaron barely noticed, caught up in why the justice didn't say anything about the wedding ring he didn't bring. Maybe the man had, and Aaron hadn't heard him. Damn. Aaron turned to face his new wife. *My wife. My angel.* He forgot about the ring, and the reporter, and the littl'un, and about Mr. and Mrs. Appleton. All he could think about was Amelia Anne Polley, now Mrs. Aaron Zachary. He'd shore as shootin', in all his days, never figured on having such a woman for his wife. What had he ever, ever done in life to deserve her? The truth of it hit him. He gulped hard. He didn't deserve her. Well, he'd spend the rest of his life trying to earn his rightful, deserving place next to her.

Harvey stepped forward and hugged Amelia.

Amelia bent down and hugged little Gracie.

Mr. and Mrs. Appleton shook hands, first with Amelia, and then Aaron.

Harvey reached across and pumped Aaron's right hand.

Aaron kept his hand outstretched, hoping Amelia would take it.

She did.

His strong, warm fingers captured her cold, tremulous hand. Instinctively, she smiled at her new husband, grateful for his steadiness. At least one of them had their wits about them. Or so she thought.

When a paper was put in front of them, their marriage license, Amelia was quick to take the pen from the justice of the peace, and signed her name. She then tried to give the ink pen to Mr. Zac— to Aaron, her new husband. He seemed reluctant to take the pen from her. She noticed his fingers, steady only moments ago, seemed a bit shaky now. Once before, when she'd first met him at the *Gazette,* and took his advert from him, his fingers shook the same way. The trembling wasn't enough for most folks to notice, but she did. Something was upsetting Aaron, but what?

Aaron grit his teeth, clenching his jaw so tight he didn't know if he'd ever get it open again. This, definitely, was unexpected. *You stupid son of a bitch,* Aaron berated himself. *You didn't think on this one either.* He couldn't let his beautiful, smart Amelia find out just how stupid he was, not yet. Not before they'd even left the justice of the peace. He berated himself, too, for not telling her before she married him. *Hell, if she'd known, she wouldn't have married me. That's for damn shore. None of this is fair to her.*

Aaron shut his eyes for a moment. He could do this. He knew how to write his name. He just hadn't done it much, and for certain, never very neatly. He'd done it a couple of times before, on the deed to his place, and on deals selling off part of his herd. But now, in front of Amelia, could he sign his name and leave her thinking he could write otherwise, too? If he wrote slowly, so as to get his letters in the right order, maybe he could pull it off. That thought firmly entrenched in his mind, Aaron opened his eyes, unclenched his jaw, and took the pen from Amelia.

In the next few seconds he'd signed his name on the marriage license, next to where Amelia had signed hers. He handed the paper to Mr. Appleton as fast as he could without drawing any more attention to himself. Aaron didn't want a second look at his sloppy signature. For the life of him, he couldn't bring himself to make eye contact with Amelia. He couldn't have stood it if she'd looked unhappy with him. He could deal with hurt. Had enough of it in his life till now. But this hurt — the one he was sure to feel under Amelia's disapproving glare — would for shore go deeper than any he'd experienced before.

Amelia strained to see Aaron's signature, but the justice of the peace had already folded the paper and sealed it in a special envelope provided for the official occasion. No matter . . . she'd just wanted to appreciate Aaron's lovely penmanship again. Admiring his hand from the start, she didn't think her writing as neat as Aaron's. Now as far as printing, Amelia didn't think anyone could print better than she did. In fact she preferred printing to writing, yet ended up doing a bit of both. Only when she took her time did she use printing. At the *Gazette,* Mr. Steele told her that her printing was as good as any calligraphy that had ever come across his desk. Praise indeed, coming from Mr. Steele.

Amelia started at Harvey's touch, interrupting her musings. He'd hooked his arm through the crook of hers, turning her around and away from her new husband. Rebellious at her intruding friend, she shot him a scalding glance. Aaron Zachary should be escorting her away now, not Harvey.

Ignoring Amelia's upset, Harvey kept on guiding her toward the front door. He didn't want anything to happen at the justice of the peace's place, except the wedding. Fearful that Amelia and Aaron Zachary would discover each other's secrets at any time, Harvey determined to get them all out of there, lightning fast. Nervous on his own account, Harvey didn't want to be around either Amelia or her new husband when they did learn about each other.

Not appreciating being hauled away, Amelia tried to wrest her arm from Harvey, all the while craning her neck to see if Aaron followed. He did, with Gracie.

Aaron didn't know what to expect after the whole marriage license incident. Grateful Amelia didn't comment on his hesitancy, he didn't exactly expect his new wife to take up his hand and lead him away or anything. Might have wished it, but didn't expect it. But the littl'un. When he felt the child's hand take up his, her tiny fingers clasping his thumb and forefinger, tugging him along and away from the justice of the peace, jolted by her innocent touch, a lump formed in his throat. It hurt to swallow. His chest tightened as if little Gracie's hand tugged there, too. He forgot his worry about signing his name so poorly on the license.

It was only a short walk from the justice of the peace to the *Gazette.* The party of four, still paired, with Harvey towing Amelia, and Gracie towing Aaron, quickly arrived at Aaron's buckboard at the back of the newspaper office.

Amelia could see her satchel, Gracie's satchel, and her wooden crate of books and supplies loaded in Aaron's wagon. Mr. Higgins had obviously done the loading. He was nowhere in sight. Soon the newspaper would be out of sight, and the school, too — her family that she'd known these past six years. Soon it would all be nowhere in sight. Hit with a pang of anxiety, and perhaps regret, Amelia shook her arm free of Harvey's, and approached the wagon to make sure her things and Gracie's were properly stowed.

Gracie let go of Aaron's hand and scurried over to Amelia, nimbly climbing onto the buckboard. All giggles and smiles, Gracie began exploring the wagon and its contents.

Happy to see Gracie so happy, Amelia smiled, too. She hopped onto the wagon to help Gracie go exploring.

"Shore doesn't say much, does she?" Aaron said to Harvey, figuring Amelia couldn't hear him now.

Harvey swallowed hard. He knew Aaron wasn't referring to Gracie. Standing next to the tall, tough cowboy, Harvey felt small, indeed for more reasons than his obvious lack of height. Harvey knew Aaron Zachary could swat him like a fly and that would be that. Harvey didn't want to have Aaron mad at him. He had to be real careful now with his words. "You don't seem to say much, either, Mr. Zachary," he put forward, regretting what he said the moment he said it. He waited for Aaron to turn on him.

"Got that right, Harvey Pratt," Aaron replied, his tone mellow.

Harvey, instantly relieved, felt he should say something to ease the situation. Not just Aaron's concerns, but Amelia's plight, too. "Likely, Amelia won't say much the whole way to your ranch, Mr. Zachary."

"Call me A-Z. Most folks do." Aaron took off his Stetson, ran his fingers through his thick hair, then replaced it.

Harvey cleared his throat. "All right, A-Z. Hey, like your ranch, right?"

"Right," Aaron parroted, fighting a smile.

"Well, A-Z." Harvey smiled back, then grew serious. "Likely Amelia will be so caught up signing and talking with her hands to Gracie, she might forget all about talking to you. Don't take it personal. That's just Amelia. She'll lose her shy ways and be talking up a storm to you in no time." Aw, hell, fire, and damnation! Harvey wanted to crawl into a hole. *Why the hell did I have to go and say that to Aaron Zachary . . . to A-Z?*

183

He chanced a look at the formidable Aaron.

Aaron studied the jittery reporter. He couldn't quite puzzle out what was going on. Something was making Harvey jumpy, but what? When Aaron couldn't come up with an answer, he figured it was best to take Harvey at his word. Amelia was shy. Aaron liked that about her. He liked her, period. No matter if she wasn't one for talking. She would be, soon enough. And after all, what he liked the most about her was that he could tell she liked him, too. Aaron imagined he'd made no secret of his feelings when he looked at Amelia. He'd been around enough females in his life to know the difference in looks exchanged. That was the reason he knew Amelia liked him. She gave him that look whenever her beautiful blue eyes studied him — softening to him, drawing him in, yet keeping him at a safe distance. *For now, my beautiful wife. Only for now. You'll learn to feel safe in my arms. Won't be any distance between us then.*

Brought back to the moment by the impatient whinnying of his horses, Aaron walked over to soothe the team. He'd left Old Blue at home, preferring to use the buckskin only for riding and not hauling. Closer now to Amelia and Gracie, he watched them, charmed by their feminine presence. He'd never had much of it in his life. For certain, he had a lot to learn about taking care of a wife and a little girl, but then and there, he was just as certain that he was willing to learn.

Aaron hadn't seen the large crate of books until now. His heart sank, and his rising spirits sank along with it. Books. 'Course! Amelia was smart. She worked at the newspaper. The discovery of her crate of books hit Aaron hard. What would happen when she found out he couldn't read any of her books, and that he didn't have any of his own? *You stupid son of a bitch. Thinking you could marry up with a smart wife, a wife who thinks she's married up with a smart husband.*

Aaron knew he should be thinking more on his wife and the child, but he couldn't turn his downward thoughts away from himself. Well, he'd best find a way to do it, and quick.

Amelia climbed down off the back of the buckboard, Harvey arriving to help her.

Aaron, standing stock still, kept holding the reins of his horses.

Amelia paid Aaron little heed now, wanting to take out her pad and scribble so much to Harvey.

Her gratitude.

Her eternal gratitude.

Her avowed friendship toward him.

How much she'd miss him.

How much she'd miss the newspaper.

All she could do, as it was, was throw her arms around Harvey and hug him. Facing him, she mouthed "thank you," and "goodbye," unmindful that she'd done so. In six years she hadn't tried to pantomime with her lips. She wasn't given to mouthing her words, even when penciling her thoughts, or signing. And the fact that she had done so now was lost on her.

She hugged Harvey a second time, then turned to look at her new husband. She took one tentative step, then another, toward Aaron and her new life.

Aaron let go of the reins, and stepped away from his team, watching Amelia approach him. No time now for regrets or looking back on what he should or should not have said or done. Time now to look ahead. And he did, at his lovely, sweet . . . *seductive wife.*

Neither Amelia nor Aaron noticed when Gracie hopped down from the buckboard and came to stand between them. When they did, they both broke into nervous laughter; the child's appearance helping to dissolve their combined tension.

"Let's get you up on the wagon seat,"

Aaron said, and picked Gracie up. He could have kicked himself for talking to her. He shore didn't want to upset Gracie and have her thinking he meant for her to understand his words. Gall-darn it. This whole thing was gonna take some time getting used to, for him and for little Gracie. When the child put her arms around his neck, and squeezed hard, Aaron's worry disappeared, just as it had before. Gracie was special, all right — and not because of her deafness.

After Gracie was safely situated in the center of the driver's seat, Aaron took Amelia's elbow and guided her to the side of the buckboard. He put his arms around her slender waist and easily hoisted her up, wool cloak and all. Damn, she hardly weighed a thing. Too bashful to look her in the eye, having touched her again, he cleared his throat and quickly went round to his side of the loaded wagon and climbed up. The wagon was loaded, all right, and with more than just supplies — with his wife and his new little girl.

Finding it hard to sit still on the open seat, not just because of Gracie's playful restlessness, but because of her own restlessness, Amelia's heart skipped wildly in her chest. Aaron's warm, strong grasp penetrated clear through her thick cloak, her clothing, and her unmentionables. She still felt his fingers tighten against her skin, as if she lay bared and exposed. It was the most wonderful, yet most disturbing, feeling she'd ever experienced. Hit again by the same thought she'd had when he'd grasped her hand earlier, she acknowledged for the second time the heady power a man could hold over a woman. She couldn't imagine such power unleashed.

Glad Gracie sat between her and Aaron, Amelia dared wonder, and anticipate, what might happen now — if Gracie did not.

CHAPTER NINE

Hours after they departed Colorado Springs, Aaron scanned the darkening horizon, looking for the large evergreen that marked his usual campsite. A little stream ran right by the familiar, towering pine. Wasn't clear froze up yet. Easy enough to punch through the ice if need be. Glad he'd thrown in wood before leaving his ranch; he wanted to get a cook fire going quick. It wouldn't do — especially on *this* night — for him to have to go scavenging around for firewood. It wouldn't do, either, to roast a rabbit or any other prey over the fire, he thought. If he skinned an animal in front of his wife and little girl, they'd likely be skittish and upset. Amelia and Gracie were used to finer things, for shore. Aaron thought of his ranch, hoping they wouldn't be skittish and upset about his place.

For now, Aaron shrugged off his worry, resolving there'd be no fresh roasted meat over the campfire tonight. He'd cook up pork 'n' beans. That ought to do. Damn. He wished right now that he had some biscuits. He could make 'em. Why the hell hadn't he?

The day had turned colder the moment the trio left town. And the winds had picked up, too. Early on, Aaron reached behind him to take up two blankets he'd brought, just in case they were needed. By the looks of Amelia and Gracie, their faces reddened and their teeth chattering so, Aaron knew they needed them. Once the two were wrapped up in the blankets, they seemed a lot warmer. He hoped so. Sitting close to little Gracie for so long, Aaron worried that the child had fared more poorly than he'd expected her to on the trip, even considering the cold and all. Something nudged at him about the little one; he wasn't shore what. He'd find out, and soon. He'd ask Amelia. Gracie was his responsibility now, and he wanted to do right by her. He didn't want her getting sick.

Placing the reins in one hand, he shook off his suit jacket with the other.

Amelia looked puzzled, watching him.

Gracie, tired and chilled, had trouble keeping her eyes open.

Aaron pulled the blanket from around

Gracie, and handed his suit jacket to Amelia, gesturing for Amelia to put his jacket around the little one.

She did so.

With his jacket snug around Gracie, Aaron replaced her blanket around her shoulders, doing his best to make certain the blanket was secure. Once it was, he held the leather strapping in both hands again. The wind bit and nipped at him, but he paid it little mind. His shirt and vest would do fine. Cold never bothered him. Besides, if he got a cold, no big deal. If Gracie did, somehow Aaron thought it would be a very big deal. He didn't want to chance it.

He turned to look at the sleeping child. Her head now rested in Amelia's lap.

Amelia wasn't looking at Gracie; she was looking at him. Aaron for shore didn't feel the bite of the bitter winds then. What he saw in her luminous eyes, what he felt when he gazed into those depths, warmed him clean through. The smile on Amelia's face was for him. Aaron had never felt so pleasured, from any woman, anytime, anywhere.

Gracie had been asleep for nigh onto two hours. Aaron checked on her, and Amelia, out of the corner of his eye, not wanting to turn full to Amelia. Tempted to say something to her now, about her not saying much to him, he knew he'd best wait until he got to the ranch. Harvey Pratt had been right about his wife. She must be bound and determined to hide behind her shy ways until she got to her new home.

Anxious to talk to her and find out all about her, it didn't sit well with Aaron to have to wait. He chuckled to himself. Here he'd been worried from the start that his new wife would prattle on and disturb his peaceful and quiet life, and now all he wanted was to have a prattling, chattering wife. From Amelia he wouldn't mind prattle. From a wife such as her, he'd be content to listen to everything she might say. Unable to imagine her voice, he tried anyway.

Must be like music, like a song. Nothing else could come from those soft, rosy lips. No sir, no way. He knew he'd fall in love with her all over again the moment he heard her speak. Aaron gulped hard. The truth, Aaron had to admit now, was that he had fallen in love with Amelia Anne Polley the moment he'd first set eyes on her, way back months ago; the first time he'd spotted her at the *Gazette.* He'd refused to let himself think it, or admit it to himself. *But there it was. Love at first sight,* he figured. *And now, she's my wife.* Awed by the realization,

Aaron couldn't help himself, and he turned to look at Amelia.

Disappointed that she didn't look at him, he pulled up his reins quick, the instant he saw what she saw.

Dogie!

Aaron hadn't realized they'd arrived at the campsite, he'd been so lost in his thoughts about Amelia — until now, until too late. Hellfire. Damned if he hadn't forgotten all about the wolf. Dogie stood under the pine tree; his rabbit kill at his feet. That wasn't what scared the wits out of Aaron right now. The wolf bared his teeth, growling at the wagon's approach.

Aaron didn't dare pull the wagon an inch closer to the riled wolf. He had to try to soothe Dogie somehow. He was about to call out to the snarling Dogie, but before he realized it, little Gracie had scrambled down from the wagon.

Amelia, all her attention on the wild animal, hadn't realized what Gracie had done either.

Both she and Aaron sat frozen to their seats, each afraid for the child.

Gracie ran toward the nice doggie.

Aaron, his heart wrenching in his chest, slowly and steadily, picked up his loaded Winchester. He always kept the rifle under the wagon seat. With a quickness that years of practice gave him, Aaron had Dogie in his sights and the gun cocked and ready in the next instant. God forgive him, he'd have to shoot Dogie. If he didn't kill the wolf, Dogie could rip out Gracie's throat, and she'd be the one dead. Aaron swallowed hard, his throat burning. He didn't feel it. He didn't feel anything right now, but the pain of having to kill Dogie.

Gracie was close to Dogie now. Too close. Aaron's aim had to be dead on. Tensed and ready, his heart thudding in his chest, he moved his finger on the trigger, about to depress the cold metal. Then something made him hesitate, and told him not to shoot. Aaron blinked hard, not believing what he saw before him.

Gracie's arms were around Dogie's neck, and she was hugging him. For his part, Dogie was licking the child's face. To his dying day, Aaron would never forget the sight, or his relief at not having to kill Dogie. A tear coursed down his cheek.

Amelia noticed the tear. The second she'd seen the wolf, she recognized it to be Aaron's dog, the one that had waited for him outside the *Gazette,* when he'd come to the paper to place his advert. Scared at first, what with the wolf snarling and showing its teeth, she relaxed when she realized it was Aaron's dog, only to be stricken with fear when she saw Aaron take up his rifle. Then, the import of his gesture hit her. His dog was a wolf, a wild animal capable of killing Gracie. Fear struck Amelia, a hard, crippling fear. *Dear Lord in Heaven! Please, please save Gracie!*

She could hardly believe her eyes when she saw the wolf and the child in harmless play. Amelia thanked God and Aaron Zachary for sparing Gracie's life. At that moment, knowing Aaron would have killed his loyal pet to save Gracie, Amelia fell, without question, without hesitation, in love with her new husband. Shaken by the moment, Amelia pulled her gaze from Gracie and the playful wolf and looked lovingly at Aaron.

His hat was off, and his head was in his hands. Amelia knew how upsetting all of this must be for him. She wanted to bring him ease, to stroke his brow, and kiss his cheek. If only she could let him know everything she felt at that moment. She couldn't speak what was in her heart, but she could write what she felt. Shy, yet longing to do so, Amelia reached inside her cloak pocket for her pad and pencil. Despite the waning daylight, if she hurried with her note, he could read it and know everything she held in her heart for him. Caught up in her need to console Aaron and to tell him her secret feelings, she completely forgot that he'd yet to learn her biggest secret — that she couldn't hear.

Love has a way of making one forget, even the utmost important things.

Pencil and pad in hand, Amelia didn't have a chance to use them before Aaron got down from the buckboard and walked toward Gracie and the now-docile wolf. Shaking her head a bit to clear it, Amelia quickly replaced her pad and pencil in her pocket. What was she thinking! Buttons and bows! To let Aaron know she couldn't hear and speak, when they'd not even been married one whole day. She wanted for them at least to have one day together before he found out.

How she dreaded tomorrow.

But for the rest of today, she'd keep up her masquerade.

Steeling herself against the chill winds, Amelia climbed down from the wagon, her feet feeling as heavy as her plummeting spirits. Glad for the darkening sky, which matched her thoughts, she believed she could hide her deafness a bit longer behind the impending night, where dark secrets might go unnoticed.

Aaron turned around and eyed her as she approached. Had she been found out? Did he know? She felt sure he did, the way his penetrating, rusty-brown eyes scrutinized her so carefully. Bracing herself against more than the cold night, Amelia waited for what Aaron might say and do.

His somber face broke into a smile.

It was the most beautiful, the most handsome, smile Amelia had ever seen in the whole of her life. His even, white teeth nearly glistened. His gentle, straight mouth and sculpted lips curved into the most welcoming, warm grin ever to lift her spirits. His smile, sensual and teasing, beckoned for her to approach. She didn't hesitate, but hurried to him.

Aaron, instinctively, held out his hand for her.

She, instinctively, took it.

At just that moment, Gracie placed herself in between them, grabbing each of their legs with her little fingers as well as she could, trying to tug them over to the nice doggie.

Aaron laughed.

So did Amelia.

Aware now of their linked hands, Aaron and Amelia each quickly let go, as if they'd just been burned over a hot fire. Both equally self-conscious, they let little Gracie tug them over to the waiting animal, who sat contentedly in front of two dead rabbits, his tail wagging.

"Good boy." Aaron bent down and scratched Dogie behind his ears. "Good boy." He knew what Dogie wanted now: for him to cook the rabbits, and share the rabbits. "Sorry, pard, no can do tonight. It'll scare the womenfolk," he joked to Dogie, as if the animal understood him perfectly.

When Aaron didn't pick up the dead rabbits, Dogie whimpered a little. Maybe Dogie did understand his master perfectly.

Aaron turned away from the unhappy wolf, walking past the watchful females, and went over to his wagon to fetch the firewood he'd brought. Anxious to have a warm fire going for Amelia and Gracie, he hurried with his task. In little time, he had a cozy blaze ignited. All day the skies had threatened snow, but so far none had fallen.

Amelia and Gracie hunkered down by the fire, warming their hands over it and grinning to each other.

Content that the womenfolk were warmer now, Aaron fetched his camp skillet and two cans of beans. Damn, but he wished he'd thought to bring biscuits, too. Nothing to do now but open the beans, and toss 'em in the skillet. He tried not to notice Dogie, and the rabbits Dogie had just tossed beside the campfire. "You're lucky to be alive now, Dogie. Don't push it," he joked to the ever-watchful animal.

Dogie threw his coal-black head to the skies and howled his protest.

Gracie giggled at the sight of the nice doggie putting its nose in the air, talking like doggies must talk.

Amelia, too, found the wolf's behavior humorous. She'd started to figure out what was going on between Aaron and his dog. Obviously the wolf had brought home dinner. And, also obviously, the wolf wanted to help eat the dinner he'd brought. Why, then, was Aaron about to cook beans? Why wasn't he going to prepare the rabbits? Amelia had never eaten rabbit, but she thought it might be very tasty. Her mouth began watering, and she only now realized how hungry she was. She felt empathy, indeed, with Aaron's pet wolf. She scratched the animal behind his ears, the way she'd seen Aaron do earlier.

Dogie licked her fingers, but didn't take his eyes from Aaron.

When Aaron started to open the beans, it was Amelia who stopped him. She scooped up the dead rabbits and put them atop the skillet before Aaron could spill the beans into the pan.

Startled, Aaron shot her a puzzled look. What the hell? Then, he started to get it. She didn't have to tell him anything. Damned if she didn't want him to skin the rabbits and cook 'em up. Well, I'll be. Aaron set down the cans of beans, and picked up the dead hares. He'd need some sturdy sticks to roast them over the fire. He pulled his cutting knife from his nearby pack and took a few steps away from the fire, to get the rabbits ready to cook.

Three sets of hungry eyes were on him. Amelia's, Gracie's, and Dogie's.

Had anything ever tasted as good as the succulent rabbit? Amelia thought not. Never prone to licking her fingers after a meal, she did tonight. Of course, necessity dictated that she eat with her fingers, so why not take a break from her table manners, anyway? Gracie enjoyed the meat, too, taking seconds when offered. She'd had a full cup of water as well. The sated child was utterly exhausted now. Amelia wanted to get her to sleep right away.

Seeming to read her thoughts, Aaron laid a heavy quilt on the ground next to the fire, indicating that it was for Gracie. Amelia grinned inwardly, loving him for his attention to the little girl. He'd no idea of Gracie's illness yet. Would he be so attentive and caring when he found out she was subject to fits? That she was never to grow up like other children? Amelia wondered, afraid to find out. This was unlike her. Very unlike her, being so afraid about so many things in the course of only one day.

Once Gracie was fast asleep on the thick quilt and tucked under two blankets, Amelia wanted to go to sleep, too. She didn't want to stay awake, and be forced to confront Aaron about her secret. If she hurried to go to sleep, she wouldn't have to.

Though utterly exhausted herself, she knew she couldn't sleep if her life depended on it. Every fiber in her being was alerted to her situation, and would keep her awake. Feigning tiredness, she yawned, so Aaron would notice. Once, then again. She watched out of the corner of her eye, as he retrieved another heavy quilt from the buckboard. Instead of handing her the quilt, he laid it down next to the fire, much as he had done for Gracie. He also gave her a blanket for a cover.

Wanting to run and hide under the blanket, Amelia hastily plopped down on the quilt and pulled the blanket over her head. She'd no idea she'd done so.

Aaron warmed to his beautiful, shy wife.

She was afraid of their wedding night. That seemed obvious to him. Well, of course he wouldn't try to bed her yet, leastways not in front of the little one. Shucks, he'd never do anything like that. He hoped Amelia realized it. Amelia must be jittery over being so close to him and all, all intimate like. He wished he could tell her that he felt the exact same as she did. None of this was easy on him, either. He didn't know his young wife yet, but he shore as hell was looking forward to getting to know her. Not tonight, but soon.

Relieved that it hadn't started to snow, Aaron put more wood on the fire. He'd stay awake all night and make sure the fire didn't die. And if it started to snow, he'd move Amelia and Gracie so they could sleep dry and safe under his buckboard or the tent he'd erect. With the kindled fire as companion, he knew that Dogie wouldn't stay up and keep him company. Traitorous mutt! Dogie lay curled next to little Gracie, apparently dozing.

Aaron took out his tobacco makings and rolled a smoke. He'd pulled a saddle from his wagon, and propped himself against the weathered leather. The tobacco went down real smooth, easing his jitters a little bit, anyway. He did his level best not to look at his sleeping wife. Her blanket had fallen from her face and her upper body, and she'd turned toward the fire and him; he couldn't keep his eyes off her.

Amelia, feigning sleep, did her level best to make Aaron believe she slept. She chanced a peek, then shut her eyes hard again. Buttons and bows! He was staring right at her.

At least Aaron figured he'd been right about one thing today. Amelia was the prettiest gal he'd ever seen. Up close or from a distance, she was nothing short of an angel. Aaron took another inhale. He was still thinking like a devil. Couldn't help it, as he looked at her beautiful, sleeping face with those dark, sooty lashes flickering slightly, no doubt lost in dreams. *About me,* he hoped. Her soft features took his breath away. He coughed a bit at the smoke stuck in his throat and lungs. Tossing the remainder of his lit tobacco in the campfire, he kept watching Amelia.

Her luxurious, raven hair, undone from its ribbon, blew across her face every now and then, from the kicked-up wind. He hated the dad-blamed wind when it hid part of her face from him. Then he couldn't appreciate her delicate brow, her dainty nose, her sensual, rosebud mouth, her comely chin, or the smooth line of her porcelain throat . . . or lower. He thought of what she must look like under that blouse and her undergarments —

Leaning over the fire, not caring if his arm singed a little, Aaron quickly pulled Amelia's blanket over her, clear up to her chin. At least if she were more covered up, he might have a chance of a relaxing moment or two before morning.

The instant she felt Aaron's touch, Amelia knew she would, most definitely, not know a moment's rest during this stirring night. Shutting her eyes harder against her new husband, Amelia tried to quell the ache forming deep in her core. Never in all her life had she experienced such a sensation. It frightened her, tormented her, and yet, thrilled her.

Against her will, Amelia couldn't help but wonder if Aaron, too, had such a feeling. Did men and women feel the same, at such a moment? When they were in love? Amelia tried to calm her shattered nerves. She knew she loved Aaron, but did he, could he ever . . . *will he ever love me, too?*

It was going to be a very long night for both of them.

Snow! Eight inches at least, and still coming down!

Angry as spit at himself for dozing, Aaron shot up off his horse blanket. The fire was out, and the morning was colder than a cow's frozen teat. Amelia and Gracie lay buried under their snow-covered blankets. Sam Hill! They could be dead for all he knew. Scared to find out, Aaron knelt down beside Gracie's blanket first, and gingerly picked up the portion of the blanket over the child's head. She was all right, curled up in a ball to keep warm, clutching a doll made of straw. He couldn't believe the little one still slept, with him disturbing her blanket and the snow still falling. He brushed the flakes from her sweet face, and lightly replaced her blanket.

No need to see if Amelia lived and breathed. She'd thrown off her blanket and stood, by the time he meant to check her. Aaron had never been so glad to see anyone in his life. Right now he knew she had to think poorly of him for allowing her and the little one to sleep out in the open, in the snow and frigid temperature. But at least Gracie seemed all right, and Amelia, too. At the moment, that's all Aaron cared about.

He acted quickly, unmindful of Amelia's sleepy, muddled stare, as if she didn't know where she was. First thing, instead of turning on him, she'd looked up at the snowy

205

skies. He expected her to do or say something now, even rail at him for not providing properly, given the snow and all, but Amelia surprised him, by ignoring him. She seemed more interested in the white flakes landing on her face and clothes than in going after him. Hell, she didn't seem to mind the bad weather one bit.

Aaron climbed into the back of his wagon, grabbing up the canvas tarp he always carried. Shaking the snow from the canvas, he put it back down, and reached for the sturdy hickory supports to contrive a tent. The effect was the same as on the wagon trains headed west, and cook wagons, too. In no time, Aaron had the supports in place and the canvas draped and secured, creating a warmer, drier place for Amelia and Gracie. Worried about them both, he hopped down from the wagon.

Amelia had got the child up and guided her around to the back of the pine tree. Aaron turned his back to the pair, giving them a few moments of privacy. He took the opportunity to step around the side of the wagon where he couldn't be seen, and took his morning relief, too.

As far as a cook fire and hot coffee, not on a morning like this. No breakfast, either, except for jerky. He shore hoped the womenfolk would take to the dried beef. He kicked himself all over again for not bringing better eats for Amelia and Gracie. That would have to wait until they arrived at his ranch. With the snow coming down and all, it would take longer to get home than he'd planned for. At least the wind had died down, making travel easier. A blizzard would make for a harder trip for shore. Quick now, Aaron checked his team. They were strong, tough horses, used to all sorts of weather. Still, he grabbed their feedbags, glad he'd remembered them. They'd at least have some breakfast. In anticipation of possible snow, he'd thrown the feedbags into the wagon before leaving his ranch yesterday.

Yesterday.

Yesterday, I got married.

And, I got a little girl.

I got my family.

His new family was still out of sight. Aaron picked up their camp gear, shaking off the sugans and blankets, and folded them up as well as he could, before setting them inside the tented wagon. He made sure, too, to brush the snow from the floor of the buckboard. It wouldn't do for Amelia and Gracie to ride in the covered wagon if they were knee-deep in snow and slush.

Once the floor of the wagon was drier and cleared of snow, he spread one of the sugans down. The heavy quilts were pretty much dry. With everything set to his liking, Aaron hopped down from the back of the wagon.

Where the hell was Dogie?

Damn, he didn't want to have to wait at the camp for the wolf to return. This was no time for Dogie to be out hunting for breakfast. Aaron figured that was exactly what Dogie was doing. Hunting. Dogie was tough, like his horses, and would find his way back to the ranch soon enough. Hell, the way Dogie had taken to little Gracie last night, curled up next to her and all, Aaron figured the animal would be hard-pressed to leave her even to hunt. Aaron softened inside, thinking about his pet and his new little girl, happy as anything that the two had taken to each other. This morning could have been a very different one if he'd had to shoot his wolf. He would have done it, if Dogie had attacked Gracie. He thanked his lucky stars that Dogie was out hunting, instead of lying in some snowy grave.

Amelia and Gracie walked up to Aaron then. They were all grins and smiles. Their good cheer delighted yet utterly surprised Aaron. He touched the edge of his Stetson, returning their smiles, then gestured at the wagon step. He wanted them to climb in and warm up before they caught their deaths.

Once Amelia and Gracie sat safely inside the wagon under the canvas tenting, Aaron spread the other dry sugan over their laps. Grabbing the canteen of water he'd filled from the nearby partially frozen stream, Aaron handed the water container to Amelia so she could help Gracie drink. He took out the small burlap bag of jerky, and handed this to Amelia, as well. Tossing both his wife and child an apologetic look, he touched his hat again, and then went around to climb into the driver's seat and head for his ranch. He put a hand on his Winchester under the seat, to make sure of it. He was glad he always kept his oil slicker rolled up near his rifle; he'd need it for this ride home. He put it on, then his gloves, then took up the reins and giddy-upped his team.

The buckboard creaked and lumbered along in the deepening snow. Aaron, certain of his team, didn't worry about them slipping, or of having any accidents on the trail home. If the drive went well, they'd all be back at the ranch in a couple of hours.

Relieved to be inside the wagon and away from Aaron, Amelia offered Gracie another piece of jerky. The child was hungry. *Good,* Amelia thought, relaxing now that she didn't think Gracie would fall into a fit over the rugged journey, inclement weather, and all. She was relieved for another reason, too. Amelia wouldn't have to sit next to Aaron and face the prospect of revealing her secret to him. Not yet. She'd have to do it soon. After all, today was today. She'd been married one whole day . . . well, almost. And this was the day for secrets to be revealed.

Gracie held up her unfinished piece of jerky, offering it to Amelia.

Amelia signed, "No" and "I'm not hungry, thank you."

Gracie, her face puckering into a questioning frown, lost her frown in the next moment and shoved the rest of the jerky in her own mouth.

Amelia's stomach did flip-flops. She couldn't eat a bite of the jerked beef. She did take a sip of water. It soothed her dry throat, but little else. There was nothing that could soothe on a day like today — a day of reckoning.

CHAPTER TEN

Twice on the rigorous journey home, Aaron stopped his team and opened the tent flaps to check on his wife and little girl. Each time, the pair had nothing but smiles for him, grinning as if they'd just been interrupted, and were up to something. Suspicious, Aaron smiled back, then re-closed the flaps and was on his way again. Anxious to get home and actually talk to his new wife, he'd leave Amelia alone for now. But as soon as he'd unhitched his team, he'd sit her down and insist they start getting to know each other. Not using their hands to talk, like Amelia did with Gracie, but their tongues. Without meaning to, Aaron's simmering frustration with his too-shy wife had begun to bubble. It was certainly not boiling over yet, but bubbling all the same.

"Amelia!" Aaron hollered at her back. "Get Gracie! She's too close to the open well!

She might fall in!" Aaron was in a panic, suddenly noticing that the child was already out of the wagon; Aaron had just pulled his team up near the barn at his ranch. And danged if Gracie hadn't gone straight for the well, the open well. He could have kicked himself for not making certain the heavy, wood cover was secure yesterday. Should have checked it for shore.

"Amelia!" Aaron cried out a second time, not believing she wouldn't help. She was much closer to Gracie than he was. All she had to do was turn around and she'd see the trouble the little one was in. "Amelia, get Gracie!" Aaron yelled again, charging toward the open well and the child in danger. In the next instant, he'd reached Gracie and scooped her up, saving her from a fall that could have killed her.

Little Gracie screeched when he picked her up, but he paid her no mind. His disapproving attention was fixed on Amelia, who'd turned to face him and the child he held.

Stunned, startled, and scared for Gracie, Amelia didn't know what to make of the situation. Gracie was crying, and Aaron looked at her with a critical, even accusing, eye. What could be wrong? She looked past Aaron and Gracie and saw what was wrong.

An open well!

Gracie could have fallen in!

Now she understood why Aaron looked so upset with her. She hadn't tried to help little Gracie. He must have called out a warning. *And, I didn't hear him!*

When Amelia stepped toward Aaron, to take Gracie in her arms, she couldn't look him in the eye. Not with him knowing she was deaf, just like Gracie. Saddled with two deaf females, he wasn't going to know another moment's peace or happiness in his life.

For now, Gracie was all that mattered. To get her inside, warm and safe, was critical. Hurrying ahead of Aaron, she rushed toward the ranch house, with Gracie clinging to her for dear life. Her husband was right on her heels.

Opening the door for them, his jaw tight, Aaron let the two go inside then went over to kindle the stone hearth. He had to warm things up, quick. Working fast, he didn't want time to think about what he'd just discovered. He didn't want to accept the fact that Amelia was deaf, too. Didn't fault her for not telling him before — not exactly, anyway. He had a secret himself, for crying out loud. And right away, that was the problem. How in Sam Hill was he gonna talk to Amelia now?

With my hands?

No damned way!

And if he couldn't read or write, how in blue blazes was he supposed to make himself understood, or to understand her? Panic rose in him, just as it had moments ago when he'd been afraid for little Gracie's life. Amelia would find out about *him* now.

She'll find out how stupid I really am.

She's smart.

She won't want to stay with a stupid husband.

Once he had the fire going and the frigid main room began to warm, he brushed right past Amelia and Gracie, and went back outside. He didn't have a word for them.

Word, hell.

This was a fine how-do-you-do.

Amelia set Gracie down. Her spirits followed, blacker than she could ever remember them being. With her focus on Gracie, she watched the child go near the hearth and sit in front of the warm fire. This time, Amelia watched carefully, not wanting Gracie to get hurt. It hit her again that she'd not helped outside, by the open well. If anything happened to Gracie, anything she might have prevented, Amelia would never

214

forgive herself. As it was, Aaron had saved Gracie. The harsh look on her husband's handsome face when he left told Amelia there was no saving her or her brand-new marriage.

When Aaron came back in, she knew what would happen. He'd make ready to pack her and Gracie back up and return them, as if he'd bought the wrong goods or something. *That's me,* she reflected sadly. *I'm the wrong goods for Aaron Zachary. He'd have fared far better with Bertha Hildebrand for a wife,* she thought, and she meant it.

His team unhitched and stabled, and after having secured the lid to his well, Aaron began unloading the wagon. He'd take Amelia and Gracie's things inside, all but the wood crate. "Dad-blamed books," Aaron muttered aloud. He easily grabbed the heavy crate, as if it were already empty, and took it inside the barn. He shoved it into a corner; he didn't want to look at the gall-durned books! A sore spot for shore, because Aaron didn't have any of his own to put with them.

No sign of Dogie yet. Aaron was way too worried about his own fate at the moment to worry about his companionable wolf.

He could see no way in hell to get around

this one. When he went back inside the ranch house, he'd have to sit Amelia down, all right, and somehow make her understand that he wasn't book-learned. That he couldn't understand her. Once he confessed his shortcomings, he knew what she'd do. She'd pack up herself and Gracie and want to leave for Colorado Springs. She'd want to get away from her stupid, son-of-a-bitch husband as soon as possible. He wouldn't be angry with her for it, or blame her for wanting to leave him. At least he understood that well enough. He understood that someone as smart as Amelia wouldn't want to be saddled for the rest of her life to an ignorant husband.

It had been an hour since Aaron had left, and Amelia couldn't wait a second longer to get things over with. She'd tucked Gracie in the iron bed, in the only bedroom of the spacious ranch house, and was happy the child fell fast asleep. The ordeal of her move wore on the child. It wore on Amelia, too. For Amelia's part, it wasn't just the rugged journey that had worn her down and grated her insides. It was the pained, hard look on Aaron's handsome face, the look he'd given her when he went outside an hour ago. The look that said, "I know you're deaf now, and

216

you didn't tell me before I married you."

Putting her hand on the outside door latch, Amelia sucked in a breath for courage, and opened the door. She'd scout around and find Aaron, come hell or high water. She'd take her medicine, and that was that.

She didn't have to go far.

Aaron stood right in front of her.

In the next instant, he'd walked right past her, again, coming inside this time. He hadn't even bothered to shake the snow off his boots. Her own frustrations mounting, Amelia was getting tired of him brushing past her. Maybe a little bravado would be better than timidity. She gulped hard and closed the door, turning around to face Aaron straight on.

He faced her, straight on.

Good. He wasn't running from any of this. Because, she couldn't help thinking, *he's not a coward, like I am.* A line from Shakespeare's *Hamlet* came to mind: "Screw your courage to the sticking place!" Setting her feet a little apart and squaring her shoulders, Amelia struggled to do just that.

There was nothing to do now but wait — wait for Aaron to make the first move.

Aaron, struck again by how beautiful his wife was, and how proudly she stood before him, waited for the ax to fall on him. Amelia didn't know yet that he was ignorant of books, but he felt exposed, as if she already did. When Amelia gave no indication of her thoughts or feelings but stood stock still, her lovely face unreadable, Aaron did the same. He didn't try to speak or gesture or anything. He'd no idea how to let on to her about his not being able to read and write.

The two stared at each other for long, impossible minutes before Amelia made the first move, breaking the tension between them. If either of them had been clear in their thinking, both Aaron and Amelia would have each observed that the other didn't wear a disapproving look of recrimination and rejection, but a look of exposed vulnerability instead.

Amelia took her notepad and pencil from her skirt pocket, where she'd transferred them from her serviceable wool cloak. With her pad and pencil in one hand, she gestured with her other for Aaron to join her at the table near the hearth.

Aaron understood, and mutely followed.

Once he sat across from her on one of the two benches, she hurriedly scribbled her feelings.

Aaron, I'm so sorry I didn't tell you that I'm

deaf. I should have. You must be angry. I understand. Write how you feel, please.

Amelia berated herself the moment she finished, thinking she should have taken her time and printed instead. Her printing was so much better than her chicken scratches. But — she needed to know Aaron's feelings, and fast. She hoped her script was legible enough for him to read. Carefully now, and oh, so much slower than she intended, Amelia pushed her pad across the table until her note was right in front of Aaron.

Aaron looked at the note, and then at Amelia, and then back down at the note. Sam Hill! This wasn't going to be easy. Carefully now, as slowly as she'd done, he pushed her note back in front of her.

Their gazes locked.

His eyes hooded over.

Her wide eyes communicated her utter, profound, disbelief. She had no trouble understanding his grave gesture. *He can't read!*

Panic rose in Amelia, nauseating her. It wasn't the discovery that Aaron couldn't read or write that panicked her, but the bitter reality that she wouldn't be able to write to him. She wouldn't be able to make herself understood. A lot of men out west didn't have a good education. She'd met some of them at the newspaper, even during the few short months she'd worked there. It had never meant much to her, other than making her feel sorry for their plight in trying to communicate in a growing, fast-paced world. Not being literate left a body handicapped, for certain.

What to do? What to do?

Amelia took up her pad and pencil and put them back in her pocket, and then folded her hands in front of her. She looked straight into Aaron's unreadable eyes and stony expression. A part of her knew how upsetting it must be for him to have to admit such a thing to her. It had to be hard for him to look her in the eye. Buttons and bows! Hadn't she dreaded, worse than the plague, looking him in the eye and telling him about her deafness!

Queer, Amelia thought, that he didn't seem to be angry with her — for being deaf and not telling him, that is. She had the oddest feeling that he was angry with himself instead. Was it possible? Could Aaron not mind the fact that she couldn't hear? Could Aaron one day . . . *love her* . . . in spite of her deafness? Could he simply be upset now, because she'd found out his secret? Maybe, Amelia reasoned. Maybe.

She'd give him the benefit of the doubt and put her theory to the test.

Signing slowly, despite knowing he didn't understand sign language, as calmly as she could, Amelia put her hands in front of her chest, wanting to talk with them to her husband. She'd gauge his reaction, and then she'd know if her theory was correct. If he were put off or offended by her deaf language, she'd find out soon enough.

"I am deaf," she signed, by first positioning her right "I" hand with her palm facing left and her thumb touching her chest. Then she placed her right "A" hand thumb on her lips, and moving her right hand straight, forward; followed by touching her right ear with her right index finger. She ended by placing both of her down-turned, flat, hands to her front and drawing them together until her index fingers and thumbs touched. Repeating her movements, watching Aaron's face carefully as she did so, she repeated in sign, "I am deaf."

His eyes opened wider as she signed. His stony expression vanished, and he looked like an innocent child trying to understand his first words. If she could have done it without seeming indecent, Amelia would have got up and thrown her arms around her dear, wonderful husband's neck. He wasn't disgusted with her at all! His reaction took away some of the hurt from long ago, the hurt inflicted by Avery Bingham and nameless others. She shook off her bad memories and breathed a sigh of relief, unable to take her eyes from her handsome and so, so wonderful new husband.

Damned if Amelia didn't have the most beautiful hands he'd ever seen on a woman, so delicate and moving so pretty, like music. Like a song. Aaron wanted to reach out and take her hands in his, and kiss them, then bring them against his breast. Imagining what they'd feel like against his naked flesh, he gulped hard. No time for this! Hell, she just tried to say something to him, and he didn't have a clue. But, maybe, the way she put her hand to her ear, maybe she was telling him that she couldn't hear. Well, he could let on that he understood *that* well enough.

Her liquid blue eyes were on him, warming him, melting him inside. Hard to keep his focus, wanting to speak clear as he could, he said low and quiet, "I know." He felt like an idiot, speaking out loud, knowing she couldn't hear him, but he suddenly discovered he had to say it, to mouth it. It would be like driving a team without a wagon behind if he didn't. Anxious for her response, he wanted to gauge her opinion of him, faults and all. He'd know soon enough if she couldn't understand his words — or didn't want to. Why should she bother, him not being able to write to her and all? She shouldn't and she wouldn't. She'd get up from the table, march over to her satchel, pick it up, get Gracie, and leave!

Amelia did none of those things, surprising Aaron yet again.

She studied Aaron's lips, then his eyes, and then she nodded her understanding by smiling at him.

She didn't get up and leave!

She's smiling at me!

If it wouldn't have scared his new wife half to death, Aaron would have got up from the table, come round, taken Amelia in his arms and given her the biggest kiss he'd ever planted on any gal before.

Amelia smiled because Aaron accepted her, faults and all.

Aaron smiled because Amelia accepted him, faults and all.

Or so they thought.

Content for the moment to gaze lovingly into each other's eyes, the newly married couple sat at the table, in front of the cheery hearth. Aaron took Amelia's delicate fingers in his callused, weathered hands, suddenly believing they just might have a future together after all.

Getting through the rest of the afternoon and evening, using basic gesture and facial expression, Amelia and Aaron managed to communicate, at least on a rudimentary level. They conveyed their intended meanings in much the same way they'd done on the trip from Colorado Springs.

Amelia, able to lip-read about fifty percent successfully, tried to read her husband's lips. She'd no way, yet, to let him know she didn't fully understand everything he said to her. Maybe, just maybe, Aaron would let her teach him, as she had Gracie, *his* ABCs. Then, maybe she could even teach him to sign. But would he want to learn? Signing would require a lot of time and effort. Aaron, the Aaron she knew so far, was worth it.

Aaron, unable to comprehend what Amelia and little Gracie had said to each other with their hands, visualized their hand movements, trying hard to find some rhyme and reason to them. He wondered if he could ever learn such a language. Then, remembering his learning troubles, he decided that he couldn't. He knew his numbers and all. But if he didn't know how to keep his ABCs in the right order, he shore as hell wouldn't be able to follow sign language. For now, all he could do was rely on Amelia's skill at reading his words on his lips. Grateful she could understand that much, at least he could make himself understood when she was looking at him straight on. His heart tugged in his chest. He wished he could understand what was in her head and her heart. That was the pity of it all. The real pity.

Aaron stepped outside into the dark night. Snow blew inside when he did. The wind hadn't given up on this day yet, Amelia could see. She'd watched Aaron take his rifle down from above the door before leaving. He evidently kept his rifle there for safekeeping, she thought. Good. Little Gracie, ever curious, couldn't get to the gun then. Amelia wondered if there were other guns stored inside the ranch house. She'd need to find out, somehow, from Aaron.

Alone now — with Gracie having been put to bed in the other room, and now sound asleep behind the closed door — Amelia had a chance to more closely survey the ranch house. She loved the cook stove. She'd never imagined such a luxury out in the middle of the open prairie, far from any town. She might even enjoy cooking up meals on such a stove. Humph. She chuckled. *Well, I'll try,* she told herself. *For Gracie's sake, and for Aaron's.*

At that moment, Gracie reappeared in the main room. Surprised the child had already awakened, Amelia knew Gracie must be hungry. Aaron returned then, too, and replaced his rifle over the door. Good. She needed Aaron to help her fix something for Gracie to eat, and to help her with the stove. Glad for Gracie's company, her trepidations about facing Aaron again, alone, gone for the moment, Amelia focused on helping Aaron understand, through simple gestures, that Gracie needed to eat.

Happy she'd successfully communicated to Aaron that the child needed sustenance, Amelia watched while Aaron took down a jar of peaches from a shelf near the double washtub sink. The sink sat under a good-sized window in the kitchen portion of the spacious room, right under the loft. No curtains adorned the window, but then, Amelia wouldn't have expected them. *My, but a little lace would be pretty. Oh, buttons and bows,* she scolded herself, *I've never been one for such frivolities.* Then why did she want to see lace curtains on the kitchen window? Never a girlie type of girl, why did she feel like she wanted to be girlie around her new husband? It made no sense at all to her.

Refocusing her attention on Gracie and her meal, Amelia watched Aaron take out a tin, a bread tin, and open it. Biscuits. He took two out for Gracie, and then replaced the large, square tin on a second, nearby shelf. *Aaron can make biscuits.* The revelation surprised and pleased Amelia. *Aaron can share in the cooking.* Amelia, being a very forward-thinking, nineteenth-century young woman, liked the idea of a man and woman working alongside one another. *Partners, yes. That's how any marriage should be. Aaron and I will be good partners,* she lightheartedly concluded.

Once Gracie had finished her meal of peaches, biscuits, and another portion of dried beef, Amelia took up the water jug in the kitchen and poured a Mason jar full for the child. She'd been surprised to find such fine dishes and cups, and cast-iron pots. Amelia had expected chips and scratches and broken odds and ends. To have a nice set of dishes at the ranch pleased her very much. Very unlike her, to be so girlie.

With Gracie safely tucked in for the night, Amelia sat patiently waiting for Aaron to return. He'd stepped back outside while

Gracie was eating. Exhausted herself, she wanted to wait for her husband to come back inside, so she could bid him good-night. She'd take one of the two lit kerosene lamps from the sawbuck table and light her way into the bedroom, to crawl in next to Gracie. How wonderful that Aaron gave them his bed and his bedroom. Amelia sighed in approval. Laying her head against the back of the slatted wooden rocker, she closed her eyes and reveled in the comfort of the well-made chair and her thoughtful husband.

My husband. His bedroom. His bed!

She shot out of the rocker, but had no idea on earth, where to go. What to do?

Any second now her husband would return. Her mail-order husband. She'd heard what was expected of mail-order brides. *We're supposed to do our new husband's bidding, in all things, including the bedroom. Including the bed in the bedroom!*

In sheer panic, Amelia plopped back down in the rocker. If she hadn't sat down, she might have swooned. *Be logical, Amelia Anne Polley . . . Zachary* — she gulped as she mentally said her new full name. *We only just met, really. We're both mail-orders,* she reasoned, so serious in thought she didn't laugh at her use of the term. *I've no inten-*

tion of . . . of assaulting him. She forced herself to think the unthinkable. *I'm sure he won't assault me, either. After all, he didn't last night. He could have, and he didn't.*

Amelia got back up and began pacing in front of the fireplace.

No, he didn't lay a hand on me last night. It might *have been because of Gracie.* She sat back in the still-rocking rocker. *Of course, it was because of Gracie. Aaron is a gentleman. He'd never touch me in front of the child.*

Amelia shot up again.

Right now she was alone. Gracie lay sleeping in the next room, behind a closed door. If Aaron came in now and . . . wanted to . . . demand his rights as her husband . . . well, he could. With little Gracie none the wiser.

Amelia made a dash for Gracie's door to open it before Aaron returned.

Too late. Her husband interrupted her intentions, walking back through the front door. A cloud of snow followed him in.

Amelia turned around to face him full, without opening the slumbering child's door. Gingerly, trying not to draw further attention on herself, Amelia offered Aaron a wan smile and sat back down in the rocker she'd just abandoned. Concentrating hard on the blazing fire, she hoped with all her heart the embers wouldn't die, thereby signaling bedtime. No matter how much she needed to yawn, since she was utterly exhausted and frazzled, Amelia refused to open her mouth. She'd swallow every yawn that tried to form in her thudding chest. No way would she let Aaron think she was tired and ready for sleep.

She watched Aaron shake off his slicker and hang it on one of the pegs by the door. His hat followed. Then he picked up his rifle that he'd set inside the door, and re-hung the gun overhead. *Brrrrr,* he seemed to say, smiling at her while giving his shoulders a shake and rubbing his hands together. *No doubt, shrugging off the snow and chill in his bones,* Amelia thought.

He was walking toward her!

Amelia stopped rocking, abject fear taking hold.

The way he smiled at her now, the way his sculpted mouth formed a teasing smile, full of promise . . . *of what he was going to do to her . . .* brought on a swoon, even though she was sitting down. She felt faint. Maybe if she fainted, it would be a blessing.

Chapter Eleven

Aaron, worried that Dogie hadn't come home, wondered if something had happened to him. If he didn't have Amelia and Gracie to think about, he might have saddled Old Blue, despite the snowy night, and gone looking for Dogie. As it was, he'd have to wait for him to come home.

Home. Aaron had a home now, a true home. He had a wife and a little girl to come home to. It was a damned good feeling. Yes, in-deedy. Had a ranch and a family. He had no reason now to worry over anything, except Dogie's return. But one more thing had nagged at Aaron earlier in the day: when he'd gone to make an accounting of his livestock and check on things around his ranch, he'd found more of his herd with his brand changed from A-Z to L-A-Z-Y B. Didn't make sense.

Aaron had it straight from Ned Bingham's mouth that the aged, well-off rancher wasn't messing with his herd and his brand. Then who was? Aaron asked himself. Hell, if some thieving no-account was stealing his cattle, that would make more sense than this. Somebody was messing with his stock. Somebody, if not stealing from him, was playing a hell of a practical joke. When Aaron found out who it was, he'd send the bastard straight to hell, all right. Maybe not kill him, but mess him up enough to make sure it wouldn't happen again.

Aaron needed every cow on his ranch healthy, hearty, and accounted for. His life, and the lives of his wife and child, depended on it. If he couldn't make a go of his cattle ranch, if he went into debt and lost his ranch, they'd all suffer. It wouldn't do for his wife and little girl to suffer. It wouldn't do for them not to have a safe and secure home. Whoever was messing with his livestock might do something even worse. Cattle theft was a hanging offense. Aaron didn't relish the thought of anyone decorating a cottonwood over his ranch and herd, but he'd hang the son of a bitch himself, if he ever caught anyone stealing from him, and his family. There was enough to worry about, what with range pirates, put-up fences, bad weather, and no-account bastards trespassing and up to no good, without worrying over thieving rustlers.

It felt good to be back inside his home now. Aaron shook off the cold and his nagging worries the moment he stepped back inside the door. Things looked real different to him tonight. The lonely ranch house wasn't so lonely tonight. Especially not with his beautiful wife sitting by their stone hearth, waiting for him. Wanting him.

Aw, hell, I don't know if she wants me or not.

Aaron shore wished he did know. Then maybe he could act like a proper husband to Amelia. Here they'd been married for a whole day and he'd yet to bed her. He'd wed her. So she must for shore expect him to bed her. For his part, it wasn't from lack of wanting to.

A quick look around the room told him Gracie was asleep in the next room. Sunup tomorrow, he'd start fixing up the loft so the little one could have her own room — close, so he and Amelia could keep watch, but far off enough so he could be private with his wife. With his gaze fixed on Amelia, he approached her and the kindled blaze. Aaron didn't know which to do first. Should he put more wood on the fire or put his hands on his wife and bed her? Unsure if he should touch Amelia yet, he brushed past her and grabbed a piece of wood, tossing it onto the already well-tended fire.

Amelia couldn't believe it. She didn't know what she'd wanted or expected Aaron to do, but it made her mad that he'd brushed past her, yet again. Was it going to be like this their whole married life? Her waiting for him . . . to keep brushing right past her? She shot up from the rocker, needing to pace again. Of course, she shouldn't pace. How silly would that look? Instead, she did her best to sit demurely on one of the benches at the table. She couldn't help it; she stared holes through Aaron's back.

When Aaron, his innards doing somersaults, turned around to face Amelia, he couldn't fathom why she glared at him, as if he'd just done something wrong. Dammit! He had! He should have taken Amelia's hand, and her, and carried her over to the camp bedding he always kept opposite the hearth. The quilted sugan looked real inviting to him now. That's what Amelia wanted. Not him tending to a fire that didn't need any tending to. Not when the fire in both of their bellies needing seeing to.

Something scratched loudly at the front door, momentarily taking Aaron's attention from his upset wife. He walked over to the door, taking down his loaded Winchester, before opening it.

Dogie!

"Good boy," Aaron squatted down to give the wolf his usual scratch behind the ears.

Now it was Dogie who brushed past Aaron.

"What the — ?" Aaron couldn't believe it. Dogie had actually come inside the ranch house. Two years, and the wolf had never crossed the threshold. Aaron stood up, replaced his rifle overhead, and shut the door. Shaking his head in disbelief, he turned around to his pet, only to find Dogie . . . nowhere in sight. He looked to Amelia for answers. She smiled at him. At least she was smiling and not glaring at him anymore.

Standing near the now partway-open bedroom door, Amelia, her anger gone, gestured to Aaron that the wolf went inside to sleep with Gracie. Amelia pointed through the open door, then folded her hands together as if in prayer, and leaned her cheek against her hands, mirroring sleep, as well as she could. Doing her best to remain serious, she nearly burst out laughing at the dejected look on Aaron's face. She didn't know if the animal usually slept with Aaron or not; she couldn't tell from his surprised look. It wouldn't do for her to laugh at him. Quickly now, she

gestured that she was going to sleep, too —
inside the bedroom with Gracie and with
Aaron's wolf. Her face broke into a smile
before she could control it.

She couldn't help it.

The wolf had solved her dilemma for her,
and now she didn't have to worry about
fulfilling her mail-order wifely obligations to
her mail-order husband. For tonight, at
least. Not daring a look at her doubtless-
upset husband, Amelia forgot to fetch a
kerosene lamp before stepping through the
bedroom doorway and shutting the door
behind her.

Paying for her forgetfulness, she tripped
over something the moment she turned
around. Bending down, and feeling around,
it felt like a pair of boots. Men's boots.
Aaron's boots. His room. His things. Even
his wolf was inside with her and Gracie. Did
she belong there, with his things? Did
Gracie? *Of course we do,* Amelia muttered
her thoughts to herself, standing up and
feeling her way over to the iron bed.
Shrouded in darkness, she felt for little
Gracie to make sure the child slept peace-
fully. The wolf licked her hand instead.
Amelia giggled at the friendly, affectionate
wolf's touch, and scratched the animal
behind its ears.

Dogie had already jumped onto the bed and was curled up near Gracie.

Slipping off her boots, but not daring to slip off anything else, Amelia sat at the foot of the bed. Tired beyond belief, she felt as if she could sleep sitting up all night. With the wolf in bed, too, there wasn't much room left. Amelia's eyelids closed, so weary and exhausted that she couldn't keep them open. Slumping forward inch by inch, she soon slept next to the wolf, which slept next to little Gracie.

On the other side of the door, Aaron, disappointed in himself and in Dogie, put another piece of wood on the fire and lit up a smoke. He was tired as hell, but he needed a smoke worse than sleep.

Aaron woke with a start. "What the — ?" He sat up on his bedroll and rubbed his eyes, more to clear his hearing than his sights. Blinking through his still half-asleep vision, he saw Amelia standing at the cook stove, skillet in hand. She gripped the heavy cast iron with both hands. *Must have just dropped it, to make such a clanking,* Aaron sleepily thought. A figure dashed in front of him. What the — ? Then another figure ran past. He rubbed his eyes again. It was Dogie, chasing Gracie! Of all the —

Everyone, obviously, was already up. His family had got up before he did. Wasn't like Aaron to sleep in; he was always up at sunup. A glance through one of the two ranch house windows told him it was well past sunup, and the sun was shining this morning. No snow fell. *Good,* he thought, as he pulled himself to a stand. *I've got a lot of work ahead of me today, and I'm late getting to it.*

Something smelled real good. Coffee. Fresh-brewed coffee. He loved Amelia, but now he fell in love with her all over again, with her and her fresh-made coffee. Soon as he stepped out to the privy, and then washed his face and hands outside in the basin he kept on the front porch, he'd have a cup of his wife's aromatic coffee. Before he could do it, Amelia stepped between him and the front door, her back to him. He chuckled at her obvious attempts to usher Dogie out, and not him.

His wife stomped her foot at Dogie, opened the door, and pointed for the wolf to leave.

Dogie, no longer in a game of chase with Gracie, sat, staring at Amelia, his tail wagging, and his dark head cocked to one side.

Amelia stomped her foot once more and pointed outside again.

Gracie tried to run past her and go outdoors, but Amelia caught the child's arm, only to let her go and begin signing. Aaron watched Gracie scrutinize Amelia's delicate movements. When Gracie walked over to one of the benches and sat down, her curly-topped head low, as if she'd been scolded, Aaron figured his wife had instructed Gracie to sit, and not go outside and play.

Dogie still didn't move, however.

Amelia stomped her foot harder.

Dogie cocked his head again, this time to the opposite side.

Aaron couldn't help but laugh, and went outside himself.

Dogie followed.

Amelia practically slammed the door behind them both, almost breaking into laughter herself. Almost. Happy the wolf had gone outdoors, at least for the time being, she turned around to the cook stove and to Gracie. She'd already discovered the hen house, built inside the barn — for warmth, she assumed. Amelia would prepare eggs for breakfast. Eggs and biscuits. Actually, Aaron's biscuits. Today, she'd make fresh bread. Plenty of flour in the larder for it.

Sorting through the supplies in the storeroom in back of the ranch house before

Gracie rose, Amelia had surveyed the sacks of flour and sugar, jars of peaches and pears and tomatoes, along with barrels of vinegar, apple cider, and cured meat suspended from the low ceiling. She recognized ham, venison, and beef. A rich store of food, indeed.

Her foot stumbled on something. A root cellar door? She pulled up the small, planked trap door, and found she'd been right. Inside the space, she could see potatoes, squash, carrots, peas, apples, and even a crock of butter. My, oh my. They certainly wouldn't starve this winter. Amelia fell in love with Aaron all over again for his thoughtfulness and ability to provide.

The new family of three — four, counting Dogie — made quite a sight, gathered around the ranch house table.

Happy her eggs turned out all right, and happy to see Gracie and Aaron enjoying them, Amelia sneaked a bite or two to the wolf under the table. Gracie did the same. And damned if Aaron didn't throw down a biscuit for Dogie, too.

Clouds gathered outside, darkening the bright, sunny skies. Aaron needed to finish his meal and get to work, but he knew better than to get up too soon. That would be disrespectful of Amelia. Besides, he didn't want to leave his family. Not just yet.

Two weeks passed, two weeks without fulfilled marriage vows, two weeks of restless nights, two weeks without Amelia and Aaron getting to know each other as well as they'd have liked. The barrier between them was obvious: communication. Muddling through as well as they could, each day like the one before it, Amelia, Gracie, and Dogie slept in one room and Aaron in the other.

Gracie appeared healthier, to Amelia's thinking. Thank God the child hadn't had even so much as a headache since their arrival at the A-Z Ranch. Amelia thought of her husband, who had no idea about Gracie's troubles. Maybe Aaron never needed to find out. Maybe a Christmas miracle would happen, and Gracie wouldn't have any more fits. That would be the best present of all. Christmas was only two days away, according to her *Harper's* calendar. She didn't know if Aaron celebrated Christmas, but she'd love to make a wonderful holiday for Gracie. Remembering her treasured copy of *'Twas the Night Before Christmas,* still outside in her crate in the barn, Amelia decided to fetch the children's book for little Gracie. She hated that her treasured books still sat in the barn where they might become damp and ruined, and wished they were inside the ranch house. Even in a crate stuck in a corner. If the books were inside the house, they'd at least be safe from harm.

Suddenly feeling guilty over the lapse in the child's lessons, Amelia realized she should have brought her books inside before now — her books and the teaching supplies she needed. She'd been self-conscious about doing so; she hadn't wanted to cause Aaron any upset. After all, he couldn't read, and it might disturb him to see her reading with her hands to little Gracie.

"What's this?" Aaron asked, before he realized that he'd spoken when Amelia wasn't looking at him. He pulled the booklet around on the table to have a look. Full of numbers in squares, Aaron knew it had to be a calendar. At least he could read the numbers. The twenty-fifth was circled. Had to be the twenty-fifth of December that Amelia had circled. It was, after all, December. He recognized part of the word beginning with the big D. He looked at Amelia for answers about what she meant by putting the calendar under his nose.

Her bright smile distracted him. Damn, she was so beautiful and capable and kind and sweet as clover, and seductive and sensual — damn. Aaron forced another look at the calendar, then back at Amelia.

She picked up the calendar, pointing to the twenty-fifth, and then met his eyes.

He understood. She was referring to December twenty-fifth. 'Course. Christmas. Aaron nodded his understanding — that he knew Amelia wanted his attention about Christmas — not that he knew much about the holiday. Ranching families celebrated Christmas. He'd pressed his nose against their windows enough times to see families gathered round a decorated tree with presents under it. He'd never celebrated it in the bunkhouses where he grew up. Hell, all he knew about Christmas, really, was that ranchers gave out liquor come holiday time. Did the same at Thanksgiving. He never got drunk like the rest of the cowboys. Didn't much feel like drinking, then or now.

Amelia set the calendar down on the table, then pointed to the twenty-third of the month.

At first Aaron didn't understand. He did when she held up two fingers in front of him and then pointed to the twenty-third, moving her index finger to the twenty-fifth. She held up two fingers again, but Aaron took hold of them this time. He gently pulled her fingers away from his face, fighting the urge to kiss them, and nodded that he understood, and then mouthed, "I know. Two days till Christmas." By now he'd figured out that she couldn't understand his each and every word. About half, maybe. Only half.

The instant he'd finished, Amelia vigorously nodded her head, yes, and beamed at Aaron, thinking him the smartest of pupils. She had to get Aaron to help her with Christmas.

Amelia flipped through the pages of *'Twas the Night Before Christmas* for Aaron's benefit. She watched his wondering eyes as he studied the colorful Christmas scenes of Santa and the reindeer and the children nestled all snug in their beds. She knew then, that he'd never nestled all snug in his bed, waiting for Christmas morning. Her heart reached out to him. Just as it had in the wagon, when she'd seen how upset he was about almost having to kill his wolf, when she'd wanted to touch him and kiss his cheek —

Buttons and bows, Amelia Anne Polley, she chastised. *Gracie will be up any moment.* Amelia didn't want the child to see the special storybook until Christmas Eve . . . *oh my goodness, that's today!*

Shutting the picture book on Aaron's fingers, she made a dash for Aaron's bedroll and hid the book beneath his quilt.

Aaron found both actions quite interesting and fought a smile. To see his wife touching his bedroll, smoothing the sugan out after she'd hidden the book beneath it, interested him for shore. He could only imagine what it would feel like to be on his bedroll now, with his wife. Reaching for the first thing he could find, Aaron gulped down the rest of his coffee. All of it. The hot liquid hit his stomach like a bullet from a Colt .45, a bull's-eye shot! He got up from the table and headed for the door. Work waited outside, lots of it. He'd no time to sit around inside, wasting time — good ranching time. The second his hand touched the front door latch, Amelia stopped him.

When Aaron tried to free her hand from his arm, she protested and stomped her foot at him. *Damn. She's stomping at me, like she did at Dogie.* A little irritated, what with being kept from going outside, Aaron didn't hide his feelings from Amelia. His sour expression said it all.

Frustrated, Amelia took quick action. She pulled her cloak down from the peg next to Aaron's buckskin jacket, then took Aaron's arm again, this time to drag him outside.

Dawn had just broken. They didn't need to go far for Amelia to make her point known to him. Gracie still slept, secure in the bedroom with Dogie. It had taken effort, but Amelia finally extracted the wolf's name from her husband. He'd mouthed the name to her repeatedly, until she understood.

Aaron grabbed his jacket and let Amelia usher him out the door, curious as to what she was up to.

Amelia made a beeline for the woodpile and the chopping block. Aaron's ax rested atop the block. It upset her a little to go near the ax and the block. It was the spot where Aaron likely chopped off the heads of the cute little chickens from the hen house. No matter, her task was too important to think on that right now.

Grabbing up the heavy ax, she dragged it around back of the ranch house, to the grove of pine and spruce, turning once to make sure Aaron followed. The grove offered protection from the open prairie. The ranch house also backed onto a hill, where more pine trees dotted the rise.

Gracie loved to run up that hill and play beneath the swaying pines. It didn't seem to matter to her whether the ground was snowy or muddy, or whether the temperature was biting cold or mild, she'd run up the hill all the same.

Aaron studied the rise of the hill. He wanted to make a swing for his little girl come spring. A swing would do fine for Gracie. He knew just the tree. The largest pine had a sturdy branch, perfect for a rope swing.

Brought back to the moment by his wife, Aaron let Amelia take up his hand and guide him over to the grove. With his hand in hers, he didn't care where she led him. Her delicate fingers were cold. He quickly reversed their handhold, grasping her fingers in his, wanting to help warm her.

Amelia jerked her hand free, stomped her foot, then took up the heavy ax in both her hands. She did her best to point to the perfect Christmas tree she'd spotted.

When Aaron made no move, obviously not understanding her intentions, she dragged the ax over to the tree she'd decided on, and put the tool in front of the lovely, fragrant spruce. The pine trees were also lovely, but too large to go inside the house. The spruce would do nicely. Amelia put her nose to the prickly tree. The needles smelled good, and would smell even more wonderful indoors. Some pine boughs would smell good, too. She'd bring several in, along with their Christmas tree.

Amelia turned around, unable to hide her Christmas smile. She couldn't wait to get the tree inside for little Gracie. Oh, how much fun she and the child would have today, decorating the tree and baking Christmas goodies! Amelia's heart brimmed with love at the thought of the child having her most special Christmas ever, with her very own tree and her very own fam—

Dare she think it?

Dare she think of Gracie as family?

Of course!

Gracie was her family now, wasn't she? Like a little sister . . . like the little sisters Amelia had lost so long ago. Their deaths still plagued her, and would until the day that she joined Ivy and Hannah in heaven. Somehow, some way, she'd make up for their unjust, unfair, unthinkable deaths. Amelia squared her shoulders. She had Gracie to consider now. Gracie to take care of.

Her head began to pound, panic rising in her frightened breast. Little Gracie, she knew, would soon join Ivy and Hannah in heaven. As much as she didn't want to admit it, since coming to the A-Z Ranch and with Gracie looking so well, Amelia yet knew Gracie's time on earth would be short. Like her sisters. And, as with her sisters, Amelia was powerless to do anything to help. Yet she felt responsible for Gracie, the same way she still felt responsible for the deaths of Ivy and Hannah.

No, I didn't cause Gracie's brain fever and bring on her fits, but I should be able to do something. Dear Lord, please, I should be able to do something for Gracie. If this is to be her last Christmas, please . . . let it be her best Christmas.

Amelia began to sob, the sadness inside her welling and then spilling down her cheeks. She wanted to die, too. Just as she had wanted to do so many years ago, when she'd wanted to die along with Ivy and Hannah. *Why didn't you take me too, Lord? Why?*

Unable to do anything else, Amelia fell into Aaron's strong embrace, needing to disappear in his arms, to forget. She pressed hard against him, nestling into his inviting warmth, putting her arms around him, and holding on for dear life.

CHAPTER TWELVE

This spate of tears wasn't over cutting any Christmas tree down. Something else tore at Amelia. Aaron figured she cried from a hurt, way deep down. One she'd kept inside for a long time. He kept his arms around her slender, quaking body, wishing with all his heart that he could take the hurt away. Whatever upset her, maybe, in time, she'd let him know. He'd give her all the time she needed. Right now, with her clinging to him, needing him, he'd do anything in the world for her. He loved Amelia. He didn't know everything about her yet, but he knew enough about her to love her, and cherish her.

She pulled slowly, deliberately, out of Aaron's arms, embarrassed at her behavior. Glad it wasn't full light yet, she wanted to stay hidden, along with her secrets. With no thought to dry her eyes, or to explain her actions, she turned around and walked away from Aaron, toward the spruce tree. Christmas wasn't going to wait for her to get everything ready, for mercy's sake!

Aaron grabbed up the ax and began chopping the young spruce.

Amelia, relieved beyond measure that he'd done so, nodded her appreciation and stepped out of harm's way.

Gracie clapped her hands in glee, excited to wake and find a Christmas tree in the house. She ran across the room and touched the branches reverently, as if the most beautiful and magical of Christmas ornaments hung from the short-needled evergreen.

Ornaments! What to do? Amelia hadn't brought ornaments from the deaf school. She had brought their Christmas stockings. She'd sorted through one of the boxes at school filled with Christmas decorations, and luckily found the right stockings with the right names, but took nothing else. The only other boxes she'd sorted through were in the sewing room. The seamstress let her, and so she did. Other than two balls of red yarn, ribbons and a bit of prized lace to adorn dresses for Gracie, Amelia took nothing. Why she'd removed such frivolities — other than the wool, of course — when she should have taken sensible materials for dresses, she'd no idea. But then . . . maybe she did.

Helping Gracie with her boots and cloak, Amelia ushered the child out the door and to the privy. When they returned, Amelia would set to work baking Christmas cookies, but only after Gracie ate a nourishing breakfast. She and Aaron had already eaten theirs. After Aaron pulled the tree inside and secured it in the corner near the stone hearth, he'd gone out to work, mouthing to her several times that he'd be home late. Glad she understood his intentions, she reasoned that he must have to ride out farther than usual to check on the livestock. It was a cloudy, cold day, and Amelia thought it might snow. How wonderful. To have snow on Christmas! But there was no time to daydream — Amelia and Gracie had a lot to do to prepare for the happy celebration. The moment Gracie stepped out from the privy, Amelia rushed the child back inside the house.

It nagged at Aaron something fierce that he had no presents for his wife and little girl. Mad as a hornet at himself for forgetting about getting presents, Aaron paced back and forth in the barn. Dogie lay nearby with his head on his paws, his eyes following Aaron's every move. Aaron was grateful for the wolf's company. Of late, he'd missed Dogie's constant companionship, since Dogie spent most of his time with Gracie. Aaron stopped pacing, bent and scratched Dogie behind the ears, and then resumed his pacing.

It was Christmas Eve. Tomorrow was Christmas morning, and he had no idea what to do about it. He couldn't let Gracie wake up to nothing. The moment he'd brought the tree inside and set it where Amelia wanted it, he remembered the Christmas picture book, and he remembered himself when he was little, with his nose pressed against the window, looking inside at ranch house families. Presents under the tree! If it took the whole damned day, he'd figure something out. Damn. He had to.

As it was, in an hour's time, Aaron charged out the barn door and inside the ranch house. This time Dogie didn't come in, no doubt choosing to wait for his master to return. Aaron walked right past Amelia and Gracie, ignoring their puzzled looks — they were cooking up something that smelled real, real good — and went into the bedroom and closed the door. He reached way under the bed for his money jar, having hidden it from the playful Gracie, and took out the amount he'd need, glad he had enough left for extras. He worried that one day he might not.

As hurriedly as he'd come in, Aaron went back out, nodding to the watchful Gracie, and the even more watchful Amelia. Smiling to himself, he couldn't wait to see the looks on their faces tomorrow morning, when they saw their presents.

So far, today had been one of the happiest days in Amelia's memory. To have Gracie with her, in their own home at Christmas, brought more joy than she'd ever imagined. And to be in their home with Aaron . . . that was the best present of all for them both, Amelia knew. A kinder, more wonderful husband — and father for Gracie — she'd never find in the whole state of Colorado. Or the entire country, for that matter. Her heart missed a beat when she thought of Aaron as a father for Gracie, and she became dispirited, not about Aaron, but about her own father. He'd been kind and wonderful, too. Humph. She shrugged off her memories. She had no time today for such thinking.

No sooner had they finished baking

Christmas cookies than Amelia put Gracie to the task of sprinkling sugar on top of the yummy rounds. To see Gracie so happy made Amelia happy and less worried about the little girl's health. After all, it was Christmas, a time for high spirits. Saving the rest of her baking for later, Amelia left Gracie, who now seemed content to decorate the cookies, and rushed outside to the barn and to her storage crate.

Rummaging through the box of books and supplies, she found her ribbons and lace, intending to turn the frivolities into Christmas ornaments. Then she found the Christmas stockings. Gracie's was red, and hers green. She pulled the stockings out, along with the ribbons and lace, and stood up, setting her things straight so she wouldn't drop anything on her way back into the house.

Buttons and bows! Aaron! I've no stocking for Aaron! It won't do for him to wake up tomorrow, with no stocking, and no present.

Amelia dropped her gathered things beside the crate, and knelt down to rummage through the wood box, for ideas for Aaron. She ran her fingers over all of her books and supplies, disappointed when she saw nothing there for her husband. Or did she? Her fingers traced back over the contents of the crate, stopping on one particular item. *Christmas is the time for miracles,* she thought, and snatched up Aaron's gift.

Once back inside the house, Amelia set Gracie down to sign the rest of the day's plans to the child.

Gracie clapped her sugarcoated hands in glee.

Amelia cleaned off the table and put down the ribbons and lace. She reached for her scissors from a high shelf over the washtub sink. With Gracie watching, Amelia cut the red ribbons and ivory lace into short strips, long enough to make decorative bows for the tree. As soon as she'd cut a strip, she'd give it to Gracie, who kept them all separate. The cutting finished, Amelia led Gracie, with decorations in hand, over to the tree. Gracie tried, but she couldn't make a bow. She giggled instead of crying at her failed efforts, and handed all the ties to Amelia. Amelia placed a quick kiss on Gracie's cheek, letting Gracie hold everything for her, and then took up ribbon and lace in turn and tied bows onto the tree.

A star! Buttons and bows! There was no star for the tree!

Amelia pivoted in the spacious room, hoping to spot something that might do for a Christmas star. Her gaze landed on an unlit candle in its holder, set on the mantel over the hearth. *Perfect,* she thought, and walked over to the mantel to take the candleholder down. Pulling a bench over to the tree, she climbed onto the bench and did her best to set the candleholder, just so, atop the tree, happy to find a flat spot for the candle to stay put. She'd not light the candle until later. It wouldn't do for the wick to burn down, before they could all enjoy Christmas together.

As soon as she'd returned the bench to its proper place under the table, Amelia went over to Aaron's corner of the room — or at least, the corner where he stowed his things now. Surely he had a wool sock she might borrow for his stocking. Clapping her hands together when she found a large, clean pair, she put one back but took the other. She knew just how she'd decorate Aaron's wool sock to turn it into a Christmas stocking.

With the cookies baked and the tree decorated, Amelia set about finishing the stockings and hanging them on the mantel. They weren't filled, yet, of course. Amelia would put her presents for Gracie and Aaron in first, and then pile wrapped cookies on top. She wished she had oranges to put in the stockings, too. Maybe, if she ferreted through the storeroom, she'd find some fruit. Dried apples would do. With Gracie at her heels, Amelia hurried out the back door to see.

Amelia had no gold nugget or new doll for Gracie, but she had a gift for her all the same. After Gracie was asleep, for a week now, Amelia had labored to knit her a warm and cozy red wool hat and scarf. Her knitting and purling might not be the neatest, but Gracie's gifts had been made with loving hands, at least. Happy she'd had the yarn to fashion the hat and scarf, Amelia couldn't wait to see how they'd look on Gracie.

Dear, sweet Gracie. Earlier, the child had come out from the bedroom, with her straw doll in hand. The sad look on Gracie's face had frightened Amelia at first. Did Gracie feel ill? Amelia knelt down to Gracie's level, her heart pounding. But when the child offered her doll to Amelia, Amelia began to relax. This wasn't about a headache coming on, thank the Good Lord. But then, what was the matter?

Once Amelia had taken the doll, Gracie held up her little arms and began to sign her intent. She touched her right temple with her right index finger, then dipped it straight until her index finger pointed forward. Then she repointed her right index finger at Amelia. Gracie next repeated the movement of her right index finger to her temple and then pointed it forward again. Her little face scrunched when she tried to finger-spell the letter A. She'd yet to learn all of her letters. Frowning still, Gracie seemed to give up on the spelling, choosing sign instead. She touched her forehead with the thumb of her right open hand, wiggling her fingers slightly. Taken all together, Gracie had signed, "For you. For A . . . father."

Amelia's chest tightened.

Gracie put up her little hands again. She had more to say. She moved her right "C" hand in a sideways arc to the right, with her palm facing forward, meaning, "Christmas." Then she resigned, "for you."

Touched by Gracie's generous gift to her and Aaron, Amelia shook her head, refusing to accept the child's treasured doll.

Gracie began to cry, shoving her straw dolly back into Amelia's hands.

With little choice if she wanted Gracie to stop crying, Amelia accepted the doll. For one so young, Gracie was wise beyond her years. Never in her life, Amelia knew, would she again encounter a child so giving, so selfless, or with so much heart. Hugging

Gracie, then tickling her to make her laugh, Amelia decided to wrap the doll in brown butcher paper, and add it to Aaron's stocking.

Aaron pressed his nose against the front window, staring inside at his wife and little girl sitting on the hooked rug before the blazing stone hearth. Dogie whimpered beside him. Aaron absentmindedly gave Dogie an ear scratch, keeping his eyes on the scene inside. Amelia had the Christmas picture book in her lap and was telling the story to Gracie with her hands. The child gazed in wonder at Amelia's hand movements, hanging onto every sign, with eyes and mouth wide open in concentration. Aaron's heart lurched at the intimate scene. Tonight, this time, this Christmas Eve, he was going to walk into his own house and spend Christmas with his own family. He swallowed hard, then stepped away from the window to go inside, with Dogie running ahead of him.

Aaron shook off the snow from his slicker and heavy work boots, then removed his Stetson and placed it on one of the nearby door pegs. His coat followed. Rubbing his hands together for warmth, he stood frozen to the spot, when he noticed the decorated tree. *Well I'll be. Christmas bows.* The instant he saw the unlit candle resting at the very top, he took some matches from his pocket and stepped over to the tree. Once kindled, the candle shone brightly. When Aaron turned around, both Amelia and little Gracie stood close, smiling ear to ear at the wonder of the Christmas star.

The delicious smell of beef stew emanated from the cook stove. Aaron's nostrils flared at the pungent aroma. His mouth watered. He didn't remember being this hungry, ever. He only now recalled the wild turkey he'd shot earlier in the day. Aaron had left the fowl hanging outside for Christmas dinner tomorrow. With the night being so cold, the meat wouldn't go bad. He'd be sure to bring the feathered critter in, plucked, at sunup.

For now, Gracie and Aaron took their seats at the table, while Amelia served up the stew she'd cooked. Fresh bread, too. Dogie hunkered beneath the sawbuck table in anticipation of handouts. The merry trio was all smiles during supper, each with visions of sugarplums dancing in their heads.

After supper Aaron was the first to get up from the table, quickly clearing away the plates so Amelia could finish her story for Gracie. Aaron wanted to watch and enjoy the story, too. As well as he could, that is.

The candle still flickered atop the decorated spruce. The fire still blazed in the hearth. Outside, the snow fell, blanketing the night with a white Christmas — a time for peace, a time for love, and a time for joy.

Gracie had fallen asleep in Aaron's lap, in the rocker near the hearth. The child had, unexpectedly, climbed into his lap the moment Amelia had finished signing *'Twas the Night Before Christmas.* Aaron stared down at Gracie's innocent sleeping face now, gently pushing the curls away that had fallen across her rosy cheek. He still couldn't believe it — that Gracie was his little girl now, and that he had a girl at his ranch, and not a boy. Right now Aaron couldn't picture anybody but sweet little Gracie at his ranch. Tightening his arms around her, he knew he held in his arms the best Christmas present any man could want. Holding the child now made up for all the years he hadn't got any presents. Gracie made up for it all.

Aaron placed a kiss atop Gracie's curly head, and planned to take her sledding tomorrow. And after that, when the weather broke, he'd teach her to ride. He had the perfect horse, his gentle mare, Daisy. And after Gracie was able to ride, he'd take her with him to check on his herd, showing her where the best watering was, and the best grazing. Boys? Who needs boys, when there's Gra—

Amelia touched Aaron on his shoulder, interrupting his reverie.

He nodded to his wife, understanding her wishes, and stood up. Glad Gracie didn't waken, he started to hand the child over to Amelia, to put to bed.

Amelia backed away, indicating "no" by shaking her head.

Aaron understood. She wanted *him* to tuck Gracie in for the night. The tug in his chest tightened. He swallowed hard and began walking toward the open bedroom door, nervous about doing so. He'd never tucked a littl'un in for the night. Turning to see if Amelia followed, he looked at his wife for encouragement more than for anything else.

Amelia did follow, lighted kerosene lamp in hand, smiling inside and out at the sight of her husband holding little Gracie, a part of her own heart. Dogie followed, too.

Pleasantly surprised when Amelia came back into the main room and shut the bedroom door behind her, Aaron stood up. The Christmas picture book fell to the floor. He'd been sitting in the rocker, leafing through the pages, enjoying a smoke, intending to go out to the barn and get Amelia and Gracie's presents and put them under the tree. He'd even put the room in order, getting the dishes in the washtub sink, bringing more wood in for the night, and blowing out the kerosene lamp on the table. He cleared his throat. Amelia usually went to bed when Gracie did, or soon after. Aaron wanted another smoke, but decided against it. He wanted to sit back down, but decided against that, too. Bending down, he picked up the fallen book and set it on the table, locking gazes with Amelia the moment he'd done so.

Over the past weeks, he'd learned to read his wife pretty well — her moods and such, that is. When her blue eyes glazed at him, piercing straight through him, she was mad. When her eyes opened wide, she was upset, even scared. When her eyes twinkled, she was happy. Never one for staring blankly at anyone or anything, Amelia always showed her moods to him. Always, until now. The fire in the hearth burned bright, bright enough for him to see the expression in

Amelia's eyes — it was one he hadn't seen before.

Amelia suddenly looked down at her clenched hands, unable to keep her gaze locked on Aaron's. Nonetheless, she kept walking toward him, slowly, deliberately, with purpose in her heart. Nervous, yet determined to show Aaron how she felt about him, she hoped she'd do all of this right. She needed to let her husband know that tonight she wanted to become his wife, in the true sense of the word. But how? What to do? What to do?

With her eyes still trained downward, she'd reached Aaron, but couldn't make herself look at him. Not yet. Not until she knew what to do. The hint of new tobacco wafted in front of her. Her nostrils flared slightly at the pleasant aroma. She breathed in more deeply, this time taking in a whiff of leather and earthy, clean woods. And musk. Closing her eyes, she languished in the seductive, aromatic mix in the air around her. Her heart skipped in her anxious chest, and her body began to stir.

Aaron's strong fingers caught under her chin, lifting her head and her gaze to him. Amelia's heart stopped. Time itself stopped. Drawn to him, drawn to his mesmerizing brown eyes, holding her, touching her with their tender promise, Amelia rubbed her chin against Aaron's fingers, relishing their feel. No touch, ever, had felt like this. Rough, yet smooth. Soft, yet hard. Cool, yet burning hot. Soothing, yet arousing. She leaned into his touch, vowing to chase after it should he try to remove the magical hold he had on her.

Aaron leaned into her, too, lowering his head and his lips for a kiss.

The instant Amelia felt Aaron's lips on hers she opened her eyes wide, then slowly pulled them shut, unable to do otherwise. At first she kept her mouth and lips shut, too, but slowly, then more urgently, she began opening to him — to the feel of his lips on hers, to the delicious taste of his inviting mouth, to the man in him touching the woman in her.

Amelia pressed more against Aaron than her mouth now, wanting to lose herself in his masterful grasp. His heart thudded, too. She could feel it, she was so close against his rock-hard chest. Each drumbeat drew her in, lulling her, enslaving her, conquering her — unafraid of capture, at the hands of such a man. Instinctively, although she was utterly inexperienced with men, Amelia knew she was born for this moment — to be with Aaron Zachary, to be his wife, to be his mate. Everything else paled in comparison. Any other reason she might be on earth had to be no more than a ridiculous notion.

When his arms came around her, drawing her even closer, Amelia warmed to the heady feel of his strong, muscled arms on her back. She was afraid, for a moment, he might stop — his kiss and his arms around her. When his hands moved down her back, and onto her derriere, pressing her seductively against him, she was afraid of something far more provocative — that she might not know the way of a man with a woman, joining together as husband and wife. That she might not know Aaron! Ever a good pupil, a ready pupil, Amelia turned her body, heart, and mind to one thing now and one thing only: to truly know her husband. Somewhere inside her, she knew her thoughts were wanton, but she didn't care. All she cared about was Aaron, and joining with him. She had to know how it would feel or she'd surely die! The craving in her belly cried out for Aaron. Her head swooned. Her thoughts fogged. Her alert, aroused, anxious body was ready for her handsome husband to take her, wherever he wanted.

Flooded with disappointment, Amelia couldn't believe Aaron had let go of her.

What happened? What had she done wrong? She stared at him, her accusing eyes showing her hurt. Her lips pulsed and burned. Her face felt chafed from his whiskered touch. Her body ached . . . for Aaron to hold her again. Both hands moved to her stomach, though she instinctively wanted to place them lower . . . she hurt *there*, for Aaron.

Gracie! Oh my! It was Gracie standing in between her and Aaron now. The child had awakened and come into the room. Aaron hadn't pulled away from her because he'd wanted to, but because the child had come in. Amelia crouched down immediately to give Gracie a huge hug.

For her part, little Gracie woke up thinking it might already be Christmas morning. She wanted to check her stocking and see what Santa had left. When she saw Amelia and Aaron hugging, Gracie ran in, wanting a hug, too. When she looked at her empty stocking hanging over the hearth, she needed an extra hug.

Amelia pulled Gracie's arms from around her neck, quickly signing that Santa hadn't come yet, and that Gracie needed to go back to bed. Then Amelia signed that Gracie should go back to bed on her own.

Gracie shook her head, fighting tears, and

grabbed Amelia's hand, obviously insisting Amelia should put her to bed, then go to bed, too.

Amelia couldn't refuse the child, and she let Gracie lead her away from her beloved, handsome, wonderful Aaron, all the while knowing she'd not get a wink of sleep herself tonight.

Hours later Aaron finally fell asleep on his unforgiving quilt, believing that he never would sleep, either.

CHAPTER THIRTEEN

The first to awaken in the morning, Gracie shot out of bed and ran for the door, with Dogie right behind her. Outside, the dawn was just breaking, and snow continued to fall. A soft, easy, Christmas snow.

Gracie charged toward the cold hearth, ready to jump up and pull her Christmas stocking down, but out of the corner of her eye, what she saw under the tree stopped her. Gingerly at first, rubbing her eyes as if still lost in a holiday dream, she approached the dolly under the tree. Kneeling down, afraid to touch the beautiful toy, Gracie hesitated. Then she grabbed the dolly, beautiful calico dress, long brown braids and all, and hugged her, and kissed her baby on the cheek. The child couldn't believe Santa had brought her a new dolly. How did he know she'd given hers to Amelia and Aaron?

Gracie looked at the beautiful tree, wondering if Santa might still be there, maybe behind it. She looked to the sides and then upward, to the very top of the tree. Yes, he was still there! The Christmas candle flickered, telling Gracie he was. She gave her dolly another kiss, then waved to the top of the tree.

Amelia and Aaron had awakened, and both now stood behind the kneeling child. Neither could believe the candle atop the Christmas tree still burned. Gracie couldn't have put another candle there. Aaron knew he hadn't. Amelia knew she hadn't. They both looked at each other, knowing then that neither one had put another candle in the holder and lit it. Then they both stared again at the top of the tree, at the Christmas star. A miracle, indeed, to be heralding in this Christmas morning.

Aaron, not a praying man, felt like dropping to his knees next to little Gracie. He glanced over at the cold hearth; he had forgotten to put more wood on the fire last night. How could the sizable logs be out and cold, with not even an ember glowing, and the little candle still burn? Swallowing hard, Aaron believed then and there in a higher power. Because of Gracie. Gracie had brought this miracle into his life — Gracie was the miracle. He bent down and gave the precious child a kiss on her cheek.

Gracie held up her new dolly to Aaron, then quickly set the doll down, and began signing to him, "Look what Santa brought me!" As soon as she'd finished signing, she re-collected her dolly in her arms.

Aaron didn't have to understand sign language to know that Gracie liked the doll he'd purchased at Mrs. Gannon's place yesterday. He'd remembered seeing the doll in the Gannons' small, general store, weeks back, and decided the doll would be the perfect Christmas present for Gracie.

Amelia, her heart already brimming with emotion over the gift Aaron had given Gracie, choked back a sob when she spotted other gifts under the tree. Her crate of treasured books! Aaron had brought them in. And right next to the full crate was a handsomely crafted, mahogany bookshelf with three shelves — empty now, but not when she'd placed her books on them. Oh, for Aaron to do such a thing . . . to bring her things in, when she thought he never would . . . and then to provide her with a special place for them on the beautiful shelves. The lump in Amelia's throat tightened. As gingerly as Gracie had, Amelia knelt down and ran her fingers over the smoothly carved wood, already organizing which books she'd place where.

Aaron, how to thank him? How, indeed? She would have thanked him last night, if Gracie hadn't awakened. But she and Aaron would have tonight. She would thank him tonight for such a genuinely, perfectly, wonderful gift. To signal her gratitude and her intentions for the coming night, Amelia stood back up, and turned to Aaron. With all the love she felt in her heart, she took his hand and rubbed it against her lips, then kissed his palm, all the while keeping her gaze locked with his.

Aaron got her meaning, all right. His blood stirred, and his heart longed for nightfall. Tonight he would take her to bed, and make her his wife. Tonight he would make her his.

Once again, little Gracie stood between them, this time tugging on them to take down the Christmas stockings and open them. Smiling, reluctantly letting go of each other, Amelia and Aaron let Gracie lead them to the hearth.

Amelia and Gracie made Aaron sit at one of the benches, then put his stocking in front of him. His laden wool sock was decorated with red ribbon, tied in a bow. Aaron undid the ribbon, humbled by any idea of a present . . . for him. He didn't chance looking at Amelia or Gracie, but kept his eyes on the brown paper package just inside his stocking. Opening the paper, he was delighted to see Gracie's old straw doll. There were no words to describe how he felt, as he realized that the child wanted him to have her treasure. He gulped hard, his chest tight. After long moments, he smiled at the watchful child, and was happy when she smiled, too. He was about to put the stocking down when Amelia reached over and put it back in his hand. He felt around inside, and found another package. A book. His smile faded. He took out the gift and unwrapped the little book. Unable to read the exact title, it looked like a reader to him. *P . . . Pe . . . et . . . Peet's* something.

Amelia had given Aaron *Peet's First Lessons for Deaf Mutes,* hoping for a Christmas miracle for Aaron — the miracle that he'd let her teach him to read and to sign. It wouldn't be easy for either of them, but she wanted to try. For Aaron's sake as well as her own. Nervous as could be now, worried that Aaron might be upset by her gift, Amelia forced herself to look at his face for a sign, any sign, of whether or not he'd accept her present.

Nervous himself, Aaron was afraid to take the book, but if he didn't —

Working up to a smile, he held the book up, then nodded to Amelia.

Amelia let out the breath she'd been holding. How very wonderful. Aaron was going to read and write and sign. How absolutely, amazingly wonderful! She fell in love with him even more at that moment, if such a thing were possible.

Gracie interceded, yet again. Pulling her red stocking down from the mantel, she jumped onto the bench next to Aaron before looking inside. With quick hands, she pulled out her present and ripped open the butcher paper, beaming from ear to ear the moment she unwrapped her red wool hat and scarf. Hopping back down off the bench, she put the hat on and wrapped the scarf around her neck, dancing in circles.

Amelia and Aaron laughed, happy to see Gracie so happy.

The rest of the day proved just as merry.

After Aaron rekindled the fire, he went out back to pluck the turkey. After breakfast, he'd fetch the sled he'd borrowed from the Gannons, and then he'd take Gracie sledding down the hill she loved so much. Amelia set the breakfast table, excited to pull out the Christmas scones she'd made. She'd filled them with peaches and hoped Aaron and Gracie would like them. Later, for Christmas dinner, she'd make mashed potatoes and peas to go with the turkey. And cider. They'd have delicious apple cider with their meal. Of course, she'd also made a special apple pie yesterday, too. It was all going to be the best Christmas ever!

And it was, for all three of them.

And Dogie, too.

Amelia noticed that Gracie seemed overly tired, but then, they'd all been celebrating merrily throughout the day. Of course, the child would be exhausted. Time for bed. Gracie still played with her doll — and Dogie — on the rug by the fire. Aaron had just helped Amelia finish putting the dishes away, working side-by-side at the washtub sink. Amelia gave Aaron a shy smile, then turned to scoop up Gracie and her new doll and put them both to bed.

Dogie howled.

Aaron pivoted fast, expecting trouble. Dogie never howled, except outside, at the moon or at wild critters coming close.

Gracie was in trouble. She lay on the hooked rug by the kindled hearth, her body stiff and her new doll flung from her. Dogie stood over the child's lifeless form, howling, then whimpering. Aaron was right behind Amelia, both reaching the prostrate child at the same time.

Aaron had never been so scared.

Amelia had . . . for Gracie.

Fighting for calm, and trying to remember every detail the matron at school, Mrs. Kennedy, had shared with her, about fits and what to expect with little Gracie, Amelia examined the unconscious child.

Gracie's teeth are clenched. It's too late to insert a wooden spoon to prevent her biting her tongue. She's blue and not breathing, but should start to take in air any second now. Saliva is foaming at her mouth, which is expected.

Quickly, Amelia dropped to the floor, put her hands to the sides of Gracie's head, and turned it laterally. The moment she'd done this, coincidentally, Gracie's lungs filled with air. Amelia, relieved to see the inspirations and Gracie's improved color, kept her hands at the sides of her head. She knew what came next.

Gracie began to shake violently. Amelia kept hold of the child's head, to keep it safe and still and prevent further injury. This stage could last seconds, even minutes. Gracie flung her limbs about, much as she'd sent her doll to land in a limp pile. Her shaking soon slowed, and the color returned to her face. Her breaths were even now.

Relieved that she was coming out of her fit, Amelia carefully watched Gracie's eyelids. They'd begun to open. Gracie looked confused, but she was going to be all right. *This time, dear child. This time.*

Gracie tried to sit up.

Amelia, undone, her own strength exhausted, tried to scoop Gracie up.

Aaron, needing to help, took Gracie from Amelia and walked toward the bedroom. Gracie put her weak arms around his neck and hugged him. Amelia followed, picking up Gracie's new doll as she went. Dogie, no longer howling, was close behind.

With Gracie sleeping and Dogie standing guard, Amelia and Aaron left them alone and went back into the main room, leaving the bedroom door open. Everything looked the same in the main room. The fire blazed. The dishes were done. The fragrant Christmas tree, a new candle lit, stood proudly in the corner, marking the special day. Amelia's new bookshelf, stocked now, and organized with her things, sat against the wall near Aaron's bedroll. Yes, everything appeared to be in proper order, but things were not the same. After tonight, after Gracie's terrible fit, one that could have killed her, Amelia knew, everything was not the same, and never would be again.

And there was Aaron. Now he knew. He knew how sick Gracie truly was. Amelia, unreasonable in her fear, shot him an accusing glance, as if he might try to kick her and Gracie out this very night. After all, she'd not told Aaron about Gracie. On top of her and Gracie being deaf, Aaron had now discovered her double lie to him. *Well, I don't care. I don't care how he feels. Gracie is ill. I don't care about anything else now. Even Aaron.*

Aaron took Amelia's hand.

She let him at first, and then pushed his hand away.

Aaron didn't understand the scathing look Amelia shot him. Her icy blue eyes cut through him like a knife, a new cut. He'd been cut through the heart when he set eyes on Gracie's lifeless body. He didn't understand what exactly was wrong with the little girl. For a long time now, he'd known something was wrong with her, but not what. Well, now he knew she suffered from fits. Helpless to help, Aaron felt hopeless, too. He didn't know much about doctoring and illness, but he knew that fits couldn't be good. And Gracie's seemed real, real bad. He would have gone for a doc if Amelia had let on to him that's what needed doing.

As things were, Aaron figured Amelia knew best. She appeared to know how to watch over Gracie and what to do and all.

Trying again, Aaron started to reach over and take up Amelia's hand. He wanted — no, he needed — her to try to tell him about Gracie and how bad off she was. Aaron pulled his hand back. *Son of a bitch! Amelia can't tell me. I can't read. I can't sign. I'm a useless son of a bitch.* Aaron got up, kicking the bench out from under him, and went for the front door. He needed some air and some time to think on what to do.

Amelia watched Aaron leave, and she put her pad and pencil back in her pocket. She'd been about to take her writing implements out, despite her guilt over having lied to Aaron about herself and Gracie, and despite knowing he couldn't read and write. If Aaron wanted to know anything from her, from now on she'd write it down. If he didn't understand, then so be it. She'd no intention of trying to mouth and gesture her meaning to him anymore. It was too hard. She didn't have the heart or the energy to try.

Unable to admit it to herself, Amelia needed someone to blame for Gracie's illness.

Her husband made a very convenient

target.

Aaron woke with a start. Dogie was whimpering. He could hear the forlorn animal despite the closed bedroom door. Aaron scrambled off his bedroll in a panic, not bothering to pull his pants on over his long johns. *Gracie. It's Gracie.* All he could think about was the fragile child. The sky was already light, Aaron could see his way to the closed door. Once there, he hesitated to turn the latch and go through the door, scared to death for little Gracie.

Dogie came running the instant Aaron opened the door, then ran back to the bed. Aaron rushed over to Gracie's side. Amelia still slept, with Gracie cradled in her arms.

Gracie didn't sleep. Gracie was dead. The child looked so peaceful, as if she were sleeping. Just like Amelia. But Aaron could tell without even touching the little girl, that she slept in heaven now, in God's arms.

Aaron's heart broke, his own spirit ripped away with little Gracie, a part of him dying, too. He willed himself to reach down and touch Gracie's cold cheek and her unmoving chest; he had to check her, to confirm that she'd passed. He pulled his hand away once he'd made sure. Dogie found his hand and licked it, whimpering still. Aaron scratched Dogie's ears, unmindful of the hot tears escaping down his own face. Right now he didn't know what to do. He didn't know how he could keep Amelia from waking and finding Gracie dead.

And then Amelia's eyes opened.

Aaron's heart stopped for the second time that morning.

Amelia smiled at her husband, her handsome, wonderful husband. Certain she was lost in dreams of Aaron, she shut her eyes and sighed heavily, wanting to dream on.

With little choice, Aaron reached down and touched Amelia's shoulder gently, yet urgently.

Her eyes flew open at his touch. She cuddled Gracie closer, confused and upset by Aaron's presence in their room. Why was he here? What could be wrong? She pulled Gracie's lifeless, stiff body toward her . . . and was suddenly struck by horror, by the impossible, agonizing reality of the moment. *Gracie has died!*

Amelia pulled Gracie even closer, as if her life spirit could join with the child's and bring her back to life. Amelia would willingly exchange her life for Gracie's. *Please God. Take me. Not Gracie. Not Gracie!*

Amelia sobbed in her silent coffin, cradling the dead child. Hugging Gracie tight,

Amelia waited for the dirt to pour atop them both. She'd never let go of Gracie. Never! She'd let go of Ivy and Hannah. Her sisters had died without her. She wouldn't let Gracie die without her.

Amelia felt Aaron's hand on her shoulder again, but she refused to respond or even look at him. Annoyed by his presence, she couldn't imagine what he wanted. *He's no part of this. He's no part of Gracie and me.* Wracked with grief, Amelia lashed out at Aaron the instant she felt him touch her again. "Go away!" she screeched, unaware she was doing so. "Go away!"

It was the worst, and best, moment of Aaron's life — to know his precious little girl lay dead, and yet, to hear his precious wife speak. Overwhelmed by the moment and the emotions warring within him, he stepped away from the bed, and leaned against the nearest wall for support. Sad to the core, Aaron felt helpless to do anything but stay in the room with Gracie and Amelia. His wife had pushed him away, had even screamed for him to go away. His wife didn't want him to help. His wife didn't need him. Amelia didn't want him. The truth of it all, the harsh reality of Gracie's death and the bitter knowledge that Amelia shunned him, sent Aaron out of the room.

Soon he'd have to return and collect Gracie in order to bury her. Desperate to do something to help, Aaron got dressed and went outside, heading for the barn. He'd make Gracie a coffin out of his smoothest pine. He wanted to do right by the child.

The ground was hard, but it wasn't impossible to dig a grave. Aaron finished Gracie's pine box, then walked up the hill out back of his place and began digging a grave for Gracie, under her favorite pine tree. He'd meant to build her a swing in the spring, not to dig her grave here. He knew he was being selfish, choosing a place for Gracie without asking Amelia. But Aaron wanted to be able to look up the hill and imagine little Gracie, swinging and playing there, for the rest of his days. Flowers, too. He'd plant flowers for Gracie come spring.

He hoped and prayed Amelia would be there with him when he did.

Feeling dead inside herself, Amelia laid Gracie's body out on the bed, intent on dressing her and preparing her for burial. No need to lay her in the main room, waiting for mourners to come by. With no church, no preacher, and few neighbors close, Gracie should be buried this very afternoon, Amelia decided. She'd have to be laid to rest on the A-Z Ranch.

Why did I ever bring her here? Gracie might still be alive, if I hadn't been bound and determined to be a mail-order bride. Aaron Zachary's mail-order bride.

Ruing the day she'd ever laid eyes on the handsome rancher, she blamed them both for Gracie's death. Aaron, for being so handsome and seductive, and herself, for being so weak and giving in to his powerful allure.

Gracie might have had more time back at the Institute, instead of out on this God-forsaken ranch.

Amelia straightened and choked back new sobs. None of this melancholic thinking would do any good now, not with her needing to take care of Gracie. She'd put the little girl in her finest calico. There was a bit of lace at the collar and the sleeves. Her boots and cloak, too. Amelia reached for them. *Gracie will want these — and her new hat and scarf. She'll need them, for the day is bitter cold,* Amelia told herself, as if she were a child dressing her dolly for a winter outing.

Aaron returned.

Amelia spotted him out of the corner of her eye, but ignored him. She hadn't finished dressing Gracie. The child's new Christmas doll was still in the main room. *Gracie should be buried with it,* Amelia decided, and walked past Aaron to fetch the doll.

Aaron understood his wife's distress. He understood why she behaved so coldly to him, too. It wasn't just because Gracie was gone. It was because of him, as if Amelia blamed him, and held him responsible for the child's death. He blamed himself, for not being able to talk proper and communicate proper with the little girl. He'd suffer Amelia's shunning for now. It ached inside him something awful, that Amelia wouldn't let him bring comfort to her at such a time. Aaron needed to hold Amelia and to have her hold him. He needed her comforting arms around him, too.

Aaron let Amelia pass by him, hurriedly going in and out of the bedroom, fixing things just so for Gracie. He didn't disturb her preparations. When she was all done, he'd take care of the burying part.

Figuring Amelia and innocent little Gracie were ready, Aaron took down Amelia's cloak from the peg by the front door and brought it back into the bedroom. He put it around Amelia's shoulders. She'd jumped at his touch, but let him place the cloak around her all the same. Then Aaron tenderly, carefully, scooped up Gracie and her Christmas doll and started for the main room.

Amelia, her emotions drained, stared blankly at Aaron's back. It took her a moment to realize he'd taken Gracie. Practically jumping into her boots by the bed, she charged into the next room in order to stop Aaron. But the moment she thought about it, she realized Aaron was taking Gracie outside to bury her. Aaron had disappeared out the front door with the beloved child. Amelia, shivering in her nightdress despite her warm cloak, hurried over to her bookcase and found her Bible, then rushed outside herself.

Where was Aaron? And Gracie? Panicked, Amelia started for the barn, but then caught sight of Aaron and Gracie out of the corner of her eye. Aaron was walking up the hill, the hill Gracie loved. He'd chosen the perfect place to lay Gracie to rest. The perfect place. Wanting with all her heart to thank him, Amelia hung her head, knowing she couldn't find it in herself now to do so.

Aaron lovingly placed Gracie and her Christmas doll in the pine box he'd made for her. Amelia stood behind him. He choked with emotion when he watched Amelia kiss the child and sign goodbye.

Dogie was right there with them, too. The wolf lay down at the side of the open grave, resting his head on his paws, ever watchful. The pain of losing Gracie, for all of them, hit Aaron hard. His parched throat burned. When he swallowed, the ache in his throat burned clear down to his gut. Burdened by the sad day's events, he tried to find the strength for the grim task ahead.

When Aaron finished lowering the little pine coffin into the partly frozen earth, Amelia caught his arm before he could put the first shovel of dirt over Gracie. He shot her a questioning look, but then understood, when he saw the Bible in her hands. 'Course, there should be some words said. 'Course. Aaron stepped away from the grave, and dropped his shovel to the ground.

Amelia smoothed down the page, and the Psalm she'd selected from her Bible, to sign over Gracie. The wind had picked up enough to rustle the pages. She felt like crying, she was so exasperated and upset that she couldn't even do this right for Gracie.

Aaron stepped forward and took the Bible out of Amelia's hands. He figured out her intentions, and wanted to help.

She let him, and placed her Bible, just so, in his hands so she could clearly see the Twenty-Third Psalm. "The Lord is my shepherd, I shall not want . . ." Her hand movements were sure and steady, clearly, reverently signing the holy words for Gracie.

When she was finished, she shut the pages of the Bible and took it from Aaron's hands. She'd appreciated his help, but didn't have the energy or will to try to tell him so. No matter. It wasn't important. He likely wouldn't care to know, anyway.

Aaron took back up his shovel and began covering the pine coffin. The frozen mixture of snow and dark earth went down heavily. The wind blustered now, making his efforts all the more difficult. Dogie stood at his side, watching every shovelful cover Gracie's coffin. Amelia watched, too. She wanted to help, but her stamina had drained away along with her spirit — as if each shovelful of earth buried her, too.

CHAPTER FOURTEEN

It had been three weeks since little Gracie had passed — three, long, lonely, miserable weeks for both Amelia and Aaron. Lost in their own melancholy, neither tried to console the other. Neither tried to communicate on any level, other than preparing obligatory meals and getting through the day's routine.

Every night Amelia went into the bedroom and closed the door. Aaron took to his bedroll, knowing sleep would come hard. Every morning, they avoided eye contact, each unwilling to face the other and forgive the other their trespasses. Even Dogie was affected. The wolf no longer slept in the bedroom, but outside under the pine tree on the hill, beside Gracie's grave. Together, yet alone, Amelia and Aaron got through the empty days and nights.

The truth of her mistake haunted Amelia.

She should never have married Aaron Zachary and brought Gracie to his ranch. Her selfishness had caused Gracie's early death. Despite the fact that her first impulse to marry Aaron had been to help him, and save him from marrying the awful widow Hildebrand, none of that mattered now. She should have reconsidered when Gracie came into the picture. That she hadn't done so ate away at her every day, just as the deaths of her own little sisters still did.

Amelia believed she deserved her fate now. She deserved to be sentenced to a life with a husband who couldn't read or write or communicate with her. She deserved to be away from her beloved deaf community in Colorado Springs. Oh, how she missed them all. Even Minnie Gilbert and her sourpuss expression. At least she could sign with Minnie, and everyone else at the Institute. What a relief it would be to talk with her hands again. What a blessed relief.

Amelia missed her position at the *Gazette,* too. There, she could easily write to Mr. Steele and Harvey and all the others working at the newspaper. And there she had purpose, *real* purpose. She did illustrations for the *Gazette,* important illustrations for the whole country to see, illustrations that would bring tourists to the resort area. And

Amelia loved typesetting, priding herself on how quickly she could complete her assigned tasks. Maybe she could have become a reporter like Harvey. How interesting that would have been. No, she shouldn't have so easily given up on the job she'd fought so hard to get in the first place.

What purpose did she have now? She wasn't a rancher. She knew absolutely nothing about caring for livestock, or checking the herd, or about watering places, or range pirates, or rustlers, or shooting a gun, or roundups, or any of the other vital aspects of ranch life. Aaron should have taught her, and included her in his business before now. She couldn't even ride a horse. Aaron should have taught her to ride long before now.

And he should have at least tried to read and write. Why he didn't try harder both puzzled and angered her. Well, she certainly hoped he didn't expect her to help him. She'd offered, and he'd refused. As for Amelia, she refused to be honest with herself and remember that Aaron had agreed to learn, on Christmas day.

Amelia bolted up from the rocker, leaving it to swing back and forth without her. What to do? What to do? *Nothing. There's nothing to do, about any of this,* she told herself dejectedly, then slumped back down in the rocking chair. The fire burned low, ready for more wood. The kindling box, she could see, sat empty. With a heavy heart, and even heavier feet, Amelia got up to go outside and fetch more wood. She pulled her cloak off its peg by the door, chancing a look outside at the weather before opening the front door.

Avery Bingham!

No matter that six years passed — she'd recognize her so-called childhood friend, anywhere. Amelia grabbed the heavy Winchester rifle from its rack above the front door with no idea how to shoot it, yet grateful that Aaron hadn't needed the gun this morning. She most definitely had need of it now.

Aaron spotted the riders approaching the moment he stepped outside the barn, leading Old Blue. He had finished stacking the hay and wanted to ride out and check his herd for strays or any trouble. He'd smelled trouble in the air the moment he'd come outside this morning. When he saw who rode up just now, he knew exactly what kind of trouble it was. Aaron holstered the rifle he kept with his saddle gear, and tied Old Blue to the hitching post. Much as he wanted to use a gun on Avery Bingham, never having liked Ned Bingham's no-account, no-good son, he wouldn't shoot him. Not yet, anyway. He walked toward the three men.

Dogie charged down from Gracie's hilltop grave, growling and snarling, getting in between the riders and Aaron.

Aaron put a hand down to Dogie, all the while keeping his eyes on Avery. "Easy boy, easy."

The wolf kept growling, but pulled back. He didn't leave, but stood at Aaron's side.

"Howdy, A-Z. That's some watch dog," Avery said, his two men beside him. "I guess I should say wolf," he added, unable to hide the fear in his voice. He holstered his six-shooter the moment Aaron called the wolf off.

None of them now, man or beast, made a sound or a move.

None of the riders got down from their horses.

None were invited to do so.

Aaron didn't say anything, but waited to see what in blazes Bingham and his riders wanted. They'd never come up like this before, to his place and all. To his house. Suspicious of Avery, Aaron eyed the three warily.

"Like I said, A-Z. Howdy." Avery smiled.

Aaron nodded, more accustomed now to gesturing than speaking.

Avery started to get down from his horse, his eyes on the wolf.

"Don't bother, Bingham," Aaron snapped.

Avery sat back in his saddle, his phony smile gone. "Listen, A-Z," Avery spat back, "I'm only here cause my pa asked me to come. Don't go getting all riled at me about your troubles."

"What troubles?" Aaron shot out his question, mistrustful of Avery.

Avery's sardonic smile returned. "Well, my pa says you're having a mite of trouble with your herd, your brand being messed with or some such. Pa wants me to help you find out what's going on."

"Yeah, well, thanks, Bingham," Aaron said, low and even. "But no thanks."

Avery straightened the reins in his hand and centered his hat. "Suit yourself, A-Z. No skin off my nose." Avery started to turn his horse, but just then the front door of the ranch house flew open.

Amelia dashed out, aiming the heavy Winchester rifle at Avery Bingham's traitorous, cold-hearted chest. She should have killed him long ago.

Aaron easily took the gun from her and

held on to her arm when she started for Avery Bingham. He looked at Amelia, and then at Avery. The two knew each other. He could tell that much. And Amelia evidently didn't like the son of a bitch any more than he did.

Amelia tried to wrench free of her husband. If she couldn't shoot Avery, she'd tear Avery's eyes out, and rip out his throat, and stomp on him, just as any reasonable woman would. Angry with Aaron now, too, she fired him a scathing look, then turned around and rushed back inside the house. She'd have to wait another day to kill Avery Bingham, thanks to her unhelpful husband.

Aaron let Amelia go back inside, grateful she did so, but he was pure puzzled about her reaction to Bingham. Something made her mad as hell at the no-good cowboy. Wary of Avery for more than trouble with his herd, Aaron wanted him gone and away from his place.

"*Your* wife?" Avery accused more than asked.

Aaron didn't answer, but waited. He didn't want Avery to know anything about the trouble between him and Amelia.

"She was supposed to be mine," Avery oiled out, all smooth and friendly-like.

Aaron could have kicked the horse out

from under Avery then, and let him hang. "Git," he ordered instead.

"Sure thing," Avery touched his hat brim, a knowing smile on his spiteful face. "Yep, I knew your wife way back," he pointedly intoned, then turned his horse and rode away, his men close behind.

Watching Avery and his riders leave, Aaron knew he'd live to regret not hanging Avery Bingham from the nearest tree, right then and there.

Furious with Avery, Aaron, herself, and the world, Amelia gave her bread dough another punch. Then another. *Of all the nerve! I should have shot Avery Bingham!* She balled her fist tighter and punched the unfortunate dough yet again. Tendrils of hair fell across her face when her hair ribbon loosened. Amelia blew the annoying strands away. Flour dusted up in her face. She waved it away with a floury hand, creating even more white dust in the air. She turned the bread dough over and gave it another whack.

Humph! The thought of eating bread, or anything else, made Amelia sick to her stomach. So did thoughts of Avery Bingham. Buttons and bows! No matter that he was handsome as ever — in fact even more so, with his curly blond hair, mustache, and muscular build. It was likely Avery was as tall as Aaron, too. So what that Avery was good looking? So what that six years had passed? So what that she still found him attractive? Nothing she might think of Avery now could change what he'd done to her six years ago. He'd hurt her badly. She gave the poor bread dough a fatal blow, sending the floury mixture clear across her breadboard and onto the floor.

Amelia hated Avery Bingham.

She hated that she still liked him.

Aaron chose that moment to come into the main house. The sight of Amelia, with flour on her pert nose and comely chin, her raven hair loosened and softly falling over her beautiful face and down over her shoulders, her apron tied on backward and crooked, her delicate hands balled into fists and resting on her slender, curvy hips, her luminous eyes sparkling with fury, and her rosy lips puckered into a delicious bow made Aaron jealous . . . of Avery Bingham, and the fact that the son of a bitch knew Amelia long before he'd ever met her.

Aaron couldn't ask Amelia about Avery. Even if he could, would she tell him? Would she tell him exactly what she and Avery Bingham had been to each other? Would she tell him why in blazes she'd been going to marry the likes of Avery Bingham? Aaron pictured the two together, touching and kissing. He fought the urge to take Old Blue, find Avery and his riders, and kill all three of the sons of bitches. At the very least, he could have let Dogie have at the bastard!

Aaron clenched his teeth so tight his jaw hurt. He clenched them harder. Damned if this wasn't a fine fix. Bad enough what he and Amelia were trying to sort out, without no-good Avery Bingham in on things. Avery didn't belong on his ranch, at his house, or with his wife. Aaron wanted to charge over to Amelia and shake her shoulders enough to force her to tell him — in sign language or some way or other — what had gone on between her and Bingham. Then again, maybe he didn't want to know.

Aaron turned and went back out the door, without so much as a nod for his wife. He needed some time alone. He needed to check the herd. He needed to find a way to drive all the trouble, riding up on him, away.

A week after Avery showed up on her doorstep — on Aaron's doorstep — Amelia was still keeping busy so she'd have little time to think about her childhood sweetheart. She baked and cleaned and washed and mended until her fingers were raw. She did it all to take care of the A-Z Ranch house. Aaron's home, not hers. Since Gracie died, Aaron's home didn't feel like hers anymore. She felt as if she was living with a stranger. And, after all, wasn't she? Heavens, she'd known Avery much longer. She knew more about Avery Bingham than she did her own husband.

Without wanting to, Amelia wondered about Avery's life now. Was he a rancher, too? Was he married? Did he have children? She shouldn't care. It shouldn't matter to her at all. But it did. Her curiosity sparked by Avery's reappearance in her life, Amelia did want to know about Avery, conveniently forgetting her anger and upset with him. Whenever Aaron rode out to work all day on the ranch, Amelia found herself checking the front window — for Avery to ride up.

Curious about Amelia and the shenanigans on his ranch, Aaron had taken to staying out most all day — to think, and to ride the open range and his own land, checking on his herd. Dogie went with him most days. Something was rotten in the barrel, for shore. Aaron had found more of his cows with his brand changed, and something worse — fencing. Range pirates were the ones who put up fencing and closed down the open range. Public land was public land. Range pirates had no right to put up fencing. Where Aaron's land bordered public land, it should all be open for common use, for herds to graze and get to water. So who in hell was fencing his herd from getting to the Big Sandy, and good water?

His land bordered Ned Bingham's near the river. Ned wouldn't put up fencing. Ned wasn't any range pirate. Ned never said anything to him, at roundup or any other time, about putting up post and wire to keep his cattle out and away from water. Ned Bingham wouldn't do anything so low-down, but his son might.

Suddenly it all made sense to Aaron. The son of a bitch Avery Bingham was the bastard messing with his herd. And his wife, and his life. Aaron stood to lose the deed to his place if he didn't keep up his herd and land, and keep making a profit. He'd done well enough, and had savings in his money jar, but things were tight since he'd put so much into fixing up his place and providing for a family. No such thing as extra money anymore. He couldn't afford to lose any of his cattle; he needed to build their numbers. If he lost any of his cattle, he might lose everything. How could he take proper care of Amelia if he lost the ranch? He couldn't.

His jaw clenched hard, Aaron turned Old Blue around to go back to the house and fetch his wire cutters from the barn. He needed to get the blasted fence down so his cows could get to water, and he needed to find a way to prove that Avery Bingham was the culprit. If he caught the bastard in the act, he'd enjoy the fight. Aaron's palms itched to have the chance.

The wind died down enough for Amelia to more easily pull the wash off the line. Still bitter cold, the sunny January day cheered her — a little, at least. She longed for February, and then March, and then April, and then . . . what? Amelia set her wash basket down hard on the ground and pulled her shawl more closely about her shoulders. She lifted her face to the sun, shutting her eyes, wishing she could shut out her ever-present melancholy as easily.

Every day was the same. Every night, worse. She lived in a house that wasn't a home. She lived with a man that she couldn't call husband. She didn't have Gracie. She didn't have Hannah or Ivy. Separated now from the only family that had truly cared for her, her family at the deaf school, she longed to see Gabriel and Mr. Harbert and the Kennedys. If only she could lay her head in the kindly matron's lap, and pour out her troubles to Mrs. Kennedy, as a daughter might to a mother. *If only my mother were still alive. If only . . . if only . . . if —*

Disgusted with herself for the dark turn of her thoughts, Amelia snatched up her wash basket and headed for the house. It never did any good to think on her mother, dead to her now these past six years. Her father, too. Of course, she'd no way of knowing if her parents were really dead; but then, she didn't care. She'd declared them dead to her when they rejected her, deserted her, and left her at the deaf school before leaving the territory. To this day, she didn't know where they went. To this day, she told herself, she didn't care.

Once inside, Amelia set the laundry by the hearth and picked up another piece of wood to put on the fire. Suddenly chilled to the bone, her shawl wasn't enough protection from the cold, nor was the kindled fire. She pulled the rocker close to the hearth and sat down, knowing there was no protection from — and no remedy for — her own stone-cold heart. It turned cold as the grave itself whenever she thought of her parents.

Much as she fought them, painful memories of the parents who'd forsaken her managed to surface and agitate her. Amelia put her hands to her temples, the pains in her head worse than ever this time.

Twelve again, living in a cabin in Colorado City with her mother, father, and two little sisters, Amelia could still hear and talk and find laughter and joy in everything she did. She worshipped her father, James, and couldn't do enough to help her mother, Emeline. Of course, her mother had to cajole her into helping with the cooking, cleaning, and washing, as Amelia was ever the tomboy. But Amelia loved her mother, despite her mother taking to her bed for days at a time. She tried to please her by helping with her sisters. Amelia helped Hannah and Ivy with their schoolwork and enjoyed teaching the little ones to read, write, and learn about the world. Why, they could grow up to be anyone they wanted and to do anything they wanted. The world, she used to tell them, was at their feet.

All three of the Polley girls nagged at their father nearly every day to take them with him to the mines in the mountains. He promised them that one day he would. But — not yet — not until they were older. The mines, James lectured, were no place for girls, especially not his. Not yet. Too rugged, too tough, where too many things could happen to his precious little ones. Amelia thought her father must be the best miner in all of the Pikes Peak region, and beyond. No matter that he hadn't made his fortune. At least, not yet. Gone much of the week, he'd return tired and worn with little to show for his work, but he always had a hug and a smile for his family. He'd tell Amelia, "One day I'll bring you a present from the mines. A gold nugget just for you, Amelia Anne."

And, as promised, one day he did.

Amelia put her hand to her throat to feel the nugget and run her fingers over memories of her beloved father once again. The moment she realized her nugget wasn't there, Amelia swallowed hard, then leaned her aching head back against the rocker. The unforgiving wood provided little cushion for her upset.

Here Amelia's exact recollections started to fade. For here marked the day her family broke apart, never to be put back together again.

Happy as could be when her father put her new necklace around her neck, she remembered having trouble holding her head up for him to do so. She felt sick and

305

weak and scared. Put to bed with her sisters that night, Amelia tried to console them, but was too sick herself to bring them comfort. Her parents were in the room, she remembered. Her mother cried, and her father kept putting cold cloths on her head, and on Hannah's and Ivy's. There might have been a doctor. Amelia couldn't remember.

The room was hot, so very, very hot. Her head flamed, and her stomach heaved. It hurt to move her arms and legs, and she couldn't find a comfortable position to lie in. She turned to her sisters, scared now for them both. Their eyes had glazed over, and they appeared lifeless. Alarmed, Amelia wanted to help, but her body wouldn't move or cooperate. She was too weak to do anything but turn her fevered head toward her sisters. What was wrong? What was going to happen to them? She looked at her father and her mother, both at the bedside, and read the sorrow on their faces. Fighting renewed panic, Amelia could see her parents were upset, but calmed a little, knowing that surely her mother and father would be able to help her, and Hannah, and Ivy. *Surely they will . . . surely . . .*

That was her last thought before she succumbed to a feverish sleep.

When Amelia finally awakened from her fitful illness, her life — her entire world — shattered.

She found herself in bed, alone, without Hannah and Ivy next to her. In fact, no one was in the room; not her parents or any doctor. Her body ached, her head most of all, but still, Amelia tried to sit up in bed. Something else was wrong, besides the torment of her headache: she couldn't hear. She shook her head, trying to shake away the odd sensation and clear her ears. Silence. Complete, numbing, deafening silence.

Trying not to panic about her hearing loss, Amelia worried for her sisters. They must be all better now, and up and playing. Despite her fuzzy, painful, head and weak limbs, Amelia managed to get out of bed. She needed to find her sisters and her mother and father, and let them know she was awake and fine.

When she entered the only other room in the small cabin, Amelia fell to her knees, more from horror and shock than her weakened state. There in front of her, laid out on the table side by side, dressed in their Sunday finest, each with her hands folded and her eyes shut, lay Hannah and Ivy . . .

dead! Amelia wanted to die, too, but fainted, instead.

The next days somehow passed. It was hard for Amelia to remember them. One thing, however, she'd not forgotten: the horror on her parents' faces when they looked at her, deafened now, and unable to talk right. Her mother would turn away and her father would hang his head when she tried to speak. That's when Amelia knew a monster lived inside her, and she vowed never to speak again, ever. That's also when Avery Bingham came to visit, never to visit again, turning away from her much as her own parents had done. Amelia didn't feel that her father shut her out — not completely, anyway. There were moments when he looked at her, even held her, and she knew he cared for and loved her. But her mother — well, Amelia didn't think her mother could love a deaf daughter.

And just when she thought things couldn't get any worse, they did. One day her parents packed her up, satchel and all, and took her to Colorado Springs, to the deaf school on the hill. Her father hugged her goodbye, but her mother did not. Her mother sat in the buggy, dabbing at tears Amelia knew she didn't *really* shed. Amelia didn't know why her parents left her, or where they were going. But she sensed that they were leaving the Colorado Territory — and their only surviving daughter — never to return.

Only later did Amelia learn the name of the illness that had taken the lives of her sisters and left her profoundly deaf. She'd had brain fever, known also as acute congestion of the brain. She was told she was fortunate to be alive, as many died from the catastrophic brain illness. It took Amelia a long time to feel fortunate to be alive. She missed her sisters, and wished she'd gone to heaven with them. For all of her days, she'd feel guilty about surviving, when Hannah and Ivy did not.

The day her parents drove off in their buggy, leaving her at the Colorado Institute for the Education of Mutes, was the day Amelia declared her parents dead and forever lost to her. If anyone asked, she'd say that her parents had died. For indeed they had died, in her mind and in her heart.

Managing as best she could, Amelia determined to learn to sign and talk with her hands. No use in pining away, wasting time and worrying over her hearing loss. At least she had her mind, and she was alive. She'd nothing to complain about. It helped that she'd been a good student at the Grout School in Colorado City. It helped, too, that the teachers and caretakers at the deaf school paid close attention to her and treated her kindly, especially the matron, Mrs. Kennedy. They all wanted her to learn, and Amelia wanted to learn and to fit in.

Amelia refused to give up her tomboy ways — to give up on her dreams of becoming someone more than "just a girl." If the boys achieved something at school, Amelia wanted to excel in the same thing. If the boys learned printing, she wanted to learn printing. Never mind that the girls at school, Minnie Gilbert at the top of the list, teased her when she'd sneak out of dressmaking class early and run off and catch the tail end of Mr. Harbert's printing class. Amelia always tried to get a seat right next to her best friend and bosom pal, Gabriel Moore. He was smart, like her. She liked Gabriel for more than his brain. He became the brother she'd never had. Gabriel was the beginning of her new family, along with Della, Mary, and Gracie, her little charges. They all became her new, her only, family now.

That her true parents had left her was unforgivable. Never would Amelia forgive them their trespasses. Never. No matter that her parents had once been kind and loving. Their rejection of her, their inability to accept a deaf daughter — a deaf daughter who lived while their other daughters did not — buried her parents in Amelia's mind forever.

Amelia tore herself out of such dark reverie, and got up from the rocker. Digging up old memories did no good at all. None.

CHAPTER FIFTEEN

As usual, Aaron had ridden out early, at sunup, with Dogie. And, as usual, Aaron and Amelia barely gave each other notice before he left, sitting down at the table with their eyes on their morning meal and not each other. She'd made coffee. He drank it. He'd made eggs and bacon. She ate it. He got up to leave for the day. She let him.

The February days seemed the same to Amelia, as all her January days had been. And March would be no different. Something needed to happen. Something needed to change in her pitiable life. How much longer could she and Aaron pretend to have a marriage and a home together? How much longer could they pretend to have ever had any feelings for each other?
We never did.
She admitted the truth: that she and Aaron were together only because of his

advert in the *Gazette* for a mail-order bride, and her accepting the business agreement. There were no feelings involved. They'd made a deal. That's all.

Only a deal.

Amelia refused to admit the whole truth about her marriage to Aaron: that it wasn't just a deal. Somewhere, deep down inside her, she knew it. But deep down, buried now along with dead memories of her parents, she knew she'd killed any hopes she might have had of life — and love — with Aaron Zachary.

Amelia shrugged off the uneasy inkling in her gut and headed for the barn. She'd teach herself to ride — so she could leave the A-Z Ranch and Aaron. She should have done it long before now. This was no life, for either of them.

A rider was coming.

Amelia turned toward the approaching horse and rider.

It wasn't Aaron.

It was Avery — her childhood sweetheart.

She stood stone-cold still and waited for him to ride up. Her heart, warm when she'd thought of him since he'd showed up in her life weeks before, turned cold now. Avery was her enemy. She'd best remember that. Avery had deserted her, just as her parents had. He'd rejected her because she was deaf and couldn't talk.

Amelia set her feet apart, squared her shoulders, and locked her gaze on Avery. She didn't have a gun, but she had her fists and her wits about her. She was ready for a fight, and she'd get rid of Avery Bingham, and quick.

Yes, Avery was still handsome. His blond good looks, if anything, had improved over the years. Yes, he cut a dashing figure astride the big bay, dressed in a fine black western jacket, white shirt, and Stetson. Like Aaron, but not like Aaron. Somehow, she'd never thought of Avery as the cowboy type, despite the fact that he came from a ranching family. He'd never seemed interested in what his father or his family did for a living; he was always talking of faraway places and adventure.

Evidently Avery had ended up on a ranch, after all. His father's or his own; she'd no way of knowing. And evidently, judging from the fine cut of his clean clothes, he didn't have to work too hard. Others must do the work for him. Suddenly Amelia remembered that part of Avery, the part where he was always trying to get her or one of his friends to do his schoolwork. It wasn't that Avery didn't have the know-how; he just didn't want to waste time working when he could be playing.

Amelia studied him. Perhaps he'd changed for the better by this time. Perhaps he'd learned to shoulder responsibility and treat others seriously and with respect, instead of always playing jokes on them. She'd never laughed at his jokes and pranks, finding nothing funny about taunting others. But Avery was popular with all the kids, boys and girls both, so Amelia had overlooked his faults. Besides, she loved Avery Bingham. He loved her. In time, he'd grow up, and give up his childish ways. She'd wait for him.

Much as she did right now . . .

Avery rode up, then slid off his horse, tying his mare to the post near Amelia. Damned if she wasn't the prettiest gal in Colorado. His manhood stirred, just looking at her. Yeah, she was deaf, but it didn't take away from her looks. Not anymore, at least. Couldn't talk then, probably can't now. Sounded awful when she did. He hoped she wouldn't open her mouth now and ruin it for him.

But hell, any gal as pretty as her . . .

Avery took off his hat and smiled at his childhood sweetheart, satisfied that Amelia had grown up into such a beautiful woman

— much prettier than his wife could ever be. It grated hard against his insides that Amelia had married the unwelcome newcomer, A-Z. Zachary. Colorado didn't need any more Texas cowboys punching into his ranching territory. He'd tried to spook A-Z into leaving, but so far it hadn't worked. Now he'd need to do something worse to get rid of A-Z for good — not just because he didn't want outsiders in his territory, but because he didn't want Amelia in A-Z's bed anymore. Avery wanted her in his.

Amelia untied Avery's horse, and shoved the reins at him, meaning for him to leave, now.

Avery stepped away, his hands at his sides, all the while smiling inside and out at her feisty spirit. This all-grown-up Amelia interested him, for sure. Avery looked around to make sure A-Z wasn't riding up on them, then smiled at Amelia again. He didn't know how to talk to her, her being deaf and all, but then, talking wasn't what he had in mind.

Amelia shoved the reins at him again.

He stepped away again.

Frustrated and angry, at Avery's refusal to take his horse's reins as much as his unwanted presence, Amelia dropped the reins and turned toward the house. She needed her pad and pencil to tell Avery to leave the ranch, and leave her alone. She didn't bother to look around and hope for Aaron to ride up and help her, confident she could take care of Avery Bingham, all by herself.

Once inside the house, Amelia made a beeline for the bookcase to fetch her notepad and pencil. She'd put them away almost two months ago, right after Christmas. Easily finding what she wanted, she pivoted and ran smack dab into Avery's rock-hard chest. Circling around him, she charged over to the table and sat down hard on one of the benches.

Avery took the other bench across from her.

Fighting to keep her hand steady, she scribbled her angry thoughts at Avery.

You must leave, now!
And don't come back!

The moment she'd finished, she shoved the pad under Avery's nose.

He read her note, then smiled, slow and teasing, before he took her pencil from her and wrote:

No.

Amelia couldn't believe his rudeness. His arrogance. His stubbornness. His nerve. Or his penetrating stare. His blond mustache over his inviting smile. The set of his sculpted jaw. His square shoulders and well-muscled arms. And the feel of his chest. Avery had been good-looking as a boy — and was even more handsome as a man. Amelia's heart skipped one beat, then another. Forgotten memories returned. The good times of old returned. The longer she gazed into Avery's boyish, playful blue eyes, the longer she took in his handsome countenance, the more she fell under his wicked, mesmerizing influence.

Avery knew the moment Amelia fell, and he was more than ready to pick her up.

He took the notepad from her, and penciled his thoughts.

You've missed me.
Admit it.

She laughed, although she would have done well to run.

But then, it felt so good to write, to communicate again, as if a cloud had suddenly lifted, taking away the strain of the past few months. Never mind that it was Avery and not Aaron who sat across from her. Never mind that it was unscrupulous, uncaring Avery, and not her all-but-forgotten scrupulous, devoted husband, Aaron.

Amelia picked up the pad and took her pencil from Avery, asking the questions that had been on her mind about him for weeks now.

Little did she know that Avery had no intention of being honest with her, and every intention of doing and saying whatever it took to get her to his bed.

How wonderful that Avery has been such a help to his father in saving their ranch and keeping a roof over their heads. Amelia wouldn't have thought the Binghams would have had trouble with money, but they had. And Avery, being their oldest son, had saved the family from financial ruin. Avery wrote that his younger brother, Seth, still lived at the ranch and was married with two little boys. He'd helped them, too.

How wonderful, Amelia repeated to herself. Evidently Avery had straightened out and straightened up, and had grown into a good man. *How wonderful,* she thought again, already looking forward to Avery's next visit. He told her he'd come back. She hoped it would be soon. Her only thought now for her husband was to wonder: when would he be away from the ranch, so Avery could more easily visit? Amelia could tell that her husband didn't care for Avery, the moment she first saw them together. She'd no idea why Aaron didn't care for Avery, and she was irritated with Aaron for bearing a grudge against her kindhearted, benevolent, hardworking childhood friend.

Something had changed with Amelia. Aaron couldn't put his finger on it, but something was different about her, for shore. He'd grown used to her being mad at him — for lots of reasons, he supposed. Accustomed to her cool indifference, Aaron almost preferred her disdain and distance to how she behaved now — as if nothing in the slightest was wrong between 'em; as if the past didn't matter; as if *he* didn't matter. She actually smiled at him once in a while, more like to a brother than to a husband. That upset Aaron most of all. He'd rather she be angry as spit at her husband, than be all roses and sunshine to a brother. It didn't make sense, the change that had come over his wife.

He wished to hell he could talk to her. It wasn't her fault that he couldn't. It was his. Maybe he could get her to sit still across from him long enough to let him speak his piece. Maybe she'd understand most of what he was saying, and somehow she'd answer him. Aw, hell! As agreeable as Amelia seemcd to be lately, he didn't think she'd take to the idea. Besides, it would just point up how ignorant he was. Maybe that's why she'd started to like him less, and think on him all brotherly, instead of as her husband. Maybe she didn't think of him as a man, an able, educated man. Maybe that was the whole problem now. Aaron slid off Old Blue and let his horse free-graze on the grassy patches the snow didn't cover. He jerked out his tobacco makings, then quickly lit his smoke. Dogie stood by, alert to Aaron's changed mood.

Charlie Goodnight would be stopping by his ranch, any time now. Spring roundup was close, so Charlie would be coming. If Aaron could lean on his friend to stay at his ranch and watch over Amelia and his live-stock, Aaron could head for Colorado Springs and Amelia's deaf school. Maybe the folks there, the teachers and all, would be willing to teach him what he needed to know in order to talk to his wife. Maybe he could learn. Aw, hell. Aaron doubted it. Folks at the school would likely laugh him right out.

Maybe he should try, anyway. Anything would be better than this — than not know-ing what the hell was going on inside his

321

wife's head. He had to figure a way to win back her affection. He'd had it once. He'd be no good for anything else in this life if he couldn't win Amelia's love again. No good for anything.

The sooner Charlie Goodnight rode up, the better. Aaron would chomp at the bit every day, until the venerable trail boss arrived.

Amelia returned Avery's smile as she watched him climb down from the buck-board and tie his team. Funny, he usually came on horseback, not by wagon. It was almost noontime, and she'd prepared a special lunch for him. Mutton stew. Not her favorite, but most men liked it. Aaron did. It was the first time she'd thought of her husband since early that morning. He'd left, as usual, at sunup — gone for the day and gone from her mind until evening. Buttons and bows! She'd no time to think on any-thing, but Avery's visit, and Avery's lunch.

Delicious, Amelia.

Amelia warmed to Avery's note about the meal, and to his seductive smile. Before she could comment in return, he slipped an-other note to her.

Delicious, just like you.

Embarrassed, flushed, and unnerved, Amelia got up from the bench where she'd sat across from him at the table.

Avery got up, too.

Her back to him, Amelia started when she felt Avery's hands at her waist, then at the back of her neck, untying her hair ribbon. More frightened than enraptured by his touch, Amelia stepped out of his reach. She needed time; time to sort all of this out, time to take her measure of the situation.

Avery didn't want to give her any time.

He took hold of her hand and easily steered her back to the table and to the pad and pencil. The moment she sat down, he started writing, then passed her his note.

Amelia, I want you to come away with me. Now. Today. To any place in the world you want. Just like I promised you.

Dumbstruck and shaken, Amelia read and reread Avery's note, looking at his words and not him. This was all too fast. Too soon. She'd had no time to think on things the way she needed to. Yes, she liked Avery. But love? Did she love Avery? Did she love Avery enough to leave her husband now? Yes, she'd wanted to leave Aaron and the A-Z Ranch but . . . like this?

Amelia chanced a look at her childhood sweetheart. His lazy, deceptive smile made her think of a hungry bobcat about to pounce on its next meal. Her stomach churned. Avery didn't write that he loved her. He wanted her to come away with him, but he didn't write that he loved her. Should she ask him, or was it too soon to ask for such a declaration? Did she even want such a declaration? Buttons and bows! That was the problem, precisely. She didn't know what she wanted as far as Avery was concerned.

All she knew for certain was that she did plan to leave Aaron and his ranch, and soon. Would it be wrong to go now, with Avery? Would it be wrong to go to Colorado Springs now and obtain a divorce from Aaron? Things hadn't been right with Aaron since Gracie died, and they'd never be right again. Amelia had tried, hadn't she? Hadn't she made an effort to have a life with Aaron? Well, it hadn't worked.

Besides, deep down, in her heart of hearts, Amelia knew Aaron had stopped caring for her somewhere between holding her Christmas Eve and letting her go after Gracie was laid to rest. Aaron had let go of whatever marriage, whatever life, they'd had together at the very moment the last shovel of dirt covered dear little Gracie. The sadness of that moment, of that pain, still burdened her. It was so heavy at times that it was hard for her to catch a decent breath. Sighing heavily, Amelia made her decision.

Gracie was gone, along with any love Aaron Zachary might have once felt for her. Just as she'd never see Gracie again, Amelia knew she'd never again know her husband's warm, welcome, powerful, loving embrace. Leaving Aaron now was the right thing to do, for the both of them. Not just because Aaron didn't love her, but because he deserved to have a wife who could hear.

Yes, the right thing to do was to leave Aaron Zachary this very day. Amelia was sure of it. But whether or not it was right to leave with Avery Bingham, Amelia couldn't be as sure.

Nothing to be done for it now. Her decision made, Amelia quickly penciled her response to Avery.

I'll leave with you for Colorado Springs.
As for the rest, we'll wait and see.
All right with you?

Avery frowned when he read her quick scrawls. Dammit! It might be a little harder than he'd figured to get Amelia out of A-Z's bed and into his own. For a mute, Amelia was smarter than he thought. But then, he should have remembered how smart she was before she became a deaf-mute. Avery had no intention of marrying Amelia, for God's sake! He'd never marry a pathetic mute, pretty or not. He'd have to get her away fast, so she wouldn't catch on to things. If Amelia caught on that he was already married with children of his own and living off the good graces of his pa, he'd never get her to leave with him.

Avery relaxed, shooting his best smile at Amelia. Smart or not, he didn't think he'd have much trouble bedding her once they got to Colorado Springs. Hell, at camp tonight, he'd bed her. She liked him plenty, he could tell. Always did. Always will.

Fine, he penciled his answer.

You get your things packed, and I'll load up my wagon.

Amelia nodded her agreement, then got up to pack, starting with her bookcase.

Avery used the time to rifle through all of Aaron's things, his money jar and personal papers included. Pretending to help Amelia, all the while Avery plotted new ways to bring ruin to A-Z Zachary. The Texas cowboy hadn't been welcome in Colorado before, and he certainly wasn't now — now that Avery knew A-Z was Amelia's husband. No one should be bedding his childhood sweetheart but him. Avery would get rid of A-Z and run him out of Colorado, one way or another. He knew just what to instruct his men to do.

Amelia carefully placed the envelope for Aaron on the hearth mantel, waiting for Avery to leave the house before doing so. This was a private thing, and no one should see what she wrote to her husband. It hurt her that Aaron wouldn't be able to read it — knowing how it would hurt him — but it seemed wrong to leave his ranch without a word. At least Aaron would always have the note, in case he wanted to know her intentions and her whereabouts and her feelings. She should at least give him that.

The moonlit evening did nothing to brighten Aaron's flagging spirits. He was tired, hungry, and just plain mad. He'd found three more of his cattle with his brand changed. There must be others, but how many he couldn't know. And with roundup coming soon, his cattle could easily be herded up with the Binghams'. Convinced that his trouble was brought on by Avery Bingham, seeing as how his brand was changed to the Binghams' L-A-Z-Y B, Aaron didn't need to be hit over the head with his own branding iron to know the truth. What he needed was proof so he could go to the law or Avery's pa. He stood to lose his ranch if he didn't get the proof he needed. As soon as Charlie showed up, he'd have Charlie help him and —

Aaron slowed Old Blue to a walk. Beaten down by worry, Aaron's shoulders slumped. He needed Charlie's help all right, but not to catch Avery Bingham.

Aaron needed Charlie's help to keep his wife from leaving him.

He hoped Charlie would be willing to stay at his ranch, missing out on spring roundup and leaving his share of work to his partner Oliver Loving. Aaron didn't know Oliver, but Charlie always spoke well of him. The cattle business was a hard, serious business that could make or break a man. Every cattleman set his store on every cow herded and brought to market. Dollars mattered. Every cowboy working the drive earned forty of 'em a month. Aaron didn't want anybody losing income and wages over his problems, but he hoped Charlie would take the risk.

Amelia was worth it. He'd make sure Charlie knew she was worth it.

Old Blue whinnied.

Dogie whimpered.

Aaron, lost in his thoughts, didn't realize he was home.

His animals did.

Something was wrong. Aaron could smell it as much as see it. The fact was, there was nothing to see in the windows of his house and no smell of supper on the stove. No firelight or lit kerosene lamp. No light at all. No sign of Amelia through the window, at the stove, or sitting at the table, or in the rocker. Aaron slid off Old Blue and took his rifle from the saddle sheath. He wouldn't let himself think something might have happened to Amelia. He could take anything, but not that.

Dogie beat him to the door, scratching to get in.

"Easy boy." Aaron spoke low and quiet. "Easy." Hardest thing he'd ever done, opening the front door to his place. Scared of what he might find, he turned the latch, then poked the barrel of his rifle through the gap before opening the door full. Dogie was already inside, growling at something. Aaron shot a glance at the hearth but saw nothing. He checked the main room. Luckily the moon shone brightly enough inside the ranch house for him to see. Nothing. Same in the bedroom. No one and nothing. No sign of Amelia, hurt or otherwise.

Relieved she wasn't hurt or worse, Aaron let out the breath he'd been holding.

Dogie growled again. This time Aaron walked over to the alert wolf to give him a scratch behind the ears and ease his worry. Amelia didn't lay dead by the hearth. Aaron stopped in his tracks before reaching Dogie. Then where was she? No sooner had he formed the thought in his head than he knew.

Amelia was gone.

His heart fell. She'd left him. But surely she wouldn't have just up and left. She couldn't. He clutched the cold steel of his rifle, wanting to turn the barrel on something . . . on someone . . . on whoever took his wife. She didn't even know how to ride a horse. How in blazes did she leave? She couldn't have left him on her own. If some bastard took her, kidnapped her, killing wouldn't be good enough for him.

Aaron swallowed hard. He had to stay steady and concentrate. Then he lit one of the kerosene lamps and went out in front of the house. He'd check for tracks and the direction of the horses' hooves. All he saw were new wagon marks. He set the lamp on the ground, for a better look. The tracks weren't from his wagon, but he thought he knew the wheel impression. The wheels were larger than most wagons and set apart wider. They were like wagons on drives — and like the Binghams' wagons.

With killing in his heart, Aaron cocked, then un-cocked, his Winchester, and charged inside. He'd ride over and kill the son of a bitch Avery Bingham, with his first bullet, right between Avery's double-crossing, double-dealing, thieving eyes!

Dogie hadn't moved from the hearth. Aaron went to fetch Dogie, to take the wolf with him to the Binghams' ranch. Hell, he'd let Dogie tear out Avery's throat this time.

"C'mon boy," Aaron snapped out, expecting his loyal animal to follow.

Dogie growled . . . at the mantel.

This time, Aaron followed the direction of Dogie's stare, and spied the envelope on the mantel. Amelia's. It was Amelia's.

Aaron's rifle fell from his hands, and he dropped into the rocking chair.

Dogie's growls turned to whimpers. The wolf moved over to sit in front of Aaron, and then put his head on Aaron's knee.

Aaron immediately let go of any thoughts of going after Avery Bingham and killing him for taking Amelia away. Amelia had left because she wanted to leave. She'd left a note in an envelope on the hearth mantel. If she'd been taken against her will, there wouldn't be any note. No, his wife was gone because she wanted to be gone . . . from him.

Could he blame her? No.

Could he blame her for leaving a husband who didn't know enough to write to her or talk to her in her own sign language? No, he couldn't blame her. He had only himself to blame, not his beautiful loving wife. None of this was her fault. It was his. All his!

Aaron shooed Dogie away and got up, reaching for Amelia's note. He took it in both his hands and held the fragile paper against his heart. Right now he was glad he couldn't read her words proper. He didn't want to read what he knew she'd written in her letter — that she didn't love him, and that she never could.

CHAPTER SIXTEEN

Thus far, the drive had been uneventful for Amelia, but for Avery Bingham's occasional advances. She'd merely look the other way when she caught him smiling at her. She was already melancholy about leaving the A-Z Ranch, and Avery's leering grin didn't help matters. It only made her uncomfortable.

She instinctively shifted a little away from him on the jostling wagon seat, hoping Avery thought her action was caused by the movement of the wagon. She didn't want to attract any more attention to herself. Only once did Avery try to touch her, reaching his gloved hand up to stroke her cheek. Deliberately turning her head to avoid the gesture, she didn't bother to disguise her displeasure with him. Buttons and bows! Melancholy and tired, Amelia wasn't alert to her precarious situation — being alone with a man who was not her husband.

When Avery Bingham pulled his wagon team to a halt, to make a camp for the night, Amelia's thoughts returned to her wedding night, on the trip out to the ranch with Gracie and Aaron. That night had been bitter cold, with snow coming. Amelia remembered being undaunted by the weather or about leaving Colorado Springs, and being happier than she'd ever been — happy to be married and to have Gracie with her. She'd been looking forward to a brand-new life.

Jarred back to the reality of the moment, she let Avery help her down from the buckboard. She wanted to run and hide . . . and cry. The last thing she wanted was for Avery to witness her sadness. This was private. This was between her and Aaron, and Avery Bingham had no part in it.

The instant her feet touched the hard prairie, Amelia tried to wrest her arm free of Avery, but he wouldn't let go. Angry and upset, Amelia glared up at him, sickened by his lecherous expression. He was too close. Warm panting breaths that smelled of onion mixed with whiskey wafted against her face, making her stomach churn. Avery's other arm went round her waist, pulling her even closer. Buttons and bows! If she had a gun right now, she thought she might use it on him. In that wretched moment, with Avery's touch revolting her, Amelia knew she'd no intention of spending the rest of her life with Avery Bingham. She didn't love him. She didn't seek his touch. She didn't like his touch. Not anymore. Too much time and too much pain lay between them. Better to live life alone than with someone you did not, and never could, love.

She could not have a life with Aaron, and for certain, she had no intention of having a life with Avery Bingham. Perhaps she should feel guilty about her recent flirtation with Avery, her being a married woman and all, but she did not. She didn't have time for guilt. Besides, it would end here, and it would end now. Amelia wasn't a stupid woman, and she forced herself to stay calm. Avery was a man. He had strength on his side, but she had wits, on hers. They were alone on the open prairie. He could have his way with her easily, with no one close by to help her. *This whole situation serves me right,* Amelia fumed to herself, more angry than panicked.

Avery tightened his hold and bent his head to kiss her.

His dry, whiskey breath made her gag, but she stood still, letting him kiss her, letting him think she would go along with his advances. She needed to play on his weakness. In her heart, she knew — she had known all along — that Avery was weak where it counted. But he was also cruel. She mustn't forget how cruel he could be — and might be again with her. He might get angry enough to hurt her . . . or worse. And no one would ever know. Acutely aware that she might not get through this night unscathed, Amelia held herself even more still, to think — to find a way to get away.

Avery wore a six-shooter, and it was no doubt loaded. Amelia, for the briefest of moments, thought of trying to get his gun from him. But then, he was stronger than she. He might even kill her. His stiffened manhood pressed against her. It felt like a loaded Winchester poking at her belly, ready to shatter and scatter her body into helpless bits. Her head reeled. Amelia tried to keep standing, all the while wanting to pass into blessed oblivion — a cowardly escape from his stale kisses and scratchy pawing.

What would repel Avery now? What would make him recoil from her as much as the threat of a bullet in his chest? A bolt of lightening couldn't have hit her harder. Suddenly Amelia knew the answer. She remembered Avery's weakness as far as she was concerned, and she'd use it against him.

Jerking her mouth from his, her hands balled into fists against his chest, Amelia fought to keep her gaze deceptively soft. She opened her mouth — not for another kiss, but to speak, to awaken the monster inside her, the monster that would slay Avery Bingham.

"Avery . . . we must . . . not . . . rush things," Amelia managed, her energy for the fight intensifying. She'd no idea how she sounded, but hoped her voice was shrill and grating and unappealing. She tried to make her words sound worse than they already did, and she knew they already were having the desired effect on Avery.

He stood stock still, his hold on her loosening. He looked alarmed.

Good, she thought.

Avery hadn't let go of her yet, not completely. It was as if he were waiting for her to undo what she'd just done to him with her unsavory, unpleasant words. He just stared, his eyes glazing in disbelief.

Amelia seized the moment. "I think . . . we will be . . . happy together, Avery." In a state of disbelief herself, Amelia didn't know where her words came from. She hadn't spoken in over six years.

Avery let go of her and took a step away.

Good. It's working. It's all working!

Avery looked sick to his stomach now. Amelia went in for the kill, literally, as she took a step toward him, her arms reaching out to him. "Just you and me . . . together forever. How wonderful . . . that will be!"

Avery's face twisted as much as his stomach must be churning with nausea. Amelia began to relax, knowing she'd won. He wasn't going to rape her or kill her. Avery's attempt to seduce her had failed. His mood for any kind of intimacy with her was gone, killed by the monster inside her. Never again would Amelia be afraid of the voice hidden inside her. The monster inside her, her voice, wasn't the death of her after all, but her salvation.

His hands up, palms facing her, Avery gestured as if to push her away. He took more steps back, then turned. She watched as he scouted around for wood for a cook fire. She'd no desire to help him. She was relieved beyond measure that he was every bit as repelled by her now as he'd been years ago. For the rest of this night and the trip to town, Amelia had nothing more to fear from Avery Bingham.

By the time Avery and Amelia pulled into Colorado Springs, the last trace of Amelia's childhood dreams of him had vanished.

Here she thought she'd only been deafened as a child, when all the time she was obviously also blinded — blinded to Avery's cunning and false charm. Despite their lack of communication on the remainder of the wagon ride, Amelia took Avery's measure, more closely now. She found him sorely lacking. They did exchange brief notes, brief civilities, about his family and his life, and her life at the Institute before marrying, but they stopped short of expressing any past or present feelings. Avery didn't try to tell her how much he cared for her or how beautiful she was. He didn't try to lie. He didn't want her around. She was a deaf-mute girl.

Amelia purposefully had prodded him again, about his family, sensing his lies.

Avery became angry, so angry, in fact that he shot the truth at her, not realizing she could read lips, and understood a fair amount of what he'd just said.

So, Avery's already married with two little boys. Amelia wasn't hurt by his confession, but angry — with herself. She'd allowed herself to be taken in and duped by him, just as she'd done before. Doubtless he'd lied to her, too, about helping his pa and his brother. Lies. All lies. She could get the rest of the truth out of him if she wanted, but she neither wanted nor needed to. She'd no heart for the battle. She'd no heart at all for Avery Bingham.

Grateful to arrive safe and unmolested in Colorado Springs, Amelia scribbled a quick, insincere, thank you to Avery, then watched as he practically shoved her crate onto the ground, before driving away from the Institute.

Avery seethed inside. Mad as a stirred-up hornets' nest at plain, pathetic, deaf-mute Amelia Anne Polley. Yeah, he hated her muffled, garbled, horrible, pathetic voice. It was even more pathetic than her being a deaf-mute. Still, she might have been real good in bed. He should have got over his wanting to puke last night and taken her. Dammit! He shoulda done it. He hated Amelia now. He hated himself for letting her go without taking her.

He'd show her and get even. He knew just how to do it. Less angry now, he slowed his team and turned toward his favorite Colorado Springs saloon. He needed to bed a pretty gal, a willing gal, a hearing gal with a silky-smooth voice, and down a good bottle of whiskey, before heading back to his pa's ranch.

Amelia was gonna be real sorry about all this. Real sorry.

■ ■ ■ ■

Amelia breathed in the fresh springtime air once, then again, to help fortify her and steady her nerves. She set her satchel down by her loaded crate of books, then slowly took the school steps one at a time. Rather than thinking about what she ought to be thinking about — enlisting the help of the Kennedys and Principal Kinney in allowing her to live at school again — Amelia worried over running into Minnie Gilbert. The last person she wished to see again was sour, dour Minnie Gilbert!

Relaxing, letting out her breath the moment she entered the vacant reception area, Amelia decided to sit and wait on the bench in the hallway for the receptionist, Mrs. Beale, to return to her post. She leaned her head against the wall and shut her eyes. *Home. I'm home. Back with my friends and my family. Back with Gabriel and Della and Mary . . . but not Gracie.*

Welling tears forced Amelia to open her eyes. She tried to swallow the lump formed in her throat. Dear, sweet Gracie. How she dreaded telling everyone about Gracie's death. *Everyone will be so upset. Everyone will miss her so. Everyone . . . but —*

Minnie Gilbert walked up, at that moment, finishing Amelia's thought. Minnie's pouting lips curled into an insincere smile. She raised her devious hands and signed her greeting for Amelia, first pointing the fingers of both of her bent hands down, then placing her hands back to back, and then revolving her hands in and upward, together, until her palms were flat and facing up. Next Minnie placed the fingers of her right, flat hand at her lips before moving her hand down into the palm of her left hand, with both palms facing up. Continuing, Minnie held her left index finger up and moved her right index finger toward it, but not touching her fingertips. Then, with her palm facing up, she placed the fingertips of her right "V" hand near her eyes and moved her right hand forward. Lastly, she pointed her right index finger toward Amelia; taken together, signing, "How good to see you."

Before Amelia could respond to Minnie's disingenuous greeting, Minnie hastily signed a question, sarcasm dripping from her fingertips. "Why Amelia . . . or, should I say, Mrs. Zachary? Wherever is your husband?"

Amelia stood up, dried her eyes, and then diverted them from disagreeable Minnie.

She wouldn't respond to Minnie's barb, predicting Minnie's mean thoughts — that a hearing husband didn't want a deaf wife. Mrs. Beale had returned. Amelia brushed past Minnie and approached the counter. She signed hello and then asked the receptionist if Mr. and Mrs. Kennedy were about. She was directed straight away to Mr. Kennedy's office. Amelia would much rather deal with the kindly, generous steward and matron than nosy, unkind Minnie Gilbert.

"Oh, Gabriel," Amelia signed heavily, "it's still hard to believe Gracie is gone. Della and Mary are still so forlorn, even after a week. It took me an hour to settle them to sleep tonight."

Gabriel sat across from Amelia at the oak table in the study room. The room was crowded with advanced pupils, and would be for the next hour. The two steadfast friends had much to share with each other after so long an absence. Had they not been so embroiled in their own conversation, they might have noticed Minnie taking in their every signed word.

"Tell me, Amelia. What happened with Aaron Zachary? I know you left him, but why?" Gabriel sat back against his chair, ready for Amelia to share what had transpired between her and her mail-order husband. A lovely brunette girl, about Amelia's age, brushed past their table. Gabriel gulped and sat up straight, momentarily distracted by the passing girl.

Amelia took notice and grinned at her oldest and dearest friend.

Gabriel turned crimson, then smiled bashfully at Amelia.

Amelia couldn't resist, and signed to Gabriel that she'd only tell him about Aaron Zachary if he told her about the new young lady at school.

Grinning ear to ear now, Gabriel signed, "deal."

Amelia shared much of what had happened between her and Aaron. She left out what took place between them Christmas Eve, believing her few shared intimate moments with Aaron far too personal to mention to anyone else. This time, however, she told Gabriel all about Avery Bingham, not just what happened recently, but what had happened so many years ago in Colorado City. Amelia also revisited losing her sisters to brain fever and losing her parents after they learned she was deaf. It felt wonderful to pour her heart out to a trusted friend.

If only the burden of bad memories of her

parents would lift. She stressed to Gabriel that she'd rather die than ever face her mother again. How could she face the mother who'd forsaken her? How could one bear such a pain? "It's all I can do now to deal with the burden of leaving — of losing — my husband. I failed him, Gabriel," Amelia weakly signed, the energy suddenly draining from her hands. "He's a wonderful man, Gabriel. Truly, he is. I've had the divorce papers drawn up. I've signed them, but I can't bring myself to take them to the courthouse, yet. They're in my room, under my mattress. I should take them this very day, and start proceedings. I should, Gabriel. Aaron deserves better than me. He deserves a wife who can hea— "

Gabriel took hold of Amelia's hands, refusing to let her finish. He held her fingers firmly in his, wishing he could take away her pain, her heartache.

Amelia sighed heavily, took her hands from Gabriel's, and placed them in her lap. Through with going over hurt feelings and more hurtful memories, she squared her shoulders and tossed Gabriel her best, pretend smile. If she smiled long enough on the outside, maybe some of it would trickle inside.

■ ■ ■ ■

Everything at the *Gazette* looked the same, and yet it looked completely different to Amelia. It all seemed so easy. Too easy. The Kennedys had welcomed her back to school with open arms, as did Principal Kinney. He'd asked Amelia to consider becoming a teacher now that she'd returned, but said he would understand completely if she wanted to work at the newspaper in town. When Amelia approached Mr. Steele at the *Gazette,* he'd welcomed her back, too. It was as if she'd never left and time had stood still, waiting for her. She felt undeserving of such solicitude. Grateful to have a place to live among her friends in the deaf community, and grateful to have her old job at the *Gazette,* Amelia thought she'd not complain ever again for the lack or want of anything.

And to have dear, dear Harvey *not* ask her questions about Aaron Zachary — she was the most grateful for his silence. In the weeks since her return to work, Harvey hadn't pressed her even once for answers. He did seem sullen, even a bit irked with her, but she chose to ignore Harvey's cool attitude, given his silence on the matter of

her marriage. She did miss her companionable rapport with Harvey, and she hoped
he'd soon snap out of whatever had annoyed him. If it were she who'd irritated
him, maybe in time he'd forgive her for
causing so much trouble for Aaron Zachary.
Harvey had liked Aaron from the start.
Amelia could tell.

Harvey, she knew, would never have liked
Avery Bingham. She could only imagine
Harvey's glee at the way she'd treated Avery.
Harvey wouldn't be moping around the *Gazette* now if she'd left Avery Bingham. He
wouldn't have helped her message notes
back and forth to Avery, or stood up as witness in any marriage to him. Humph. Marriage to the likes of lecherous, lazy, and
disloyal Avery Bingham.

She'd just hit upon another thing to be
grateful for — that she was Mrs. Aaron
Zachary, and not Mrs. Avery Bingham!

*At least for the present, I'm Mrs. Aaron
Zachary.*

She'd yet to take the divorce papers to
court and was unsure when she would. Why
hurry? No need, really. *I'll take the papers
soon, perhaps tomorrow.* What Amelia
couldn't admit to herself was that she didn't
want to sever her marriage to Aaron. Not
yet.

For the first time in all the weeks since her return to Colorado Springs, Amelia let herself think about Aaron. She'd managed to shut him from her mind and her thoughts until now. She wondered how he was doing, and what he was doing. Dogie, too. At precisely that moment, Amelia looked up from the work piled on her desk to see Harvey coming toward her. He wore a grim expression. Amelia stiffened in her chair. At least Harvey intended to speak to her again, even if he was still mad at her. Watching Harvey approach, Amelia saw a commotion behind him, a stir at the news counter. Men were gathered; some appeared to be shouting. Alarmed, Amelia quickly stood. Harvey must need her help.

Harvey motioned for Amelia to sit back down.

She did, albeit reluctantly.

Taking out his pad and pencil, Harvey quickly passed his note to Amelia.

Trouble with spring roundup.
Livestock poisoned.
Livestock stolen.
Aaron Zachary's.

Amelia froze, reading, then rereading, Harvey's writing. With as steady a hand as

she could, she needed to know more from
Harvey.

What do you mean Aaron Zachary's?
What else do you know?

Harvey understood.

Not much.
Aaron's been wiped out.
The men are all riled.
They're worried about their own
cattle being stolen or worse.
Came here to get the sheriff.
Aaron's not one of them.
He's not here.

Amelia wrote so fast, she broke her lead
and had to grab another pencil from her
desk. Her heart drummed in her chest.

Is Aaron all right? Is he hurt?

Harvey put his hand over hers, then
smiled at her, indicating Aaron was fine. He
was quick, however, to pencil to her that no
one had said anything about anybody getting hurt.

Amelia stood up, then sat back down to
write her intent to Harvey.

I have to go to him.
Will you help me, Harvey?

Harvey slowly penciled his answer.

I can't.

Disappointed, yet understanding Harvey's unwillingness to help her, Amelia wrote back:

That's all right.
I'll go myself.

Harvey read Amelia's words, and, shaking his head, wrote another message.

I can't help you because it's too late. Aaron's gone. Rumor has it he's already left for Texas. He's plain gone, Amelia. I'm sorry. I truly am sorry.

Amelia carefully laid her pencil down on her notepad, aligning the items just so. Her work, too, needed tidying. Harvey was forgotten. When she'd finished setting her drawings in proper order, she straightened the ties of her canvas apron, then made sure her hair ribbon was secure. Everything was the same, and yet everything had changed. She leaned back against her slatted chair and shut her eyes. She could almost hear the shouts coming from the front of the news office.

It wasn't at all proper to shout at a funeral. Someone should settle the cowboys down and tell them to show respect for the dead. Thank the Good Lord, it wasn't Aaron's funeral, but hers. She'd never imagined roughened cowboys and ranchers shouting over her grave. Unbidden, Amelia began wiping her face, wiping away clods of dirt tossed over her shaken yet dead-inside body.

Aaron is gone, gone to Texas.

A fitting epitaph for her gravestone, she thought.

Harvey's heart broke for Amelia. He saw the tears streaming down her face, saw her trying to wipe them away. He shouldn't have wasted so much time in being upset with her for leaving Aaron Zachary, especially when he didn't know the reason she'd done it. He should have asked Amelia what happened and tried to help. Now it was too late to help her. Her husband was wiped out and gone, gone to Texas. Without Amelia. Poor Aaron Zachary had nothing now, not even his mail-order bride — a bride who obviously loved him.

Harvey walked around to Amelia, and placed a hand on her trembling shoulder, wishing to console her.

Startled by the touch, Amelia blinked hard, then turned her tear-stained face up to Harvey. She got out of her chair and fell into his friendly, lanky embrace. Harvey had known Aaron, too. Harvey liked Aaron. Harvey had helped her marry Aaron. Harvey understood her feelings. *He knows I love my husband. He knows. He knows. He knows.*

Amelia didn't know how long she cried in Harvey's arms — because they were not Aaron's.

"Listen, Aaron." Charlie Goodnight got down from his horse and hitched the reins near Aaron's. "You can't just go a-charging over to the LAZY B and hang Avery Bingham from the nearest cottonwood. Be reasonable, son. Next thing you know, you'll be the one swinging from a rope. Now come on inside your place, and let's get some coffee and work this out."

Aaron knew if there was any working out to do, it would be putting enough lead into Avery Bingham to sink him into the ground, all the way to hell. Killing was too good for him. Aaron wished he could deliver the bastard to the meanest, maddest Indians left on the plains, for *their* brand of justice. The Indians knew how to deal with dirty, low-down, cowardly killers and thieves. No need for any prolonged trial as far as Avery Bingham was concerned.

Proof. Aaron needed proof.

The cattle that hadn't been stolen from his herd had been poisoned. The brand problem, he knew about. But to poison his herd, and leave 'em to rot on the prairie . . . *ain't nobody I know could do such a thing but Avery Bingham. Nobody in these parts is low-down and mean enough.* What Aaron knew of Avery, he didn't like, never would, never could. His shifty eyes gave him away as much as his shiftless disposition. So did his actions, the day he rode up all how-do-you-do to Amelia. Then Aaron put the two side by side — trouble and Avery Bingham. Aaron just didn't know the how or when of it — until he came home and found Amelia gone, along with his money jar and the deed to his place. Then he knew the how and the when, for shore.

Avery had taken everything from him — Amelia, his money, and his deed. Couldn't be anybody else doing the stealing but the bastard son-of-a-bitch Bingham. Aaron would have ridden over to the LAZY B and taken Avery down — if he didn't believe Amelia had gone willingly.

She'd left a note.

Deep down in his gut, Aaron knew Amelia hadn't stolen from him. Lying and stealing wasn't in her nature. She didn't steal his money, and didn't know Avery had. Aaron knew it, was certain of it in his gut, and his gut never lied. Aaron predicted what Amelia's note said: she didn't want him coming after her. She wanted to leave him. She wanted him to leave her alone. And that included Avery Bingham, Aaron reckoned, shuffling inside the ranch house behind Charlie.

It killed Aaron that Amelia wanted Avery Bingham over him. If she wanted the bastard Bingham, Aaron wasn't gonna mess things up for her. If she didn't love him and if she'd left him for Bingham, then that's how things would be. Bingham likely was educated and could write. Avery Bingham could give Amelia everything that Aaron couldn't. There was something else Aaron couldn't give Amelia now: a decent roof over her head. The bank would take his place, forcing him back to Texas, working for other people, on *their* ranch, in *their* bunkhouse, taking care of *their* land and livestock. Not his own.

"Say, what's that on the hearth?" Charlie asked, the moment he looked over and saw the envelope. "Looks important," he added, then pulled a bench out from the table and sat down.

"What makes you think it's important?" Aaron muttered back, wishing he'd left Amelia's letter under his bedroll. He reached for kindling to light the stove; coffee sounded like a good idea.

"Well, seeing as how you've got the letter sitting up there like a Bible in church or something, I think it has to be from someone special, that's all," Charlie said, his tone matter of fact.

Aaron trusted Charlie. He didn't feel like talking about Amelia, but he trusted Charlie. "It's from my wife," Aaron spoke low and quick, dumping coffee into the pot on the lukewarm stove.

"Your what!" Charlie repeated, incredulous.

"Amelia Anne Polley." Aaron turned to his friend, speaking loud and clear now. "My mail-order bride wife, Amelia Anne Polley."

"Well I'll be damned." It was Charlie's turn to mutter. "Son, I'll take a shot of that whiskey on the shelf over your coffee."

"So will I," Aaron agreed, moving the pot off the stove, then reaching for the whiskey and two Mason jars. Aaron wasn't a drinking man. He kept the whiskey around for medicinal purposes, but right now a drink sounded real good. He poured an inch of whiskey in each jar, handed one to Charlie, and quickly downed his drink, all of it at once. He poured himself another and sat down across from Charlie.

"I got all day, son," Charlie said, the corners of his mouth twitching into a smile. He downed his drink, too, and poured himself another.

Aaron talked for the next hour, finishing his story about meeting and marrying Amelia, and about little Gracie. Then he finished the bottle of whiskey, with Charlie's help.

Dogie had followed Aaron and Charlie inside earlier and still lay under the table, his ears pricking at the sound of their voices.

"I'm real sorry about the little one, Aaron. Had to be hard on the both of you." Charlie rested his arms on the table, his glass empty, and his heart full of sadness for his young friend. He glanced over at the mantel, at Amelia Anne Polley's letter. "Say, Aaron, want me to read the letter for you?" Charlie asked, knowing he wouldn't offend Aaron by doing so. After all, he'd written Aaron's advert for the newspaper in the first place.

Aaron fixed his gaze on Amelia's letter, admiring again her printing of his name.

Looked like a drawing, her letters were so neat and pretty. He was tempted to take Charlie up on his offer. Aaron wanted to know what she said, but he dreaded knowing, too. How many ways could Amelia say, "I'm leaving you. I'm leaving you with Avery Bingham." Much as he wanted to know, Aaron didn't want to know.

"Charlie, if I ever read her letter, it will be 'cause I can read it. I don't deserve knowing what's in it, if I cain't." Aaron stared hard into Charlie's weathered gray eyes.

"Understood," Charlie replied, sad that Aaron still couldn't read or write, and sadder still that Aaron's new little girl had died and his new wife had left him.

Aaron got up from the table, a little unsteady from the whiskey.

Dogie came out from under the table.

Charlie didn't move.

Aaron dropped onto his bedroll in the main room, still unable to bring himself to sleep in his bed. Amelia had slept there, and Gracie. He couldn't sleep there yet. Might never again. Aaron drifted off to sleep the moment he lay his head down.

Dogie curled up now against Aaron, the same way he had against Gracie — and continued to do, curled up most nights on her hill, under her tree, by her grave, where the child slept still.

Charlie got up and went outside to fetch his gear. He'd take the empty loft and not the barn. For some reason, Aaron wasn't using his room, so Charlie didn't want to either. Aaron's feelings ran deep, deeper than most cowboys Charlie had ridden with. Tough on the outside, but not so tough on the inside. From the first, when Aaron was no more than a kid and joined up to ride on one of Charlie's cattle drives up from Texas, he'd taken to Aaron like the son he'd never had. With no family of his own, Charlie thought of Aaron as family. Aaron was a straight talker and a straight shooter. A good man, through and through. Charlie had encountered far worse, but none better.

Right now Aaron needed him. Like a son would need a father.

Charlie intended to help. Like a father would help a son.

CHAPTER SEVENTEEN

A . . . my name's Amelia. I'm going to marry A—

Amelia woke with a start, and sat up in her bed. She'd not had a dream about her past, about her childhood and her childhood fancies, for a very long time. Old wishes died hard, she supposed as she laid her head back on her pillow. Old memories, too. Shutting her eyes against the dark night did little to shut away her dark reverie and memories of times past.

A . . . my name's Amelia. I'm going to mar— Buttons and bows! Amelia turned to her side, punching her pillow. Why on earth she tried to hold onto something that could never be, the promise of wedded bliss with the man of her dreams — her knight in shining armor, her storybook hero — she'd no idea. She'd ruined it. *Aaron doesn't want me. Aaron is gone.* No whimsical rhyme she could conjure from childhood or womanhood would ever bring him back.

Sobs caught in her throat, forcing Amelia to sit up. She swallowed hard, then pulled her knees to her chest and stared out the window at the starry night sky. No use wishing upon a star for her husband to come riding up and rescue her from her misery, and no use wishing that her parents ever would, either. Dreams don't come true; they die before they do.

Amelia began to sign to the heavens, not caring if anyone was awake and witnessing her prayer: "Dear Lord, please watch over Aaron and keep him safe. Please be with him and guide him to a life of peace, happiness, and fulfillment. He deserves that and more, so much more. Thank you, Dear Lord. Amen."

She'd no such prayer for her parents or for herself.

Minnie watched, frustrated that she couldn't see all of Amelia's hand movements from her bed near the opposite end of the dormitory. Amelia had been praying, but about what? Minnie didn't know why she hated Amelia so much; all she knew was that she did. She'd never admit to herself that she was jealous of Amelia. *How silly! I'm way more beautiful than Amelia Polley. My family is rich, too. I'm smarter and prettier and richer than Amelia Polley could ever be. Principal Kinney should single me out as a teacher, not her. I should work at the* Gazette, *not her. I should have a handsome, hearing husband, not her.*

The bright night allowed enough light inside the spacious dormitory for Minnie to see that Amelia lay in bed now, wracked with sobs. At least Minnie had the satisfaction of knowing that Amelia was upset enough to cry. *Good! I'll do my best to keep her that way,* she promised darkly, then lay back on her bed. Instead of sleeping, Minnie plotted what she might do next to Amelia.

Minnie couldn't believe her luck the next morning. She was alone at the reception desk because Mrs. Beale was visiting family, and so it fell to her to greet the stranger who'd just entered. No one else was about. Minnie liked her job as assistant to Mrs. Beale. She often learned about things before anyone else did. She liked that most of all.

The attractive middle-aged woman, clad in black taffeta with only a touch of ivory lace at her collar, spoke to Minnie. Minnie caught the "hello" part and the "my name is" part, but not the name part, at least not all of it. Her heart began to beat faster, excited by the hope that this woman might be Amelia Polley's mother! Very carefully Minnie took out a blank sheet of paper, and wrote her intent across the top, asking the woman to write her name and her business, and then turned the paper for the woman to see.

The woman smiled.

Rather uncomfortably, Minnie thought happily, and watched as the woman began writing. Minnie already planned what she'd do next — to Amelia. The moment Minnie read the woman's name and business was the happiest moment Minnie'd had in a long, long time. She remembered every detail of the conversation between Amelia and Gabriel, particularly about how Amelia would rather die than face her mother again.

This is going to be too wonderful, Minnie thought gleefully, practically running up the steps to fetch Amelia — to face her mother . . . and die.

Amelia had spent another sleepless night wondering if she'd ever know a night's rest again. Tired and drawn, she supposed it mattered little. Nothing to be done for it. Della and Mary were already through with breakfast and in class. Amelia had come back to her dormitory to fetch her shawl and head down the hill to the *Gazette.* Mr. Steele had been so kind in giving her job back that she didn't want to disappoint him by being late. The moment sour, haughty Minnie Gilbert showed up in the doorway, Amelia knew she'd not only be late, but her day could only go downhill from here. Minnie's crooked, satisfied smile told her as much.

Minnie began signing, forming some of her words on her lips.

Reluctantly, Amelia waited to see what Minnie had to say.

"Say again," Amelia forced her own hands to sign. Faint and disbelieving, Amelia stood her ground. This was no time to swoon.

Minnie smugly signed and mouthed her same message. "Your mother is downstairs waiting to see you."

A fist in the stomach couldn't have hit Amelia harder or upset her more, she was so stunned and wounded. Forced to sit despite her earlier resolve not to swoon, Amelia collapsed in a heap on the nearest bed. Her head buzzed and her stomach churned, the ache inside her trying to get free. Was there any escape from this impossible news? Was there anyone in the world she wanted to see less than the mother who'd deserted her, rejected her, and stopped loving her? Even Minnie Gilbert would be better! Even Minnie . . .

Shutting her eyes tight against the horrible news of her mother's sudden, unexpected, and unwanted visit, Amelia tried to will her mother away — from her school and from her thoughts. It hurt too much. Not just this, but Aaron's leaving, too. Unable to bear getting up, yet unable to sit still a moment longer in Minnie's oppressive presence, Amelia opened her eyes and managed to pull herself to her feet. Somehow finding her footing, she darted past Minnie and ran down the outside back stairs. If she hurried, she could be at work, and out of harm's way, in no time at all.

Amelia tried to work, to get something, anything, accomplished, but she failed miserably. If she looked up once at the front news counter, she looked up a thousand times to see if her mother stood there. What to do? What to do? Worse, Harvey was gone on assignment today and wasn't around to offer his shoulder to cry on. She felt like crying and screaming and — dying. Despite the fact that her mother had killed her years ago. Where to go? What to do? School wasn't safe. Aaron's ranch didn't exist anymore. She didn't have the money for a ticket out of town on the Union Pacific. Who could hide her? Where could she hide?

Looking up for the one thousand and first time at the clock on the wall, Amelia got up from her desk chair. Time to go home. She didn't bother to collect her work or put her things neatly away, as she usually did. Unlike her. Very unlike her. Time to go home. Thirty minutes past four. *But where is home for me now?* Where could she go, and not see her mother?

With little choice but to return to the Institute, Amelia decided she'd go in the same way she'd gone out, using the back stairs. If she had any luck at all on this unlucky day, her mother might have left the Institute and be far, far away from Colorado Springs by now. This thought and this thought only kept Amelia on the path back to school.

Another sleepless night for Amelia. This time she was kept awake by thoughts of her mother and not Aaron. Her mother hadn't been waiting for her when she returned to school. No one came running up from reception to persuade her to go downstairs and visit with Emeline Polley. Amelia sat up in bed and glanced across the dormitory to Minnie's bed. Minnie appeared to sleep soundly. *Well, fine. Just fine. I couldn't care less that she's not over here, jarring me awake to see a mother that I definitely, certainly, absolutely do not want to see.*

If Minnie had been awake, spying on Amelia now, she would have seen Amelia wracked with sobs, just as she'd been the night before.

Finished with her morning tasks, including getting Della and Mary and her new charge, Lettie, organized for their day, Amelia was anxious to arrive at the *Gazette* and immerse herself in work. Maybe today she'd actually get something done. Maybe today could erase yesterday and all that had transpired. Maybe . . . maybe . . . Amelia's dispirited thoughts trailed off, going along with her worn-out body down the front steps of school. She didn't take the back way this morning, seeing no need to avoid a mother who'd left her yet again.

Passing hurriedly through the empty reception area, Amelia put her hand on the doorknob to leave. Another hand, someone else's, clasped her elbow, stopping her. Amelia didn't have to look up at the face to know whose hand it was — her mother's. Despite all the years between them, all the sleepless nights, hurtful days, and old memories fading into new, Amelia recognized, and remembered, her mother's unmistakable touch.

So many years she'd longed for it.

But not now.

Jerking her elbow free, without even a glance at the mother who'd forsaken her, Amelia put her cold, clammy palm on the knob again, this time making it outside before Emeline Polley stopped her. At the bottom of the steps now, suddenly having a change of heart, Amelia turned to her mother — ready to face her, ready to fight her, and ready to forget her.

But this mother, this still-slender yet gently smiling, finely dressed, beautifully groomed, bejeweled, elegant lady, couldn't be her mother; at least she wasn't the mother Amelia remembered. She remembered a mother who rarely smiled, whose face was deeply lined, who was prone to melancholy, who dressed in plain, unadorned calico, yet who was refined all the same. Amelia remembered her mother's eastern ways, always wondering where they'd come from, since their family lived out west on the frontier. Amelia's books took her many places during her childhood, including the cities in the East. She'd seen pictures of eastern, citified ladies, looking much like her mother did now.

How could such a change have happened? How could her mother be looking at her now with such loving blue eyes, with such a soft, sweet smile on her lips, and with such concern written on her lovely, scarcely lined face? Not believing what she saw — whom she saw — Amelia glanced at her mother's hands, as if her mother might suddenly explain everything and tell her why she left and why she returned — and about Papa, too.

Emeline's hands lifted, not to sign, but to put her arms around her daughter.

Amelia stepped away, out of reach.

Emeline choked back sobs, her hands still outstretched.

On the verge of tears herself, Amelia wanted to run into her mother's arms, but she held back. Suddenly she was a child again, a little girl needing her mother, a little girl needing to forgive her troubled mother. She was a little girl who needed forgiveness herself. The longer Amelia stared into her mother's pleading blue eyes, her resolve to hate her mother until the end of her days melted away. Drawn into her outstretched hands, Amelia took one step, then another, into the welcoming arms of a dream she thought dead long ago.

Time hung suspended while mother and daughter stood holding each other, shedding pent-up tears and letting go of long-held burdens.

There was so much Amelia wanted to know.

There was so much Emeline wanted to say and to make up for to her daughter.

Only one person would Amelia trust to help her sign and communicate with her mother. Gabriel. Too impatient to take out her pad and pencil and write every word back and forth, Amelia wanted to learn everything right now. With her best and brightest smile for Emeline, Amelia grabbed her surprised mother's hand and pulled her up the steps and inside. Amelia needed to find Gabriel. He was excellent at lip-reading, much better than she was at deciphering the spoken English language. If they had problems with lip-reading and signing, she'd take out her notepad.

Rushing now, more lighthearted than she could recall being in years, with her mother's hand held fast in hers, Amelia chanced a look at her feet to make sure they still touched the ground.

Amelia put down her sketching pencil, proud of her drawing of the new hotel in

Manitou Springs. She couldn't wait to show Harvey and get his opinion. One or two sessions with Gabriel, and her illustration would be ready for print — if, that is, Mr. Steele approved. With energy to spare, Amelia got up to set the afternoon type she'd been assigned. The clock read three. There was plenty of time to finish before heading back to school, see to her evening duties and her dear charges, then meet her mother at the Colorado Springs Hotel for supper.

With summer coming, she wanted to make a plan at supper tonight for her mother to visit school soon, for a picnic out on the lawn. Rejuvenated by such a happy prospect, Amelia's sure hands completed her typesetting in record time. No need now to linger at her upstairs dormitory window, staring outside at other families having a picnic, like Minnie Gilbert's. Amelia would be outside on the lawn, too, with her mother, her family.

Sadly, Amelia's father had died two years ago. "His heart," her mother explained. "He didn't wake up one morning, and the doctor said his heart just gave out. A broken heart," her mother added, then wept yet again, telling Amelia she felt responsible. "My melancholia, my low spirits, kept dear

James back east, when he'd rather have been out west with you, his cherished Amelia. And then after his passing," Emeline wiped away new tears, "I knew I should find you, and tell you, but I dreaded it. I'm ashamed that it took me so long. I'm ashamed that I was weak. I want to be strong for you now, my dear, brave Amelia."

Despondent herself over the news of her father's passing, Amelia better understood her mother's lifelong melancholy. She'd remembered her mother's dark times, but as a child, she hadn't understood the import of such an emotion and the hold it can have on a body. Evidently, the tragedy of her sisters and her coming down with brain fever had proved too much for her mother, worsening her already poor state of mind. Then, when Ivy and Hannah died, her mother told her, "I couldn't get my mind around such a horror. I couldn't cope with any of it. James knew I couldn't, and he feared for my life, too. Amelia, he didn't want to leave you. It killed him to leave you. Later, when I was in my right mind again, he told me so. Please, you mustn't think ill of your father."

Robbed of so much, how could Amelia ever have a bad thought about her father again? He hadn't left her, deserted her, because she was deaf. Nor had her mother. All her years at the Institute, thinking her parents didn't want her because she was deaf and because she lived when her sisters died — it wasn't true, any of it. Her parents hadn't stopped loving her, after all. On the contrary, her father had taken her mother back east to her family in Philadelphia, hoping for a cure for her deep melancholia. There he began to weaken physically. As Emeline's condition improved, James Polley's worsened. "He couldn't get over leaving you at the deaf school. He couldn't get over leaving you. It broke his heart."

It broke Amelia's heart, too, that her father was dead, and that he'd suffered so, over the past years. How hard her father had worked for her and the rest of the family, going to and from the mines every week, hoping to strike it rich on his claim. Evidently, he had done precisely that. Amelia remembered the day he put the gold nugget around her neck, but she'd been too sick to think about what the necklace might mean. His claim turned up vein after vein, proving the richest yet in the region. He'd turned everything over to a trusted friend to manage before leaving for the East. And now, according to her mother, "You are a very wealthy young lady, dearest Amelia."

It mattered little to Amelia if she had money or not. What mattered was family. Her father had gone to rest with her sisters in heaven, but her mother was alive. Amelia had her mother. And she had her hus—

No, she didn't have her husband. Aaron was gone. She didn't have all of her family, but she did have her mother. To ask for more would be greedy. Even so, Amelia had yet to take the divorce papers out from under her mattress and file them at the courthouse. She should do it and free Aaron to marry again. The very thought made Amelia sick to her stomach — to lose Aaron to another woman. But then, she'd never had Aaron. Not really. Not on honest terms.

Aaron had thought she could hear when he agreed to take her on as his mail-order bride. Aaron likely thought he'd married a wife who would stick by him, too, in good times and bad. She didn't and she hadn't — she didn't hear and she hadn't stuck by him when he lost his ranch.

Mercy sakes! I could help Aaron get his herd and his ranch back! I have money. I can help!

No. She could not.

Aaron was gone, goodness knew where. Maybe to Texas, maybe to Mexico for all she knew. Maybe he'd gone to find another bride. Amelia thought again of the divorce

373

papers. Filing them would free Aaron. She'd be free, too. Amelia couldn't imagine ever being married to anyone but Aaron. In fact, she couldn't imagine being with any other man. Not now. She'd come close to knowing Aaron intimately, dangerously close. What if she had, and now carried his child? That would have been a fine fix. Amelia's heart sank. Yes, it would.

Unfortunately, she didn't carry his child. Nor did she live with him on his ranch, or have the pleasure of sharing meals with him or the luxury of gazing into his mesmerizing, mischievous brown eyes; nor could she touch him and have him touch her. She imagined her trembling fingertips tracing over the lines of his handsome features, then his broad shoulders, then down his well-muscled arms —

Buttons and bows! Amelia tore herself out of her wishful reverie. Such thinking did no good, no good at all! Aaron was gone, from her life and from Colorado. But she was still married to him. At least she did have that.

And she had money now. Money wasn't the answer to her problems with Aaron, even if she could find him to give him the funds to keep his ranch. Their problems went deeper, too deep. How could he ever trust her after she'd lied to him when they got married, not telling him about her deafness and poor speech? Equally disheartening, he couldn't read and write and might never be able to. He had a learning problem; of that she was certain. Why else could he not read by now? His math and accounting skills were too good for Amelia to believe that Aaron didn't read because he was ignorant. Far from it. As much as she cared for Aaron and loved him, how could she live with someone when they couldn't communicate? Beyond gesturing and partial lip-reading, what did she and Aaron have in common? Frustration with each other, that's what!

Amelia wouldn't be a hypocrite. She refused to speak. How could she fault Aaron for his refusal to read and write? She had her reasons for not speaking. He had his for not learning to read and write. That was the end of it. Their story was over; the chapter in her life with Aaron Zachary was closed. They were not meant to live happily ever after. Fairy tales don't come true. Nor does childhood whimsy. *A . . . my name's Amelia* would end there, with her name, and with no other name alongside it.

Aaron hadn't come for her, after all. Why she thought he would, with her leaving him — even if he could have read her letter —

she couldn't imagine. Unlike her. Very unlike her. Burying her disappointment and despair as well as she could, Amelia took in a cleansing breath and squared her shoulders. Nothing to do now but look ahead at what she could do, at what she could accomplish.

If she couldn't help Aaron with her newfound fortune, at least she might help others at the Institute. Tonight at supper, besides planning a picnic with her mother, she'd share her plan to contribute to the Institute. Many of the pupils could use new clothes. Amelia warmed to the thought of tossing out their patched clothing and filling the wardrobes in each room with warm cloaks, jackets, shawls, and boots for the winter; and with new calico dresses and britches for the summer. Supplies, too. And perhaps new classrooms and more dormitories. Yes, her money could do much good at the school. One thing, however, she would insist upon. After conferring with Principal Kinney and the Kennedys, she'd be resolute that they say nothing of her charitable donation.

No need for anybody to know. It served little purpose. Besides, she had no interest whatsoever in changing anything in her life now. Amelia liked what she wore, where she lived, and where she worked. Content now to stay in the confines of the deaf community at school, she'd no intention of leaving.

Leave?

Amelia couldn't believe what her mother wrote! Quickly retrieving her pad, she scribbled her reply.

Mother, what do you mean, leave?

Emeline Polley wrote slowly and surely.

I want you to come to Philadelphia with me.
My parents, your grandparents, are there.
I can't be parted from you, again.
Please think about it, Amelia. Please.

Amelia hadn't thought about going east with her mother, or about her mother leaving. She thought her mother would stay with her, here, in Colorado. She didn't want to be parted from her mother, either, but . . . Easily lost in dreams gone by, Amelia closed her eyes and imagined being surrounded by her family again, her mother and father and her dear sisters. And her grandparents, although she'd yet to meet them. It would be wonderful, now that she was reunited with her mother, to see her grandmother and grandfather. It would be. But to live in Philadelphia and not Colorado, away from the deaf community, away from her deaf family, away from the only home she'd known? Amelia opened her eyes and studied her mother's gentle face. So peaceful now, so at ease. Gone were any signs of worry and brown studies as in days past. Gone were any signs of her melancholia. If she said no to her mother now, her mother might fall into despondency. Amelia couldn't bear to see her mother sad again.

But if she said yes, could she bear to leave Colorado, and live in the East?

Amelia fought the headache coming on, putting her hands to her temples to ward off her anguish. In her heart, she knew she couldn't disappoint her mother, but in her head, she knew she'd best not leave. To leave her friends and her deaf family when they'd been steadfast companions to her these many years, and to leave a job she loved — and to leave Aaron and be even farther away from him in Philadelphia, and not Colorado Springs? She'd said in her note, "I'll be in Colorado Springs." She'd said more than that . . . much, much more.

One day, one day, he might come for her.

Amelia felt like crying, but instead she picked up her fork to take a bite of the meal in front of her. She needed more time to think about what to do before answering her mother. Feigning hunger, she took a second, then a third bite of her steak, taking her time in cutting small pieces. Her stomach rebelled. She took a sip of water, praying she'd keep it and her steak down.

Amelia decided that the best she could do in answer to her mother was to make a promise to think about leaving. She picked up her notepad and scribbled her answer, then quickly went on to the subject of making a generous donation to the Institute, hoping to steer her mother away from any more talk of leaving Colorado Springs.

After more exchanged notes, Amelia was happy that her mother thought it a good idea to donate funds to the school, albeit anonymously.

Emeline didn't understand why Amelia needed to be secret about it, but she would comply with her daughter's wishes.

Mother and daughter spent the remainder of the meal enjoying their shared company and sharing more details of their separated lives. For now, there was no more discussion of moving to Philadelphia.

Summer might be a good time to go back east with her mother and meet the grandparents she'd never seen, Amelia reasoned. As gingerly as she could, without upsetting her mother, Amelia broached the subject with Emeline. Amelia had decided to commit to living in Philadelphia for the summer, with lengthy visits thereafter, appealing to her mother to agree to the arrangement.

Her mother did so, but only on the condition that Amelia agreed to agree to keep thinking about living permanently in Philadelphia.

Relieved that her mother approved her plan, Amelia felt as if a heavy black cloud that had been hovering over them both had magically lifted. Emeline hadn't fallen into despondency and melancholia when Amelia suggested a summer visit for the time being. Her mother was much improved. *Thank you, Dear Lord. Thank you.*

Mr. Steele agreed to give Amelia the summer off. The Kennedys would miss her, but supported her desire to visit the East and her family. They would ask one of the new advanced students to take charge of Della,

Mary, and Lettie, older now, but rambunctious as ever. Upon her return in the fall, perhaps Amelia would consider taking a position as teacher at the Institute alongside Gabriel. Of course, Amelia didn't need to work, but she might want to. Mrs. Kennedy was quick to add how upsetting it was that women were not accepted at Gallaudet College in the East. Amelia would be a wonderful pupil, and surely graduate with honors!

Quick to thank Mrs. Kennedy for her kind words, Amelia shared her hopes about her return with the Kennedys. She thought she might try to become a reporter, a journalist, like her friend at the *Gazette,* Harvey Pratt. With his mentoring and Mr. Steele's permission, she might learn the profession. Even though women couldn't attend Gallaudet, surely nothing could stop a woman from becoming a journalist. Besides, it would present a challenge to learn a new trade. Right now, a challenge was just what she needed to take her mind off Aaron Zachary.

She'd no hope of a future with Aaron or of being in love again, but she might have a future in journalism.

CHAPTER EIGHTEEN

Halfway to Texas, a disheartened Aaron slowed his buckboard team. Dogie had run ahead. No telling where he was now. He glanced over his shoulder to check his horses. Aaron had tied Old Blue, along with his other three horses, in a line behind the buckboard. All of 'em could use a break. Aaron pulled on the reins, stopped his team, and then climbed off the buckboard. A stream ran nearby. Aaron guided his string of horses over to the water, letting Old Blue loose to drink and graze. Old Blue wouldn't go far, but his other horses might spook and run. Aaron didn't feel like chasing after 'em now, his horses or anything else.

He wasn't up for any chase, no sir. He'd found that out the moment he'd saddled Old Blue weeks ago, to chase down Avery Bingham. Didn't even have the saddle cinched before he changed his mind about running down and gunning down the bastard. It didn't matter that the no-account murdering thief stole his cattle and his livelihood from him. What did matter was that Amelia was with Bingham. How in hell was he supposed to go after Avery Bingham with Amelia at Bingham's side? It would look like nothing short of sour grapes to go after Bingham and would only give his wife another reason to have left him.

Aaron gritted his teeth, his jaw so tight it hurt. Hell, he needed a smoke. Taking out his tobacco makings, he rolled a cigarette, then lit it. After a deep draw, he felt better, if only a little. He inhaled again, then walked along the stream. He was disgusted with himself. He'd never run away from anything in his life. Any time trouble came knocking, Aaron always answered, with his fist or his gun or his wits. Even when he was no more than a kid and the bunkhouse boys decided to have a little fun with him, locking him in with fancy dance hall whores and all, he hadn't run then, either. 'Course, the whores had proved to be no trouble at all for him.

That he'd left Avery Bingham, pretty as you please, in Colorado and not taken care of business with the bastard who'd robbed him of his place and his wife ate at him real bad. He threw his smoke in the water, disgusted with himself all over again. So what if he didn't have proof? Avery had gotten away with everything.

There ain't no justice to it.

Charlie had been willing to help, rounding up his boys from their end-of-the-drive celebrating in scattered saloons in the area. Charlie would go to Colorado Springs with Aaron, or Ned Bingham's ranch, or wherever it took, to find the lying, thieving son of a bitch, Avery Bingham. When Aaron turned him down, Charlie offered to partly stake him in buying another place, giving Aaron what he could. Aaron turned him down on all counts, because of his pride, and because of Amelia.

Because she'd left him.

Because he'd let her down.

Amelia had a right to happiness now, even it was with the likes of Avery Bingham. If she wanted to throw away the life she might have had with Aaron, so be it. Aaron ran his hand over the still-sealed envelope in his shirt pocket — Amelia's unread letter.

Aw, hell.

Aaron's mood changed. Something inside him changed. In that moment, Aaron knew he could never look himself in the mirror again unless he stood up to Avery Bingham. A man's gotta do what a man's gotta do.

Upset turned to anger and then to getting even with Avery Bingham. *Ain't no way any sheriff can right the wrongs that bastard done to me. I gotta do it.*

Bingham might have taken his wife, her being willing and all, but by damn, he didn't have a right to take Aaron's herd and his ranch. Aaron had worked plenty hard to fulfill his dream of having his own place, plenty hard. No, he didn't have the wife and the family he'd wanted, or thought he'd wanted. In Texas, Avery Bingham would already be dead. In Colorado, Aaron didn't need to kill Bingham, but he shore as hell needed to mess him up a little. Aaron took his fingers from Amelia's letter, both his hands forming tight fists. He itched to get at Avery Bingham.

In a hurry now, Aaron guided his horses back over to the buckboard, retied them, then whistled for Old Blue. Dogie showed up, too, waiting for his usual scratch behind the ears. Whimpering a bit when none came, Dogie followed Aaron to the front of the wagon, and then watched him climb up into the driver's seat. Jumping back a little, out of the way of the turning wagon, Dogie ran on ahead, same as always.

Aaron pulled his outfit, buckboard and all,

up to the front of Ned Bingham's huge, stately ranch. The drive back to Colorado, and to the LAZY B, had taken over two weeks, with a few stops only to rest, feed, and water the animals. Aaron had slept little, his determination and anger at Avery Bingham enough to keep him going. The sun shone high overhead. Aaron pulled off his hat, ran taut fingers through his hair, then reset his Stetson, the brim lower than usual. A couple of ranch hands headed toward him.

Dogie growled, but stayed by the buckboard. Aaron spoke to the wolf in a voice that was low and even. "Stay, fella. Stay." The last thing he wanted was for Dogie to spook the cowboys, who'd think nothing of shooting a wolf. Damn. He should have waited until Dogie had run off to hunt before passing under the gateway to the Bingham place. He'd never tied Dogie before, but he thought about doing it now, so nobody would have an excuse to hurt him. Slow and steady, his eyes on the cowboys, Aaron climbed down from the buckboard and put his hand on Dogie's head, then scratched behind the animal's ears. He needed the cowboys to know Dogie was a pet and not on the attack.

Aaron didn't recognize the men. At least

they weren't the same two that had ridden up with Avery to his place. These two had their gun hands ready, but didn't go for their holstered pistols. More men approached, coming out of the bunkhouse and out from behind the barn and livery, their stares more curious than anything else. So far, there was no sign of Ned Bingham or his bastard son. Aaron had two loaded Winchesters with him in his wagon, along with his Colt .45. He didn't go for his rifles or his strapped-on pistol. He didn't need them yet.

The front door of the large, Spanish-style adobe ranch house opened. Aaron waited to see who'd come out first, Ned Bingham, Avery Bingham — or Amelia. He relaxed his gun hand. Hell. He didn't want her getting hurt. No, he'd have to go real careful and get Avery alone.

Ned Bingham walked toward him now, all smiles. "Glad to see you, A-Z," the veteran rancher greeted, and put out his hand for a shake.

Against his better judgment, Aaron took it.

Dogie started to growl, then stopped.

"Heard about your troubles and was sorry you up and left for Texas. What happened, A-Z?"

Ned Bingham's friendly tone did nothing to ease Aaron's agitation. The old man acted like he didn't have any idea what his rotten son had been up to. But then, maybe he didn't. "Where's Avery?" Aaron shot back, in no mood for a parley with the father. He wanted the son.

"Avery? What do you want with him?" Ned replied, less friendly now.

"It's between him and me," Aaron gritted out.

"Come on inside, son, and we'll talk," Ned invited. "No need to talk out here."

"Suits me." Aaron nodded, ready to follow the older rancher inside. He figured Ned didn't want all the cowhands in on this. Uneasy he might run into Amelia before Avery, Aaron forgot all about Dogie and left the wolf outside alone.

Once inside, Aaron followed Ned down a highly polished, clay-colored tiled hallway, past a big parlor and an even bigger dining room, to an office at the end of the hall. No sign of Amelia, or anyone else, for that matter. Where the hell was Avery? Aaron would hit the bastard right in front of his father if he had to. As it was, Aaron refused the seat offered, waiting for Ned to sit at his desk before he said anything more. The room was filled with heavy Spanish-style furniture, like in Texas, like in Mexico. The air was close despite the open window and the door standing ajar. Ned must have forgotten about shutting the door. Aaron didn't close it. He didn't give a damn if anyone overheard them.

"Please, son. Sit down," Ned coaxed.

Aaron sat this time, only because Ned reminded him a little of Charlie. Older than Charlie by at least ten years, Ned's aging shoulders slumped. He looked worried. Aaron had little choice but to pile more worries on the man.

"Listen, Mr. Bingham —"

"Ned," the veteran rancher corrected.

"Listen," Aaron said again, trying to hold his temper, and save it for Avery. "Avery's caused me a lot of trouble, and I'm here to settle things with him."

"Avery?" Ned looked astonished. "I sent him over to your place a long time ago to help you out of your troubles, not cause any."

"Yeah, well, *Ned,* your son is the reason for it all. He's no good. Took my place, took my cattle, and took my wife." Aaron's gravelly voice stayed low and even, but he couldn't sit still any longer and got up.

Ned stood, too, and pointed an accusing finger at Aaron. "You're wrong! My son doesn't need your cattle or your wife! He already has his own — cattle, and a wife, and two boys!"

"Tell *him* that!" Aaron shouted back, his temper flaring and his control breaking down at the news that Avery was married and two-timing his wife with Aaron's!

Ned glared at Aaron, then slowly, dejectedly, sat back down at his desk. He sighed heavily once, then again, and fixed his gray, watery eyes again on Aaron. This time they were full of appeal rather than fury.

"A-Z, tell me what you know. Everything," Ned quietly insisted.

Aaron did, not leaving anything out.

Ned Bingham listened carefully, his old eyes tired and his body worn down by the telling.

"A-Z, I believe you," Ned stated flatly, straightening in his chair. "Join me in a shot of whiskey, son?" he offered, pouring himself a glass of whiskey from the decanter on a nearby table.

Aaron refused, shaking his head no.

"I do, too," a soft voice, a woman's, came from the hallway.

Aaron turned to look at the same time Ned Bingham did, to see who it was.

A lovely blond woman, trim, neat and composed, stepped through the open doorway and came inside the office. She held something behind her back, all the while looking at Aaron. "I'm Mrs. Avery Bingham, and I believe you, too. I have proof, Ned." She turned to her father-in-law. "Here," she said, showing them both what she had hidden behind her.

Aaron recognized his money jar and his personal papers. The bastard had some gall-darned nerve to steal his stuff and then bring proof of everything home. Hell, the poison Avery used on his cattle had to be around here somewhere, too. And Amelia —

"Excuse me, ma'am." Aaron cleared his throat, unsure of what to say. "My wife, Amelia. Is she . . . do you know where she . . . excuse me . . . but have you seen —"

"Lydia. My name is Lydia," she interrupted, melancholy now, less angry and more distracted, her mood unreadable. "Your wife isn't the first one my husband has spirited away, Mr. Zachary. And she won't be the last. I'm sorry for your troubles. I've lived with my own for years now, with Avery. He's the father of my children, but it ends there, Mr. Zachary . . ." Her voice trailed off.

"Lydia . . ." Ned whispered, in surprise and resignation.

Aaron felt sorry for the both of them, but it wasn't getting him any farther, at getting to Avery. "Mr. Bingham . . . Ned . . . where is Avery now? I need to find him — and my wife."

Gunshots rang outside. Out front.

Aaron bolted for the door.

Dogie!

He'd left Dogie alone!

Sickened with dread, Aaron knew now exactly where Avery Bingham was! Yanking his Colt .45 from his holster, Aaron cocked it, ready for anything, once he was outside. But he wasn't. The moment he saw Dogie's body at Avery's feet, he slowed his step and replaced his gun, the murder in his heart replaced by fear for Dogie. Ignoring everyone but his wounded pet, he checked to see if Dogie still breathed. Despite all the blood, and the animal's two obvious wounds, Dogie was alive.

Noise buzzed around him and men shouted, but Aaron didn't hear any of it. Ned Bingham bent down with him now over his dying pet. Other cowhands, too, helped pick Dogie up and take him inside the ranch house where Ned directed them.

"Get Doc Hutchins! He's over at Farnam's now!" Aaron heard Ned yell to one of his men.

"Right, boss," somebody answered.

The next hour was a blur to Aaron. People came and went. Time passed slowly, deathly slow.

"Your animal's gonna live," Doc Hutchins said. "He's a tough one, for sure."

Aaron breathed easy for the first time in an hour. He thought back to the time, over two years now, when he'd found Dogie wounded, trampled, and close to death. He gulped hard, choking back the lump in his throat. "Thanks, Doc," he managed, and put out his hand to shake the doc's.

"Gonna take some time to heal up, but he should be good as new when he does," Doc Hutchins added. "The bullets passed close to his heart. Lucky they didn't hit it."

Aaron studied Dogie's chloroformed body and gave the animal a gentle scratch behind one of his ears. Yeah . . . lucky. Dogie was all he had in the world. He didn't know what he'd have done if the wolf had been killed . . . by the no-good son of a bitch, Avery Bingham.

His wits returning, Aaron shot a glance around the bedroom. Only Doc and Ned Bingham remained. The others must have left. Aaron turned on Ned Bingham. "Where's your son?"

Ned walked toward Aaron, not speaking

until he stood close. "You'll get your shot at my son to talk, only to talk. You deserve that much, seeing all that he's done to you. But he's my son, A-Z. I'm going to take him in myself, to the law in Colorado Springs." The elder rancher's face was drawn and his voice shook, but he stood his ground in front of Aaron. "I was just waiting to leave until Doc here finished with your wolf." Two ranch hands showed up at the doorway, no doubt to help their boss, in case Aaron went for his gun and the boss's son.

Aaron's jaw clenched. "Lead the way, boys," he said, madder by the second, when the two didn't move.

"Take him to Avery," Ned ordered from behind.

The surly ranch hands led the way, down the hall and then outside, to a storage build-ing near the barn. One of the cowboys unlocked the door for Aaron to go in. "Give up your gun first," the other cowboy or-dered. "Boss says you've got five minutes," he said, before locking Aaron in with Avery Bingham.

The space was dark, with only narrow slits in the thick walls allowing light inside. The stale, musty air suited Aaron's mood. He quickly spotted Avery hunkered down in one corner, having a smoke.

"Join me, A-Z?" Avery oiled out, friendly-like, yet oozing with cunning.

Like a snake, Aaron thought. *Like the sleazy, slippery, snake that he is.* "Stand up, Bingham." Aaron would only ask once.

"Not until I'm through with my smoke, A-Z," Avery spat back, his earlier pretense at friendliness gone.

"You son of a bitch," Aaron got out, grabbing Avery by the collar and pulling him to his feet. "You murdering bastard. You stealing, murdering, lying bastard. I could kill you for taking everything from me — for taking my wife!"

"Yeah, your wife . . . was the . . . best part," Avery gasped out. "I took her . . . all right . . . more times than . . . you can count . . . you stupid cowpuncher —"

Aaron didn't listen to the rest. His fist found Avery's lying, filthy mouth, knocking him down and out cold in one blow. Aaron clenched his jaw hard and stomped out Avery's lit smoke when he'd rather crush Avery's last breath out under his boot. One punch wasn't enough.

The heavy wooden door creaked open.

"What'd ya do to him?" the first cowhand coming inside asked, his voice holding no anger or upset, as if he didn't care much for the boss's son, either. He didn't even bend down to check on the fallen man.

Aaron unclenched his jaw and relaxed his fists. "Not near enough," he gritted out, his tone deadly. Brushing past both cowhands, Aaron charged outside. His holstered Colt .45 had been hitched over a post. He grabbed it, fighting the urge to turn around and unload his gun into Avery's Bingham's no-good, cowardly body. Instead, he turned toward the ranch house to fetch Dogie.

Amelia saved her last goodbyes for Harvey and Gabriel.

A quick glance at the clock above Mrs. Beale in school reception told Amelia she'd best hurry. She'd promised to meet her mother at the train depot at noon, in two hours. Minnie worked in the reception office this morning along with Mrs. Beale, but Amelia had no goodbye for Minnie, especially not since Minnie glared at her now. Amelia shrugged, realizing yet again that she'd never understand what went on in Minnie Gilbert's ungrateful, unfriendly, self-centered mind.

Gabriel rushed into the office and set his stack of books down hard on the counter. "Amelia, I'm glad I caught you before you left," he signed quickly, trying to catch his breath while he did.

Amelia beamed at her dear friend. She raised her hands and in sign reassured Gabriel that she'd never have left for the summer without bidding him goodbye. "Never," she underscored, then threw her arms around him, hugging him tight.

Over his shoulder, she noticed Minnie glaring at both of them now, but shrugged Minnie off just as she'd done only moments before.

"Gabriel," Amelia broke their hug and began to sign to him again, "I'm so happy for you and Rachel." She finger-spelled the last.

Gabriel blushed, then touched his lips with the fingertips of both his flat hands, moving his hands forward until the palms faced up, signing "thank you," smiling and nodding all the while. He then traced his right jawbone from his ear to his chin with the palm side of his right "A" thumb, then pointed his index finger forward. Next he moved his right "I" hand forward from his mouth. He followed this by moving both of his flat, open hands up, and forward a few times, with his palms facing out. Taken together he signed, "She *is* wonderful!"

"I know," Amelia signed, with just as much emphasis as Gabriel.

"Amelia," Gabriel turned serious. He

slowly positioned his right "I" hand with the palm facing left and his thumb touching his chest. Then he placed his right "A" hand thumb on his lips and moved his right hand straight forward. Next, he rotated his right "A" hand in a few circles over his heart.

Amelia's own heart wrenched. She knew what was coming, yet she let Gabriel continue.

Gabriel moved his right index finger in a forward, circular direction around the fingers of his left "and" hand. Then he moved his flat hand across the front of his body from left to right, with his palm facing outward. He followed this by clasping his hands in a natural position with his right hand above the left. Taken together, he signed, "I am sorry about your marriage."

"Don't be, Gabriel," she signed, more lightly than she felt. Her hands felt like weights . . . around her heart. "I'm not sorry. I'm grateful for every day I had with Aaron Zachary. Every day," she signed, smiling, fighting her welling tears. "I'm still married. I'm not divorced yet." Amelia gulped down the lump in her throat. "I can't make it official, Gabriel. I just can't."

Gabriel took Amelia's hands in his, then gently let go to sign. "It's all right. The papers can wait until you're ready. For now, for the summer, and for as long as you want, you stay Mrs. Aaron Zachary."

"Thank you for understanding, Gabriel. Aaron's name is all I have left of him. I can't part with him. Not yet," she fought for composure, not wanting to give in to self-pity and doubt.

"Tell your mother goodbye from me," Gabriel quickly signed, wanting to change the subject, and see his friend smile again.

"Oh, I will." Amelia warmed immediately to the mention of her mother and spent the rest of her time with Gabriel on the topics of her family, the East, his girlfriend Rachel, and his summer plans. There was no more discussion of marriage or divorce.

Why don't you try to find Aaron?
I'll help.

Amelia appreciated Harvey's offer, but she didn't want his help — or anyone's — in finding Aaron. What good would it do? Aaron didn't want her or need her or love her. In Texas or Mexico or wherever he was now, Aaron hadn't made any effort to come for her. He knew her feelings from her note. By now, surely he'd have found out what her note contained, despite needing someone to read it for him. Someone must have by now.

She gave some thought to Harvey's offer for another reason altogether. Amelia worried over Aaron's fate, since he'd lost his herd and his ranch. She'd like to find Aaron to help him out, to help him get back all he'd lost. Feeling partly to blame for Aaron's troubles, Amelia knew he'd spent much of his time and attention on her and Gracie and not on his ranch. Maybe if she and Gracie hadn't been with him, he could have found out about everything before it happened!

Harvey, do me a favor?

She jotted her quick note and passed it to Harvey.

Anything.

Amelia smiled her appreciation, and wrote more slowly this time.

If Aaron comes back, I want you to help. Do not tell him where I am. That's not important. What's important is that you give him money. I want it given anonymously. He mustn't know it's from me.

Before Harvey could read what she'd written him, Amelia took her pad back.

Harvey, can you find Aaron for me? Can you find him, and give him the money? He's probably in Texas.

Harvey finished reading, then answered.

Do you want to know when I do?

For the briefest of moments, Amelia's heart fluttered with hope at the thought of seeing Aaron again. But just as quickly, her heart sank. There was no use hoping for what could never be.

No, Harvey.

There was nothing more to say, and only one thing left to do. Amelia worked out the money transfer for Harvey. For Aaron.

After exchanging hugs with Harvey, Amelia opened the door of the *Gazette*, watched its bell jingle, then left for the train depot. Sad to be leaving Colorado Springs, even if just for the summer, Amelia took in a deep, resigned breath, turning her thoughts away from Aaron and toward her mother and Philadelphia.

CHAPTER NINETEEN

"There you go, boy," Aaron soothed, laying Dogie down on his bed as gently as he could.

Dogie whimpered at the movement, then settled, his eyes closing again, one paw over little Gracie's straw doll. Aaron had left the child's doll on his bed, unable yet to sleep on the bed himself.

The trip back to his ranch was hard, with Aaron worrying over Dogie. Every bump, every rut, grated against Aaron's unsettled nerves. He didn't want Dogie's wounds to open up and start bleeding again.

Once home, he'd put his wolf in his bed, the same bed where Amelia had slept with little Gracie — the same bed where Dogie had watched over them, and protected them. Amelia was gone. Gracie had died. Only Dogie remained for Aaron to watch over and protect.

Leaving his bedroom door ajar, Aaron

walked back into the main room and headed for the front door. He needed to take care of his horses and see to the barn. He'd been gone for a long time, and plenty of things on his ranch needed seeing to. The instant he grabbed for the door latch, something caught in his chest. It wasn't a pain, but it was enough to get his attention. He took his hand from the door, and put it over his heart. Right away, his fingers grazed the edges of Amelia's letter jutting out from his vest pocket. He'd forgotten about her letter, with everything else going on, especially with Dogie. There was no forgetting now. Aaron yanked the letter from his pocket and stamped over to the mantel, but stopped short in front of the cold stone hearth.

He took the letter in both hands, running his fingers lightly over the clean edges of the envelope. If the fire were lit now, he'd toss the envelope into the flames. Then all traces of Amelia having ever lived here would be gone. Easy enough to do, to reach into his pocket, get his matches, and start a fire. Easy enough to get rid of Amelia's letter, but not so easy to get rid of her — to forget her, to stop wanting her, and loving her.

Aaron slumped into the nearby rocker, Amelia's letter still in his hand. He placed it back over his heart, and for the first time wanted to know what was inside. And he didn't want anybody else doing the reading for him. He didn't want anybody else knowing what was between him and his wife.

Something wasn't right about Amelia leaving him. If she ran off with Avery Bingham, then where was she? Old Ned had nothing to say about Amelia, and neither did Avery's wife. The bastard Avery had plenty to say, but right now Aaron was thinking everything he'd said were lies, all lies. If Amelia had run off with Avery in order to be with Avery, wouldn't she be with him at the LAZY B?

Aaron shot out of the rocker and quickly replaced Amelia's unopened letter on the hearth mantel. Amelia could be anywhere by this time, but he guessed she'd be in Colorado Springs. At her school or at the newspaper, more than likely. Maybe if he found her, she'd come back to the ranch and to him. Maybe they could get a fresh start. *If I learn to read, and to write to her, then maybe she'd be willing to give me another chance.*

Suddenly the idea of him not reading, because he figured everybody would think he was stupid, seemed genuinely stupid. It didn't seem to matter much now, especially if his learning to read might bring Amelia back to him. It didn't matter much that he mixed up his letters. What mattered was somehow, some way, learning to read so he could understand Amelia's letter. Then maybe he could find Amelia and bring her home where she belonged, with him and Dogie and little Gracie's hill.

His heart raced with determination, while his head filled with plans for what he had to do. First, he had to wait for Charlie, who should arrive in a week's time. Charlie could watch over Dogie and his place. Fortunate to have his place back, Aaron took Ned Bingham up on his offer to make good on all the trouble his son had caused and everything he'd stolen from Aaron. Ned offered to pay Aaron back in money and in cattle. Aaron could cut out the makings for a new herd from Bingham's stock, if he chose. Aaron had already made up his mind to combine some of Ned's Colorado stock with stock he'd bring up from Texas. He and Charlie could drive the cattle up together.

Aaron knew how lucky he was to be able to call Charlie Goodnight "friend." Sometimes Aaron came close to calling Charlie "Pa," but then quickly caught himself. Hell, Charlie would likely laugh his socks off, at that. Still, it felt good to know Charlie was usually around when he needed him. And now Aaron needed him more than ever. With Charlie taking care of Dogie and things at the ranch, Aaron could make the trek to Colorado Springs and stay as long as it took, to learn to read and get his wife back. Getting his ranch up and going again was nothing compared to the two most important things in his life now — Amelia, and learning to communicate proper-like with her.

With things set right in his mind, Aaron breathed a little easier. He checked on Dogie one more time, then headed back outside into the warm sunshine. He had a lot of work to do, and he didn't want to leave it for Charlie.

It was a hot day. Aaron figured it had to be at least eighty degrees, a high for June. He'd already lost his vest, and now rolled up the shirtsleeves of his boiled shirt, steadying Old Blue a moment to do so. He was in Colorado Springs now, only a street away from the *Gazette* Newspaper and Printing Office. Aaron wasn't too sure about going any farther; not yet. He slid off his horse, letting Old Blue drink from a nearby water trough. He needed a drink, too, and wished it were whiskey in his canteen, and not water.

He might see Amelia in a few minutes. It had been months since she'd left him and the ranch. What would she do when she saw him? Get mad? Run? Leave him again? Damn, he didn't know if he could take it if she ran from him. Aaron didn't fear much in life, but he feared the look he might see in Amelia's radiant blue eyes. Would they gleam with happiness or glint with anger and regret? He didn't know which, but he had to risk finding out.

Beads of perspiration trickled down the sides of his face. Yanking his bandanna from his saddlebag, Aaron wiped the wetness away, taking off his Stetson to do so. He put his hat back on, put his bandanna away, and sucked in a deep breath for courage. "C'mon, boy," he gritted out, more for his own benefit than his horse's, putting a heavy, booted foot in the stirrup and mounting up. He gripped the reins tightly so the leather strapping wouldn't slip clean out of his sweaty palms.

Any other day, the streets of Colorado Springs would have looked normal to Aaron, with so many passing wagons, men on horseback, and folks walking here and there. But this wasn't a normal day. Today the whole city felt deserted except for him, Old Blue, the *Gazette* newspaper office, and his wife waiting inside.

"Gone, you say?" Aaron parroted Harvey Pratt's words, scarcely believing what the reporter had just told him. Glad to run into Harvey right away at the front counter, he wasn't glad to hear that Amelia was gone.

"Yes, gone." Harvey tried to keep his voice steady and sure.

"Where? When?" Aaron raised his voice, refusing to accept Harvey's disappointing news.

"Can't say, Mr. Zachary," Harvey said, barely able to speak above a whisper.

"Cain't? Or won't?" Aaron asked accusingly.

"Mr. Zachary." Harvey found his voice again. "I can only tell you what I know, which is that Amelia is gone. As to where or when, I can't say."

Aaron clenched his jaw. His hands balled into fists. He wanted to hit something or someone. Even Harvey. He shot a threatening look at the unhelpful reporter.

Out of instinct, Harvey backed away from the counter. This was all going wrong. If Aaron Zachary showed up, Harvey was supposed to say nothing about Amelia and only give her anonymous envelope to Aaron. The rancher was supposed to accept what he'd been told, take the money, and that would be that. It wasn't supposed to happen like this.

Aaron stared holes through Harvey, but he didn't raise a hand to him. It wasn't Harvey's fault that Amelia was gone. It was his. Defeated, Aaron backed away from the counter then turned to leave.

"Mr. Zachary," Harvey called behind him. "I have something I need to discuss with you."

Aaron turned around. "Is it about Amelia?" he leveled.

"No," Harvey had to say. Amelia didn't want Aaron to know she was his benefactress.

"Then I'm not interested," Aaron said, and walked out, slamming the door behind him.

The bell jangled hard, jarring up and down Harvey's spine. He never wanted to be on the end of Aaron Zachary's anger again. The rancher could tear him apart with one hand. Whew! He hoped Amelia appreciated his help. Dejected himself, Harvey felt as if he hadn't helped Amelia just now with her husband.

Buttons and bows! Frustrated with herself for forgetting to ask Harvey to routinely send her the *Gazette,* Amelia thought she'd best write him and ask him the favor. She didn't want to get behind in the news of Colorado, despite living in Philadelphia for the summer. If she had any hopes of securing a job in reporting upon her return, she wouldn't impress Mr. Steele if she wasn't in the know.

She'd forgotten something else, as well. But then, she could do little about it now. She'd wanted to return to Aaron's deserted ranch just once, to retrieve Gracie's straw doll. Surely Aaron wouldn't want it. The doll would only be a reminder of the woe Amelia had visited on him by marrying him. If someone else lived at the ranch now, he wouldn't want an old straw doll. He might have thrown it away. Amelia sat up in bed, putting her hands to her aching temples. This night wasn't getting any better. Why hadn't she got the doll back? Why didn't she think to take Gracie's doll when she left in the first place? Worse, someone else, a stranger, might be living at Aaron's ranch, in possession of his house and property and little Gracie's hill.

Amelia lay back down in bed, turning onto her stomach. Maybe the renewed pain there would go away. Pressing her cheek against her pillow, she shed new tears, easily soaking the fine cotton sheeting. She'd been in Philadelphia a week now, with her mother and her dear grandparents, yet still she couldn't relax and enjoy her time away from Colorado Springs and her school and her job — and Aaron.

Amelia abruptly rolled onto her back, glaring at the starlit sky outside her bedroom window. In spite of her tears, she pulled her arms out from under her covers and began signing to the heavens: "I *will* make the most of my summer with my mother and my grandparents! I *will* try to be a good daughter and a good granddaughter! I *will not* miss my life in Colorado Springs! I *will not* pine away for my husband who does not want me or love me! I will not!"

Amelia flopped back down in bed, pulling her covers up under her chin and setting her jaw. She felt much better. Well — a little better at least.

"Gone?" Aaron could barely speak to the receptionist at the Institute for the Education of Mutes, so dispirited and disappointed was he to find Amelia gone. He swallowed hard, trying to clear the lump in his throat. Why ask where or when? He already knew the answer. There wouldn't be any. Not anymore. Not for him where

Amelia was concerned. If she'd wanted him to come after her and find her, she would have left word, or some sign of where she was going. Upset that Amelia was not at the school, and blinded by love, he forgot all about the letter she'd left him — the letter he'd yet to read.

"Mr. Zachary," Mrs. Beale began. "I'd be —"

"Thank you, ma'am." Aaron stopped her from saying anything else. "I'll just be going," he managed and walked out into the hallway, his energy drained. Instead of leaving, he sat down hard on the nearest bench. He'd no idea what to do next. Sitting down was the only activity he could come up with.

Minnie Gilbert walked by, slowly entering the reception office, staring back over her shoulder at the well-built, handsome man in the hall. She'd have to find out from Mrs. Beale who he was.

Gabriel, too, walked by, hurrying into reception, the same way he always did. He took little notice of the stranger sitting alone on the hallway bench. But once inside, as he waited to get Mrs. Beale's attention, Gabriel couldn't help but notice the conversation between the receptionist and Minnie. The man who sat alone in the hallway was Amelia's husband!

"Mr. Aaron Zachary is looking for his wife, Amelia Polley Zachary," Mrs. Beale signed to Minnie. Gabriel next wondered exactly what Aaron might have been told about Amelia and where she was.

It wasn't his place or Mrs. Beale's to say anything about Amelia. It was Amelia's. Certainly not Minnie's! Worried now, Gabriel closely studied what transpired between Mrs. Beale and Minnie, and only let out the breath he held when he learned that Mrs. Beale had said little other than that Amelia was gone. Gabriel would take over from here.

Unaccustomed to using speech, since he was far more comfortable with sign and lip-reading, Gabriel had to try. He stepped out into the hallway and stood right in front of Aaron Zachary.

Aaron got up and walked past the stranger, intending to leave. This was no place for him; not anymore, with Amelia gone.

"Mr. Zachary," he heard the man yell at his back. Aaron turned around, unsure of what the young man could possibly want with him.

"Thank you," Gabriel said and signed at the same time. He walked up to Aaron. "Come with me, please," he said, slowly and as deliberately as he could pronounce the words.

Aaron nodded yes, and followed the young man into an empty office, struggling to understand what he had said. The words sounded foreign. Aaron didn't know what he was being thanked for, but he did want to know what this was about.

Gabriel shut the door, then took a seat at the table, gesturing for Aaron to do the same.

Aaron sat down, across from the curious young man.

"My name is Gabriel," Gabriel pronounced carefully, signing all the while. "I am deaf," he said. "My speech is poor. My lip-reading is better. Talk slow. I'll get most of what you say if you do."

Aaron listened attentively to what Gabriel said, but paid far more attention to his hand movements, like Amelia's. He was suddenly envious of the young man for his skill in signing, because Gabriel could communicate with Amelia and he could not. Aaron absentmindedly shrugged his shoulders, still studying Gabriel's hands.

"I am Amelia's friend," Gabriel spoke and signed.

Watching Gabriel spell out "Amelia" on his fingers mesmerized Aaron. On its own, his hand tried to mimic the letters.

Gabriel took notice, heartened at the sign.

"Teach me," Aaron abruptly blurted out, still staring at Gabriel's hands and not his face, barely aware of what he'd said to the young man. Aaron waited for Gabriel's hands to talk to him. Aaron gulped hard, afraid to move for fear he was dreaming all this up and it wasn't real. But maybe, just maybe, Gabriel held the key in his hands — the key to unlock the door keeping him apart from Amelia. Aaron could have kicked himself that he hadn't thought of this before. He'd come to Colorado Springs to learn to read and write. Why not to sign? Maybe if he could learn enough to get by, and talk to Amelia with his hands, she might come back to him. It was worth a try. He had nothing to lose.

"Mr. Zachary," Gabriel began.

"Aaron."

"Aaron." Gabriel smiled and began again, finger-spelling Aaron's name as he did. "You want to learn our deaf language?" Gabriel spoke and signed slowly, to make sure Aaron understood him.

"Yes," Aaron said, making sure Gabriel watched his lips. "Will you teach me?"

"I will do it for you and for Amelia." Gabriel carefully spelled Amelia's name, more slowly than before.

Aaron understood what Gabriel said. He also understood that Gabriel must be a good friend to Amelia, and that he wanted to help her and Aaron stay together. Why else would he help out a perfect stranger? Aaron liked Gabriel. He had a good heart and a strong character. A man like Gabriel would be worth a lot out ranching and running cattle. He'd be someone to trust.

"Gabriel," Aaron didn't know where to start. "I'll just say it straight out. I caint read or write much. I know some of my letters and a few words, but that's all. I mix things up, always have. I don't know if I can learn. I want to try. I want to sign, too. I'm good with ciphering. That comes easy. I'll give it all I got, if you'll help me."

The two men sat eye to eye.

Gabriel's brow furrowed as he thought over Aaron's words. He knew what Aaron's problem was, but he didn't know if he could help. Some pupils didn't see letters in a word in proper order, much the same as some pupils might not hear all of the sounds in a word. Things come across backward, if at all. Evidently Aaron didn't have any problems with numbers. With effort, he hoped he could help Aaron, to read and to sign. Sign language wasn't easy to learn, but maybe, with a lot of practice, Aaron could become knowledgeable enough to communicate on a basic level. Aaron certainly seemed motivated, and would work hard. Gabriel could read as much in Aaron's determined, intelligent eyes.

Gabriel thought of Amelia, trying to imagine what she'd think now if she knew her husband sat in front of him, wanting to learn to sign in order to win her back. Gabriel was happy that Amelia need not worry over divorcing Aaron. He couldn't wait for her to return in the fall. For now, however, he wouldn't give anything away, to her or to Aaron. Best now to leave things be.

"Aaron," Gabriel finally began his answer, "I will try. I have heard of your learning problem before. It will make things hard, but not impossible. If you're willing to try, so am I."

Aaron let out the breath in his constricted chest, relaxing for the first time since he'd sat down across from Gabriel. It was damned hard to understand Gabriel, and damned hard for Gabriel to understand him. It took a lot of close concentration. He guessed they both got most of what the other said. "Thank you," Aaron at last replied, his answer humble and from the heart.

Gabriel grinned and spoke again. "You know, Aaron, I am deaf, which makes things harder for you and for me."

Aaron smiled, too. Like Amelia, Gabriel didn't think on himself in a bad way, being deaf and all. And, like Amelia and Gabriel, Aaron decided he'd best try to do the same, and not think on himself in a bad way, just because he didn't have proper learning.

"When can you start?" Gabriel asked, his hands talking, too. He held his left index finger upright with the palm facing right, then made a clockwise circle around his left index finger with his right index finger. Then he held both of his "S" hands to the front and moved them down firmly together. Next Gabriel pointed his right index finger toward Aaron. Finally, he held his left, flat, hand forward with the palm facing right, then placing the tip of his right index finger between his left index and middle fingers, and then twisting in a clockwise direction twice.

"How about now?" Aaron was serious, too, his intense concentration on Gabriel's hand movements.

Gabriel grinned again. "Tomorrow will have to do. All right, Aaron?" Gabriel spoke and signed.

"All right," Aaron answered, and nodded.

418

"Come at nine in the morning. We'll work here every day for the whole summer, if that's what it takes. All right?" Gabriel ended with the same question, putting his hands on the table when he'd finished.

Aaron reached over the table to shake Gabriel's hand, then stood. "I'll be back at nine sharp, Gabriel." He tipped his Stetson and left, more lighthearted than he'd felt in months.

Minnie had been fuming all morning. She could hardly wait for her lunch break to run upstairs and go through Amelia's things, and find Amelia's divorce papers. She remembered what Amelia had told Gabriel. She hadn't missed any of their signs about hiding the signed divorce papers under her mattress, and being unable to take them to the courthouse yet. Minnie seethed with jealousy, especially now that she'd seen Aaron Zachary in the flesh. She knew he was a handsome rancher, from Amelia's conversation, but Minnie'd had no idea how handsome, how well built, and how masculine he actually was until she saw him this morning. It wasn't fair that Amelia should have Aaron Zachary, when Minnie didn't have a handsome husband, too.

Glad Amelia had left for the summer,

Minnie hoped she'd stay away for good. Good and good riddance, Minnie fumed, green with envy of Amelia Anne Polley Zachary. If Amelia did return in the fall, Minnie would make sure it wouldn't be to her legally married husband. At least Minnie could make sure of that.

The moment Mrs. Beale returned from lunch, Minnie rushed upstairs to the empty dormitory. Many of the pupils were on summer break, and those who remained were in summer school classes now. Fortunately, no one lingered about to watch her. She reached under Amelia's bed and snatched the divorce papers out from under the mattress. Quickly, she rushed over to her own bed and put the papers under her own pillow possessively, as if they were hers.

First thing tomorrow morning, she'd head into town and to the courthouse to file Amelia's divorce papers. Minnie's family was due to arrive and take her away for summer vacation in the afternoon. She would make sure that Amelia was no longer Mrs. Aaron Zachary before she left.

CHAPTER TWENTY

Aaron glanced over the titles of the three books Gabriel had given him to take home. He pronounced their names aloud, proud to be able to do so. "Mc . . . Guffy's Pri . . . mary Read . . . er. Web . . . ster's Dic . . . tion . . . ary, and Peet's First Les . . . sons for Deaf Mutes."

He'd accomplished a lot over the past two-plus months, with Gabriel's patient help, knowing he at least had the building blocks to learn. But it was time now to head back to the ranch. Charlie couldn't stay any longer. Aaron knew that. Besides, Aaron missed Dogie.

The Turley Rooming House had been comfortable enough for the summer and conveniently close to the Institute. Aaron had stabled Old Blue, taking him out for a ride most afternoons after his studies with Gabriel. If Aaron could do it, Gabriel wanted him to come back again so he could check on his progress. He needn't send ahead, but should just come. Aaron couldn't thank Gabriel enough, and felt himself to be indebted to Gabriel for teaching him the basics of reading, writing, and signing. He still had much to learn and needed to practice every day, especially his signing.

There wasn't much else to pack besides his new books. He hadn't brought much with him since there was no need, it being summer and not winter. Opening his satchel wide, about to drop his books inside, Aaron saw Amelia's envelope at the bottom of the empty case. He'd forgotten he'd left her letter there, unopened and unread. He couldn't believe he'd forgotten about it! Blue blazes! That letter was only the most important thing in the world to him. Aaron dropped his books on the bed and carefully, reverently, took out Amelia's letter. It was time now to read it.

Turning up the wick of the kerosene lamp, Aaron sat down in the chair next to the bedstead, ready to finally discover what Amelia had written to him so long ago. This wasn't gonna be easy. He knew that much. For the past several months he'd been trying to learn so she'd take him back, and now he was about to learn something, all right. He feared he'd learn that Amelia couldn't live with him and couldn't love him. He closed the letter he'd just opened, afraid to read it. Steeling himself, he re-opened the letter, promising aloud, "Dar-lin', I'm gonna change it all. You'll see. If I ever find you, you'll see."

Aaron,
I've gone to Colo . . . rado Springs. I just need time. So much has happ . . . ened. In time, if you want, come for me. I'll try a . . . gain, if you will. I love you, Aaron. Nev . . . er for . . . get that I love you.

Your Amelia.

Aaron read the letter again and again, at first disbelieving Amelia's words. He was afraid now of his poor reading skills. Maybe he wasn't seeing things right. But there it was, in beautiful print. Amelia had closed her letter *Your Amelia.* He shot up from the chair, and then sat back down. And then got up.

Someone rapped on his door. Without a thought for anyone or anything but Amelia's letter, mindless of his actions, Aaron headed for the door, to open it.

"Harvey Pratt?"

"Yes, that's me," Harvey joked, seeing

right away that Aaron was upset about something. It couldn't be about losing his ranch and his herd and his money. Harvey knew he had not. After the ruckus at the *Gazette,* with the ranchers in a stir over cattle being stolen and poisoned, Harvey made a point to nose out the news and find out from the bank, from the Cattle Association, and from anyone else, what happened to the A-Z Ranch and Aaron Zachary. He'd been pleased to find out that the culprit had been caught and justice meted out. Harvey learned that Aaron's property and money had been returned to him.

He'd stalled all summer in giving Aaron the money envelope from an anonymous Amelia, knowing that Aaron hadn't been ruined after all. Truth be told, Harvey didn't know how to go up to Aaron and hand him money from an unknown source and then expect Aaron not to raise questions. But, ever a good reporter, he knew Aaron was leaving in the morning. And if he didn't give Aaron the money, Amelia would have his head on a platter.

"Come on in, Pratt," Aaron ordered, more than invited. "You're just the person I need right now."

Stunned, Harvey mutely obeyed.

"I got something for you. Wait a minute,

will you?" Aaron fumbled around for a pad and pencil.

Even more stunned now, Harvey watched Aaron write something down!

Finished, Aaron handed his note to Harvey, which Harvey promptly read.

Purrsonal Avdert
Looking for my wife. Amelia Anne Polley Zachary. Pleese come home. I love you, to.

Aaron

"The spelling might not be right, Pratt. You fix it for me, all right?"

"All right," Harvey parroted, reading Aaron's note yet again.

"Pratt, does your paper go outside of Colorado? If you put this advert in the *Gazette* for me, is there any chance Amelia, wherever she is, might see it?"

"Oh yeah, I think so," Harvey answered, knowing he'd put tomorrow's edition, with Aaron's advert, in the post himself to Amelia in Philadelphia!

"I have to get to my ranch now, but I'll come check with you every Friday to see if Amelia answers." Aaron spoke fast, his tone anxious. He took out some money from his pocket for his advert, but Harvey refused it.

425

"This one's on me," Harvey insisted, trying to contain his joy for Amelia. He wished he could be there when she read her husband's advert. He'd circle it in red, to make sure she didn't miss a word. Out the door, and down the street before he thought of it, Harvey still had the money envelope for Aaron in his pocket. Oh well, Amelia wouldn't be too mad at him now for not having delivered the money to Aaron. Harvey was going to do her one better, and deliver Aaron to her!

Amelia tried to eat a little something on the train, but nothing wanted to go down, much less stay down. She tried to sleep, but couldn't manage that, either. It had been the same on every train she'd taken from Philadelphia back to Colorado Springs and to Aaron. Was it really only two days ago she'd received the *Gazette* and discovered Aaron's personal advert? *Please come home. I love you, too.* Is that really what he'd said? Amelia picked up the *Gazette* from the seat next to her so she could read Aaron's words again and again. *Please come home. I love you, too.* Whoever helped Aaron pen those words, whoever Aaron trusted enough to do so, Amelia wanted to meet that person and bestow gifts aplenty. She had the money to

426

do it if she chose — for that or anything else.

Sad to leave her mother and her grandparents, Amelia promised them all she'd return for a visit when she could — with her husband. More than her grandparents, her mother understood why Amelia needed to be with Aaron.

"The time that we have with our loved ones is short, my dear Amelia. Short, indeed," Emeline said, making her words clear as possible on her lips so Amelia would understand her bittersweet goodbye. She kissed her daughter's cheeks as only a mother can. "Go with my blessing and with my love," she added, tenderly holding her daughter. It would be her last opportunity to do so for a long time.

Amelia's heart had never been so full. Tears began trickling down her flushed cheeks. She touched them, remembering her mother's goodbye kisses. No sooner did her cheeks dry, than new tears welled in her eyes. The tightness in her chest took her breath away. Nervous beyond anything she'd ever imagined, she couldn't wait to see Aaron, but couldn't imagine what she'd do, when she did. Embarrassed by her disturbing womanly feelings for him, she tried not to think about how her body tingled everywhere at the thought of seeing her husband and of being with her husband.

Unsure what exactly she wanted from Aaron when she saw him again, Amelia was absolutely sure that she wanted it more than anything else in the whole of her life. She started to imagine all sorts of things, then caught herself, quickly glancing around at the other passengers in the train car as if they might be reading her wicked thoughts. No one looked at her. Relieved, Amelia straightened in her seat, cleared her throat, and tried to think about something else besides seeing Aaron again. Finally, she gave up and soon fell asleep, dreaming of falling into her husband's waiting arms.

Amelia's hand froze, caught under her mattress in the dormitory at the Institute. Her signed divorce papers were gone! She'd made sure of them before leaving for Philadelphia. They couldn't have been thrown away by accident, not with her so carefully hiding them. No one at school would take them. Certainly not Gabriel. No one would be so mean and go through her things and steal . . . Amelia thought of Minnie Gilbert. She slowly pulled her hand free, then used both hands to pull up the entire end of the mattress, knowing all the while the divorce papers were gone, taken by Minnie Gilbert.

For reasons known only to her, Minnie must have searched out Amelia's signed divorce papers. She must have taken them to town, to the courthouse, to file them — to make certain the divorce went through. Amelia tried to feel sorry for Minnie and her spiteful, vindictive ways, but she couldn't muster any emotion at all for Minnie; not anymore. Amelia felt dead inside. She couldn't muster the energy to do anything but let the mattress drop back down onto the bed, then sit down herself. The finality of the moment — of her divorce from Aaron — took everything from her suddenly, with one swift stroke, leaving her devoid of purpose and incapable of emotion.

At once, her intellect ruled where her heart could not.

Aaron is on his way home, to me. Aaron loves me, too.

Her dulled senses started to clear the more she repeated the truth to herself. She had the newspaper with her still, evidence of the truth that Aaron loved her and wanted to be with her. Amelia stood, shaky at first but determined to find, not Minnie, but the clerk at the courthouse. She needed to see for herself the evidence of Minnie's cruelty.

Amelia wanted the clerk to officially tell her she and Aaron were no longer married.

Harvey, isn't it wonderful!
I'm not divorced, after all!
No one can file but the parties involved!
The clerk tore up the papers in front of me!
I'm so happy, Harvey!

Harvey wrote back.

Me, too!

He jotted more down.

Tomorrow is Friday.
Aaron comes on Fridays, to see if you've answered him. What should I say?

Stirred head to foot at the thought of at last seeing her husband, Amelia put her hands to her fiery cheeks, hoping Harvey wouldn't notice. What to do? What to do? She took her hands from her flushed face, thought for a moment, and then slowly began to write.

Tell him I'm at the Colorado Springs Hotel.

Waiting for him.

Harvey read Amelia's nervous scribbles, then nodded, yes, tickled pink that Amelia and Aaron would end up together after all. It tickled him, too, that he believed he'd had more than a little something to do with it. He'd neglected to mention to Amelia that he still had her envelope full of money for Aaron. That could wait.

Noon! Amelia checked her watch pin once, then again, and then again. She hadn't eaten any supper last night and didn't take anything this morning but a cup of steaming tea. Even that threatened to come back up. Unable to sit still after a sleepless night, she paced back and forth on the thick Oriental carpet, trying to take in a good breath, and failing miserably. The wardrobe door in the elegant Victorian-style room at the Colorado Springs Hotel stood wide open. On the large brass bed atop the burgundy satin quilt, Amelia had thrown outfit after outfit, unsure what would be perfect to wear when she saw Aaron again. Though she'd checked her watch pin, in truth she'd lost track of the time — and the day and the place and

431

everything else except what to wear for Aaron.

Her nerves were so on edge, she needed to calm down. A hot bath would help. There was a convenience down the hall with a beautiful, gilded-trim tub. A soothing soak was just what she needed now, to ease her nerves. Without a thought for the possibility that Aaron might show up any second, Amelia fumbled with the buttons on her white lace blouse, undoing them as quickly as she could. She ripped the grosgrain ribbon from her hair, needing something more to tie up her heavy locks so her hair wouldn't soak, too, when she immersed herself in the hot bath. Untying her black lace-ups, she quickly kicked off the soft leather boots, ridding herself of her lightly woven stockings, too. Next came her navy taffeta skirt. She tossed it on top of all the other outfits on the bed. For the briefest of moments, Amelia shook her head at the pile of dresses, remembering the day in Philadelphia her mother had insisted she buy them. Well, she did. And now what use were they?

None. None whatsoever.

Down to her cotton chemise with its ivory ribbon stays and her pantalets, silk fastenings and all, it finally dawned on Amelia that she couldn't march down the hall in her unmentionables! Oh, buttons and bows! Maybe she could just grab up the quilt or a blanket or . . . maybe her robe. She did have one, for pity's sake. Hurrying over to the wardrobe, she stopped dead in her tracks when the door to her room opened.

Aaron slowly opened the door to Number Eleven, Amelia's room . . . happy it was unlocked and hoping he wouldn't scare her by doing so. The moment he saw his beautiful wife, half undressed, her smooth, creamy skin beckoning, her raven hair flowing wild to her waist, her soft pink mouth open in surprise, her luminous cobalt eyes sparkling, her delicate feet bare and her shapely arms held over her partially exposed bosom, Aaron couldn't imagine finding her waiting for him any other way than this. He shut the door behind him, and locked it.

Amelia stood frozen, her thoughts racing ahead of her stunned limbs. If it were possible, Aaron was even more handsome than she'd remembered. And so tall he towered over her. His mischievous brown gaze teased, touching her everywhere. Even from across the room, his masculine essence reached her, bearing with it the pleasing aroma of leather, tobacco, and musk. Captured by his essence as much as by the man,

Amelia felt herself being drawn to Aaron, yet she couldn't move.

He didn't either.

She wanted to put her arms around him and have him put his arms around her, and never, ever, let go. Alarmed and scared that she wouldn't know what to do, still she wanted Aaron to do other things besides put his arms around her. She'd desired his touch for oh, so very long. She yearned to know what it truly meant to be a wife. Although her feet refused to move, her hands did, of their own volition. She had to do something, express something, sign something to release her building tension. Besides, Aaron didn't understand sign. He wouldn't understand that she harbored such wicked thoughts for him. For the first time since she'd met Aaron, she was glad he didn't understand.

Dropping her arms from her bosom, forgetting her state of undress, Amelia raised her hands and began signing, slower than usual, to help quell her nerves. Unable to tear her gaze from her husband, she pointed her two "F" hands forward and moved them up and down alternately, with her palms facing each other. Then she pointed her right index finger toward Aaron, next pointing both "C" hands down to the front and moving them simultaneously, first to one side and then the other. After this, she placed her right "A" thumb, palm left, under her chin and moved it forward and away from her chin. Gulping hard, Amelia then placed her right open hand forward and drew it into her chest, while simultaneously forming a closed hand, followed by pointing her right index finger toward her chest. Taken together, thus far she'd signed, "If you do not take me — " The rest of her sentence followed.

" — in your arms now, and take me, I'll die. I'll absolutely die. Aaron, please, if I have to die, let it be in your arms!" She'd sped up her movements on the last words, unaware she'd done so, although she was aware of Aaron's changing expression.

Amelia felt better at releasing some of her mounting tension, but then, Aaron didn't seem upset with her at all. He didn't look puzzled or agitated or concerned that she signed to him, instead of trying to mouth her words to him. He stood there, staring at her, first smiling, then serious, his intense concentration on her hands, as if he actually followed her signing. Something was different about Aaron, beyond his even better good looks and taller frame and sheer masculinity. It was in his smile, his knowing smile, and his . . . understanding countenance.

Even before Aaron raised his hands to her, she knew. She knew that Aaron did understand her! It was written all over his face, in his tender eyes, in his teasing grin and the set of his tensed jaw. He knew her deaf language! He'd learned to sign! Although utterly, completely embarrassed to have Aaron know her intimate, wicked thoughts, Amelia was overjoyed to know Aaron had somehow, some way, learned to talk in sign. The import of such news overwhelmed her, humbled her, rendered her unable to imagine how hard it must have been for him. She had so many questions, but now was not the time. Amelia hadn't believed she could love Aaron any more than she already did, but she'd been wrong. She was the luckiest of women to have such a man love her.

Fighting tears, her chest tight, she fixed her gaze on Aaron's intelligent, heartfelt hand movements. Like magic, Aaron's tanned fingers answered her earlier plea. She felt, more than read his signs. His hands touched her with each gestured word.

Aaron pointed both of his index fingers toward each other and rotated them around each other, while, simultaneously, moving them toward his body. Then he held both of his flat hands to the front, with his palms facing up, making forward semicircles in opposite directions. Taken together, he signed, "Come here."

Amelia, entranced, began moving toward her husband, her gaze remaining fixed on his magical hands. Afraid of him, yet wanting him, she didn't know how to be a wife in bed, his wife in bed. Her body ached for him, but she didn't know what to do about it.

Aaron did. He signed slow and easy so not to frighten her more. He read it in her anxious eyes, on her tense, unsmiling face, in every gesture of her trembling body that she'd never been with a man before. She wanted him, but she was afraid. He was afraid, too, afraid that he wouldn't make her first time the best time. He'd hated that he'd have to hurt her and cause her pain. The best he could do was to love her, the best he knew how. With all the love and passion he felt for her, Aaron tenderly signed to her, "We'll die together, my darling Amelia, in each other's arms."

Her husband stole her breath, deliberately, seductively, with his words. Amelia had never known such a moment, and was at once afraid yet fearless. Aaron had power over her, passionate, sensual power, and she welcomed it, invited it. No longer worried about the power a man could have over a woman — the power Aaron had over her — she realized she, too, had power over him — the power of love.

All the barriers keeping Amelia and Aaron apart fell away in that one enchanted moment. Stripped now of everything but the love growing inside them each for the other, Amelia and Aaron stepped closer, their passions rising and their fears melting away.

Aaron put his hands in Amelia's thick, luxuriant hair, threading his fingers at her temples, pulling her to him for a kiss.

Lost from the instant his hands touched her and his lips found hers, Amelia prayed for passion's death — in Aaron's arms.

Aaron deepened his kiss.

Her body instinctively cleaved to his, her soft, aroused shape molding against his hardness, against *him.* Despite the layers between them, Amelia felt his manhood against her female center, and couldn't get near enough, her agitation mounting. Buttons and bows! Why ever did she wear them? What cruelty, what obstacles to her happiness. She fumbled with her bodice lacing, all the while keeping her lips molded to the urgent press of Aaron's demanding mouth, tasting him, touching him, opening to him.

Bitterly disappointed and confused when he broke their kiss, Amelia shivered in protest, attempting to re-tie her bodice, to get warm again. Her lips burned for his touch, just once more, *please, oh please.* When Aaron swept her up in his arms, she let go of her satin ties and leaned into her husband's body, going with him now wherever he chose to take her.

Right now, it was to bed.

Aaron laid Amelia atop the brass bed, atop the dresses she'd scattered there, not bothering to move anything but his wife, so he could take off his clothes. He thought he'd already died, too, just looking at his gorgeous, seductive wife, lying amid buttons and bows and soft, mysterious female clothes. He'd had no idea, when he married her, what a pleasing handful she'd be, but he knew now that his hands would never be full enough, from want of her.

His hat off, his vest gone, Aaron unbuttoned his shirt, ripping the bottom two buttons clean off. Angry that he couldn't kick his boots off he bent down and jerked each one off, as if they were shackles. Undoing his Lee jeans, he yanked them down and off, tossing them at the foot of Amelia's bed, his worn jeans landing on top of her new lace nightdress. He didn't know much about female things, but he recognized the nightdress. It flashed across his aroused mind that he'd love to see Amelia in the lacy thing, but for now, he didn't want her in anything. Pulling his long underwear off his shoulders, Aaron jerked it down his body until he could kick the nuisance clean away.

Amelia's underthings were next. Aaron clenched his jaw and steeled himself, needing to hold himself back for his wife. As gently as he could, with as much restraint as he could muster, he reached for her.

Merciful heavens! Amelia had never imagined this moment. Instead of fear, her insides, right down to her female center, began to throb and ache. Had she ever, in the whole of her life, seen anything, any drawing or any painting of the human male body, so absolutely perfect? It was as if Aaron had been molded and sculpted by one of the great masters . . . *all for me.* Amelia's thoughts turned even more wickedly wonderful. The more her insides pulsed and burned, the more convinced she was of why a woman's body was made as a vessel: to receive such a man. She held her arms up to Aaron, waiting, wanting, and needing to be filled.

He didn't disappoint.

Amelia reveled in the feel of Aaron's skilled hands at her bodice and her hips, easily ridding her of her bothersome buttons and bows. She melted at his taste, his touch on her mouth, down her throat, over her naked chest, and below. She wouldn't stop him; she couldn't. She let his lips brush her female triangle. He kissed her, at first gently and then with more pressure. Her molten center burned, each flame more powerful than the last. At that point of impossible, agonizing arousal, Amelia knew what it was to be on the brink of ecstasy and passionate death. Now she knew what her body craved from Aaron, what she had to have or die.

Answering her passion with his own, knowing what his wife wanted and was ready for, Aaron moved up, over Amelia's aroused nakedness, kissing her mouth now, his tongue probing, deeper and deeper, before he entered her with his stiff manhood. He waited for her cry of pain, dreading it but needing to hear it, so he could enter her more fully for his own release. He waited, needing to give her all of the love and passion within him.

She didn't disappoint.

Amelia arched her hips to him, her pain

forgotten, marveling in their union, more surprised by the pleasure of it than anything she could have ever imagined. Though innocent in the ways of lovemaking, out of instinct she knew her husband sought the same pleasure, the same satisfaction and release, she did. Oh, the pain of such pleasure. The pain of such a death. Suddenly, Amelia thought she heard bells . . . bells as she remembered them . . . church bells . . . clanging . . . tolling . . . ringing. This wasn't a death knell at all, but wedding bells, bells of celebration, blissful, wonderful, beautiful bells chiming so loud now that her head, her heart, her whole body, exploded at such a miracle!

Amelia woke first, lying in her still-sleeping husband's arms after they'd made love a second time. It was dark outside now, moonlight and shadow. She wondered what time it must be. Neither she nor Aaron had gotten out of bed since he'd laid her there hours and wonderful hours ago. In between their lovemaking, they'd shared themselves with each other, telling each other everything that had happened since they'd parted.

Amelia nestled closer to Aaron, realizing she hadn't told him everything. She hadn't told him she was a rich woman, and that he was a rich man now. That could wait, perhaps until their children came along. For now she'd return to the A-Z Ranch with her husband — her amazing husband who'd learned to sign, thereby making their communication and their lives together far easier — content to live on the ranch as it was, ready to support Aaron in any new cattle venture or land purchase.

She was anxious to learn more about ranching and the cattle business herself, and thought it would be wonderful to invite some of the pupils from the Institute to visit the ranch during their vacation time. Some might want to become ranchers themselves, and learn the trade. Surely Aaron would agree to take the children under his wing.

Amelia nestled even closer against her husband's powerful nakedness, not a bit chilled. The bed was still in disarray, with her clothes scattered everywhere, but it didn't matter. What mattered was that her life was no longer scattered with dreams of Pikes Peak and beyond, but rooted and firmly planted now alongside her husband, in Colorado. She wasn't just a mail-order bride, but a true bride, a wife, in every sense of the word — Mrs. Aaron Zachary.

Aaron stirred and pulled Amelia closer,

but he didn't awaken.

Amelia ran the fingers of her right hand over his encircling arm until her fingertips met his. Gently, so not to awaken Aaron, she threaded her fingers through his until their hands clasped. Raising her left hand, enough to see the gold wedding band Aaron had placed there, Amelia choked back tears of joy, turning her ring hand to catch the moonlight. But in her right hand she held the greatest gift, the greatest bond symbolizing their love; she held Aaron's hand. In his hand was the gift of communication and understanding, the promise of safety and security. She knew she and Aaron could sign to each other, intimately, and privately — two together, with no need for anyone else to come between them.

Suddenly Amelia's thoughts turned to childhood whimsy. She was eight years old again, back in her bed in the family cabin in Colorado City. She gazed out the window at the starry, moonlit night, much like this night, her head filling with romantic notions of old. *A . . . my name's Amelia . . . I'm going to marry —*

She stopped herself. Correcting herself, Amelia began again.

A . . . my name's Amelia . . . and I married Aaron . . .

ABOUT THE AUTHOR

A . . . My Name's Amelia is **Joanne Sundell**'s second published book, and no one is more surprised than she is! Happy to bring yet another strong, western heroine to the printed-romance page, Joanne continues to search through Colorado archives, leaving no silver mine, dance hall, or mountain stone unturned, to breathe life into the adventuresome, exciting, brave women who helped settle the West.

Her first novel, *Matchmaker, Matchmaker,* won the Land of Enchantment Romance Authors/Romance Writers of America top prize for series historical in 2004. A member of RWA, CRW, and WWW, Joanne admits she has lots to learn and considers her involvement in these noted writing groups an honor.

Joanne (her children grown and off on their own adventures) lives Rocky Mountain

High with her husband, two cats, and two dogs.

Email Joanne: author@joannesundell.com

The employees of Thorndike Press hope you have enjoyed this Large Print book. All our Thorndike and Wheeler Large Print titles are designed for easy reading, and all our books are made to last. Other Thorndike Press Large Print books are available at your library, through selected bookstores, or directly from us.

For information about titles, please call:
(800) 223-1244

or visit our Web site at:
http://gale.cengage.com/thorndike

To share your comments, please write:
Publisher
Thorndike Press
295 Kennedy Memorial Drive
Waterville, ME 04901